WHERE I'VE NOT BEEN LOST

PB ISBN: 978-1-7395269-1-7

eBook ISBN: 978-1-7395269-0-0

For my lovely wife, Kate

LEMON MARMALADE

Mum was calling again as I stepped from my train. There was a scream and an odd scene at the platform across the tracks where a thin white-haired man strode purposefully towards its edge as a passing train arrived. There was a tug at his raincoat, slowing his progress as the engine clattered through horns blaring, somehow never colliding with the man.

He lay on the ground as the noise dissipated, the emptied contents of a plastic bag spilt by his legs. And a pair of teenage girls stared down at him, asking if he was okay. The enquiries seemed genuine until one began to film him on her phone.

'If I want to fucking die, that's my business!' he yelled, with his head against a pillar.

My pocket vibrated again. 'Hi, Mum,' I said, answering – unable to look away.

'Hi, Bab,' she chirped. 'I'm letting you know we're on the ferry.'

'Okay. That's good.'

'You sound all shaken up.' The old man screamed at the girls as a third, muscular onlooker stepped in to calm him down. 'What's that noise?'

'Nothing.' I gripped my guitar case and turned towards the concrete walkway. 'Do you think that could have been a text?'

'Oh, well.' She sighed. 'You're in a bad mood.'

'I'm not,' I insisted as I descended the staircase. 'Sorry. I don't know what to say, Mum. Bon Voyage. Have fun in Spain.'

'I thought you'd want to know.'

'I do. I'm just about to meet Frank. I'm busy, and you keep calling.'

There was a bar built into the railway arches, and I knew it well. Frank was sitting among the long, crowded tables as I arrived at the concrete beer garden. It was warm, and he was easy to spot with his lank, grey hair. We shook hands and gripped forearms. I told him I couldn't stay for long, with other plans in the diary for later.

'It's a bit of a hipster hang-out,' he noted, scanning the younger faces around him. 'Oh, congratulations, by the way. On your tutoring qualification. I saw it on your mum's Facebook.'

'Oh, thanks.' I slotted onto the bench opposite and fumbled to balance my guitar case against it. 'It's just a fallback if work continues to slide.'

Frank pushed a bottle of beer my way. 'It's good to have options, though, right?'

'Yeah. Sure.' I shrugged and took a swig of my drink.

'Well, I'm proud of you, mate.' Frank smiled and pushed his hair to one side. 'I might grow it longer. I'll fit in these sorts of places then. What do you think?'

'I think that's an awful idea.'

He cackled with an odd musical noise. 'So….' He flexed his fingers. 'How'd it go with Naomi?'

'Um. Yeah, I don't think I can do it.'

Frank frowned like it was a disappointment. 'Okay. It's just….' He smacked his lips. 'It can be good for streams if a journalist of her quality randomly pops up to do a piece. Her stuff goes viral all the time. People will get interested.'

I shrugged. 'Ask Amber, then Frank. I'm not sure I'd do it justice.'

'Well, it would be good if you got involved,' he said, wiping his manicured beard after a thirsty guzzle. 'It's just what with us bumping into each other last week, Luke's band potentially breaking up. And now this. Maybe the stars are aligning.'

'Hmm.' I snickered and polished off my drink. 'Getting a little carried away.'

Frank finger drummed at the table, and our conversation pivoted to the old days, because of course it would. He said it had been five years since Dorothea split up and then frantically scanned through his phone to check when I told him it had been eight. Time was melting away, he said, as we reminisced fondly on that time, dancing around its unhappier end. And we drank more until the laughter came.

'Frank, I am in a bad way,' I said suddenly.

I hadn't wanted to leave our hastily arranged catch-up on a bitter note, but the news escaped my lips and jolted us both. I had been losing days, I explained, unsure if I should. Perhaps my brain was broken and had stopped imprinting memories – like my entire day before I arrived there.

Frank didn't say much in response. He gave only a perceptive nod and scratched nervously at the same spot on his forehead between his eyebrows. I forced a carefree chuckle, wanting to turn the clock back ten minutes when we were both smiling.

Frank tapped the bridge of his nose. 'I'm sure it'll pass, mate.'

'Maybe.' I winced, with a sudden sharp pain in my head – like fingertips gripping into my skull. 'I think there is something wrong with me.'

'Look, I've got a friend if you want to see someone. Professionally. Have you done that?'

'No.' I shook my head and stood, strapping the guitar case to my back. 'Sorry, mate. I'm running late.'

'Right.' He grabbed my forearm as we shook hands again. 'Just give me a call if it gets bad. I'll sort it, anything you need. Anything.'

'Okay. Thanks.'

I trudged back to the station platform, where a train home awaited. My head throbbed as I slipped inside the busy carriage and gripped a pole.

Esther was staring into the wooden mirror perched on top of the tall chest of drawers in the corner when I told her about my migraine, holding my forehead for effect. She didn't say anything at first and had a brush poised at her freckled face as the walls of our tiny bedroom shrank inwards. The timing of my announcement was awful. We were minutes before we were due to head out with friends, who were her friends, really.

'You've had too much to drink,' she suggested.

'Yeah. Sorry. Maybe it is that.'

Esther had been upbeat about catching up with her old friends too much to let her down. She liked the new green dress she had purchased that morning – a smock, she called it. 'This isn't about Manchester, is it?' she asked.

I sighed, dreading a revival of the previous evening's argument – how she was feeling homesick and wanted to be nearer old friends and her family. 'No.'

'I only suggested it because the tenancy is coming up. And Liz's rent went up by twenty per cent. And we could buy up there. You know.'

'Yes, you said.' I played with my hands. 'I don't want to think about that. Not now.'

'Okay...' Esther returned to the mirror and dabbed at her lips again. 'It'll look bad if I cancel now.'

'Of course. Yeah, go and have a good time,' I insisted. 'I might go to bed early. I'm still not getting enough sleep.'

I wanted to poke the dimple in Esther's chin, a weird thing of ours which always seemed to lighten the mood. But I hadn't done that in a while, and it wouldn't have been right under the circumstances. Instead, I retreated to the beige dog-eared sofa in our narrow living room. I scrolled through my phone, dimming its screen in the darkness with my feet planted on the coffee table.

There was another message from Naomi.

So when would be good to speak? I was such a fan of Dorothea! Xx

'Oh!' Esther leaned against the living room door where she was poking her chubby hooped earrings in. 'Did your mum and Bill get away okay?'

I nodded. 'Yeah. Mum called.'

'That's good.' She chewed a fingernail. 'I was talking to her about your thirtieth next year. Perhaps we could go to Spain and see them after the party.'

'Maybe.' I tossed my phone to one side and groaned.

'What's up?'

'It's such a fucking big number, isn't it?'

'Sorry.' Esther wandered inside and nudged my cheek. 'I'm just trying to organise something nice for it.'

'No, I'm sorry.' We looked at each other and smiled, all mouths, no eyes. 'You look nice.'

'Thanks.' She stepped back to check her outfit from all angles in the mirror above my head. It was unusual for her to like anything she had on. 'It looks okay, doesn't it?'

'Yeah.'

'I think green might be my colour, you know.' Esther perched herself on the sofa arm and rested her head on my shoulder. She pulled at the neck of my jumper to sniff at it. 'That lemon smell is everywhere. It's never going to leave us, is it?'

'Maybe in a few months.'

'Maybe.' Her laughter petered quickly. 'Are you okay?'

I nodded. 'Yeah.'

Her phone vibrated. 'Oh God, the cab's here.' She crept across the room and peered between the vertical blind at the window. 'I hate getting them on my own.'

'I'm sorry...' I squeezed her hand. It was too late to change my mind now. 'Shall I wait up?'

'See how you feel.' She kissed my head and moved into the hallway a few steps away to slip her shoes on. 'Babe. What set me off to make lemon marmalade?'

I smiled. 'I don't know.'

'So funny.' Esther snickered and reached for her going-out jacket. 'I don't know what I was thinking.'

I snickered, too. 'It's funny.'

'Yeah.' She grabbed the door and opened it. 'Take some painkillers.'

'I will.' I smiled. 'Have a nice time.'

My head growled as the front door clunked shut, fingers pushing and gripping. I held my wrists into my eye sockets to dull the pain and then skulked into the kitchen, where the citrus tang hung most. Packets of painkillers and sleeping tablets came tumbling onto the worktop as I reached into the narrowest corner cupboard. Lacking the want to file them away again, I scooped up what I could and headed back to the living room, plucking a bottle of dark rum and a glass from the side on my way.

The old broken-in sofa was ready to absorb me as I plonked back onto it and poured a drink. I swallowed an assortment of pills to defeat the pounding for a night – a blotting out that couldn't come soon enough. And fuck Manchester and Naomi, and fuck Frank and Dorothea.

I squeezed my head with both hands as it pounded and wouldn't stop. Perhaps it was impatience, but I popped more blister packets and sunk their contents. My throat charred as I washed them down, so many and then again. It was strange not to flinch, to sit quietly instead and kick at the sheepskin rug fibres beneath my feet. Perhaps I knew what I was doing and was okay with it. Perhaps I was miserable and seduced by the sudden possibility of that going away.

My phone buzzed from between the gaps in the back cushions. There was a message from Esther.

It's fun here. I think it would have cheered you up! xx

It was a slap of reality, and I panicked, full of pills – wishing I wasn't. And my breathing had lost its depth and rhythm. I stood up and immediately reached for the sofa arm, unable to suck in enough air. What if I passed out and choked? Esther would have come home, still on a high from her night out and in love with her dress and the French fringe her hairdresser had talked her into that morning. She would have seen my limp body wherever it had landed – all of that optimism for nothing. The utter selfishness of it.

I typed a reply, and it was clumsy and awful. But I wanted to die far less than I wanted Esther to find my body.

I think I'm going to the A & E. Don't worry xx

A pair of kindly paramedics observed me first at the flat after my call. We talked about what I had taken and joked about the smell. But then it went dark, and suddenly I was being coaxed out of the building and into the rear of their ambulance waiting outside. One stayed with me in the back. She was an older woman, a recent trainee, she said, after a career in finance. And she squeezed my hand and said they were worried I was losing consciousness.

'Do you want me to call your dad?' she asked, the vehicle rumbling. 'You're talking about him.'

'No,' I told her, cognizant and embarrassed. 'He's dead.'

That foggy humiliation intensified as I arrived at the hospital and was ushered inside a curtained cubicle. I was wasting their time when bombarded with questions I couldn't form sensible responses to. I was sorry, I kept saying. Perhaps it was the distraction of the machines beeping nearby or the other patients screaming beyond the fabric walls.

I drank a black liquid the doctor handed to me. It would help prevent my body from absorbing the tablets, she said. A seasickness knitted the floor and ceiling when she left again. And my phone was buzzing relentlessly in my pocket, perhaps filling with frantic messages and missed calls from Esther. I managed to free it just as the latest note landed.

WHAT DO YOU MEAN?? BRIAN!! WHERE??

My head pounded again, filling up, unable to contain the pressure. My skull was surely fracturing or about to pop open like a lid. And I had to reply to Esther in case I died there. It seemed possible when a young nurse slipped inside the curtain, flustered, and daunted. She was softly spoken, and it was difficult to absorb what she was saying beyond the thumping and the outside.

'Which hospital is this?' I asked, interrupting her.

'Guy's.'

I'm at Guys Hospital. I'm so sorry Es. I've ruined everyone's night xx

The nurse asked me to put my phone away. She fumbled with the back of my hand, and a jet of blood sprung as she tried to attach a tube into a vein. 'Shit.' She whispered that like it wasn't supposed to happen. She held her mouth, pinned down the gushing with cotton wool and taped it there before rushing from the cubicle again.

I leaned forward and vomited, thick and black, some landing inside the cardboard bowl resting on my stomach. The nurse returned, this time with a colleague. 'He's been sick,' she said.

'That's okay,' replied her coworker, like he had seen it a million times. 'Just ignore that for a second.'

'Oh, God. I'm having such a bad day,' the young nurse whispered.

I must have started to pass out then, a shutdown rapidly looming. Somebody called for a doctor, and a tube scraped across my throat sometime later. The scuffing against my gums was the last moment I was vaguely aware of anything.

Esther was slumped in a pink chair beside my bed in the morning, still wearing her dress. And I yelped and clutched at my ribs after trying to sit up, an unbearable bitter agony yelling from there.

A nurse paused by my bed. 'Are you okay?' he asked. I nodded and grimaced, unable to summon a helpful verbal response. 'I need to check what we can give you for the pain.'

We sat in silence on that ward of sad souls between the requests for blood and the bag changes for my drip. Eventually, the doctor arrived with news. She said I was lucky there were no apparent signs of organ damage and handed me a form for my GP. I could go home once I had received a psychiatric assessment.

We returned to our tiny bedroom that night, and the walls closed in, touching the sides of our bed. Perhaps I had died as Esther turned away, shifting suddenly when our feet glanced.

'What are you thinking?' I asked.

'Um. I'm just trying to make sense of it.' There was the sharpest pain in her voice, slicing me in two.

'You know it was an accident.' I hovered my hand over her arm and let it rest on her waist.

'Hmm.' Esther wriggled until I moved it away again. 'I just need to sleep.'

The days after were long and quiet, and the smell of lemon ebbed away. Eventually, over dinner, Esther said she saw my version of events differently, or at least there was an alternative explanation she couldn't get out of her mind. She worried I had intended to kill myself and planned to do it when she was out but couldn't follow through. And if that was true, she didn't know how to deal with feeling upset that I hadn't left a note, that I thought so little of her it didn't occur to me.

We had been propelled so far from the long, lazy mornings we would spend coiled around each other, and I was contented only there. And in the years together, we had slowly emptied our eggs into the same basket until there was no obvious way out. Perhaps we weren't in a healthy relationship and were codependent – welded together and afraid to separate for the damage it would cause the other. Perhaps what I had done was seismic enough to wake us up.

After days of awful silence, I decided to leave. Perhaps the execution of my quick departure was as clumsy and impulsive as my overdose. But it solved more problems than it created. Or so I reckoned. At the very least, I couldn't torture Esther with the prospect of more attempts now that I had set such an ugly precedent. So I called Frank, and it was a ludicrous phone call to have made.

ONE

A noise outside woke me from a brief nap – a commotion by the park across the way. I climbed onto the bed where the eaves almost touched and opened the skylight window. A pair of dogs growled and barked at each other outside, their owners struggling to pull them away. And there was still a vehicle-sized space on the street three floors down, where Frank's had been before he left to sort some early-morning errands.

I sat down again and rested my feet on a packed suitcase when the phone rang for the third time. 'Hi, Mum,' I said, answering.

'Hello. You're speaking to me now, are you?'

There was a barely disguised anguish in her voice. Still, it was soothing to hear her Brummie tones again, how words boinged from her mouth like treacle.

'Yeah.'

'We haven't spoken for six months, Brian.'

'Yes.' I leaned back across the bed and closed my eyes again. 'I'm sorry, Mum.'

'I've been out of my mind, worried. I was about to fly back or call the police.'

'I can keep apologising if it makes it better.'

Mum hissed a deep nasal exhale. 'And your message said you're moving to Devon today. Is that right?'

'Yeah. I'm looking after a house.'

Mum blew a sharp puff of air like she couldn't understand it. 'On your own?'

'That's the plan.' It fell quiet. Perhaps she was taking it all in. 'How about you? How's sunny Spain?'

'It's nice, especially now the Wi-Fi has been sorted. That's been a long saga.' Mum clicked her tongue several times as if she was whirring back to where we were. 'So, will Frank be checking in on you?'

'I don't know.' A low-pitched off-key singing echoed out of sight. 'Is that Bill?'

'Yes.' There was a mumbling between the two for a moment. 'Bill says to check your emails. He's sending you a link for the photos.'

'Okay, I will.' There was a tap at the door. 'I better go. Frank is here, and he'll want to leave soon.'

'Okay, bye then. I love you, Bab. Keep in touch.'

'Love you too, Mum. I really am sorry.'

There was a second knock at the door. 'Brian?' Frank called. 'Are you ready, mate?'

'Yep.'

I saw the suitcase up onto its wheels and tapped the velvet chaise lounge on my way to the door. Half of one year disappeared inside that top-floor escape – a perfectly preserved mid-century triangular prism which once belonged to Frank's auntie. She had died in the chunky ornate bed, a fact he gleefully relayed to me when I moved into the flat with its own kitchen and shower room. I barely needed to leave most days other than to maintain a stock of sleeping tablets to knock myself out each night.

It was raining again, as it had been all month, and the downpour pelted Frank's white car. After dashing for it, we climbed inside, tossing my suitcase in the boot first. What had started as a throwaway suggestion a month before was now happening for real.

'You've got your glasses on,' Frank noted as he clicked in his seatbelt.

'Yeah.'

'They look alright. What's it like being able to see properly?'

'Fine.' I shrugged. 'Helps, I guess.'

'Good.' We pulled away, and Frank was apologetic for being late back. He had been to see an estate agent that morning. 'I'm selling up. It's too big for me.'

'Oh wow. Where will you go?'

'Maybe I'll get a flat somewhere with a little garden. I don't even know where's good in London anymore.' He yawned into his fist. 'Perhaps I'll go to Provence, retire there, and live my days peacefully. Maybe I'll do that. Sometimes I feel ready for the pasture.'

'Sounds nice.'

'Obviously, I won't.' We pulled out of the narrow street and immediately stopped at a zebra crossing where a procession of school kids headed across and into the park. 'It'd beat driving round here. Come on, little cunts.'

Our conversation sputtered as we slowly wound out of London. Frank had to deal with a constant flow of incoming calls being answered automatically via the in-car entertainment system. 'I need to sort this fucking thing out,' he would say, with each call prompting another round of fruitless jabbing at the touchscreen.

After complaining about his flagging energy reserves, we stopped at Reading Services so Frank could fill up on caffeine. It was busy inside, and we queued for refreshments at separate providers.

When I finally slid back onto the passenger seat, the car had been filled with the aroma of Frank's double-strength takeaway coffee.

'God, I miss those,' he huffed as I lifted a slumping burger from its box.

'That's a shame.' After an untidy bite, I placed the fast food back into its packaging, too tense for an appetite anyway. 'I'm worried your car is going to smell.'

'I don't mind that.'

We pulled away, and I clamped the closed box between my knees. 'You can have it if you want.'

'No, no. I'm getting acid burn just thinking about it.' He belched and rubbed his chest. For a well-spoken man, there was a gruffness to Frank. 'That's years on the road for you, drinking and eating nothing but bollocks.'

'You look good for your age, mate.'

'I'm sixty-seven this year. How did that happen?' He chuckled onto the rim of his plastic cup and pushed his hair aside. 'I need a haircut, too. I've decided to age more gracefully.'

'Good idea.'

Frank flicked on the radio as it started to rain again. His finger raised immediately as a mid-tempo danceable groove played. 'I could have signed these years ago.' He snorted. 'This shit's everywhere now. Unbelievable. You can never tell.'

'Rough luck.'

'Story of my life.' Frank said he thought about the misses more than the hits, not that there was much of the latter to ponder over. Dorothea were his most hurtful miss, and he regurgitated that sentiment for the millionth time. 'Did you read the Naomi Bennifer *From There to Where* piece?'

'Yep.' I nodded emphatically – though I had only given it the briefest skims. 'A couple of months ago. Why?'

'Just noticed the streams up ticking.' Frank drained the remnants of his drink and placed the plastic cup back into the holder by the gearstick. 'Remember that's money straight into your account.'

I snickered. 'What shall I spend that three pounds on?'

Frank chuckled at my scorn and flicked the wipers on. It was raining again. 'Think big picture. You get Luke back in the fold, and suddenly you're in the studio finishing off that album. People will fall in love with the narrative.'

I shook my head. 'Jesus fucking Christ, Frank.'

'I'm serious. We'll get you rested in Devon, and then I'll send the bat signal to let you know it's back on.'

'Sounds incredible.'

I snickered. It was weird that Frank felt he had to speak to me as if we still had a professional relationship. He did seem to have a genuine affection for my band, but perhaps it was the only way he could make sense of our arrangement. Or, perhaps, he had been conditioned by forty years in the music industry, and that was how he spoke in hype and promises. Perhaps it was much easier to laugh along than to believe there was anything to it. It was safer that way.

Another call dropped in, but Frank stabbed at the screen before the caller could get going. 'I thought it was fascinating, anyway, that article. Lots of people read it. She goes viral all the time, big-time Twitter following.'

'Yeah.' I stretched in my seat. 'It's just a bit surreal to read about yourself like that – like reading your obituary.'

'I bet. It's pretty heavy in places.' Frank clicked his fingers like he was trying to recall something. 'What did she say, now? *Those outside the industry might have forgotten Dorothea, but those from within it haven't. They are a cautionary tale to every up-and-coming band. They blew it, mostly for themselves – but also for everyone else.*'

'Lovely.' I removed my specs and cleaned the lenses on my t-shirt – hating them. 'It's nice you've committed that to memory. I thought she was a good writer.'

'Well, I'm paraphrasing. Naomi worded it much better.' Frank rubbed at his stubbly face. 'Amber did a good job I thought – seeing the rest of you bastards were too lazy to get involved.'

'Yep.' Perhaps she did.

'She said you and Luke got the band's name from studying Middlemarch together. Dorothea Brooke.'

'You didn't know that?'

Frank shook his head. 'I'd forgotten, but it reminded me how much I liked that,' he said. 'A little story behind the name, not something just thrown together.'

'Yep. Dorothea wanted to change the world. That was the headline in the Guardian's *Band of the Day* article.'

'That's right.' Frank snickered as another call threatened to drop through, and he jabbed at the screen again. 'Well, you didn't do a very good fucking job, did you?'

The rain stopped as I located the setting for automatic call answering and switched it off – as if the two were connected. Buoyed by the peace it brought, we continued our journey towards South Devon with the sun peeping through the clouds.

'Does Niall know about your move?' he asked.

'Yep. He said I could call if there were any major issues. That was the gist.'

'That's good.'

Frank began speculating about the renovations that had taken place inside the house as we moved closer to our destination. It had been a pet project for Tamara, his daughter, who had wanted to revamp the holiday home that once belonged to his parents – a place they used for their summer sailing interests. Now, she had accepted a job offer in Berlin to begin a new adventure, leaving the home empty.

'What's Tam like these days?' I asked. 'I've only met her once, and she was off her head.'

'Good question. We don't seem to speak as much.' Frank sighed like it was a source of angst. 'Now she's all sensible. Or supposedly sensible.'

I had never been to Totnes before and assumed it was a sleepy spot full of retirees and seasonal holidaymakers. But Frank said it was more interesting than that. The town was eccentric and a champion of commercial independence, new-age thinking, and the arts. He said there was a real community feel there, and I would like it. Perhaps I would draw inspiration from the place and start writing again.

I drifted into a doze as we coasted past Bristol, and the previous night's restlessness finally caught up. The remaining journey was a flickering slideshow of fields, rolling hills, roadside signs for farm shops, and amusingly named hamlets.

I woke again once the car bumped onto a curb, and a tall powder blue terraced cottage loomed outside between identical buildings in pink and pastel green. We were there, Frank announced, outside what was to be my new home for a while. It was a stone's throw from the high street and, according to the street signs, a nearby castle.

After cycling through his answer messages, Frank explained he would have to make the house tour brief. He had a flight the next day and needed to return to London at a reasonable time.

I retrieved my suitcase from the boot, and Frank pulled a chunky key from his jacket pocket shortly after joking that he had left it at home. The door swung open into a small, carpeted hallway. There was a closed seventies-style frosted glass panelled door to our left and a wooden staircase directly ahead.

Frank puffed his cheeks, disheartened. 'Well, this looks just how I remember it.'

The narrow staircase squeaked as I gripped my suitcase and followed Frank up the steps and into the room at the top of the landing, now mine. It was the larger of the two bedrooms on the first floor, painted lilac and likely had been some time ago. But it was clean, at least, and housed an old Chesterfield sofa bed folded open and a writing desk under a large window.

'Think of it as a blank canvas, mate,' Frank said, stroking his chin.

'Yeah, okay.' It wasn't easy to think of it as anything else.

Frank placed himself on the sofa bed, which peaked in the middle. He bounced up and down to test its buoyancy – not very. 'Get yourself a proper bed if this isn't very comfortable. I don't know how long it's been here.'

'Sure.'

We walked inside the bathroom at the end of the landing, with its dated cream fixtures and brass fittings. Frank pursed his lips as we exited. He pointed at the staircase ahead, which turned to a second floor. 'I assume Tam was up there, in the master. She's probably left a load of her shit behind.'

'Right.'

He turned and headed back towards the stairs. 'Right, let's see where my money has gone.'

'Yeah, okay.'

I hung back as Frank pushed open the retro hallway door. 'Oh wow.' He clapped his hands after stepping through. 'She's opened it right up and knocked it through.'

I poked my head inside, where Frank was rotating and drinking it all in. The room was long and had a partitioned social space nearest the hallway with varnished wooden floors and a vast lime-coloured sectional sofa that spanned two walls. Several long-leafed indoor plants loomed in the corners, and a series of enormous abstract photographs hung along the walls.

'Tam's had the falcons reupholstered,' he beamed and pointed at a pair of architectural chocolate leather armchairs. 'God, Dad loved those chairs.'

'That's good.'

Frank wandered into the kitchen beyond a supporting beam in the ceiling and examined its new dark grey units. He watched a cupboard close softly, then drifted to a dining table by the patio doors. 'This is gorgeous.' He rubbed its surface with the back of his hand. 'Must be repurposed polished concrete or something like that. What do you reckon?'

'Maybe.'

It poured outside, with the rainfall rapping at the glass patio doors. Frank pointed to a raised stone terrace in the courtyard garden where a jumble of weeds and spindly buddleias had reclaimed a garden table. 'There's an old photo of my mother and father enjoying a bottle of wine up there. They were looking back at whoever took that photo, where you are, smiling away. Seems quite sad out there now.'

'Maybe I could trim it down,' I suggested.

'Yeah. Or I could get a landscaper over.' Frank's phone blared with an unpleasant metallic ringtone, and his eyes popped when he pulled it from his jeans. 'Speak of the devil. Hey, Tam. Did you get my text?' He disappeared from the room with the mobile at his ear as the downpour washed the mossy slabs outside. 'What do you mean?' he asked, his voice disappearing into the hallway. And then, 'Well, where the fuck are you?'

I tapped at the concrete table, with the phone call now a series of tense, far-off murmurs.

Frank slapped his hands together as he wandered back inside.

'Everything alright?' I asked.

'Hmm.' He made a series of shushing sounds as if he couldn't find a suitable way to communicate whatever news had just arrived his way. 'Tam's been down in Kent, visiting her mother.'

'Oh.' I scratched my week-old beard, not knowing how to process the news. 'She's not in Germany?'

Frank shrugged. 'She's just sorting out a few things first.' He glanced at his watch. 'Fuck. I've got to fly in a second.'

'What does that mean, then?'

'Look, you're here now.' He glanced outside, where it was still hammering and buttoned up his jacket in preparation. 'Obviously, your stuff is coming down in a few days.'

'Yes…' I followed Frank to the hallway, not enjoying where this was all headed. 'So, is she coming back here? I'm just trying to get this straight.'

'Yep. Maybe tonight, but probably not. She wasn't sure.' He gave me an apologetic smile and pulled the front door open. The rain was slapping his car outside, the drains overspilling. 'Look, I know it's vague. It's always vague with her.'

'Right. But she knows I'm here?'

'She does now.' Frank patted me on the shoulder and failed to pull off a sufficiently comforting smile. 'There might be a tiny overlap, but it's all good. She's fine.'

'Okay...'

'You can always come back if you can't get on with it.' Frank winced as his offer tumbled out like it wasn't what he wanted. And who could blame him? I certainly couldn't. He handed me his key and asked me to look after it. I told him I would, but I could only think about that first awkward interaction with Tam as he made his dash for it. Why would she want me around? She couldn't. It was absurd.

A creeping anxiety prickled as Frank's car splashed around the bend and disappeared out of sight. I had stopped taking my antidepressants – a plan hatched only that morning. I wanted to test my rehabilitation, but perhaps I was reaching for them again already.

I closed the front door, unsure what to do next. Eventually, I headed upstairs to my new room instead of going outside to explore the town. I didn't fancy the soaking I would get, and besides, it made more sense to remain inside the house if Tam did show up rather than surprise her with a re-entrance later on.

The bedroom door scraped the carpet as I struggled to close it. I then made my bed and folded my clothes inside the compartments of an ancient hanger-less wardrobe spanning the length of the far-end wall. Its sliding door came away from its track as I pulled it shut and spent the next ten minutes trying to manoeuvre it back into place without it toppling outwards.

I froze after the exertion, unsure if there had been a noise elsewhere inside the house. It was an old home that let off tiny creaks and cracks, but perhaps Tam was home already. I waited for another sound, footsteps or a door opening.

My stomach growled after a period of silence. Confident I was still alone, I flicked on the landing light and headed to the kitchen to see if there was anything I could eat and perhaps replace later. When I swung its door open, the fridge was mostly empty, except for a small block of cheese and a couple of eggs about to go over.

The concrete dining table had its own hanging spotlight, and I ate an omelette underneath it, my reflection lurking in the patio windows where the wind whistled. It was impossible to relax, a buzz of tension in my limbs when I pushed my finished plate to one side.

I scanned through my phone to try and distract myself, but it led me back to an idea I'd had the previous evening – that I would contact a selected group of people and let them know I was okay. Perhaps the distance made that easier now and would cushion any anger or upset. Perhaps it was indifference I feared the most.

After nearly an hour of tweaking and fine-tuning the catch-all note, I left the message unsent. I had decided it was absurd to have tried to reaffirm my existence with such an inflated sense of self-importance as to announce it. Instead, I reactivated my old social media accounts and quietly hoped someone would notice.

I headed upstairs after deciding to soak in the cream bathroom's corner tub to relieve the friction. The water bobbed at my neck as I remained coiled and ready to spring out should there have been a noise resembling a returning Tam.

There was a vibration from the floor where I left my phone on a towel. I dried my hand and read the note from Frank.

Tam says she's back tomorrow. I've given her your number.

Okay cool thanks mate

After my bath, I locked up, and the bedroom door fought against the thick olive carpet resisting underneath as I tried to close it. After finally winning that battle, I slotted my phone charger into an old plug extension coiled underneath the desk. It whirred, disconcertingly so, as I slipped under the covers. And what would I say to Tam when she was home? It was insane.

Eventually, my eyes closed under their weight, and thoughts drifted to Esther instead. It had been my nightly routine for some time.

TWO

I perched myself on the writing desk after finding it solid enough. It was a good vantage point at the front of the house with a view of the street below. Mum had taken the iPad onto her tiny balcony with its glass railing to show me the sea view. 'Can you see it?' she asked.

'Just about.' I squinted at the grainy sunlit beach on my phone screen. 'There's a castle or something.'

'Those are the old city walls. It's beautiful up there.'

'Ah, cool. It looks nice.' The screen became fuzzed and pixelated. 'Are you zooming in?'

'Yes. I've zoomed in so you can see it.'

'It might be too much. Is the town really called Tossa?'

Mum sighed. 'Yes, Tossa de Mar. And I know what you're getting at.'

'I'm just asking.'

'Can you see me now?' There she was, sitting at her bistro set and smiling proudly at her technical mastery. Mum never aged, her round cheeks grinning back at me as she removed an enormous pair of sunglasses. 'I've turned the camera around.'

'Yes, I can see.'

'And I can see you.' She laughed like it was magic. 'Since when do you wear glasses?'

'Since I got my eyes tested.'

'Okay.' Mum grinned with a cigarette at her lips. 'Well, they look nice.'

'Maybe. You're smoking again.'

'Yes. I'll stop it again soon.'

'Well, you look nice and tanned.' I flinched as a sudden clunking noise rattled inside the house, or perhaps it hadn't.

'What's up? You look on edge.'

I told Mum about the situation, how Tam was supposed to be in Berlin, but now she wasn't and could be back at any moment. 'I've no idea what to do. No idea.'

'Well, be careful!' Mum gasped, never one to play a situation down – even for my benefit. 'You might scare her if she thinks you're an intruder.'

'Well, she knows I'm here, apparently.'

'Even so, be careful how you introduce yourself. Don't jump out at her.'

'This is incredible advice, Mum.'

She laughed. 'Well, I wouldn't want a strange man moving into my house if it was me. Sorry.'

'Jesus, Mum – *a strange man*?'

'You know what I mean.' Mum's partner, Bill, appeared behind her and waved at me with a watering can in his grip. We shared greetings, and he gave me a comedy salute. It was nice to be reminded of his perpetual cheeriness and commitment to a short grey side parting. 'Bill doesn't like the heat when it's like this.'

'Oh, dear. That reminds me. I'll look at that email when I get a moment.'

'Okay.' Mum stubbed out her cigarette into a yellow ashtray. 'There are lots of photos of us when we moved into the house and lots of you playing your guitar in the workshop with your friend when he was over.'

The screen froze, and I switched the camera off. 'It's gone again, Mum.'

'Okay, Bab. I think it's the Wi-Fi playing up.'

'That's alright. I need to get up anyway.'

'Okay, I'll let you go. Tara-a-bit, darling. Stay in touch, won't you? And let me know how you're settling in.'

'Yeah, I will. Bye, Mum.'

A shard of warm light peeped through the window and warmed my legs as I scanned over the instructions in Bill's email whilst it was fresh in my mind.

I wasn't braced enough when the outdated website loaded, and Dad's face immediately appeared in a picture of us together on my tenth birthday. We were standing in the sloping garden of our rented pebbledash terrace, and his big arm was tight around my shoulders. A fag jutted between his fingers and tufts of hair poked from his vest like puffs of greying candy floss.

He had a trustworthy face, Dad. He was handsome too, in a careworn way, as if much was on his mind. And it was wild how pre-puberty me was still me – the same mound of brown hair and wide-set panicked blue eyes, almost seeing what was coming.

I pushed myself off the desk and headed for the once-opulent brass-fitted shower. I spent an age under its shower head, micro-adjusting a dial in the tiled wall. It blasted me with thin water jets before it convulsed and sputtered for minutes. I was about to give up entirely when it suddenly sprung to life after stumbling upon a precariously perfect position. Suddenly there was a noise, just as the newfound flow had washed its comfort over me – a cry of laughter from somewhere inside the house.

I shut off the shower, and water dripped like thuds onto the base. Two distinct voices were engaged in a conversation echoing downstairs. It was Tam. Tam was home, and someone was with her.

I snuck out of the shower, grabbed my folded towel from the closed toilet lid, and tip-toed to my room. I dried off in a panic, wanting to get the moment right – needing to be clothed at the very least for that to happen. I carefully slid the faulty wardrobe door across, leaning a knee to prevent it from toppling again, and grabbed whatever outfit I could pull from inside.

'Hello?' A tentative voice called out, clearly aware of my presence.

I moved onto the landing, pulling a sock onto my damp foot.

'Come down and meet us,' a second voice insisted. 'We won't bite you.'

'Hi ya,' I called, and the laughing renewed. 'On my way.'

I began the hesitant journey down the creaking steps of the staircase. A vaguely familiar face suddenly appeared in the hallway below, all cheekbones, and I wasn't ready for it.

'Tam?'

'Hi.'

'Hi.'

'Hold up a sec.' She held up her palms as if she wasn't ready for something and disappeared again. The frosted glass door clunked out of view. 'Sorry, Brian. Can you wait? I'll call you inside in a moment.'

'Oh. Okay.'

The situation was already stranger than I had imagined our meeting would be – something suitably brief and frosty. I removed my glasses, folded them into my shirt pocket, and pushed my damp hair into what I estimated was at least a barely presentable style. I shuffled down the hallway and placed my ear on the frosted glass panel. It sounded like they were filming something in there, a daytime television show. There were muffled mentions of a yellow dress and how it was perfect because the sun was shining.

'So, everybody, Tam's housemate has moved in. We thought meeting him with you for the first time would be fun, which I know is insane. So come on in, Brian, let's see what we have.'

I froze. What the hell was going on? 'Do you want me to come in?' My hand moved onto the door's curved handle, no desire to lever it open.

'Yes, please,' Tam called. 'Come on in, Brian,'.

I poked my head into the room. It was bright, the light flooding through the patio doors at the far end as Tam held a camera clasped to an extended selfie stick by the concrete dining table. Her oversized earrings glinted as I moved inside, my entrance presumably being filmed.

'Here he is, everyone,' said Tam. 'This man will look after the house when I leave for Berlin.'

'Hello,' I replied. I gave a 'this is odd, but perhaps I don't mind' sort of shrug.

Tam chuckled. 'Brian, don't look so terrified! It's just Connie and me. You are with friends, I promise.'

A tall red-haired girl with thin arms waved from within the kitchen with both hands. She must have been Connie, in so much that she was wearing the aforementioned yellow summer dress. I waved back as Tam beckoned me forward with her hand and held her palm up when I reached a spot underneath the supporting beam between the two spaces.

'Am I being filmed?' I asked, nervously scratching at my face.

'Yes! You are.' Connie sniggered as she adjusted the bandana in her hair.

Tam started laughing too. I forced out a polite chuckle, trying my best to join in with the spirit of whatever this was. It was a fun project. Perhaps I had to seem like I was fun too.

The camera panned back to Connie, prompting her to speak. 'Brian, we listened to your music in the car this morning. We really liked it. It's not normally my thing.'

'Just bear in mind that Connie's been listening to Hamilton exclusively for two years,' Tam said.

'Oh.' I shrugged. 'I don't know what that is.'

Connie gasped. 'Oh, my God! Heresy!' she exclaimed in a theatrical yell-singing.

Tam clapped her hands, perhaps a reminder to stay on topic. 'Your band had an intense vibe. We were really into it, actually.'

'Thanks.' I pawed at my face again and couldn't stop touching it. 'Guessing that was our EP.'

Connie held a finger to her chin. 'Not sure.'

Tam returned the camera glare my way, and I dried up instantly. 'Well. Glad you enjoyed it.'

'It was great,' enthused Connie. 'One of your songs had thirty thousand listens. I thought that was good.'

'Maybe,' I said. It wasn't something I checked in on. 'We peaked pre-streaming, I guess. If you can call it a peak.'

Tam looked at Connie. 'You can talk about how I know Brian. We'll edit this.'

'Yeah, so guys, Brian was in this incredible underground band Tam's dad used to manage. She had the pleasure of seeing them once when she was younger.' Connie winced. She was running out of things to say, and they giggled as Tam panned back to me.

'Did you want me to say something?' I asked, running on empty.

The pair collapsed into a fit of laughter. 'We'll edit. We'll edit,' Tam said.

'Sorry. It's my fault,' Connie tutted. She pouted and extended her bottom lip to its fullest. 'I think I get flustered when we talk about you leaving. I don't like thinking about it.'

Tam popped the camera on the table. She played with her septum ring as the pair mooted the possibility of re-shooting my entrance. But they were concerned about losing the organic nature of our meeting for the first time, even if it lacked impact.

'So, what was that?' I asked. I attempted a carefree chuckle, but it caught the back of my throat and led to a mild coughing fit.

'Are you okay, Brian?' Tam asked as I continued to sputter with my thumb raised.

'Yeah, fine,' I replied, eyes watered. 'Fine.'

'You're probably wondering what the hell is going on, right?'

'Yeah. Probably accurate.' Based on the laughter it inspired, it was the most amusing thing I could have said.

Tam gave me a warm hug. 'You look terrified. That wasn't the intention, sorry.'

'No, it's fine,' I insisted. 'I just wasn't expecting this. Was it a prank?'

Tam shook her head. 'No, no. God, sorry. Con does a thing–'

'It's *our* thing!' Connie exclaimed. 'Or was.'

'It still is.' Tam insisted. 'And we had this funny idea to film meeting you. But we're both tired from having fun at Mum's, so perhaps it wasn't.'

'Do you want some tea, guys?' asked Connie, filling the kettle. 'Or coffee.'

A coffee would be lovely, I told her.

The girls sat side-by-side on the opposite bench as we moved to the dining table once our hot beverages had been made. I had long lost the ability to make small talk. Either I was out of practice, or my social confidence was in ruins. I explained this problem to Niall that I didn't know what to say to people anymore and that sentences didn't queue like they used to.

It was helpful that Connie was proudly extroverted, and I was thankful for it. She talked about her tattoo sleeve, more or less unprompted. It covered the round of her right shoulder, continued down to her forearm, and featured pirates and sea serpents, who all had names. She said her friend was an artist and had designed it for her.

'So, what's this thing?' I asked, circling back to the filming from earlier.

'Oh, yes!' Connie had set it up the previous year, she said. She filmed herself recreating songs from musicals in her room and amassed a loyal following. Now she just filmed whatever she was up to, as well.

Tam laughed. 'You're Totnes Kim Kardashian.'

'Hardly!' Connie gasped after glancing at the clock on the wall. She needed to head over to her parents' house to take the dog for a walk and pick up the few things she had promised to get. 'Shall I pop back later?'

'Yes, please.' They both smirked. There was an energy between them entirely their own.

'Nice to meet you, Brian!' Connie beamed. She drifted into the living room and paused by the frosted glass door. 'We should introduce Brian to James. If he's staying here on his own.'

'Yes!' replied Tam. 'I was thinking the same.'

'Great minds.' Connie continued on her way and called from the hallway to say she would grab some things for dinner on her way back, just before the front door banged shut.

'Who's James?' I asked, which was another great question.

'Con's older brother. He doesn't have many friends – not around here.'

Tam fetched a laptop from a yellow hard-shelled suitcase parked by the patio doors. She said she needed to check her work emails, which she did at the table in relative silence. I pretended to browse through my phone there, unsure if leaving her to it was the polite thing to do.

'This is the best spot in the house for the Wi-Fi signal,' Tam said suddenly. 'If you're planning to work here.'

'Oh. Cool. I'll remember that.' I drummed at the table with my fingers. 'So, what do you think of Totnes?'

Tam lowered her laptop screen, grinning as if we were discussing an eccentric family member. 'I do like it. It's different. I've never lived in a small town before, but it's got its vibe. It's quite artsy, which is nice. And there are a few interesting characters around.'

'I've heard it's quite eccentric.'

'Yeah, it is. But maybe less than its reputation.'

'Are you going to miss it?' I asked.

'Mhm.' Tam tapped her teeth with her fingernails. 'Some things, for sure.'

I was on a roll with questions and decided to go for it. 'Do you mind if I ask when you're going to Berlin? Your dad gave me the impression the place would be empty.'

Tam smiled, her eyes narrowing. 'Are you trying to kick me out of my family's home already?'

'No! God. Sorry.'

She laughed and grabbed at her arms. 'I'm kidding. To be fair, I forgot to tell Dad I needed to sort a few more things first.' She flattened the laptop screen and looked me in the eye. 'So, what's your plan anyway? Dad was super vague about why you were coming here. Not that it matters.'

'The plan?' The plan was to find a way to get back to Esther, and this was just another stepping stone towards that goal – an odd side-step, perhaps. But I needed somewhere to get my head together again because I hadn't quite achieved that during our time apart. 'I might get a job or something for a bit. And write some music. I might be here for the summer. I think I'll miss London, then.'

'Oh, cool. I'm just being nosy.'

'Well, that's fair, considering.' I smiled. 'I think your dad thought I might be some sort of temporary guard dog in case of another break-in.'

'Has he met you before?' Tam chuckled into her fist. It was a fair point. 'I mean, the place did get broken into. But it's not exactly a crime town.'

My phone buzzed on the table. There was a message from Esther.

Hi. A removal guy has just been. He said he was bringing your stuff to you tomorrow.

I reread the brief message, scanning each word for any hint of fondness. 'I'll let you get on, Tam.'

'Okay.' She yawned. 'I'm sorry about earlier. We thought it would be funny.'

'It was funny.' I kept nodding as I reversed into the living room, not wanting to leave Esther hanging. 'Catch you in a bit, then.'

I sped up to my room because nothing else mattered. I jumped onto the sofabed and typed a thousand responses. Some were witty, some heartfelt, and some rambled far too much. Eventually, I settled on something painfully bland. It was no time to overdo it.

Thank you, that's good news! I hope you are well x

THREE

With one hand, I prodded at my bowl of porridge as Mum waved from my phone clasped in the other. 'Are you okay?' she asked, a soft morning sun glowing down on her balcony spot. 'You sound like you've got the flu.'

'Yeah, fine.' My spoon slipped from my fingers and rattled on the dining table. 'I wasn't expecting you to call so early.'

'Well, I was out here watching the sunrise. I didn't think you'd reply so quickly.'

'I'm up. My stuff's arriving early. Apparently.'

'Oh.' Mum picked up a mug of coffee and took a large sip. 'That's good. Are your instruments coming?'

'Yeah.'

'Wonderful.' She drew on a cigarette. 'I bought myself a little stand for my iPad, so I no longer have to hold it.'

'That's a good idea.'

'I was just using it to browse through those photos. There were some nice ones of you with your dad. Have you looked yet?'

'Yeah.' I scraped the remaining mouthful from the bowl. 'I saw a few from my tenth birthday.'

'I always remember asking what you wanted to do for your birthday that year, and your reply.'

'Go to the tip.'

'Yes!' Mum chuckled. 'You were always going. Mind you, he always had so much crap around because of his job.'

'Yeah. I think he fell out with a guy at the dump nearby, so we would take a mini road trip to get to the one he preferred. He'd get his two Beatles albums out, and we'd choose Red or Blue depending on our mood. I can't remember him listening to anything else.'

'No, he loved The Beatles.'

'Yeah.'

Mum dispatched her cigarette into the yellow ashtray on her bistro table. 'What's Frank's daughter like, then?'

'She's nice, weirdly chilled about me being here.'

'That's good! When's she off?'

'Soon, I guess. I don't want to ask again.'

'But you get along? You've not been too loud.'

I frowned as the doorbell rang. 'No, I've not been too loud....Mum, it looks like my stuff is here.'

'Okay. I'll let you go then. Tara-a-bit, then. Love you.'

'Love you, too.'

I headed for the door, unsteady on my feet – perhaps a combination of sleep deprivation and withdrawing from fluoxetine. The squatty driver belched as I opened the door, his hand gripping the neck of my favourite guitar.

There was something mildly humiliating about being confronted with the sum of my worldly possessions at 7.30 am, once they had been bundled into a loose pile in the hallway. Still, at least I had the rest of my clothes, most of which I had no recollection of ever owning as I leafed through them. More importantly, I had my guitars again and practice amps, pedals, and a giant tangled net of cables and leads.

I dragged each item into my room without any sign of life from elsewhere in the house. After packing my clothes into the wardrobe, I carefully dotted the musical things around the room. It was jarring to have everything back with me again, as if a reset had finally taken place and there were no further excuses to hide away.

I backed towards the doorway, tempted by the sudden appeal of acquiring functional furniture – perhaps a couple of stands for my instruments so they wouldn't topple over.

Perhaps I would also get a bedside table and find an alternative colour for the walls. And perhaps I would get a proper bed like Frank suggested. It wouldn't be anything fancy but could promise a night of unbothered sleep.

A sudden queasiness gripped me again. I turned and stumbled across the landing to the bathroom and spewed my guts into the toilet there, the thin warmth of porridge and coffee re-emerging. After a second and third round, I spat away the remnants and frantically brushed my teeth for an age.

My phone buzzed with another message from Esther.

Let me know when your stuff arrives! xx

It was all a bit teenage to try and decipher the purpose behind the exclamation marks and kisses. Perhaps they meant something, a fondness – a willingness to rekindle. Perhaps they were just a reflex.

It's already here, thanks. Sorry if it put you out at all! xx

After a fruitless wait for a response, I decided to take a trip around the town to get some fresh air. Tam was hunched over her laptop at the dining table when I poked my head through the frosted glass door to say hello. We had been respectfully polite to each other two days into our living arrangement. But I wasn't sure whether to maintain a respectful distance or be more outwardly friendly. Having no timeline for her departure made the balance difficult.

'How's it going?' I asked.

'Good, thanks,' Tam replied. She leaned to one side to take a bite of toast.

I rested my hands on one of the chocolate armchairs. 'Where would be a decent place to find a job? Something small and casual.'

'Hmm.' Tam clicked her tongue as she thought. She said she would ask if Connie's parents had anything going at their delicatessen. But it was a small family affair, so it was unlikely. 'Why don't you just go to the high street and ask around? It's just around the corner.'

'Yeah. I might head out and do that.'

I was about to slip away when Tam raised her hand as she was chewing. 'Oh, we're having a party here next weekend,' she said. 'You're welcome to come. I mean, you'll be here anyway.'

'Cool. In here?'

She nodded. 'Well, it's an entertaining space. It's Connie's idea. It's a sort of send-off thing. For me.'

'Ah, okay.' She was leaving soon. 'Cool, cool. That'd be nice.'

'There are loads of people coming. I just thought I'd warn you. Con knows everyone.'

'Sounds good.'

The weather alternated between stretches of gentle sun and blowy showers as I reached the pillared walkway at the tip of the sloping high street. It was significant for a small town, with potential employment opportunities in the cafes, independent bookshops, and art galleries in the immediate vicinity. Further job prospects surely lurked beyond the famous cream-coloured East Gate Arch, which spanned the width of the street at its mid-point.

I ventured inside an independent record shop peppered with solitary browsers leafing through rows of vinyl. I pulled down the hood of a bomber jacket I had been reunited with that morning and crept up to the desk to enquire about jobs. A young guy was working there with long hair and a brush moustache. He said the business belonged to his dad's friend and admitted he didn't know what he was doing. I thanked him anyway and loitered uselessly for a moment before stepping outside into the wind again.

Just as I popped my earphones back in to continue my quest, a hand grabbed my shoulder. When I turned, a large, bearded man raised his eyebrows in disconcerting tight proximity.

'Alright, mate?' inquired the man in a deep West Country burr. He was holding a wrinkled yellow plastic bag with the corners of vinyl sleeves peeping out.

'Yeah, not bad,' I replied, my hands still poised at my ears.

'Sorry, bud. I wasn't earwigging,' he said, 'but I heard you were looking for a job.'

I nodded. 'That's right. He wasn't sure.'

'He's fucking clueless.'

'Right.'

Suddenly, we were shaking hands. 'I'm Geoff.

'Hi.'

'Actually, I'm looking for someone to help me out.'

Geoff pointed at a cafe with a cheerful, wide teal fascia. 'Let's grab a drink and discuss.'

It would have been entirely sensible to decline the offer, but somehow I did the opposite of that. We gathered at a square table inside the venue. The café had a friendly ambience, with staff talking to regulars like old friends catching up.

'Nice here,' I said.

Geoff shot me a doubtful frown. 'Bit poncy.'

'Oh, okay.' I sipped at my Americano and scolded my lips. 'Are you not having anything?'

'No, I've got loads of coffee at home.'

I nodded. 'Right.'

A sudden clang of cutlery hit the floor from somewhere in the room, causing me to jump in my metal seat. Geoff pointed to a spot somewhere behind my shoulder. 'He's just dropped a load of spoons, look.'

'Oh, right.' I half-turned, but only because he was so captivated by it.

'Shit.' Geoff's eyes bulged. 'What the feck.'

'What's that?' I asked, concerned now.

'This bloke here is your spitting image.'

'Who?'

'The guy who dropped the spoons. Look.' Geoff waved an extended finger. I half-turned again. 'He's gone now. You missed it. You've got a doppelganger in Totnes, bud.'

'That's odd.' It fell quiet as he paused, seemingly, his eyebrows raised. 'So, you mentioned something about a job. Unless I imagined that.'

'Yes, that's right. So, basically, I run a music events business.' Geoff leaned forward and steepled his fingers. 'Let's call it that. And we are just about to hit up on wedding season.'

I nodded like I understood the gravity of that situation. 'Right.'

'Well, I used to run it with my brother, and he's in prison now.' Geoff rolled his eyes. 'He was drunk driving and caused a pretty serious accident.'

'I see.'

'No one died.' Geoff sighed. 'So I will have to start cancelling some bookings without help. I've got so much quality gear that it's difficult to set up on my own. Sometimes my nephew helps, but you know, he's a young lad.'

'Right.' I accidentally locked eyes with a spectacled man from the next table over. He had lifted his gaze away from a paperback. Perhaps Geoff was some kooky town peculiar everybody knew. 'Does sound interesting.'

Geoff beamed as if he had been waiting for me to show that level of tepid interest. 'I'm looking for guys like you who get the music side that can help out.' He nodded slowly, like a savant. 'Just to be clear, it's not all getting your end away like some people think.'

'Right, yeah.'

'But you get to hang out with the big dog here, and the social side is pretty spectacular.' Geoff laughed, and the unexpected barking noise drew a further glance from the spectacled man and others around. He wrestled inside the pocket of his jeans and pulled a business card from it, which was uncomfortably warm when I took it. *The Disco Inferno, Totnes* it read.

'That's a good name for it.'

'Yeah, it is,' Geoff agreed. 'But you don't say the Totnes bit. That's just the location.'

I nodded. 'I see.'

'My name's Geoff Ward. Look.' Geoff pointed at the italicised text embossed underneath.

'Right, that makes sense,' I said. 'If Ward is your surname.'

'Yeah, that's my surname.'

'Cool.'

Geoff's phone blared with an enormous thumping ringtone. He held it at eye-line and told me he needed to head off to collect his van, which was in for a service. 'Think about it, and then call me when you're ready to confirm.'

We shook hands as if departing from an interview before Geoff stomped out of the cafe bellowing into his phone.

The sun shone again, bathing the street outside with an amber glow. And the day was still young. If I was batting away job offers from a local eccentric, perhaps better prospects surely lay ahead.

I finished my coffee and hovered by the exit, where I tried to catch a server's attention. She had a cheerful face and dangling silver earrings and might have been the owner, based on my scant observations. But she was trapped in a prolonged conversation with a customer about oat milk. So I pulled the door, which was heavier on the hinges than I anticipated, and put the idea aside for another time.

I popped my earphones in once more and continued on my search. The town was livelier now, with a mix of young bohemians and older hippies, day trippers, and true-blue shoppers as I weaved in and out of the uneven, narrow pavements.

After passing the market in the square, I ventured beneath the cheerful clock of the cream-coloured arch and poked my head into the hatched window of a tiny art gallery where watercolour seascapes lined the walls. I stepped inside, and when the stern, furrowed woman behind the desk said nothing in the way of introduction, I froze and pretended to browse for a painful few moments before leaving again.

My confidence diminished via the many excruciating interactions inside the vintage clothing shops, tiny eateries, and shops that peddled crystals and new-age literature. Eventually, I lost my nerve completely, as the culmination of head shakes and indifferent shrugs took their toll.

I turned and trudged back up the slope towards home until I was back at the pillared walkway. I rounded the bend onto our street, where a yellow van had lipped onto the curb outside the house. A delivery driver was standing at the door with a cardboard package, and I signed for it as I reached him.

After deciding to hand my temporary housemate her delivery in person, I climbed the stairs with the pulsing vibrations of dance music disrupting the comforting tones in my earphones. Tam's door was closed as I perched on the small third-floor landing. I lifted a hand to knock, but the noise suggested she was busy, so I leaned the package just outside.

I slowly backed away and skulked into my room. I picked up one of my guitars, my old Squire Strat in candy apple red. It was the first instrument I'd owned, and only because my kindly guitar tutor offered to sell it to Mum for far less than it was worth. I perched on the sofa bed and picked and tuned it. The strings were old, and the heads needed replacing, but I plugged it into an old amp anyway – needing to hear it again.

It had been over six months since I had played, and a long-forgotten twinge pierced as I pressed the strings down onto the fret. The calluses on my fingertips, there since my teens, had softened enough that the nerve endings tingled away underneath. And I strummed, my digits stretching and switching between chord shapes – all muscle memory, no thought.

I played a lively, punky number called 'George is Kicking Through' – to test my finger speed as much as anything else. It was the first proper song I had written in Bill's garden workshop after he had spent days stapling old carpet to the walls before he went away for the weekend with Mum to visit family. Luke came over to stay, and after mulling the idea of throwing a party, we decided to write songs instead to see if we could.

It was incredible how much time I spent with Luke then – odd to have had so little shared chemistry with anyone until he showed up with his sideburns in my A-level music class after being expelled from posh Reigate Grammar. I wanted to hate his fine-boned, handsome face and what it did to the girls I liked – how their interest in him eclipsed any curiosity they may have had in the mysterious, outsider image I had been cultivating.

We dropped acid together for the first time in that tiny space after Luke admitted he had stolen tabs from his older sister. And we stared at each other, still playing and singing our new tune, his face slowly morphing into mine. It was wild when I told him what I was seeing, and he said the same was happening to him, that he was gazing back at himself.

The throbbing bass from upstairs ended abruptly, snapping me from my trance. The house was still, and my fingers bled through tiny punctures as I pulled the lead from my amp. Geoff's business card poked into my skin through my shirt pocket, and I slipped it out. Perhaps I'd been judgemental, and he wasn't some local weirdo. Or maybe he was and knew how to have fun with it. Either way, my phone was out, and I was calling him, perhaps only because I couldn't think of anything else to do.

'The guy from the coffee shop, yeah?' croaked Geoff, as if I had woken him up from an afternoon snooze.

'Yes. My name is Brian,' I said, already regretting the call. 'I don't think that came up earlier.'

'Well, Brian, I've got some good news.' Geoff sneezed and again several times in a row – loud, angry dad sneezes. 'Excuse moi. Yeah, you impressed me earlier.'

'Oh, did I?'

'Yep.' It was good timing, he said. A big wedding reception disco was coming up, too big that he wouldn't need a hand. 'I'll pick you up on the way to the venue if you want.'

'Right.' Perhaps he had magical persuasive powers because I found myself giving out the house address, sensing it was a bad idea, even before it tumbled from my mouth.

After the call ended, I contemplated a cowardly follow-up text to say I'd changed my mind or moved back to London. Suddenly, there was a tap at the door – a rap of fingertips.

'Brian?'

'Yeah? Come in,' I called.

Tam pushed the door open after some resistance from the thick carpet – her lips were painted pink. 'How did it go? Did you charm your way into a job?' she asked.

'Possibly.' I scratched at my neck and the prickly hair there. 'Nothing, really.'

'Okay.' Tam's eyes scanned the walls, distracted by them and perhaps thankfully. 'It's a little much in here with that colour.'

'Probably needs a lick of paint.'

'Definitely does.' Our eyes met again, and she was back with me once more. 'Did you pop a package by my door earlier?'

'Yep.'

'That explains that, then. Do you want my old laptop? It's a year old, so it still has some life.'

'Yeah, sure,' I found myself saying. 'Shall I give you some money for it?'

'If you want, not much, though.' Tam smiled. She said she was heading out for food at a small Italian restaurant in the town with Connie and James and invited me along. 'It's nice there, pretty casual.'

'Okay. Sounds good.'

'Great. I'll let you get ready.'

Tam smiled and left the room. I leafed through my collection of clothes properly, hoping to scrape over the low bar of the restaurant's pretty casual dress code. My wardrobe needed a complete overhaul, I decided. I was a man hurtling towards his thirties and still dressed like a member of an indie band who were once heading places.

The small Italian restaurant was nice with its white walls and pristine, whitewashed floorboards and menu pricing, which had me fearing for my bank balance. And I liked James, as Connie had predicted. Like his sister, he was all angles and red-haired. But he was more of a nervous talker, opening his mouth for the sake of it. That suited me just fine because the conversation flowed away from my direction, and I could drift in and out of it at leisure.

'Obviously, I don't want to be back living with my parents,' James said after expressing unhappiness at his situation. His girlfriend, Elena, was back living in Italy, and they camera-called most days, but he worried it was heading nowhere. 'I'm thirty in a couple of years. You can't be young, have a place of your own and enjoy an active social life, you know? Not without creating some financial black hole for yourself.'

'At least it's a nice big house, so it's not like you're all on top of each other,' Tam said. She picked up a glass jug and filled her tumbler with water. 'I bet it's nice for your parents to have you both back with them.'

James laughed and pointed out that his sister spent most of her time at ours, anyway. 'They probably think we're both massive failures.'

'Well, I'm not a failure!' Connie argued, mock shocked. 'I'm building my brand.'

'Of course.' James snorted and pushed at his fringy ginger stack of hair. 'Dad congratulates me on the smallest things, like ironing my shirts. And he's genuinely thrilled I haven't burnt the house down in the process.'

'What do you do, Brian?' James asked. 'If you don't mind me asking. Con said you were in a well-known band or something. And you supported The Arctic Monkeys or something.'

'Oh, we were going to, apparently. But we split up.' I gritted my teeth, dreading a foray into the subject. 'I've been a session musician more recently.'

Connie leaned forward, intrigued. 'What's a session musician?'

I took a sip of water, my throat drying. 'A musician for hire, basically.'

'Playing live gigs and that?' James asked.

I nodded. 'Sometimes. It was mostly studio work. That was my niche.'

'That sounds exciting,' Connie said. 'Ever worked with any famous people?'

I shrugged. 'Once or twice, although we'd rarely meet. Generally, I would work with a producer to add parts on a track they had recorded.'

Connie gasped. 'Did you ever work with Ben Howard?'

I shook my head. 'Nope.'

'Red Hot Chilli Peppers?' James asked.

'No.' I smirked, but James's unchanging facial expression suggested his enquiry was sincere. 'Maybe I've made it sound more glamorous than it was. I'd often just record pieces that might get used on a daytime television show – that sort of nonsense.'

Tam's eyes narrowed. She was intrigued. 'Do you still get booking offers?'

I shrugged. 'I haven't checked, really.' I scratched at my face, nervously. 'It's probably not something I want to go back to.'

The server cleared away our plates as an unfamiliar warmth of heavy carbs began to sink. It was strange to have a full stomach again.

'Well, I suppose that's handy. I heard you might be looking for something,' James said after being glared at by Connie.

Tam laughed. 'We've not been gossiping about you.'

I smiled. It was nice. 'Yeah. I'm keeping an eye out. Something small to keep me ticking over on my break.'

James said he worked for an IT consultancy firm. Whilst it was as dull as it sounded, temporary jobs were always available at the office on the edge of town. And I didn't need to worry when I suggested my CV wouldn't be a good fit. I could send him something, and he would tweak it for me.

'Well, I think it's a good idea,' Tam said. 'You could use your laptop to write a CV.'

I nodded. 'Sure.' It didn't exactly sound like a thrill ride. But perhaps there was an appeal to the structure of office work, or at least in how I imagined it when thinking about Esther's job – five days per week, knowing exactly how long her day would be. 'Maybe.'

It was karaoke night at The Dartmouth Inn, Connie then announced, and the four of us were going. She had made that decision for us. 'Connie, we've been through this,' Tam said as she quietly settled the bill when the server returned with the card machine. 'The singing –sometimes I wonder if there's too much of it.'

Connie pouted. 'Well, I'm not going to stop.'

A spontaneous staring contest broke out between the girls, grins rising as their eyes locked like everything around them was floating away. It would have been the polite thing to do in the circumstances.

The pub was open for another hour when we arrived and snagged a tall table with green cushioned stools. I sat alongside my housemate as our sibling friends took to a tiny makeshift stage and murdered a rendition of 'Mr Brightside' and a pub regular in a denim cap heckled them from the bar. Tam said she couldn't work out why Connie and James were so endearing. There was a relentless theatre school energy about them, but it was charming far more than chafing.

After closing time, the four of us assembled in the paved square courtyard outside the pub. Then, as we went on our separate ways, it was jarring that Connie turned back with her brother towards the cobbles at the bottom of the high street.

'Is Connie not coming?' I asked as we ascended the climb in the opposite direction.

'No. We're trying not to spend all our time together,' Tam replied as if that would be difficult for her. 'Berlin and all that.'

'Right.' My phone buzzed as we walked past the high street's closed shops and orange street lights. It was Esther again.

I'm visiting Mum and Dad in Ilfracombe soon. That's probably not far from you x

Perhaps I should have stayed calm and not instantly replied like I had been living for every scrap of communication.

Oh cool! North Devon isn't it?

Yes. Maybe we could meet up? Just a thought x

My mind raced a million miles ahead. I had no idea if Ilfracombe was far beyond being in the same county.

Yes! We should. I would love that x

What were the chances? We were like magnets, drawing towards each other again. Seeing her again was impossible, magical, and it would be the sharpest reminder of what we had.

I gasped as I slipped my phone back into my pocket – a huge happy *pah!* My excitement had erupted to the surface as I narrowly missed the lampost already threatening to take it away.

'Everything okay there?' asked Tam. 'Did you get some good news?'

'Yeah! Yes. Possibly.'

'Good.' Tam looked at the sky as we rounded onto our terraced street and its tall pastel-coloured houses. 'There are so many stars tonight.'

She was right. It was sparkling up there. 'It's amazing.'

I couldn't stop talking as we headed inside. Whole sentences arrived in my mouth like gifts, propelled there by the dumb luck of it all. I made tea, and we sat together on the lime sofa. We talked about what it was like to move from London to an unfamiliar small town, even as the tingling possibilities of leaving again were spreading through me. Tam was easy to talk to, and it was a miracle she had bothered to deal with me, given our situation.

My head was swimming and alive when I finally headed to bed, long after Tam had decided to. I lay there on my sofabed, leaning into the fullest potential of a reunion with Esther. Green shoots were springing from the ground, and a thousand hopeful possibilities danced over the cracked ceiling. And I held our chubby babes there, the inevitable culmination of those tentative steps towards each other. And I told them how their parents got back together, a sanitised version of events that made sense to their tiny ears.

FOUR

Mum's lips trilled on the laptop screen, cigarette smoke lingering around them. 'I sent you both a card at Christmas,' she said, tapping away the ash.

'Oh really?'

'She must have thought I'd gone mad.'

I pushed my plate to one side, chewing my toast. 'Es probably just assumed I hadn't told you.'

Mum sighed. The sun was beaming on her balcony, and she took another long drag. 'You know Bill liked Esther. He thought she was good for you.'

'Yes, I did know that because he said it every five minutes.'

'Well, she was so good for you, Brian. You had a lovely situation, and I was so proud of you, seeing how far you had come.'

'Well, maybe you need to lift that bar a bit, Mum. Just a tiny bit, so it's not on the ground waiting for me to stumble into a relationship.'

Mum rolled her eyes, her happiness tied to my own. 'It does feel like you're determined to throw away the good things in your life.'

'Wow.' I drummed at the dining table. 'This is an incredible motivational speech. I was not expecting a lecture, not this morning.'

'Sorry.' Mum tutted at herself. Her face softened with an apologetic smile. 'I am excited for you. You will say *hi* to Bubbles for me.'

I winced and then snickered. 'Still going with that nickname, then?'

'Well, she looks like Bubbles. You know, from Absolutely Fabulous.'

'Jesus. She doesn't,' I insisted during a prolonged yawn. 'She's got the same accent, and that's it. I don't even know what that show is other than what you made me watch to prove your point.'

'Well, I think the way she holds herself is similar. And not the character, because Esther is very bright, isn't she? It's the woman who played her, I think. I don't know her name.'

'Okay.' There were footsteps on the stairs, most likely Tam coming to reclaim her workspace soon. 'Well, I'll pass on your message if you want.'

'Okay.' Mum laughed. 'Honestly, Brian. Search that actress on the internet if you don't believe me.'

'Well, maybe later. I need to get going now.'

'Okay, Bab.' She blew kisses at the screen as Tam poked her head through the door. 'Tara-a-bit. I'm excited for you, really.'

'Bye, Mum.'

It was warm and grey when I stepped onto the street and caused a minor collision with a young woman carrying a baby inside a fabric sling. After an apology and a cheerful smile at the infant on her mother's back, I set on my way to meet Esther for the first time in over a year. It was a fact, still fully crystallising, as I rounded towards the pillared walkway, a ball of nervous, euphoric tension. And what would I say? Perhaps it would just fall into place.

There was little space to manoeuvre on the narrow pavements, with shoppers and day-trippers shuffling past each other and between the cars ambling on the road. The town was so active it was a struggle to find somewhere suitable to eat at lunchtime, my one responsibility.

I peered into the windows of cafes and made direct eye contact with seated customers inside as I checked for space. Eventually, I was seated at a secluded round table in the dimly lit corner of a small tearoom with low ceilings. There was an eclectic mismatch of teapots and plates adorning the walls, round cakes on stands in the window and a bright cherry-red carpet underfoot. I wasn't sure if the chintzy feel of the place would appeal to Esther, but it was all very Devon, and perhaps that made it an excellent choice.

Esther was running late, according to her message. I removed my glasses and then put them on again – unable to decide which was best in an elevated nook to ourselves as a toddler screamed at the table directly below. He hated it there, he said, it was rubbish.

I removed my jacket and placed it around a neighbouring chair to claim it, just in case. We had a space where we could be open and say what needed to be said, provided no other customer was bold enough to sit at the one table almost adjoined to ours. It would not be so easy, then.

Suddenly Esther was pushing her way inside, and she jumped in surprise at the old-school bell jangling above the door. I stood and waved as she scanned the room, drawing a cautious smile before she wandered over. We hugged across our small table, and she gripped onto my forearms as I leaned in for something warmer.

'Don't get too close,' she insisted, her eyes puffy. 'I've had a cold.

'Oh, dear.' I sat down again and pulled at the edges of the tablecloth to flatten it out.

'You should be okay, though. I'm over the worst of it.' Esther arranged a pale blue jacket over the back of her chair and placed a day bag between her feet.

'At least you're feeling better.'

'Yeah. Mostly.'

We stared at our laminated menus. Perhaps there was too much to say as Esther played with a St. Christopher, clamping it in her teeth. 'I like your hair,' I said, finally. It had been cropped short and dyed shades lighter.

Esther smirked as if there was a story behind the change and then shook her head dismissively. 'I'm not sure about it.' She glanced around the room, frowning as if it disappointed her. 'You've got glasses on.'

'Yep. What do you think? I'm not sure about them.'

Esther prodded at her chin dimple. 'Not sure they suit your face shape.'

'Right.' I slipped the specs off and folder them into my shirt pocket. 'Fair enough.'

'You don't have to take them off, Brian. Not if you need them.'

'I don't really. Slightly short-sighted. I would only need them for driving, really.'

'Do you drive now?'

'No. But maybe I'll have to round here.'

'Maybe.' Esther studied the laminated menu and prodded at her chin dimple again. I used to tell her it was her best feature all the time because it was. And I wanted to reach up and poke it like it was some reset button to melt the frosty start. 'Oh, guess who I spoke to the other week? Adam.'

'Oh, wow.'

The tension broke a little as we shared memories of our eccentric old housemate, who was a fully-trained doctor now. Then we talked about Glastonbury because he was there with our other housemates and their friends. It was a fork-in-the-road event, the last time we would see him before he left for Scotland, where he had secured a job. It was also when Esther and I decided to take our mutual fondness further.

'I started thinking about that weekend after what happened,' Esther said. She bit into her necklace again. 'Do you remember when you abandoned our group?'

I frowned, unsure of what she meant. 'When I bumped into old friends?'

'Yes.'

'It was just a surprise to find out they were there.'

'I know. But you left me. Was I not cool enough?' Esther asked. She tapped her chin, and our eyes met – hers were wounded like it was painful. She had never mentioned it until now. 'You never introduced me to your old friends.'

'Sorry. I didn't know you felt like that.'

It had been Esther's first festival, and she reminded me. It had rained, and she hated camping as much as she feared she would. 'I was only there for Beyonce.'

I raised my eyebrows. 'Not only, surely?'

She smiled, but it disappeared as quickly as it rose. 'Liz was only there to see Beyonce,' she continued. 'She was so upset we disappeared after and couldn't debrief.'

'How is Liz?' I asked, hoping for a sunnier topic change.

'She's great,' Esther enthused. 'Chris finished with her at the same time, and we've had such a great time living together. Honestly, thank God for shit men.'

Esther dropped the laminated sheet onto the table. I smiled at what I hoped was a joke. An impossible young girl arrived at our table to take our orders, so fresh-faced it didn't seem like it should be allowed. We fumbled an order of afternoon tea for two. I was too nervous for an appetite, but it sounded cheerful enough to soften the mood.

'You know it's odd just to do what you did?' Esther asked once we were alone again. 'You ran away.'

I shuffled in my seat. 'Yeah.'

'Because I don't think you would have grasped what that meant for me.' She hesitated and gave a faint and sad smile – her eyes not lifting with her mouth. 'You know, just the admin alone, having to sort everything. Even dragging your crap to Liz's place.'

'I'm sorry.'

'And where would I have gone if she didn't have the room?'

I shrugged. 'I don't know. Back to Manchester?'

'I'm not from Manchester, Brian.' Esther sighed, a face filled with conflict. 'And not just that. I've had everyone asking about you, not just Adam. People asked where you were and why we had split up. People I didn't know asked me why you had just disappeared and weren't replying to their messages. I just told them you were fine. I told them you were alive. I didn't know what else to say.'

'I'm sorry.' I bit into my thumbnail. 'I expect I'm not very popular.'

Esther laughed, short and disbelieving. 'Did you just not tell anyone what happened?'

I shook my head. 'Not really.'

'Not even your old friends?' she asked.

'No.'

'I didn't think you had. People got my number from somewhere, and I get calls asking if you're taking work. Someone called me last week.'

'What did you say?'

'I told them not to call me.'

Esther retrieved a circular tin of lip balm from her coat pocket. She circled a finger inside and smoothed it over her lip. 'It's like I'm still your spokesperson.'

'That's not good.'

The unhappy toddler rolled on the floor as his parents quietly admonished him.

Esther smirked. 'I mean, can you imagine what it was like for me on my own at our Paul's wedding? So many questions, just endless questions. *Where's Brian? What's going on with Brian? What did you do to Brian?* People were laughing about it like I should find that funny.'

'Right. I can see that would be annoying.'

'Annoying?' Esther's eyes widened. 'Yeah, it's been annoying not knowing what to say. I mean, should I have just told them you tried to kill yourself?'

'Is that what you said?'

'No, I didn't.' Esther hesitated. 'Obviously, a couple of people know. I'm sure they've been discreet about it.'

'Right.' I nodded, unsure how I felt about that – but perhaps it was inevitable. But perhaps I also needed a list of those people to avoid them forever. 'Maybe we should talk about something else?'

'Oh, no. I want to talk about it.' Esther planted an elbow on the table, her forehead onto her hand. 'I don't think you intended to kill yourself, Brian. Did you?'

The heavy artillery was out.

'Does it matter?' I asked with a protective grin.

'You didn't leave a note. And you called an ambulance.'

'You've thought about this a lot. That's understandable.'

'I have thought about it a lot. Of course I have. I've thought about nothing else at times.' Esther groaned at a separate frustration – her nose was running again, and she held a tissue to it. 'But that's all finally going now, and I'm glad. You wanted to end our relationship and didn't know how to do it like an adult. That's what I think now.'

'I did try to explain to you why it happened.'

'You didn't. You sent me that rambling note about missing your dad and your band. I mean, your band, Brian? Honestly, was that supposed to make me feel better?'

'No. I was unwell, Es. Do you understand that?' Esther lowered her eyes. She played with her pendant again, rubbing the chain between her lips. 'I was ill, and I didn't want to be. I didn't want that for you either.'

'Okay,' she said, softening again. 'Where are you living now?'

'I'm just in a house, not far from here.'

She raised an eyebrow. 'On your own?'

'Sort of…I'm looking after it.'

'What are you doing for work?'

'I don't know yet. I'll sort something.'

The young girl returned accompanied by an elderly couple in matching blue bucket hats dawdling behind her. She was sweetly apologetic and asked if I minded moving my jacket. The venue had filled up, and there were no other tables available. It was a disaster.

'Why are you looking after this house?' Esther asked as our fellow patrons sank into their chairs, and I returned their smiles without wanting to encourage them too much. 'I don't get why you're here.'

'Frank suggested it,' I said. 'And it just seemed like a good idea.'

'Brian, who is Frank?'

'He's a friend. Our old band manager,' I explained, whispering. 'I was staying at his place.'

'So, is that where you were the whole time?'

'Yeah, he offered.'

'Where?'

'Islington.'

'Islington? What is he, your fairy godmother?'

The young girl returned with our order this time and an expectant grin, perhaps anticipating an enthusiasm it usually inspired. But Esther stared blankly at the tower of scones, finger sandwiches and miniature cakes happily arranged around a tiered platter.

'I won't manage much of that,' Esther said. She lifted a lid on a toadstool-shaped teapot instead to check the brew and closed it again. 'You should tuck in. You look like you need it.'

'That's nice.'

'Sorry.' She tutted as her eyes lowered, and she gripped my fingertips. 'Your shoulders have disappeared, Brian. You look so thin.'

Our fingers unlocked. 'Yeah, I just need to eat more.' I popped a pair of cucumber sandwiches onto my side plate as a hand placed itself on my shoulder.

'Excuse me, darling,' the elderly lady said, reaching across. 'We were wondering what to order. Is that nice?'

'I think so,' I replied. I took a bite and nodded performatively. The lady gave me a crumbly smile and relayed the good news to her moustached husband across the table.

'This gentleman says it's nice,' she bellowed.

'Is it nice?' the elderly man asked, directing his question at Esther for an unknown reason.

'I don't know yet,' Esther replied. 'Looks lovely, though.'

The old couple spoke between themselves again, at a volume which provided cover for our conversation to continue.

'I thought you would have gone to Spain to see your mum,' Esther said. 'I did wonder if that's what had unsettled you. Her moving away.'

'I don't think so.' I paused for a moment. 'Mum thought we were still together until not long ago.'

'I know.' Esther poured a dribble of tea into her cup to inspect its colour. 'A Christmas card turned up from the redirect thingy I did with the mail.'

'Right.'

Esther finished pouring, content with its darker colour now. 'Poor woman. I miss her. She would have worried so much about you.'

'She was, but that's nothing new, at least. She says hello, by the way.'

'Did she say, *say hello to Bubbles for me*?'

I laughed. 'More or less exactly that.'

A fond, snuffled chuckle escaped from Esther's mouth. I was happy for as long as it lasted, a moment before she dabbed at her eyes with the tissue in her free hand.

'Does she know about what you did?' she asked.

'No.' I rubbed at my face. 'She'd been flying over. It wouldn't be fair.'

'Yeah.'

Esther tapped the table suddenly as if reminding herself of something, and removed a phone from her back pocket. She typed out a lengthy message, pausing several times.

'Everything okay?' I asked.

'Yes.' Esther looked up from the screen, finally. She placed her phone back down and tilted her head. 'Brian, you know I'm with someone?'

Perhaps it was a gut punch, winding me – and somehow not fully landing. 'No, I–' I tripped over a tumble of disconnected words, wrong-footed. 'What do you mean? A boyfriend? A partner? What are people in relationships called at our age?'

'Hmm….' Esther frowned, holding her eyebrows together. Perhaps she was unsure if I was being deliberately obtuse. 'I didn't know if you'd heard anything.'

'No, no….' I plucked a miniature butterfly cake from the platter. There was a tiny dollop of lemon curd between the sponge wings. I prodded at it as Esther's heavy news rattled around without sinking. 'Like, is this a proper thing?'

'I think so. Yes.'

'Cool.' I pinched my bottom lip, fearing it might wobble if I didn't clamp it. My ears burned unexplainably. Perhaps my body had reacted before my mind could absorb the news. 'What's he like?'

'Nice. You know him, I think. Nate.'

'Oh. Nate.' I closed my eyes and poked my ear drum to try to dull the warmth from there. 'The guy from New Zealand?'

'Yes,' Esther confirmed. 'We used to work together.'

I nodded, his face falling into place – a heavy brow and fetching aquiline nose. 'He was at a housewarming thing for your friend.'

'Probably. I think so.'

'No, he was,' I insisted, grasping at a fuzzy memory. 'Nice guy. We got talking about something. I don't know what it was. Rugby, maybe. It was sport.'

'Well, he rows. You know, recreationally. All the time, apparently.'

I held fingers in both ears, the heat spreading to my cheeks. 'No, I don't, really.'

'Brian.' Esther sighed. 'Are you going to look at me?'

'Yep.' My eyes opened, although I would have been happy to have kept them closed for the remainder of our get-together. And it wasn't because I was inclined to be childish or petty but to try and shield myself from an internal avalanche. 'Sorry.'

'I'm sorry you didn't know.' Esther reached across the table, her hands stopping short of touching mine. She smiled instead, making it known as much as she could that she understood the situation was difficult for her. And it was fucked anyway. 'I'm sorry. In general, I'm sorry.'

'Oh. Don't be sorry,' I said. I cupped my ears. 'Jesus, Esther. I should be begging you for forgiveness.'

'Okay. You're just quiet and acting a bit odd. Are you okay?'

'Yes!' I pulled my hands away again. 'I'm just trying to get my head around it. All the change.'

'Yes.'

'It feels like so much time just vanished.'

'Okay.' She nodded and sipped her tea. 'It's not been like that for me.'

'I see.' I took another bite of the sandwich. 'I'm trying to figure out why you wanted to meet.'

'To see if you were okay.' Esther half-smiled like that was obvious. 'And to get things off my chest. I think that's fair.'

'Yes.' My face was burning up again. I wiped my brow to check for sweat. 'Closure is a strong word, isn't it?'

'Well, yes.' She sniffed. 'Why did *you* want to meet up?'

'Um….' My voice cracked. 'You know, to see where we might have a friendship again.' I smiled my most charming, cheeky grin. I must have seemed insane when the corners of Esther's mouth remained still and weren't poised to explode like they always used to. I don't know why I had expected to see that uncontrolled affection again. It was just always there before. 'I mean, being honest, it would be one where something else might happen, eventually.'

'Wow.' Esther sighed, a whole six months of breath. 'I don't know what to say. Sometimes, I feel like I didn't know you, Brian. That's what scares me. Do you ever regret doing it?'

'Well, I don't think it's a good idea to talk about regretting my choices when I wasn't in a good place.'

It fell quiet, mainly because the toddler and his family were leaving, and he was wailing and thumping his father's back as he was carried away in a fireman's lift. And our neighbours had stopped speaking between themselves – their heads turned toward us. It was hard not to respect that level of oblivious invasion, in a way.

'Regret is a useless emotion,' I said, softly breaking the silence. 'It traps you in a loop. My therapist said that to me.'

Esther's eyes watered. 'I think I could have done with a therapist.'

'I could have done with more of it, I think.'

Esther pulled out another tissue, muttering in frustration as she held it to her nose. 'I think I want to go, actually. I'm really not feeling well.'

I didn't know what to say as she stood and unhooked her pale blue jacket. 'Do you want me to come, too?' It was such a ridiculous question.

'No! Thank you.' Esther picked up her bag from the floor and fished for a purse before placing a few notes beside the platter. 'That'll cover it, I think. You're not working.'

'Es, come on.'

A cold hand reached across as the bell rang above the door, and Esther had left. 'Oh dear,' the elderly lady said. She chuckled away as if she had been enjoying a piece of close-up theatre. 'She's cross with you.'

'She gets like it as well,' her husband chirped in and jabbed a finger at his wife. 'There's always something I've done wrong. Always.'

I flagged the young girl down and paid for the order before rushing outside, expecting to find Esther, just like she had wanted. And we would have held each other and cried like babies, but everything would have been okay again. It was just steam blowing off, and there was so much of it we couldn't see correctly. But it would have settled again, dissipated into the air, and she would know what she wanted again.

After scanning the immediate vicinity and dashing across both sides of the pavement, I did locate Esher. She was comforted by a handsome spectacled man in a gingham shirt outside a vintage clothing shop. In the fog of the moment, I assumed he must have been a concerned bystander, someone who had taken it upon himself to console a distressed stranger.

I was about to step across the street to let him know I could take it from there. But then she buried herself into his long frame, his eyes locking with mine. It was Nate, of course, and he clasped the back of Esther's head as she rested her cheek on his chest.

My phone vibrated, and I pulled it out. Geoff was calling, and I didn't want to answer – the last thing I could wish to do at any moment. And yet, I found myself doing it – anything to prise my eyes away.

'Alright, you fucker!' Geoff yelled as I answered.

'Hi.'

'Just kidding, mate,' he laughed. 'I'm outside your house. Are you there?'

'What do you mean?' I asked. My voice wobbled as it might have done forever now. 'Why are you outside my house?'

'We've got a wedding to get to, brother. It's disco time.'

'Oh shit.' I almost burst into tears right there. 'Now?'

'Yes, now,' laughed Geoff. 'You sound like shit, bud. No offence. A big night, was it?'

I stood glued to the ground, with nowhere to retreat now. Esther and Nate were still perched on the ledge of the shop window, his chin resting on the top of her head. And I couldn't look away, even as I wrenched my feet from the pavement and pinballed into oncoming pedestrians heading my way.

My eyes heated up as I continued up the high street. I wanted to rip them out and throw them in the air. I wanted to be reckless. I *was* a shit man, and that's what I was.

'You still there, bud?' Geoff asked.

'Yes, I'm coming,' I replied and cleared my throat. 'I'll be there soon, Geoff.'

I broke into a steady jog and was off-balance as I wove between the pavement and the cars on the road. I ran with no purpose or sense of space. And I collided with people and things and never looked at the catastrophe behind me again.

FIVE – A WEDDING DISCO

The wedding reception disco was in full swing at The Orangery – a single-storey function room in the gardens of a stately home on the edge of Dartmoor. Circles of dancing guests flung their limbs as sugar-high waistcoated children wrestled each other to the ground on the shiny wooden dance floor. And I was there but not present as a beaming carousel of lights danced over the walls. Perhaps I had died after all.

We had arrived late to the venue, having sped from a country golf club twenty miles away once Geoff had discovered it was the destination for the following week's disco. The lost time meant we had to make do with the venue's PA system, which was apparently a disaster.

Geoff was a nonsensical person, a bundle of nervous energy so caught up in the excitement of the event he hadn't noticed I had barely said a word or lifted a finger since it got underway. He was too busy performing, flinging between joy and despair and every emotion between. 'There's a hum on the left speaker,' he groaned with his chin on his chest. 'I fucking knew it. I knew this bollocks would happen.'

'Oh, dear.' I winced in performative sympathy. But then Geoff pulled on a comedy red Afro wig and began punching both arms in the air in time to Taylor Swift's 'Shake it Off'.

As the song wound up to its crescendo, the bride's mother, Helen, appeared at our booth with its flashing LED lights as she had done twice already. She handed us bottled beers as a thank-you for a job well done.

'What's your hairstyle called?' Geoff asked as he clinked the bottle in my hand.

Helen laughed and stroked a purple daisy over her ear. 'It's just a side bun.'

Geoff said he'd never heard of a side bun, and I became wedged between them as he leaned across. 'It looks beautiful.'

Helen gasped in flirtatious disbelief. 'How could you not have heard of a side bun?'

'No idea,' he replied. 'It looks great on you. That's all that matters.'

Helen told Geoff that flattery would get him everywhere and then nudged me in the stomach with her elbow. She then sauntered in reverse to rejoin the dancers out on the floor. 'Call Me Maybe' by Carlie Rae Jepson played as she shuffled backwards and appeared to be eye-fucking Geoff as she moved.

Geoff bit down on a knuckle as Helen twirled her white jacket. 'God, she looks so good, Brian.' He took a long swig of beer and gasped like he was overwhelmed with sexual anticipation. 'She's divorced.'

'Oh, right.'

'She told me.' Geoff drained his beer and then picked up the other, his eyes still fixed. 'Your name *is* Brian, yeah?'

'Yeah.'

'I was calling you Chris earlier, wasn't I?'

I nodded. 'Yeah, a few times.'

'I'll call you Bri from now on.'

'Okay.'

Geoff tapped me on the arm. 'Would you mind manning the fort, Bri? I need a piss.'

'Sure.'

He winked and removed his wig. 'I'll get that side door locked as well. They shouldn't be using it.' My thumb raised on its own as Geoff disappeared along the side of the dancefloor.

With little grasp of what 'manning the fort' meant in practice, thoughts drifted back to Esther, as they kept doing – how badly I had blown it with her and how empty life might be now. I oscillated between hopelessness and despair when a pair of white drapes blew into the room after a young boy pulled the side door open nearby. Guests used the entrance as a shortcut to the gardens to have a smoke or chat outside. Occasionally, someone would yell, 'play some ABBA,' or whatever artist or song was on their mind as they left the room.

'Oi!' A grey-suited man, hairless and angry, held his hand on the side door handle. 'Where's he gone? The twat in the red wig.'

'Having a break,' I replied. 'I think he's taken the wig off now.'

'He won't play Sweet Caroline!' Strings of saliva hung from his mouth, and he jabbed his finger in my direction. 'It's our tune, all of the boys. Why won't you fucking play it?'

I peered at the laptop. 'Looks like it'll be on soon.'

'Finally!' he yelled and slammed the door behind him.

In fact, only five tracks appeared to be in the queue if I was reading it right – it was hard to tell. Either way, our furious guest's choice wasn't on it.

A long twenty minutes trickled by as the playlist ticked down with no sign of Geoff. 'Uptown Funk' by Mark Ronson featuring Bruno Mars filled the dancefloor, but the swirl of lights obscured faces as I searched for him and could only locate his lackadaisical teenage nephew.

Jack was supposed to have been helping us but had seemingly only helped himself to the buffet. I waved with both hands to get his attention – somehow invested, now the entire event was about to grind to a halt. But he remained unmoved in his solitary chair between tables, his arms folded and a plastic plate on his lap about to topple. Perhaps he was asleep.

I made hasty plans to disappear through the troublesome door when there was a sudden tap at my shoulder from behind. 'Great work, Bri,' Geoff beamed. He planted a pint onto the desk and began tinkering with the light controllers. 'Kept it ticking over nicely.'

'There are no songs left, Geoff,' I told him.

'Shit!' He pivoted his attention to the laptop. 'Fucking hell. Good spot, Bri. What shall we play next?'

'Sweet Caroline?'

'Hell, yes!' Geoff puffed his cheeks as the trumpeted intro to Neil Diamond's signature tune kicked in. The boys rushed from the bar to the floor like a pack of dogs who had heard a fork banged on a food bowl. 'That was fucking close.'

'Yeah.'

'Fuck.' Geoff held a hand on his chest and cupped another to my ear. 'Helen gave me a blowjob in the loo.'

'Oh, okay.'

'Don't say a word, Chris,' he said, chuckling. 'There's lots of her family around, and probably doesn't want them knowing she just swallowed a load from the DJ.'

'Right. Probably.' I nodded, reasonably confident I wouldn't even think about it again. 'Jesus.'

'It took me ages to finish, you know. I was thinking of you out here on your own. Had to get her to pick up the speed.'

'Right. Lovely stuff.'

Only the hardiest of wedding guests remained as the event headed towards a climax. 'Party Rock Anthem' by LMFAO was hitting its stride, and they each held their hands and drinks aloft as the chorus hit, toasting a chandelier above them. As the song ended, Geoff pulled his red wig on once more. I didn't understand what was going on there. He sunk the remainder of yet another drink, and readied himself on the mic to sign us off for the night.

'Hello, everyone. It's been a glorious night spending it with all of you. Our very best wishes to the married couple Jeremy and Yvette Nelson.' Geoff paused as a cheer went up around the room. He was a professional, if nothing else.

'We've been The Disco Inferno, South Devon's premier mobile entertainment events service. This is it from us, DJ Geoff The Tune Train, and DJ Chris. Goodnight.'

I waved an instinctive flap of my hand as my apparent stage name of 'DJ Chris' was announced, and then immediately feared that moment might haunt me for a while.

Geoff performed his vanishing act again once the house lights were on and the remaining guests were funnelling from the venue. He said he needed to sort out an urgent invoicing issue and left his keys with Jack, who had made an unexpected and silent re-appearance.

We stacked each case and bag onto the equipment trolleys, wheeled them towards the van in the car park and bundled the gear into sloppy piles in the rear of the vehicle. Latches were popping open, and bags were half-zipped. But, this was no time for precision. I needed to get home and lock myself away.

We closed the rear doors together and climbed back inside the cabin, leaving space for Geoff in the driver's seat. And as we waited, the concrete car park slowly emptied. A misty rain washed it as residual celebrators stumbled into their departing taxis.

A prolonged chafing silence was only broken when Jack released a long resonant fart. 'You okay there?' I asked, perturbed by his lack of reaction to the sound.

'Yep,' he replied, his eyes fixed ahead. 'Just farted.'

'Yeah. Cheers.'

I edged to the driver's seat across the cocked handbrake. Suddenly, there was a full-palmed slap on the driver's window, the fright of my life. Assuming it was our absent companion, I flicked the latch and reluctantly shuffled back to the middle. The door swung open, and Geoff folded forward like falling timber, his weight onto his forearms.

'I'm so sorry, Chris. I got tangled up with Helen and some whiskey.' Geoff peered at Jack briefly and then winked at me, acknowledging our sleeping colleague. 'Has he been helpful?' he asked, whispering his question.

'Yeah,' I was whispering too.

'He's a big lad.'

'Right.'

'Like a prop forward.'

'Okay….'

'He doesn't like loud music.'

I shrugged. 'Okay.'

Geoff sighed. 'I wouldn't have guessed I would get two blowjobs tonight.'

'Right.'

'Would you?'

I frowned, unable to stay on track. 'Would I what?'

'Have guessed that I would get two blowjobs.'

I didn't know what to say. 'It didn't factor into my thinking.' I stopped myself. What the fuck was I saying? 'Listen, mate. I really just want to get home. I just want to fucking go.'

Geoff scratched sheepishly at his greying beard. 'Okay – well, confession time. I've had too much to drink, mate.' Somehow, it hadn't occurred to me until precisely that moment that his drinking might prevent us from leaving. But, of course, it did. He was a wreck. 'Luckily, Helen's invited me to stay in her room tonight.'

'Lucky for who?' I asked, increasingly annoyed.

'Well, me.'

'Okay. Does Jack drive?' I asked.

'No! He's not cut out for that.' Geoff winced like that was the worst idea he had ever heard. 'Obviously, I'd take you home first, but you can't drive in my condition, which is annoying.'

'Right.'

Geoff nodded at Jack. 'We don't want to end up like his dad. In prison.'

'No.'

'Hey, do you remember when we ran over that pony near Tavistock, Jack?' asked Geoff, tapping at his nephew's knee. 'That was from drinking and driving. That poor pony, all crumpled up like that. You shouldn't do it, Chris.' Geoff waited patiently for his nephew to respond as I tried not to think about crumpled ponies. 'Do you remember the dead pony, Jack?'

'He's asleep,' I whispered.

'Yeah, he is.' Geoff slapped me on the arm like he had remembered something. 'Hey, I spotted Al, the security guy doing the rounds. Keep a low profile. He's a fucking psycho and got aggressive last time I slept out here.'

'Wait, hold on.' I was panicking now. 'You need me to stay here with the van tonight?'

'Yeah, I'm gonna need you to, Bri.' Geoff said it was crucial to man the vehicle because of its valuable equipment. He said he was worried someone might break in, as had happened once in Torquay.

'Right.'

He slapped his hand on the seat. 'Sometimes we have to play by the rules, Chris.'

'Brian.'

'Sorry, Brian.' Geoff gave me a sheepish smile. 'Did I call you DJ Chris earlier?'

'Yep.'

'Sorry, mate.' He laughed. 'Is this alright, then? Shall I head off?'

I shrugged. There was nothing I could do. 'Okay.'

'Amazing.' Geoff balled his hands into celebratory fists. 'Get the blankets in here from the back, mate. They're fucking good ones. Keep you warm.'

'Okay.' I had either run out of other words or the will to say anything.

'Ah, shit.' He clamped his eyes shut. 'Actually, I had to chuck those. They were filthy. I won't tell you why.'

'Okay...'

'Right, then.' Geoff pushed himself to his feet, pulling his wide frame outside the van. 'I'll see if I can slip away early,' he said, tapping the van before slamming the door. 'No promises.'

I debated whether I should call a cab and bail after Geoff scuttled away, not knowing how far we had come after our two trips to get there. Jack rolled over to face the window, happy to doze away. And he was only a kid. It would have been wrong to have left him on his own. So, I rolled my shirt sleeves to warm my goose-bumped forearms and shuffled down into the driver's seat to try and find a pocket of comfort there.

Jack's snoring ratcheted up a notch as I closed my eyes and started chuckling – at the misery of it all. When I turned twenty, Dorothea were featured in an article in the NME called 'The Future of British Music'. But now I was in the future – about to turn thirty, and this, THIS, was what I was up to. And my body was embedded in shivers as I held it, and my mind was alive – a million reasons I wouldn't sleep. And I laughed at the depths I had plummeted to. And I kept laughing.

SIX

My pocket was vibrating as the early morning sun warmed my back. I leaned against the van and pissed onto a front wheel – my face pushed into a rested forearm.

'Hi, Mum,' I said, answering my phone.

'Are you outside?' she asked. 'I can hear birds.'

'Yes.' There was a lean in the asphalt, and the pool of urine forked downhill towards the other parked cars. 'Just getting some fresh air.'

'You sound half-dead. How did it go?'

'With Esther?

'Well, yes.'

'Um.' I turned, my back sliding against the vehicle's side panel as I squatted. 'Not good. Bad, actually.'

Mum tutted. 'Oh, no. Bill will be upset.'

'Jesus.' I moved a hand across my face to shield the glare from my eyes. 'Mum, I don't give a fuck what Bill thinks about it. Why is that your first reaction?'

'Don't swear at me, Brian.'

'Fine,' I whispered. 'But it's such a weird thing to say to me.'

'She's probably upset with you.'

'Yep.' I snickered bitterly. 'She was upset with me.'

'Well, maybe now you've cleared the air, she'll come round. You've got to give her a chance.'

'The air is clear now. She's with someone else.'

Mum sighed. 'Already?'

'Well. It's been a while. Long enough.'

A well-built man in short shirt sleeves slowed down inside his golf buggy. He shot a suspicious glance in my direction and then drifted past. 'Look, I've got to go. I'll speak to you later.'

'Okay, Bab. I'm sorry, love. Maybe you could channel all this into your music.'

'Right.' I laughed, short and tired and pushed myself back onto my feet. 'Maybe. Bye, Mum. Love you.'

'Tara-a-bit. Take care, Bab. Love you.'

I tucked my phone into a pocket and slipped back into the van. A warm beam of light penetrated the windscreen. There was still no sign of Geoff, and I was finally ready to switch off. But, just as I had folded away, the driver's door swung open.

'Wake up!'

I flinched in mild terror as Geoff tossed his head back, his barking amusement drawing the attention of a family climbing into a people carrier in the bay across from ours.

'Sorry, Chris,' he laughed. 'Could not resist.'

'Brian.'

'Shit, Brian! Sorry, Bri.' Geoff pointed at his outfit. There were dry streaks of mud flaking on his shirt. 'I fell over last night. I look like I've shit myself.'

'Yeah. You do.'

I shuffled back over the handbrake as Geoff climbed into the van. He said he had been guzzling water for an hour and needed to dash back for his shift at a supermarket. I suppose I was grateful by that point, knowing we would soon be heading our separate ways.

'One thing you should know about me,' Geoff said after we pulled away from the venue and onto the tight winding roads around Dartmoor. 'I never kiss and tell.'

'Okay,' I replied.

The accompanying relief of Geoff's unprompted confession was short-lived as he launched into a blow-by-blow account of his night with Helen, anyway. Luckily for me, there was a lulling, soporific quality to the vibrations of the van combined with his West Country tones. I folded my arms and drifted off.

There was a slap on my leg. It was the next moment I was vaguely aware of anything. 'I said it's your turn next time, Bri!' Geoff yelled.

I sat up and folded my arms. 'Okay.'

'To get laid.'

'Right.'

Geoff turned on the stereo, and Boston's lightly strummed intro of 'More Than a Feeling' began to play. He unleashed an unpleasant orgasmic yelp as he turned it up, already fully immersed. 'More Than a Feeling, Jack. You like this one.'

Jack's eyes opened like a newborn taking his first glimpses of the world. 'What is it?' he croaked.

'More Than a Feeling!' sung Geoff. 'Fucking hell, guys. How have I got more energy than you two when I've been pumping all night?'

Jack shuffled in his seat before releasing a long, purring fart. 'I don't know.'

'Women, Bri!' Geoff yelled, disregarding his nephew's flatulence. 'Look what they do to us!' He played air guitar as we pulled up at traffic lights. 'One minute, you're down on the floor, and suddenly you're in heaven getting your balls drained.'

'Lovely stuff.'

'Absolutely. Helen has emptied my balls!' He reached across and shook my shoulder. 'Nah, they'll be alright. They'll fill up again.'

Thankfully, the van was soon lipping up on the curb opposite the house, and I was struggling to shuffle by Jack, who made minimal effort to make my exit easier. The van's engine rumbled as Geoff leaned out the driver's window to thank me again for helping. I gave an embarrassed thumbs-up from the pavement as he blasted his horn several times and pulled away.

My head was light, and I leaned forward to rest a hand on the front door, everything hitting at once. Like Geoff's testicles, I was utterly depleted.

Connie was singing theatrically when I pushed open the front door. 'That must be Brian!' she called, incorporating that into her tune.

Despite my intent on burying myself away in my room, I reluctantly crept into the living room now my return had been clocked. Tam waved cheerfully from the dining table as I wandered inside.

'Hey, Brian,' she said over her laptop screen.

'Hi.' I held up a palm, scraping together the last remaining enthusiasm in my body. 'How's it going?'

Boxes and shopping bags peppered the worktops in the kitchen, where Connie was slowly unpacking. She stopped for a moment and pulled her hair into a messy bun. 'Here he iii-iis,' she sang. 'The dirty stop-out has ventured ho-oooome.'

Tam giggled as Connie held that final note. She flattened her laptop screen and tapped the table, ready to receive a juicy story. 'We were just wondering what had happened to you.'

'Have you been out all night?' Connie asked. She perched her elbows on the kitchen worktop. 'You look like it. No offence, Brian.'

'Thanks. Well, I just….' I fidgeted and mumbled, too tired to summarise the madness of the previous twenty-four hours. 'Um….'

Tam leaned forward. 'So, one minute you're meeting up with your ex and the next you're out all night. Should we put two and two together?'

'Heh.' It was tempting to run with Tam's insinuation – it would have been so easy. 'No. We were catching up. It didn't really go that well.'

'Aw.' Tam tilted her head in sympathy. 'I guess you don't want to discuss that with us.'

I shrugged. 'Maybe not now.'

Connie pouted like I was some wounded pet. 'But don't forget about the bash here tonight. Maybe that will cheer you up.'

'Oh, right.' I had forgotten about the party. 'Um. Do you need a hand?'

'Maybe later,' Tam replied. They were starting the actual preparations soon, she said. There was still so much to do. 'Anything would be amazing.'

'There'll be lots of single ladies there, Brian!' Connie yelled. 'Every cloud…'

I gave Connie a weary smile. 'Hmm….yeah. I'm going to go to sleep for a bit.'

I slipped out of the room and plodded upstairs with the girls laughing – about me or something else. It didn't matter as I threw myself onto the sofa bed, burying my face into the lifeless pillow. I was too tired to scream, too numb to feel anything. Perhaps Esther was gone for good, and it was too much to lose.

It was six-thirty in the evening when my eyes opened again with the murmur of pop music bubbling up from downstairs. I dragged myself out of bed, unclean and braindead, and stumbled into the cream bathroom to cleanse myself.

'Here he is, sleeping beauty,' James announced after I entered the living room – only slightly refreshed from my shower. He was mounting a speaker under one of the kitchen cabinets and had popped over early to get the new smart audio system working.

'Can I help with anything?' I asked.

He slid out from the worktop and re-arranged his floppy red hair. 'Nah, I'll do the other one in a second.' He frowned, confused. 'Is that Tintin on your t-shirt?'

'Possibly.' I looked down at the first item I had blindly retrieved from the wardrobe. 'Um, I don't know where this came from, to be honest.'

'Oh, okay.' James tossed a small screwdriver onto the worktop and pulled a phone from his green trousers. Ed Sheeran's 'Shape of You' blared from the new speaker, and he bopped his head, happy with his work. 'What do you think of this song?'

'Um. It's alright,' I replied with a shrug. 'Not sure it's my thing.'

'Yeah, it's not great.' James shook his head, eager to please, and turned his attention to a second speaker. He clicked his tongue, unsure where to place it before finding a suitable spot underneath the corner unit. 'Oh, I spoke to the boss, Trev, about you.'

'Right. How'd that go?' I asked. 'Guessing it's a no.'

'No, no. He actually thanked me for the personal recommendation. His wife Donna needs someone on her team to cover some maternity. She works in accounts. Sound good?'

I rubbed my face, unsure if we were having a sincere conversation. 'Yeah, I guess.'

'I told him it was right up your street. If you don't mind.'

'Oh, right.'

'You don't sound sure,' James said, his head underneath the kitchen cupboard in the corner. 'Are you still half-asleep?'

'No, it sounds good, man,' I assured him. 'Sorry. I've just woken up.'

James said he had given Donna my number to bump up my prospects and hoped I didn't mind. After fixing the speaker, he pushed himself from the worktop and showed me the Fryers' office location. According to his phone, it was about a half-hour walk from the house to the small business estate.

Tam called from the courtyard, and I headed outside through the patio doors. She had just finished hanging rows of fairy lights between the tall flinty side walls. They stretched over new rattan garden chairs and sofas I hadn't seen before.

'What do you think?' she asked.

'It looks good out here,' I replied.

Tam smiled. 'It was a nightmare screwing that furniture together,' she said. 'I never want to see another Allen key thing. We were ready to kill each other.'

I lowered myself into one of the armchairs. The small stone terrace had been cleared out, and the weeds trimmed away. 'It's all looking great.'

'Hold up,' called Connie from somewhere inside. She charged through the open patio doors, brandishing a camera on a selfie stick. 'I want to capture this for my TikTok.'

Tam flicked a switch, and the lights were on – but it was still relatively light outside. 'It'll look better later.'

'Cheers, colleague,' James said. He handed me a bottled beer and sank into the chair beside mine. 'Should be a good night, I reckon. What's the occasion, Tam? Now you're staying.'

Tam shot James a look like she wanted to murder him there and then. 'The occasion is that it's nice to be sociable. Isn't it, Con?'

'Yep,' Connie said. She panned the area with a careful grin. 'A lovely time to celebrate being happy with people.'

Tam played with her septum ring as her eyes met mine. Of course, it was obvious to have asked about Berlin and what had changed. But based on her reaction to James, it was too sensitive a topic to address there and then. Perhaps it didn't matter, anyway. Perhaps nothing did.

'We'll introduce you to some people, Brian,' Connie suggested. 'So you can make lots of new friends.'

'Okay.' I smiled, having already decided I would slip away once it was busy enough that nobody would notice. 'Thanks.'

James stood and ruffled his sister's red hair whilst she was filming. 'You're not clout chasing tonight, are you?'

'Shut up, mate.' Connie playfully side-kicked her brother. 'It's not my fault people are interested in my life, and yours is so fucking boring.'

'I really don't care.' He smirked. 'I just want to get bladdered. Like a normal person.'

Connie gasped theatrically as the doorbell sounded. 'Action stations! Let's go!'

She was a good party host, Connie – a natural. And although she didn't follow through on her suggestion to introduce me to anyone who arrived that night, she did greet each guest with a bespoke welcome and a camera in her grip. Like a master of close-up magic, she would tell them she was filming the event for her various social media channels, and our visitors would chuckle without any concern at all. She could say anything to anyone.

Tam had her own complementary set of skills. She was a stealthy curator, subtly re-stocking food at the kitchen table and ensuring everyone knew where to fill their glasses.

I had spent the evening drinking with James and nervously enquiring about my job now that those wheels were apparently in motion. The infusion of alcohol was starting to hit when he left to take a call from Elena in the garden, and there was little else to do but people-watch from the kitchen island.

Suddenly, there was a hand on my back. 'Too much to drink already?' a voice enquired. It was fancy and rasping.

'No, no,' I insisted. I lifted my head from the worktop surface and made immediate eye contact with the owner of that voice, disarmed already. Her face was a wonder, with large and small features working together. 'Just a bit tired.'

'Oh, dear.' She frowned in exaggerated sympathy. 'My sister has sent me on a mission to talk to people and get her some gin.'

'Right.' I scanned the worktops, suddenly eager to help. 'There's pretty much everything here, I think.'

'Are you alright? You're squinting there.'

'Yeah, fine,' I insisted. 'I left my glasses somewhere. I'm a tiny bit short-sighted.'

'Me too. Have you tried contact lenses? They work well for me.'

'No.' I winced. 'Not keen on things touching my eyes.'

'Fair enough.' She laughed – a sweet silent chuckle. 'I'm supposed to be flirting, and we're talking about eye prescriptions.'

'Oh.'

'I'm Beatty, by the way.' She leaned in and kissed me on the cheek. I recoiled, having not expected it, and it made her laugh with no sound. 'Sorry, I'm forward when I introduce myself to people.'

'That's okay.'

She closed one eye, her head tilted. 'I've seen you before somewhere.'

'Have you?'

'Yes! Somewhere.' There was a brief, insane moment as I waited, where I quietly concluded she must have been a Dorothea fan. They were still out in the wild somewhere. 'You're a musician. You were in Connie's video.'

'Fuck.' I grabbed at my face. 'I didn't know she had put that up.'

She laughed at my panicked reaction and placed a hand on my forearm, leaning so far forward she had to grip it to stop herself from toppling. 'She was sweeping around us with her camera earlier. So stealthy, I want that skill.'

'Yeah, it would be handy.' The conversation stumbled, and I whistled something nonsensical out of nowhere before our eyes met again

'What's your name?'

'Brian.'

'Brian! That's it. Aw, Brian.' She squeezed my hand. 'I remember from the video.'

Beatty urged me to come outside and meet the people she was with at the rattan furniture. I helped her to smuggle bottles and glasses there. Before I knew it, she had introduced me to her sister, Charlotte, who owned an interiors shop on the high street, and Charlotte's barrel-chested sculptor husband, Tito, with his wiry hair greying at the sides. I shook the hands of George and Hetty, too. They had recently purchased a small holding on Dartmoor where they were making artisan cheese. None of these people were relatable at all.

James wandered our way after his lengthy call was over. His shoulders were slumped like the conversation had sucked his energy away. Still, it was a relief to have some backup, and he seemed to know the others, albeit lightly. Other guests began to funnel outside, perhaps sucked towards our noise or the lights flickering as darkness fell. Suddenly there was a group of us – all prior friends and previous strangers among the garden sofas and pulled-up chairs. A garden gang.

Charlotte suggested a game of 'Never Have I Ever,' a drinking version she knew. Tito perked up and began to coordinate affairs. The game started politely and grew in hilarity as we consumed more alcohol and became comfortable with each other. And we played until it was late, and the fancy new patio heater struggled to keep us warm.

We moved back inside and made plans to hang out as unfamiliars do when buoyed by the thrill of socialising with influences bobbing in their system. Beatty announced she had to head home, and I instinctively offered to walk her there when nobody else picked up on that cue. I could walk her to the bridge, she said, wherever that was, and I nodded, still fretting I had been overfamiliar.

Suddenly we were both outside in the rapidly cooling air, wild that it was happening. 'Oh my God, I should have brought a coat,' Beatty said as a cold breeze blew again. We passed the empty market square on the high street, and she rubbed the sleeves of her white floral shirt. 'You should have worn one, too.'

'Yeah, fair point.' I was still in my ridiculous t-shirt, my body no longer fooled by the warmth of swimming alcohol.

'Are you into Tintin?' she asked, snickering. 'What's happening there?'

I shrugged. 'I don't know how. He's got a dog, hasn't he?'

'I think so.' Beatty vibrated with silent joy once more. 'Charlotte dragged me to that party. I wasn't expecting much. But it was fun.'

'It was,' I agreed. 'Do you know Tam?'

'I don't, really.' Beatty explained that she only really knew Connie. Everyone in the town knew her, but they also shared a mutual friend who taught piano to her son. He was obsessed with music, she said.

'That's cool.' I nodded enthusiastically. Beatty had a son, and I had no idea how to process that information. Perhaps there was a Mr Beatty somewhere, patiently waiting for her to return after tucking their musical child away. If there was, it made our odd flirtation, or whatever it was, a little strange.

'I was supposed to be on a date tonight with some guy. But I got blown off at the last minute.' Beatty stumbled on the pavement's edge as we walked underneath the East Gate Arch. She regained her footing, her legs splaying, and then laughed and leaned against its wall. 'Probably because I'm clumsy.'

'Are you okay?'

She waved her hands. 'Yes!'

We navigated the remainder of the slanting street unscathed and turned towards the river. 'I'm a qualified guitar tutor,' I found myself saying. 'I could teach your son if he's interested.'

Beatty grabbed my arm as we reached our agreed destination of Totnes Bridge and its three humps across the water. 'Are you serious?' I'm not even joking. Noah would love that so much.'

'Yeah. I'm serious.'

'Okay. But now I'm going to bully you for your number so you won't forget.'

'Sure.'

We pulled out our phones, and it was all so quick I was ready to dismiss it all as drunk talk. Beatty chuckled at how blowy it was, her dark hair across her face – wild enough to knock us over. 'What are you doing in Totnes, anyway?' she asked suddenly. 'Did you know it's mad here?'

I shrugged. 'I split up with my girlfriend.'

'Oh.' Beatty gave me a sweet, sympathetic frown. 'Was it so bad you had to move to the other side of the country?'

'I think it probably was.

'Oh, fuck.'

'Maybe I'll write some songs about it.'

Beatty laughed. 'Jesus, man.'

My mouth buzzed as our eyes met, and it seemed like we would kiss. And I wanted to do that, then, a long, wet, intoxicated snog – something we could dismiss later as drunken silliness. Perhaps I fancied Beatty. Perhaps there was something there, a chemistry.

I stepped away and we said goodbye at a sensible distance. Beatty turned and walked across the long gentle brow of the crossing towards the pink buildings beyond. And it rained on top of the wind when she disappeared, fine and horizontal. It tapped at the river and twinkled across my face.

When I arrived back at the house, I squeezed past departing guests, soaked from my walk. There was only a hum of conversation as I headed into the kitchen, a drowned rat ignoring glances as I proceeded to drink as much water as possible.

I headed upstairs and lost time to the speckled bathroom mirror above the sink, intoxicated enough to be unphased by the couple brazenly fucking in the shower. The groans and slapping from the cubicle barely registered as I poked at my fleshless cheeks. And God, I hated myself then – nothing to offer.

A punching pain between my ribs kept me half awake until it was light again. I unplugged my phone from the buzzing lead on the floor, the flannel bedsheet clinging to my back. There was a notification on the screen – a request from Beatty on social media. I accepted the offer and immediately scrolled through snaps from her last summer holiday in France.

There were so many photos of her with a sandy-haired boy, presumably Noah. Tito and Charlotte also featured heavily alongside who I had assumed were their high-achieving friends. It was all crumbly cottages, night-time beach campfires, straw hats, sarongs and Oxford shirts with shorts. It was so idyllic I couldn't possibly fit in.

SEVEN

Tam wished me good night as she slunk past my spot at the dining table in her dressing gown, a pint of water in her grip.

'Who was that?' asked Mum through the laptop screen. Sitting on her balcony, she had wanted to show me the Spanish night sky before bed.

'Tam,' I whispered as the frosted door clunked shut.

'Oh, how lovely. Saying goodnight to each other.'

'Yep.'

Mum glanced the sweat away from her temples. It was so warm there still. 'When is she going, love?'

'I don't know.' I shrugged. There were other matters on my mind. 'Do I look like Dad? I was looking at those photos again and was trying to figure out who I look like.'

Mum frowned as she studied her screen. 'No, not really. Your dad was bigger in the face. He had the face of a larger man for some reason. But he was quite fit and healthy. All that manual work helped.'

'He had a heart attack at forty-five.'

'Hmm. Well, that was probably from smoking. Or something genetic.'

'Lovely.'

'I'll tell you what….' Mum's face brightened, and she snapped her fingers. 'I know who you do look like.

'Oh, Christ.

'Brian Cox. Not the actor. We watched a programme about space. Bill liked it. But I thought it was boring. Apart from the fact he looked like you.'

'I don't think I'm related to Brian Cox.'

'No.' Mum frowned like it was a possibility. 'I don't think so.'

'Well, that's what I meant.'

'Oh.' Mum chuckled. She lit a cigarette, content in her outdoor sanctuary. 'I don't know, then. Maybe someone on Mum's side.'

The conversation was at a dead end. We didn't speak about Mum's side of the family, my grandparents in particular. Mum's dad left when she was young, and her mum was an abusive alcoholic. Our circle was so small.

'Could you tell me some specific things about Dad? Maybe something I haven't heard before.'

Mum tapped her cigarette into a tray. 'Well, he had an Irish accent.'

'That's unusual for someone who was Irish. I did say specific.'

She chuckled. 'Okay. Let me think of *specific* things! He used to talk with his family on the phone a lot. He would use the one in our bedroom, and I wouldn't see him for hours. Our bills were enormous, and we would argue about that.'

'I was hoping for something more cheery.'

'Well, it happened.' She puffed on her cigarette. 'You never asked about your dad when you were younger. I just assumed you weren't that curious. I have to think now.'

'I was curious!' I insisted. 'But it was difficult to ask without being reminded he was gone. You know – o*h yeah, he's not here anymore.*'

Mum tutted. Her eyes were watchful now. 'Do you still get upset?'

'Not like that. I try to recall things in detail now to check it's all there. Like the other day, I started remembering his funeral at the Catholic church in Redhill when his Irish family came. I remember staring at them and their crying and being embarrassed I couldn't.'

'Well, you were in shock,' Mum asserted. 'You barely spoke for six months, Bab.'

'Right...' I pinched my chin. 'What a weird day. They all just disappeared after.'

'Yes.' Mum drew on her cigarette again. 'I am sorry, love.'

'Don't be, Mum.' I smiled, something small to reassure her. 'I better get ready for bed. I've got work in the morning.

'Oh, yes, you better. Tara-a-bit, love you.'

'I love you, Mum. It does look nice there. So clear. It's overcast here, no sign of any stars.'

'Love you, too. That's a shame, love.'

Tam was still in Totnes. And I was still there, too, uncertain if I should be. But I was taking baby steps towards a new normality anyway. It was one where I would only face forward until I knew what I wanted. And I would look down at the tips of my shoes if I had to, but never behind me. The past was the past, and I couldn't allow it to pull me down.

I started my new office job days after the party. Donna, my new boss, had called, and I muddled through what I thought my strengths were. I was a good team player, and I said that far too often for what was a short conversation. When she then asked about my star sign, I told her I was a Leo. That was good, apparently, because Leos were loyal and dependable. Fryers needed more Leos, but I would have to watch out as there was a Scorpio on the accounts team, and we might clash. She said she would keep an eye out for any problems.

I was eating properly again, regularly at least, and I got a sensible haircut and pushed it to one side on top where my hair wanted to go anyway. I shaved periodically – no more shaggy facial hair. I fixed my wardrobe door and filled it with smart casual attire for work – as many shirts as it took to cycle me through an entire working week and back again.

The job at Fryers itself was fine, but nothing more. There were four of us on the accounts team, seemingly the least active unit in the office. Donna had a heart of gold but was often away from her desk in meetings or on extended lunch breaks. I talked to Holly the most, sometimes about her hot yoga classes and sometimes about her mum, who she cared for. David was the Scorpio on the team, but we got on okay. He was semi-retired and only seemed to talk about his German Shepherd, Diesel, who had passed away the year before. He would never get a dog as good as him again, and he would say that often unprompted – often after drinking from the mug with his beloved pet's face on.

I would exchange messages with James during work hours, panicked emails and texts under the desk. We would talk about lunch plans at least once per day, but most of my other notes were pleas for help. There was this strange assumption that I knew what I was doing. Luckily, he knew everything, and perhaps it was fair that he should help, considering how much he had oversold my skillset.

On one unseasonably warm Friday afternoon, I left work to meet Tam in a small pub at the top of the high street – a catch-up she had organised during the day. James and Connie would join us later after each had gotten waylaid with work at Fryers and the family delicatessen.

My cheek boiled as the sun glared between buildings on the high street. But there was no sign of Tam as I stepped inside our chosen venue, which doubled up as a microbrewery. It liked to remind you of that fact, with its oversized antique barrels as props and hop garlands pinned along the walls.

I talked with a friendly bartender who swiftly launched into a sales pitch as I approached the bar. His cherubic face exploded with enthusiasm as he ran through their stock and then talked me into a sampler set of five small beers on a wooden paddle.

A couple vacated a gnawed wooden seating booth which was slightly secluded, so I self-consciously carried the paddle to that spot just as Tam arrived. We exchanged waves before she ordered at the bar and then headed over with her very own paddle.

'We're paddle buddies,' Tam said, like she had also been talked into something she wasn't sure she wanted.

'Cool.'

Tam pulled off her beanie hat and plopped it on the table. Her head had been shaved. 'I've cut my hair off.'

'I can see.' I sipped at a pale ale, having plucked for it at random. 'It looks good.'

'Thanks. Does it look okay?' She rubbed her head. 'I have the right-shaped head for it, I think.'

'Yes.' I nodded. 'It's a good dome.'

'Thanks.' She had some exciting news, she said. 'Dad called earlier. He said he'll call you once he has more detail. But he was excited about your band.'

'Dorothea?'

'Yes, he was so happy!' Frank had relayed so much info that she had to type notes into her phone. She lifted her device from the table and read from it aloud. He had spoken to Luke, and they had reminisced about Dorothea during a phone call. He said it was too early to tell, but a reunion seemed possible – perhaps even likely.

'Wait. They talked about a reunion?' I asked cautiously. Frank was a hype man, and it was something he loved to do. It was important to remind myself of that fact. 'Is he serious?'

'Yes! I mean, we talked about other stuff too. But that was my takeaway.'

'Okay.' I sipped my black drink casually, unsure what it was. Tam said it was stout, but it didn't matter what it was, with Dorothea and its potential resurrection absorbing my senses. And I couldn't allow myself to get carried away. I couldn't, but I would. 'I'll wait to hear something.'

'Yeah, definitely.'

Tam sighed and became lost in her phone, shaking her head as she keyed a message before dropping it onto the table in frustration and flipping it face down.

'Are you okay?' I asked.

Our eyes met, and she twisted her lips, perhaps wondering if I was someone she could trust with privileged information. I was there, at least. 'Just arguing with Con.'

'Oh.'

She laughed nervously and rubbed her head again. 'We've stumbled into something, and it's a lot when I think about it.'

'Right.'

'Sometimes I can't get over how strange it feels. Like how quickly it's changing everything.'

I clamped my bottom lip with my top teeth, trying to summon a platitude of any value – a well-worn cliché, anything. But I was elsewhere, buried in the news of before. 'Shit.'

Tam chuckled. 'You're like, *why is she telling me all this?*'

'Sorry.' It had been challenging to get a full beat on Tam. She would flip codes – her inflexions would constantly change. She could be soft and well-spoken like you would expect, given her privileges in life. But there was an edge to her too. She was streetwise and could handle herself there. 'Well, I had thought that.'

Tam laughed again. She had a reluctant laugh, always grabbing herself afterwards like it was the last thing she wanted to happen. I was about to offer up some useless banality, perhaps something about trying to live in the moment – but she began waving to someone across the room, out of sight from my spot.

'Who's that?' I asked.

'Shit, they're coming over.' Tam smiled broadly as Charlotte and Tito from the garden gang appeared with half-finished drinks in their grips.

Charlotte clamped her cheeks in excitement. 'Oh my God, I love the hair!'

'Thanks,' said Tam.

Charlotte shuffled in beside me and opposite her husband. Her profile was just like Beatty's, with the same tiny chin and pleasing fleshy nose. But she was a foamier version of her sister, and perhaps I wanted the real thing. 'Where's Connie?'

'I'm not sure,' Tam replied. 'She might be around later.'

'Lovely!' Charlotte nodded. 'Hey, we saw Ben Howard walking past a second ago.'

'Oh, cool,' replied Tam, glancing out the window by our booth. 'I keep hearing that name.'

'Are you secretly filming us?' asked Tito. He had the heaviest Italian accent and pretended to check for secret cameras under the table. He laughed until his small brown eyes disappeared. 'Where's your camera?'

Tam chuckled along. 'Taking a break at home.'

'We've met before,' I said, shaking Tito's hand after he had extended it in my direction.

'Ah yes,' he said, finally. He looked at his wife with an extended finger in my direction as something snapped into place. 'Yes! Yes!'

Charlotte clicked her tongue and scowled at her husband. 'Titi.'

Tito cackled wildly again, his eyes behind his cheeks, before he headed off to buy a round. It wasn't clear what the in-joke was, but he had thoroughly enjoyed it. With her husband engaged at the bar, Charlotte was intrigued to learn about our living situation – as was I. Tam explained we were old family friends via Frank, and I had been looking for a change of pace for a while. It was a condensed version of the truth, at least.

Charlotte said she had also become exhausted at London life, where she met Tito. She moved back to her hometown to be near her family again, but also because it was crazy there, she said. Money had been so tight the pair had decided to rent out their beloved Putney flat, which they had been using whenever they fancied a scene change. I polished off my remaining drink, nodding as if I could relate.

Tito said it was Charlotte's birthday as he rejoined us with drinks expertly balanced on a tray. We were all locked into the celebrations as their friends showed up and food arrived from the bar. James showed up too, fresh from working late, with other familiars wandering in behind him. We pulled empty tables and chairs across the room as invited and unplanned guests created our space.

The pub was heaving when Connie arrived to cheer from our bohemian crowd enjoying their Friday night out. Seats switched as revellers returned from the bar or after a vape or cigarette outside. It was where Tam left to speak to her girlfriend – or whatever they were to each other. They talked for ages under a lamppost just beyond the pane of the window next to me. Suddenly, they hugged and swayed there.

I decided to call it a night after a lingering sense I was out of place. But as I stood, Beatty swept inside, and our eyes met as I stretched and reseated, buoyed by the sudden excitement of her presence. We had exchanged friendly messages after the party, and perhaps I had been too puzzled by any sign of interest to take it seriously. And with the timing as rough as it was, it was easier to dismiss the pain of losing Esther manifesting in a strange form that night.

Beatty slipped into Tam's vacant spot in the booth opposite me and leaned across to hug her sister. She was flustered and huffing like she had been through the wringer to get there, and as she told a story of how her babysitter had turned up late, Tito stood to serenade his wife with a bout of 'Happy Birthday'. Of course, we all joined in, and he conducted us with his hands.

'Happy birthday to my beautiful wife, Charlotte,' Tito yelled, capitalising on the moment. He puffed out his chest and held his near-empty pint glass in the air. 'Have a wonderful evening to her and everybody here!'

Charlotte recoiled in her seat and covered her face with her hands. But she was grinning too much underneath not to have thoroughly enjoyed it.

'Hello, you,' Beatty said after the fun quietened. She reached under the table and poked at my knee.

'Hey,' I replied as if I had just noticed her there. 'I like your outfit.'

'Thank you.' She touched her lips in comical exaggeration and adjusted the belt around her black dress. 'I'm waiting for someone to buy me a Negroni. I'm obsessed with them.'

'Cool. Yes.' I took the hint and squeezed my way out of the booth whilst picking up further orders from the group as I shaped towards the bar, fearing I would lose my spot.

'You look different,' Beatty said once I had slipped back into my window seat, squeezing and shuffling to get there after my duties.

'The haircut?'

'Yes, and the smart clothes.' She prodded at the spiral of orange peel in her drink. 'Have you had a sensible makeover?'

I smirked. 'I didn't know this was going on, to be honest. I've just come from work.'

Beatty pulled on a metal straw and then puffed her cheeks like her cocktail would blow her head off if she kept going. 'How's your songwriting going?'

I shrugged. 'Every time I try to play something new, I divert into old band stuff and play that instead. Bit sad, really.'

'Aw. Are you pining?'

'Possibly. Probably just lacking inspiration.' I sipped at my bottled beer, eager to change the conversation topic. 'What about you? Been on any dates?'

'No.' A slow, wry smile grew. 'I've been busy with school and planning lessons. It's either that or wrestling with Noah. Not actual wrestling. Just trying to get him to bed at a reasonable hour.'

James slid over to join us after procuring two fistfuls of vodka shots. It was perfect to have him there and how his outward quirky charm cut through any tension. And we slowly emptied the tiny glasses and shared stories in a bubble of three. Beatty was lovelier than I had remembered, self-effacing, and funny. A forgotten spinal warmth of ease tingled as I told them about my night with Geoff and how I had slept inside his van.

'Oh my God,' Beatty said, with her silent leaning laughing. It was beautiful. 'That's the funniest thing I've heard in ages.'

Suddenly Tito bellowed from the bar with a wagging finger. 'Brian, she likes you!'

I wasn't sure where to look, with those around us glancing in our direction.

'Shut up, you idiot!' Beatty tutted and gave her brother-in-law the middle finger, which he enjoyed immensely.

James gestured towards the door. He fancied a cigarette, he said, so we squeezed out of our seats. My head was light as we stood, suddenly eager for fresher air. We headed outside and paused beneath the orange-lit lamppost where Tam and Connie had been.

'Oh, congratulations, man,' said James, a roll-up clasped between his lips.

'What do you mean?'

'Con said your band were getting back together.'

'Did she?' I frowned disbelievingly and took a puff from his cigarette. 'I'm not sure about that.'

'Ah, okay. Tam said you might be heading out soon, back to London.'

I shook my head. 'Not sure about that. Unless she wants me to….'

James shrugged, unbothered. 'Well, I didn't want to say anything in front of you know who. As you're getting on so well.' The pub window had framed Beatty perfectly, where she was enjoying shared amusement inside with those who had shuffled into our seats, the bastards. 'She's gunning for you.' James tilted his head back and blew smoke into the sky. 'I felt like a right fucking gooseberry just now.'

'I don't think so.'

'Do you find her attractive? It's hard to tell with her.' He squinted. 'From some angles, maybe.'

'Don't know.' I shrugged, keen to get off the subject. 'Well, I've missed being sociable.'

James nodded like he knew exactly how I felt. 'Yeah, man. It's been a while for me, too. No wonder I'm smashed already.'

'Yeah. I feel a bit gone.'

'Do you think you're in with Beatty?' I was still getting used to this ironic uber-lad alter-ego James would slip into occasionally. He seemed to enjoy how it contrasted with his lanky nerdiness. 'Are you going to bang?'

I laughed along politely and handed his cigarette back. 'No. Nothing is happening.'

'That's probably a good thing.'

'Why good?'

'Well, on the one hand, her family are fucking loaded, so that's good for you.' He paused momentarily, blowing his cigarette smoke into the sky. 'On the other, you should tread lightly. Trust me.'

There was no opportunity to ask questions as James trod on his half-smoked fag, and Connie met us at the exit. She said there was an event at the Lighthouse Ballroom, which was more or less next door. A friend of hers was DJing there and doing a 'Guilty Pleasures' setlist. 'I'm going to get everyone in,' she said.

Tam arrived, too and leaned her forehead onto my collarbone. 'I've had too much to drink, Brian.'

'Me too.'

She laughed and stood upright again, her eyes half-closed. 'It's so good about your band.'

'Yeah…'

The Ballroom was a small historic venue with double-height ceilings and an extended balcony overlooking the dancefloor. It was where we danced and sang along to the idle joys of Limahl's 'Never Ending Story' and 'We Like to Party' by the Vengaboys. 'Teenage Dirtbag' by Wheatus was winding up to its thrilling climax as I headed off to relieve myself. And I wobbled as I pissed in a cubicle with the door left open behind, losing time as I swayed there – everything sloping and tipping.

When I finally gathered myself, the venue had swelled with newcomers – as if I had been transported elsewhere. Lights rained down in heady shafts, and our group had split into factions with new faces I didn't recognise or have the energy to get to know. And after searching for Beatty, perhaps hoping to restart our flirting from earlier, she was dancing playfully with a top-knotted man in a Breton striped t-shirt. Perhaps that was fine.

The lolloping drums of 'Africa' by Toto bounced into the room as a hand grabbed my shoulder. It was James, and he pulled me between bodies to where he was dancing with Tam and Connie. The four of us shared a group hug as the echoing refrains of the song's chorus hung in the air. We sang along, and it was dumb and ridiculous – a gentle, sozzled joy.

'Are you okay, Brian?' Connie asked, cupping her hand to my ear.

'Yes!'

She held my hand as we sang together, and nothing made sense. 'I'm so happy for you!'

'Why?' I asked, confused.

She smiled sweetly. 'About your band getting back together.'

'Oh.' I shook my head. 'I'm not sure about that.'

Tam pulled at my shirt sleeve and leaned her head on my shoulder. 'We're excited for you.'

I smiled, glassy-eyed. 'Thanks, mate.'

Perhaps life wasn't so bad as I wobbled in time to Lou Bega's 'Mambo No. 5', the least likely moment for that notion to swim into my brain. Tam and Connie touched foreheads like they were in love, and a middle-aged woman with pink hair appeared from nowhere to grind on James. There was an amused panic on his face as she reared into him aggressively.

I closed my eyes and chuckled as the light rays flickered over my eyelids. Dorothea were about to rise from the ashes, and it was safe to be optimistic about that within that tiny pocket of my own. Perhaps everything that happened over the past year had done so for a reason. Perhaps I would be okay again – no longer detached and fragmented. Perhaps I would be back to where I had been.

A wave of carefree energy soared as we left the venue at closing. The sky was black and sparkling above, and I leapt onto James's back as the four of us began the short walk home along the high street. He carried me for a while, apparently the funniest thing that had ever happened, until his skinny legs bowed, and we collapsed into the road. And we laughed because it was funnier than it hurt.

'James, you may as well stay at Tam's place,' Connie suggested as we stumbled back to our feet and checked elbows for blood. He decided he would sleep on the sofa downstairs as we passed the run of antique shops and art galleries at the tip of the high street, singing the stupid songs we had heard.

'Shush a second,' Tam said as she held a phone to her ear. 'This number keeps ringing me.' Her pace suddenly quickened until she was a few steps ahead, and James continued his awful crooning, arms aloft.

'Shut up, James,' Connie snapped, perhaps sensing Tam's sudden need for quiet.

'Oh no!' yelled Tam, a piercing despairing howl from nowhere. She sank to her knees outside the record store where three roads converged, and the colourful terraced cottages on our street lay ahead. 'Oh, no. Fuck. What.'

'What is it, baby?' Connie kept asking as we reached her.

Tam bit into her hand. 'Oh, God! Oh God,' she kept saying. I didn't know what to say as Connie cradled her girlfriend's shaved head, having knelt on the pavement to hold her there.

'Is everything okay?' I asked, the world suddenly upside down.

Tam sobbed full deep moans into Connie's shoulder. 'Dad's dead,' she said, and my blood ran cold. 'They've just found him in the house. He's dead. He's dead.'

EIGHT

I strummed my acoustic guitar on the green sofa, waiting for Mum to return. 'I'm back!' she announced through the laptop speakers. 'Where are you?'

'Here.' I switched my instrument for the laptop resting on a cushion – sliding it onto my knees again.

'Hi ya.' Her face was cast in shadow after moving inside from the balcony so she could listen in for the oven timer on her sofa. 'How's Tammy?'

'Tam. She's alright. Bearing up.'

'That's good. What did work say?'

'That I could take a few days off. Unpaid.'

'Well, that's okay. How are you feeling?'

'I don't know.' I shrugged. 'I'm all packed and ready to head up. But it doesn't feel real.'

'You could see someone if you start to struggle with it. That's what everyone does now.'

'Maybe.' I sniffed. 'I just don't know how helpful it was last time.'

'Oh.' She frowned. 'When was the last time?'

'Last year, for a bit.'

'What was it like?'

'It was okay. He was good at asking questions where you find the answers.'

'Okay. That sounds alright, Bab.'

'Yeah.' I scratched the back of my neck. Perhaps this conversation was a bad idea, but Mum was leaning forward, invested in it now. 'Sometimes I felt like he was nudging me down a certain path, you know, doing the whole, *Tell me about your childhood* thing. And I could feel where it was going.'

'Go on.'

'Just it made me worried I can't maintain good relationships because Dad died when I was young.' I plucked at the guitar again, where it laid flat on the cushion – picking, pulling. 'I guess that was the insinuation. And I don't like knowing that about myself or even pondering if it's true.'

'Well, they say it's good to talk about personal stuff so you can understand yourself, love.'

The top E-string was slightly out of tune, and I tweaked the head – micro-adjusting. 'Yeah. And it was good to talk about Dad. But it's not so simple that it's just me despairing about missing him or missing out on him and that I haven't processed my grief properly. Often, it's more subtle than that. It'll be a niggling thought whenever bad or unexpected things happen, you know – *am I taking this so badly because my dad died when I was young?* I'm trying to be more than that, you know? It's something that shouldn't have to define me forever.' I plucked at the strings again one-handed, watching, picking, pulling. 'I don't want that with Frank dying. I actually would like to be more of a mystery to myself. I think that's the key to happiness, just bumbling along – oblivious.'

Mum had vanished when my eyes returned to the screen, only a puffy-armed sofa looking back at me. 'Sorry, love,' she said, shuffling back into her spot. 'The oven was pinging. What were you saying?'

'Doesn't matter.' There was a wrap of fingers at the frosted glass door, where Tam was waving in her dressing gown. 'I better go.'

'Okay, take care of yourself.'

'I will. Love you.'

'Tara a bit, then. Love you.'

Tam pushed the door open after my thumbs-up. 'A bed and mattress arrived for you. The packages are leaning in the hallway.'

'Oh, cool.' I folded down the laptop. 'Sorry, I didn't hear the door.'

'That's okay. I knew you were talking to your mum.' She wandered inside with folded arms and parked on one of the leather armchairs opposite. 'It's lovely how close you are.'

'Yes.'

Tam said there had been a change of plan. We had been speaking all the time since Frank had died, perhaps united in grief. She had even asked me to stay with her at his house near Highbury Fields leading up to the funeral. 'You don't need to come up. Just head up on the day or whatever you want to do. I'll send the details on.'

'Okay.' I nodded. Perhaps it was a relief. 'Is Connie coming instead?'

'No.' She rubbed her face in circles from tiredness or how uncomfortable that question was. 'I was in two minds about it. Nobody would give a shit, but I don't want to do the emotional admin, not at Dad's funeral. It's just too early.'

'Fair enough.'

'Anyway, I've got a mission for you.' Tam's half-brother, Paul, was organising a mini-concert in Frank's honour during a service for him after the funeral. Considering his ties to the music industry, we agreed it was a nice touch. 'Do you think your band would play?'

'Hmm.' I reached across the sofa and plucked at the guitar strings again. 'I'm not sure how that could happen.'

'Oh.' Tam sniffed, her eyes watered. She wiped underneath them quickly with a finger. 'Sorry. I don't know why I'm so suddenly attached to that idea. It came to me last night, and I woke up excited. I want to make Dad proud, you know?'

'I understand.' I smiled, the warmest I could muster, as Tam dabbed at her eyes with the back of her hand. It was impossible not to try and soothe her at that moment. 'Maybe I can ask around.'

'Oh, my God!' Tam threw her head back and clapped her hands. 'Wouldn't it be so perfect? Like Dad's final wish coming true.'

'Maybe, yeah.' I pulled the guitar onto my lap and picked a few notes. 'It's just unlikely, I think.'

'Okay.' Tam's voice wobbled. 'But you can still try.'

'I will! Definitely.' I nodded so many times – unnerved by how much this meant to her all of a sudden. 'You never know!'

'Exactly.' Tam exhaled a weary daisy-in-the-concrete happiness. She stood again, pushing at the chair's metal arms. 'I've just got this feeling. I can't explain it.'

'Okay, cool.'

Tam hugged me around the neck and headed upstairs to prepare for her train journey.

I strummed the bridge chords Ab, Bm, F, Gm, A to a downbeat Dorothea ballad, 'Wanda', written about a wayward friend of ours. Frank always loved that song, and perhaps it was perfect for an event like Frank's funeral service. Perhaps there was something poetic about his final attempts to glue his favourite band back together and for that to happen in his memory. And perhaps it wasn't so grotty to consider the industry bods watching us. He was well-connected, if not always lucky.

Suddenly, my phone was out, and I was tapping a quick text to my once-best friend, Luke. It was no time for pride. I sent the same note to our bassist Amber and drummer Moses, who were in a relationship with each other the last time I checked in.

Hi. I've got some news. Please give me a call.

It was important not to cheapen Frank's memory by casually dropping news of his death in a text message.

It's Brian if you don't have my number.

The messages to Luke bounced immediately, his old number no longer in use. Of course, it wasn't. Perhaps it wasn't a problem. Perhaps Amber had something for him. They had practically grown up together in the leafiest part of Reigate, where their parents were friends. That was it, the tiniest obstacle left – I just needed to hear from her, and everything would fall into place.

The doorbell chimed, and I almost tripped over the tall packages balanced in the hallway to get to the front door. Connie had come over to see Tam off at the train station, where they had planned to walk together. There was an odd atmosphere as we waited for Tam to bumble her yellow suitcase down the stairs, where the two acknowledged with guarded, close-lipped greetings and then left together.

I moved into the kitchen to make breakfast, but the sink wasn't draining – the water left there taking an age to spin away. After locating an ancient plunger from a cupboard underneath, I pulled a pile of congealed slime up through the plug hole and dispatched it into the pedal bin. Strangely satisfied with my exploits, I clambered onto a dining chair to examine a tea-coloured stain on the ceiling. The doorbell chimed as I wiped and dabbed with a damp dishcloth in circles. The fruitless task had absorbed my attention when a second chime pinged and a third in close order.

Geoff was waiting on the pavement outside with a frantic look in his eye like he was about to launch into a risky sales pitch. 'Hello, mate,' he said as if we were old friends crossing paths in a random encounter. 'I haven't seen you in ages.'

'Hi, Geoff.'

'Hey, look at us! I've got a fresh haircut too. And the beard's gone.' He pointed at his gelled short spikes and his shaven face with a prickled rash blushing up from his neck.

'Looking good there.'

'And the jacket, look.' He rubbed the shiny purple lining with the back of his hand. 'Little bit of showbiz.' He reached into the inside pocket and pulled out a few notes. 'Fifty quid, there. What I owed you.'

I nodded as I took the money. 'Oh, thanks.'

Geoff had been upset, he explained. The Inferno had received a couple of bad reviews, one of which had accused him of looking like a slob. There was a real hurt when that word dropped from his mouth – a full-bodied wince. I wasn't sure what to say but suggested it was good that he was using that negative feedback to turn it into something positive.

'Listen,' he said, pivoting, 'I've been worried I'd put you off. I've been using this lad Carl, and he's a liability, to be honest. He's got a short temper. It's making Jack uncomfortable.'

'Right. That's not good.'

'No. So, did you want to give it another go?' Geoff had several 'all-dayers' in the diary, he said. Peak wedding season was around the corner, and he repeated the word peak three times. 'Listen. I don't say this often. But you've got potential, too much to throw away.'

I wasn't sure how Geoff had arrived at his conclusion, but I muttered something about being too busy. It was the best I could come up with under the circumstances and without wanting to wound his feelings further.

'Okay, Bri. I understand.' Geoff's face collapsed like a scolded Labrador, and he slumped back towards the van lipped up across the street. There was something unnatural about seeing him that way, listless and defeated.

'Actually, maybe I could help a bit,' I called.

He spun around immediately. 'You genuinely mean that?'

I didn't really. 'Yeah….'

'Yes, Bri!' Geoff excitedly tapped the side of his van. He hurried across the street and wrapped his arms around me – a full bear hug, pushing my face into his doughy chest.

'I'm not sure how often I can help….' My voice muffled before I was released. But he had heard what he heard.

Geoff pointed at the packages leaning behind. 'What's that you got?'

'Just a new bed. I'll put it up this weekend if I can face it.'

'I'll put it up for you now,' Geoff insisted. He was already trotting back across the road before I could answer. He fished between the van's rear doors before emerging with a heavy-duty metal toolkit. 'Five-second job, that bud. My treat.'

Suddenly, we were hauling the packages up the stairs and lifting the old sofa bed into the spare room. Geoff folded his new jacket and placed it on my desk. He rolled his shirt sleeves and examined the instructions before tossing them to one side because they were a 'load of bollocks.' But soon, we were scrabbling around on our knees to locate them again after quickly hitting a dead end. We searched under miscellaneous packing materials on my bedroom floor before finding them rolled up under a polystyrene sheet.

I made myself useful in small ways as the build progressed by making tea, leaning against panels Geoff fixed together, and checking my phone for any news from Amber or Moses.

'How's Helen?' I asked, having recalled their encounter. My hands gripped the headboard in place as Geoff removed a drill from its case.

Geoff groaned as he smacked the battery pack to his drill and spun the bit. 'A one-and-done job, mate.'

'Sorry to hear that.'

'Ah fuck it, Bri.' He shrugged. 'Obviously, there was plenty of chemistry. But that's how it goes. Some women want commitment, and others want a good seeing-to. You never know which is which.'

'Right.'

We plonked the new mattress atop the freshly laid wooden slats. 'That looks like a bed, at least,' I said.

'Yep!' Geoff sat on the mattress and bounced lightly – confirming his approval with a thumbs-up. 'A double bed, you dirty git.'

I nodded. 'Right.'

'I can see you getting a lot of action in here.'

I chuckled along. 'I doubt that.'

Geoff pumped both fists and thrust his groin. 'You will when we start hanging out, Bri. Women galore.'

'Right.' I scratched my face, unsure how long Geoff had planned to hang around. 'Well, thanks for your help, mate.'

'No worries. You've got your bed now, bud. They can't get rid of you.' He rose to his feet and tapped me on the arm. 'Right. I've got work, a boring shitty shift at the supermarket.'

After seeing Geoff off, I returned to the ceiling stain and scrubbed at it for prolonged periods with no real success. And Amber had no news when I stopped to check the ghost vibrations in my pocket. Nobody was calling. And the stain was still there as I scrubbed until my hands buzzed. And I couldn't get over that first hurdle. Perhaps I was the hurdle.

After retreating to the green sofa, I held a knuckle in my mouth as a prickling ran into my arms. I couldn't distract myself. Perhaps I needed to speak to someone, someone like Niall. And he would have asked me what I could have done differently in his soft Belfast lilt. Some exercise, I would have replied, and it would have been the exact answer he wanted to hear. A depressed person was inactive. They would hide inside and push their issues into the stew until the festering was too much. But a runner was active, and I had been a runner at Frank's place. Runners were positively influencing their mental health – filling their heads with endorphins.

I sped to my room and rummaged through the wardrobe until my hands landed on the polyester clothing and soft mesh trainers I was searching for. Suddenly, I was out on the street, stretching in the gentle rain, pulling at my calf muscles, and lunging to either side.

My lungs were ready to burst after jogging in spurts to each target point – a lamppost or a tree. My exertion took me across Totnes Bridge, and the sun broke through the breaks in the clouds. I had never been into that part of town before and meandered to a pause on a narrow sloping lane where wide grey stone cottages faced each other.

My breathing returned to a sensible rhythm as I rested on a low rocky wall until someone calling nearby pierced through the music in my ears. I pulled my earphones out, and Beatty was waving from across the street as if she had been teleported there. A young blond boy was with her, who must have been Noah, and he was pulling at the sleeve of her olive-coloured raincoat.

'Hey, what are you doing around here?' she asked, chuckling at my obliviousness. 'I thought you were ignoring me.'

'Sorry! I'm in my own world.'

I walked across the street, and Beatty held onto my forearm as I reached her. It was the first time we had seen each other since Charlotte's birthday, and it was wild how wide her smile was – how pleased she was. 'Are you doing active things?' she asked.

'Yeah. I've just been out for a run.' I smiled, all friendly and casual.

She smirked playfully. 'You look very shiny. All the gear and no idea?'

'Probably.' I laughed along. 'I'm panicking about getting old, I think.'

'How old are you?' She tucked her hair behind her ear on one side. 'If you don't mind me asking.'

'About to turn thirty, the big one.' I gulped. 'Christ. It's old, isn't it?'

Beatty shook her head. 'I turned thirty-two last year. You can still round down. Everything is going to be okay.'

'That's true.' The blond boy was still tugging away at his mother's arm, desperate not to be part of whatever this was. 'Is this Noah?'

'Well remembered! Are you going to say hello, Noah?' Beatty rubbed her son's straight hair, but he remained wordless and yanked at her sleeve, knocking her off balance. 'No, he's going to be rude instead.'

'That's okay.' I smiled at the boy, but he wasn't interested. 'I'm just a weird man in the street, in shiny sports clothes. It's a good instinct to have.'

Beatty's big eyes brightened. 'Oh, that reminds me. Are you still doing guitar lessons at incredibly low prices?'

'I don't remember saying anything about incredibly low prices,' I chuckled. 'But, sure. I can do that.'

Beatty gasped in exaggerated excitement. 'When can you do one?'

'Um.' I scratched at my face. The immediate timeline was so unclear now. 'I'm not sure. Maybe the weekend?'

'Okay!' She grabbed my arm again, a delight on her face like it wasn't just some guitar lesson we were arranging. 'Are we going to do this, then?'

'Yeah. Yes.'

'Great. Right. I expect Noah wants to get inside and play with his Lego.' Beatty gestured at the picture-perfect stone block cottage behind, with its primrose-coloured front door and cheerful climbing flowers bending over its porch.

'Nice! Well, we'll sort a time then.'

'Yes!' Beatty put her arm over Noah, and the pair turned to head inside, his determination finally rewarded.

A swell of ecstatic energy surged as I ran again, sprinting past the overgrown nettles in an unfamiliar narrow lane. Running would solve everything – that was so clear as I slipped through the cycling gate at the end of the path and turned towards the pink buildings by the bridge. Everything was good again until a brutal stitch punched me between the ribs, and the well-spring of momentum evaporated into a series of sputtering jogs and sad trundles to get home.

After pushing my way inside the house, I returned to the green sofa. I lay there with my phone gripped, waiting for it to vibrate.

The day ended with no news, and in the morning, I slipped into a schedule of cleaning and running. And sprinkled between were discarded plans to keep Tam in the loop with my lack of progress and ditched efforts to message Beatty with a date for our lesson. And there were discarded attempts to tell Geoff I didn't want to help with his mobile disco and that I was so sorry I had to let him down.

The kitchen table was still damp from my wiping when I sat down to eat a bowl of pasta. It was late now, a darkness in the garden as my reflection watched from the patio windows, perhaps disapprovingly.

Suddenly, my phone vibrated on the table, lighting up and rumbling. Amber was calling, and I stood instinctively to answer, unprepared to speak. But it was exciting. I just needed this call, and everything would take care of itself.

'Amber.'

'Hey,' she replied, flustered and hoarse. 'Sorry, I've only just seen your message! Are you okay?'

'Yeah, I'm okay.' I wandered into the living room and perched on the big green sofa arm. 'You don't sound very well.'

Amber chuckled. 'I've had a baby.'

'Oh wow. Shit!' It fell quiet, and I didn't know what to say. The news was so disorienting. 'What's, um, the baby called?'

'He's called Baxter.'

'That's a cool name. Baxter. Wow. Are you still in Brighton?'

'Yeah.' Amber's voice jumped as if she were jigging something, Baxter, most likely. 'Your message said you had some news.'

'Yes.' I clicked my tongue nervously, unprepared. 'Frank's passed. You know, away. He had a heart attack at home.'

'Oh no! How sad.' Amber shushed as Baxter began to cry. 'Poor, poor Frank. He called us a few weeks back.'

'Did he?'

'Yeah. To say how much he loved that article and to thank me for contributing.'

'Oh, okay. How was he?'

'In good spirits. He asked if we wanted to get the band back together – that he'd been speaking to you, Luke, and some industry bods.'

'Right.' I bit my thumbnail. 'What did you say?'

'Just that I was heavily pregnant, and Mo had sold his kit a couple of years ago. There's just no space for anything here.'

'Right...' I parked my elbows on my knees. 'Actually, there's a funeral for him tomorrow – and a concert. Frank's daughter wanted to know if we might play. I said I would ask, as Brighton's not far, is it?'

Amber chuckled like I must have been joking. 'Tomorrow?'

'I know. It's such short notice. But a couple of songs, at most. Maybe you and Mo could come up, and we could sort some gear out. We could play *Wanda* because Frank liked it best. I always loved how your voice on that one.'

'Um.' Baxter was wavering again, unhappy baby murmurs. 'Baxter's ten days old, Brian. Aren't you, baby? Shush.'

'Right...That's quite young, isn't it?' A deep, dull groan escaped my lips, and I pushed a fist into my mouth to quell it. 'It would make it tricky unless someone could have him.'

'Well, it makes it tricky because I haven't physically recovered for one.' Amber shushed her child gently as he quietened for a second. 'And Mo's fucked off for some work thing already. I'm sorry.'

'Oh, Jesus, don't be sorry.' Perhaps it was a gut punch now I had leaned into the idea again. 'I don't suppose you've got Luke's number?' I let the question slip out as if it didn't matter.

'No, I don't. He's back in London. That's all I know. I used to get all the updates when he was in America because our parents would talk.'

'Right.' I bit into my thumb. 'I still can't believe he just left us behind like that, you know? That's what still upsets me. Not to say anything.'

'Look, I'm sorry, Brian.' Amber tutted, and her baby was screeching now. 'I can't deal with that psychodrama now. Not when I've got my hands full.'

'Right. Yeah.' Baxter screamed again, a whole extra gear, as Amber cooed and shushed. 'I was a twat back then, wasn't I?'

'It doesn't matter. We were very young.' Her voice wobbled as she jigged. 'I'm sorry, Brian. I can't do this now. But thanks for letting me know. I'm really sad about Frank.'

'Of course. You head off.' I pushed my eyes into my hand, and the screaming was so loud – a guttural terror. 'Give my love to Mo. And congrats on the baby.'

There was nothing to do but slowly deflate after the call's clumsy sign-off. And with no air left to circulate my body, I dragged it upstairs and slid it inside the corner bath once it was filled with enough hot water to slow-boil in the darkness.

My phone illuminated the bathroom from its spot on the rim beside my head. I reached to the floor and wiped my hands on a towel before checking the notification – a message from Tam.

How's it going? The funeral is at 2.30 tomorrow. Are you still okay to travel up? xx

My head was gone, and I didn't know what to type other than a limp apology.

I'm sorry I don't think I can get Dorothea to play anything xx

Don't worry about that! But please come up. I need an ally xx

I set my alarm for an early hour, and a short time after it blared, I left the house on a stumbling ramble to Totnes station. The street lights were still glowing when I drifted onto a train heading for Paddington in exchange for an eye-watering price. Four hours disappeared inside an almost empty carriage before I rode the tube to East Finchley, propelled by a sense of obligation to Frank and Tam.

Fellow mourners drifted past after wandering into the expanse of the cemetery. They pulled up in their cars outside the crematorium chapel, more suitably attired under expensive umbrellas as the rain fell.

Tam waved by a concrete pillar at the front of the domed building. She had one side to herself to greet incomers who were generally veering to meet a man and woman on the other. She was so small and fragile, perhaps compressed by the weight of the event, her arms vibrating as we hugged.

I pinched at my black v-neck office jumper. 'I'm sorry. I don't own a suit.'

'You look fine!' Tam insisted, her voice shaking. She had only purchased her blazer the previous day and wished she had bought a hat too, mainly to prevent the number of guests commenting on her hair. 'Thanks so much for coming.'

I was seated in the front row on Tam's insistence when we moved inside, ignoring any curious sideglances. An enormous floral framed photo of Frank had been placed at the front of the service, catching the light from the glass dome above. The picture was well chosen, a peaceful portrait of him enjoying a pink ice cream on a park bench with yellow leaves around his feet.

Tam read Frank's favourite poem at the service, 'The Road Not Taken' by Robert Frost. His death pecked away at me then, tapping its beak until it pierced through. And she held my hand when she returned to her seat. I rubbed at my swollen face, gone at last. It was difficult not to mourn what I was losing beyond him, the briefest hope I allowed myself to drift into – how often I did that, how fleeting it always was.

The reception service was held late afternoon at an old steelworks which had been converted into a courtyard venue. The space had been smartly decorated, with foliage draped over exposed metal rafters and dressed tables facing a raised stage at one end.

Tam's older brother, Paul, guided her around the room and introduced her to the various attendees. I found myself alone and leaning against a wall after poking at the fancy spread of food. I chatted briefly with our old road manager – a small, hard man who seemed to hate us then and called our music 'student shit' at every opportunity. He was bereft now, unable to look up and speak without sputtering and falling apart. And when he left, I'd had enough and scanned my phone for train times back to Totnes – assuming I could slip away.

Suddenly, there was a hand on my shoulder. It was Niall. His jumble of black hair had been cut short since I had last seen him, leaving an island at the front.

'It's so unfortunate,' he said, poking at the coffee cake on the plate in his grip.

I nodded. 'Yes, it is.'

'How are you coping?'

The question was too open to answer neatly. 'Struggling today, I think.'

'Hmm.' Niall forked cake into his mouth and dabbed his lips with the back of his hand. 'Are you by the coast now?'

'I'm not sure. Probably. Why?'

He cleared his throat. 'Just that it can be useful, I think. Even just picturing yourself somewhere like that, paddling where the tide might be, where it was calmer. Or you might be further in the water, threatened by the depth and changing currents.'

'Right…okay.'

Niall smiled, perhaps sensing my confusion. 'Grief can get on top of people quickly. So it's important to ask yourself often where the water level might be and how that makes you feel.'

I nodded. It made sense, or at least more than it did. 'Right, yeah.'

Niall tapped me on the arm and wandered across the room – perhaps to have an identical conversation with another lost soul. And the water bobbed around my chest as he left, occasionally splashing against my chin.

Tam waved from across the room when our eyes met. She had retreated to a table near the stage, where everyone was slowly shifting. 'Do you know him?' she asked as I reached her.

'Niall?'

'Yes.' Her eyes narrowed, and she was intrigued. 'He was my therapist for like two years.'

'Right.'

Tam buried her face into the heavy white cloth on the table. 'Do you know much about wills and that sort of thing?'

I didn't, and I told her – unprepared for the sudden subject pivot. 'Sorry.'

'Don't be. It's just that I've been nodding for two days and have no idea what documents I've been signing, probably my inheritance away.'

'Shit.' I pulled a wallet from my pocket and tipped out Dad's chunky signet ring. 'My dad died when I was young. I've got this old ring of his. That's about it.'

Tam rubbed her shaved head. 'Oh, Brian. I'm sorry.'

'It's fine.'

'I need more wine.' Tam flipped over a pair of glasses and poured from a bottle on the table. 'I was trying to work out when we all last saw each other,' she said of her brother, who was chatting to musicians milling by the side of the small stage. 'I think I was eighteen, at some awkward family thing. I had an older boyfriend then, about Paul's age now. It was a scandal.'

'I'm trying to imagine you with a boyfriend.'

Tam laughed. 'I used to be a girly girl.' She pulled a phone from her blazer and showed me pouty group pictures and selfies from nights out – so many of those. Hyperfeminine Tam was jarring, with her straightened hair and tiny dresses.

'It's you, but it isn't.'

'I don't see any of these people anymore.' She smiled, holding her lips together. 'I still like girly drinks. But I'm also very gay now.'

Tam had a lot to get off her chest after days of tension. She was an outsider in her family and had grown up with that grumbling tension in her identity. Her mother had once been a promising singer and was much younger than Frank when they had their fling after his divorce, and she fell pregnant.

'Mum had this brutal post-natal depression when I was born,' she said. 'We lived in this tiny flat in Tower Hamlets, where she had a full-blown psychosis. Social services moved in, and Dad was given custody.'

'Shit.'

'I didn't know this until a few years ago.'

'I had no idea.'

'You wouldn't.' Tam downed her wine in one go and immediately refilled her glass. 'Dad did some shitty things in his life, but he could be amazing too. It makes it so complex. And I hated him for a long time, and now maybe I love him again.'

'Right.'

She scrunched her nose like there was a bad smell in the room. 'What is going on?'

'Taste bad?'

'No!' She laughed and grabbed at her arms. 'I'm unloading, and you're sitting there, absorbing – not speaking.'

'Sorry.' I shrugged. I wouldn't say I liked knowing that about myself, that perhaps I was stinted, and that was what she meant. 'I'm trying to think of useful things to say.'

'Aw, it wasn't a criticism.' She patted me on the back. 'You've got an assuaging quality. I bet I said that word wrong.'

'I've no idea.'

The lights dimmed, and Paul moved onto the stage as compère for Frank's musical tribute. He thanked everyone for coming and introduced a nervous young folk singer to kick things off. She perched on a stool and strummed the opening to Nick Drake's 'Time Has Told Me'. And the tuning was slightly off. And she stopped to tweak the heads on her guitar before starting again.

Tam whispered into my ear. 'Shall we go home? I want to see Con. I just want to see her and nothing else.'

I nodded. 'Yeah, of course.'

NINE

I balanced the laptop on my knees as I rubbed at my eyes – a morning sun beaming through the window above the sofa.

'How's your new bed?' Mum asked from her balcony bistro set.

'It's fine. I'm sleeping better.'

'Are you?' Her eyes narrowed as she sipped from her coffee mug. 'You look unwell for someone sleeping.'

'It's just weird being alone in the house again, with Tam away. You get used to the noise of other people, I guess.'

'Where's she gone?'

'Just housesitting a place in the middle of nowhere with her girlfriend.'

Mum chuckled nervously. 'Girlfriend?'

'Yes, Mum.'

'Oh, well, that's nice, actually.'

'Yeah.' I scratched my face. 'I'm just assuming she'll ask me to leave when she's back. There's no reason for me to be here if she's hanging around.'

'Hmm.' The motor on Mum's fan ran out, and she resorted to waving a paperback over her neck instead. 'Is this what's keeping you up?'

'That and thinking about lesson plans. I had written out all these notes yesterday, all the songs I learned when I started playing. I'd probably forgotten this kid doesn't even know the names of the strings yet. I should know this!'

'You need to speak to Ken. Your lovely, old tutor.'

'Yeah.' I laughed fondly. 'I wonder what he's up to now.'

Mum's mouth pulled to one side like she had imagined something unpleasant. 'Probably retired.'

'Yeah.'

'Hopefully, he's stopped drinking. He used to stink of it when he came over.'

I frowned. 'I had no idea.'

'Oh my, God, Brian. The smell. I mean, what a lovely man – I used to harass him to pay anything because he was just a nightmare.'

'I just thought he was eccentric.'

'Well, he was. But it wasn't difficult to know why the tail was wagging.'

'Right.'

'Anyway. I'm so happy you're doing it.' She clapped her hands. 'Are you going to turn this into a business?'

'Jesus, Mum. It's just a favour.' Bill appeared behind Mum and tipped a watering can into an ever-growing number of potted plants. 'Hi, Bill.'

Bill turned and comically held the brim of his cap. 'Hello, Brian.'

'You might enjoy it,' Mum said as Bill shuffled back inside. 'How old is this woman, then?'

'Not sure.' It was such a mum question, and I held up a creased Beatles guitar tab book Mum had bought for my twelfth birthday – mainly to get her off the topic. 'Hey, look what I found.'

Mum gasped and held her cheeks like it was some family relic. 'Where did you find it, love?'

'In one of my cases.'

'Oh, how precious.' She held her mouth. 'I remember saying it's no good you just learning Beatles songs all day. You've got to expand out and listen to some modern stuff.'

'I remember being genuinely shocked that they had been split up for thirty years.' I laughed. 'The way Dad carried on, it was like they were some current act to me.'

'It was nice how your dad always lit up when talking about them. They were your little shared interest.'

'Yeah. He had three CDs in his crappy Peugeot van. I remember liking them because they made him happy.'

'Aww.

'And I liked this BBC one best because of the talking between songs. They were this little gang laughing and joking. It just sounded like a cool thing to have – a posse like that.'

'Yes.'

I rubbed my face. 'Well, I better get myself sorted and rewrite these notes.'

'Okay, Bab. Good luck. I love you.'

'Love you, too.'

The heat was unrelenting on the walk to Beatty's. I wiped a veil of sweat from my face as I turned onto her sloping street with a yellow door in sight. Noah was peering down from an upstairs window as I reached it. I gave him a cheerful wave, and he wrapped himself around a rocket-ship-themed curtain and disappeared.

I gripped the brass hooped knocker and rattled it too forcefully, unable to control my nerves. Beatty opened the door in a green summer dress. 'Hey, you, come on in,' she said, so cheerful. She rested a pair of cat eye sunglasses on her head and planted a hand on my forearm and another on my shoulder. 'It's so warm today. An unnatural, clinging heat.'

'Yeah.' I slipped the guitar in its case from my back, a damp patch from my shirt there. 'It's so warm.'

Beatty called at the carpeted staircase ahead. 'Non!' We paused there and waited for signs of life to emerge. 'Let's get you set up. He'll be down soon.'

I followed across a squeaking wooden hallway which stepped up and down again. We moved into a cosy sitting room, which Beatty called the snug, with its crooked timbers and facing mustard-coloured sofas.

'It's nice in here,' I said, patting an enormous sheepskin rug with my foot.

'Yes, it's a good place to tuck yourself away with a book.'

The cottage was deep, and one room led onto another, the snug adjacent to a blush pink dining room with an upright piano. A pair of dark wood dining chairs had been positioned opposite, with a half-sized blue acoustic guitar resting against one. I removed mine from its case and started tuning.

'You look so prepared,' she said.

'Well, I've tried.' I slipped the folded handwritten notes from the guitar case.

Beatty tapped her chin as she pondered the space. 'Is there enough room in here for you? I did wonder.'

'Yes.' I nodded like an experienced tutor. 'Plenty.'

'Great, that's a relief. Let's get a drink in the kitchen. You look like you need to cool down.'

I followed Beatty through the open door in the corner of the room, stepping down the short, angled staircase there. A vast, extended kitchen lay beyond where light flowed in shafts from a lantern above and a pitched expanse of glass at the far end of the room. It was like walking into the property shows Esther was obsessed with, where a completed project was finally revealed to the euphoric peaks of a soft-rock song.

'I'm obsessed with Mojitos at the moment,' Beatty said. She pulled an ice cube tray from an enormous stainless-steel fridge freezer. 'I've grown mint in the garden and made some this morning. I'm not an alcoholic, I promise.'

I shuffled into the room, intimidated by it. 'Cool, that sounds nice.' I rested my hands on the back of a tall wooden stool tucked into a kitchen island, where Beatty began crushing leaves with a rolling pin.

'I'm in a celebratory mood.'

'Oh yeah?'

'I've organised all of my lessons, for once. I can almost smell the summer holidays.'

'That must be a relief.'

'Oh, it will be.' Beatty breathed a knowing chuckle. She turned to tidy a few items on the worktop behind, dispatching them into a wide drawer beneath an enormous nautical-themed artwork on the wall.

'Do you like sailing, then?'

'Oh no, that was my husband's thing.' She opened a bottle of soda water, topped our drinks with it, and pushed a tall glass across the work surface. 'There you go.'

'Lovely.' The mint leaves swirled, as well as a temptation to inquire more about Beatty's past tense husband. 'Thanks.'

We climbed back into the dining room, and Beatty tutted at the lack of Noah. She headed off to the hallway to call for him again, using a more insistent tone this time. I popped my drink onto the piano's lid, and he slumped inside shortly after, clutching an electronic tablet.

'You excited, Noah?' I asked. It had been some time since I had spoken to an actual child, and I had no reference. He nodded shyly and twisted himself around Beatty. 'Should be good.'

'We went to the beach earlier,' Beatty said. 'And what did Mummy forget?'

'Sun lotion,' he whispered.

'It was so embarrassing. I had to beg this couple next to us for some. I'm quite lucky. I never normally need much. But Non's just so fair. You can't risk it.'

'No,' I replied. 'You can't risk it. Not these days.'

'No, not these days.'

We both smirked at the banality of our exchange, and she said to call if I needed anything. A tingle of electricity buzzed around my mouth as our shared smiles widened. 'Cool, thanks, Beatty.'

There was no immediate sign Noah's shyness would thaw as we began our lesson. I struck upon an idea to download an app onto his tablet, which we used to help him tune his guitar. We strummed together and tried a couple of chords, the classic Em and C. We did a little more using a plectrum, which he found easier. He recognised its shape in the crap tattoo below the crook of my arm.

By the end of our first session, I had polished off my drink, and Noah could push the strings on his blue guitar hard enough to play a clean A chord. It was the perfect time to show Beatty what we had achieved as she re-joined us.

'Oh my God, that's incredible, Non,' Beatty beamed, her voice rasping. She twiddled a sunburst pendant as he continued. 'You're going to be the next Ben Howard.'

'Yep.' He smiled proudly, his tongue poking between his lips as he concentrated.

I suggested purchasing some nylon strings for the guitar, as they wouldn't be as harsh on Noah's fingers as the steel ones on there. 'I could pop into the music shop in town and pick some up for him,' I suggested.

'Aww, that's incredibly sweet,' Beatty said, a hand at her chest as if my offer disproportionately touched her. 'Right, shall we get some food? I've made a veggie lasagne. Is that okay with you, Brian?'

'Oh, wow.' The offer caught me off-guard, having half-expected to head off on my way. 'There's food?'

'Yeah, I've made far too much for just me and a fussy little eater. Unless you have plans.'

'No, this is fantastic. Thanks.'

We sat outside, around a white metal table underneath a canvas parasol in Beatty's neat country garden. Noah had freed himself from his shell and pinged questions my way as we ate. He wanted to know whether I could play an A chord as well as he could and then whether I was better than Mr

Jevons, his music teacher at school. Of course I was, I told him.

It was heady to be there as a swirling of carbs and freshly topped-up alcohol swam into my bloodstream. I had been inserted into a family scene and found myself at ease. And Beatty watched us as I spoke with Noah – a shuttering of thoughts flooding my brain, odd assessments as to whether I could be his new dad – if I were capable.

Noah asked if I would play something on the guitar as we finished up and stacked plates. He pounded on the table, wanting me to prove I was as good as I said. Beatty joined him, and they demanded I entertain them until I was determined to put Mr Jevons in his place.

After fetching it from inside, I returned with my guitar and played a couple of runs and licks. But when that didn't impress the others as I had hoped, I asked for song requests – perhaps some Beatles numbers, as they were fresh in my mind again. We got through renditions of 'Yellow Submarine', 'All You Need Is Love', and 'Here Comes The Sun' with Beatty showing Noah the lyrics on her phone. We were having fun, and I was four cocktails deep, basking in a whimsical newfound comfort.

Beatty brought the musical proceedings to a close, suggesting her elderly neighbours beyond a shrubby boundary would get grumpy soon if we continued. After some coaxing and protesting, Noah skipped off to play in his bedroom after being promised he could play on his tablet until bedtime.

Beatty was still beaming as we carried the stacked crockery towards the French doors and into the oversized kitchen. 'Oh my God, he loved that so much. He's been so quiet lately.'

'He seemed to come out of himself.'

'Yes!'

Beatty said she had been worried about Noah's recent inwardness as we slipped into a tidying routine as if it was well-known to us, rinsing plates and crockery in the sink before stacking them into a dishwasher.

I suggested that playing music might become a gateway to discovering Noah's confidence. 'It worked for me not so long ago.'

Beatty said it was a comforting thought. 'I might check on him. He normally has his bathtime in a minute.'

I nodded, unsure if events were winding up. 'Okay.'

She stretched her arms and looked out onto the garden where the low sun still throbbed.

'But he might want some of the ice cream our neighbour dropped in yesterday.'

'Sounds nice.'

'Yes! Would you like some?'

As agreed, I waited underneath the canvas parasol outside with a sobering awareness of my plusher surroundings. Beatty finally reappeared via the kitchen doors, and we ate ginger-flavoured ice cream from tiny glass serving bowls. There was a strange decadence to do that inside a pocket of quiet.

'I'm refusing to mow the garden,' Beatty said, pointing at the whites and yellows among the tall grass. 'It's for the bees and butterflies, in case you had wondered why it all looks overgrown.'

'Oh. Right.'

'Doing my bit.' She parked her teaspoon in her finished bowl. 'Small deeds from a bumpkin.'

'Right.' I stacked my bowl inside Beatty's, an odd pang as I did that as if it were an intimate thing to do. 'It looks nice.'

'Good.' Beatty placed an elbow on the table and rested her chin on her hand. 'What was your band called again?'

'Dorothea. We got the name from a book we were studying at college, and it stuck.'

'Middlemarch?'
'Yep. That's it.'
'That's my favourite book!' Beatty beamed. Her face was a wonder: enormous eyes, a large boot-shaped nose, and a teeny chin. It was a combination of features I was appreciating more and more. 'I'm not even joking. How funny. I used to think about it a lot, Dorothea and her wasted potential. I could never decide whether to be happy or sad for her.'
I tapped at my face, realising I had forgotten almost everything about it. 'I should probably reread it, really.'
'I think I want to read it again, too.' Beatty pushed her dark hair around an ear and picked up her spoon again. 'I heard it's one of those books you feel differently about as you age. It resonates differently.'
'Maybe we should both do it,' I suggested. 'We could make notes and discuss it together.'
'Yes! I'm going to force you to do that now!' An enormous tabby cat emerged from the bushy shrubs on the garden's boundary and sprung onto the table. 'Oh, it's Rupert.' She stroked the cat's neck with her fingers as he licked at the bowls.
'Rupert, is it? Even your cat is posh.'
Beatty wagged a finger. 'I'm not posh at all.'
I smiled sarcastically. 'Just someone with a posh voice and a posh house.'
'Don't be silly. The place was sort of a wedding present from my in-laws. Now it's mine. But it's not, really.'
'Okay. What do you mean?'
'Well, my mother-in-law comes over and starts gardening whenever she likes.' Beatty parked her cutlery and slowly lost herself to wherever her mind had drifted. 'Sometimes I don't know she's there, and I see her from the kitchen weeding and planting things. I feel like I'm going mad.'
'It is a weird situation.'

'Yeah....' She tutted and laughed at the same time. 'I probably need to sort bathtime.'

'Sure.' I stood, assuming it was a cue to leave.

'You could hang around.' Beatty stood up, too, and gathered the bowls. 'If you want.'

I paused, not knowing what that added 'if you want' meant. Either it was to shield Beatty from any perceived neediness on her part or that my wanting to stay was the only circumstance where it could be acceptable. Which, of course, it wouldn't be.

Without either of us willing to make what we wanted apparent, I suggested it was probably time to head back. Of course, it was the least appealing of the two options, based on Beatty's hesitant smile in response. Still, perhaps it was an excellent time to head out now that I was going – on a high.

We headed inside, and Beatty called up the stairs to let Noah know I was leaving as we gathered inside the hallway where we started.

'Bye, Brian!' He charged from his room and hung over the railing on the landing upstairs. 'Thanks for the lesson!'

I waved up to him. 'Bye, mate! See you again soon, I hope!'

'Oh wow.' Beatty held her mouth open, apparently astonished. Her ironically big reactions to small things were endearing. She was endearing. 'I normally have to beg him to say goodbye to anyone who comes over.'

'Well, we're good friends now.'

'Maybe we should make this a regular thing.' She played with her hair as we hovered by the front door. 'Actually, I should probably pay you something.'

I frowned, not wanting to sully whatever this was with a financial transaction. 'Maybe next time. Although it wouldn't feel right if I always had such a nice time.'

Beatty smiled and opened her door. 'Well, I'm glad you had a nice time.'

'Yes. I did.'

'Me too.' Our palms raised in sync as I backed out onto the street. 'Bye, then. We'll sort out another date. For a lesson.'

'Yes. Bye, Beatty.'

I turned, and the sun had almost disappeared, but the air was still warm and breathless. Everything was racing as the narrow lane widened, and the pink buildings appeared close to the bridge. And the river was almost still when I reached it, a row of moored sailboats bobbing lightly in the water. And I was going to save Beatty and Noah, and they would save me.

TEN

My legs were stretched out on the lime green sofa, having sprawled there since an early morning run. The laptop was on the coffee table a few inches away, with Mum staring back from her balcony, where she was cooling herself with a motorized hand fan. She was excited about the day trip she had taken the previous day.

'It's this monastery up in the mountains, in a place called Montserrat. Our new Irish friends across the way recommended it.'

'You don't have to call them your Irish friends.'

'Well, okay, just our friends, then.' Mum talked at length about her trip, how they had taken a train up to the mountains because Bill didn't fancy travelling up by cable car. 'It's a thousand years old.'

'Wow.'

'Honestly, Brian. It was like a film. Did you see the pictures?'

'Yeah. It looks great.'

Well, I didn't do it justice. You would not believe the scenery. We'll have take you there when you get over. Bill's still buzzing.'

'Yeah, sounds good.'

'The sofa converts to a bed, no problem.'

'Cool.' I sat up, vaguely recalling something. 'Is it near Barcelona?'

'Yes.'

'I've got some weird memory about Sam Rodgers going there.' I started laughing. 'Do you remember him?'

Mum rolled her eyes. 'I remember his mother.'

'I had this weird fantasy that you would become best friends.'

She laughed, a doubtful snicker. 'I don't think so.'

'You wouldn't even go near their door when you dropped me off there.'

'No.'

'And she would always ask Sam why Robert Towersey wasn't coming over instead of me after opening it. She would always say that out loud so I could hear.'

'Horrible woman.' Mum tutted. 'She would avoid me like the plague at the school gate.'

'She was just snobby, I think.'

'She was. Very.'

'I remember Sam asking why I spoke to her so much and telling him I wanted her to like me.'

'Why, love?'

I shrugged. 'I don't know. I think it's a problem I have.'

The front door clunked open, out of sight. 'Oh. I think Tam must be home.'

'Okay, love,' Mum said. 'I won't keep you. I need to help Bill anyway. Tara-a-bit.'

'Bye Mum, love you.'

Tam wheeled her yellow suitcase through the frosted glass door with her hands pulled inside the sleeves of a sweatshirt. Perhaps startled by the lack of prior warning, not that I was owed one, I launched into a blow-by-blow account of the cleaning I had done since she left – the patio windows and the shower cubicle.

I made coffee when Tam said she was gasping for one. We gathered at the kitchen table with our mugs, and she talked about her trip with Connie and how restorative it had been. They hadn't done much other than walk an elderly labradoodle around a quiet Suffolk village where they were housesitting for a friend. But she could work during the day, and they filled their evenings with box sets and takeaway food.

'I just want to fill the summer with dumb fun now,' she said. 'When it comes.'

'What sort of things are you thinking?'

'Just fun-sized things to propel me along.'

I nodded because it made sense. 'Yes, that's all anyone needs, I think.'

'Yes.' She sipped from her mug and gasped like it was perfect. 'Do you think you'll go back to London?'

I rubbed my hair. 'Um. Maybe.' But perhaps I couldn't just leave, not now. And where would I go? 'I should do, shouldn't I? Give you some space back.'

'Oh, I wasn't asking you to leave!' She gave me a reassuring smile. 'I was only enquiring about your plans.'

'Right.' I frowned. It was such an odd dance. What if Tam was so good at politeness it was impossible to read the signs – that my presence in her home was stifling, or worse? I clenched my hot mug, pushing my palms against it. 'I should make plans.'

'Well, Dad wanted you to stay here, and I want to honour that.' She finished her drink, her eyes widening as if she had regained a thought. 'So, Con's family garage is full of bikes. They're all cycling enthusiasts. Her dad repairs them as some relaxation, post-retirement hobby.'

'Oh, cool.'

'And now I'm stuck on this idea of going for a ride in the countryside, searching for a pub for food and beer. A little reward.'

'That sounds nice.'

'And we'll all go, the four of us.' Tam slid out from the bench and popped her mug into the sink. 'James is up for it. Are you?'

'Sure.'

Tam was good at following through with a vision, so good I found myself bumbling along the lanes of the Dart Valley Cycleway on James's spare bike. He might have been the real cycling enthusiast of his family as he bounded ahead in the steep climb to Ashprington and then onto tiny Tuckenhay where we had a table booked for Sunday lunch by the Harbourne river.

James wasn't difficult to spot in polyester neon green as we wheeled our bikes towards him, exhausted. He had balanced himself against an empty riverside table, draining the remains from a water bottle as a sailboat with a tall mast drifted by.

'James, have you got something to change into?' Tam asked as we reached him.

He held his hand up and his tight outfit accentuating an angular build. 'Nope.'

'James! You can see everything.' Connie frowned, appalled. 'It's really unseemly.'

He shrugged. 'Don't look then.'

It was difficult to be too critical of James and his attire choices, mainly because he was so unruffled compared to the three of us, who hadn't dressed or prepared for the physical demands of the journey.

Tam pulled a camera from a rucksack and panned across the twinkling water. She slipped into a jokey interview with Connie, who was panting and bent over – either the worst affected by our trip or was being the most dramatic about it.

We headed inside and were shown to our table by a window with a view of the water. As James and Connie queued for drinks at the bar, I spied a message from Beatty on my phone.

Noah won't stop asking when his next lesson is. He loved it so much! xx

'Everything okay there?' Tam asked.

'Fine,' I said, smiling as I tapped my response.

When is good for you? xx

Tam leaned over the table and pretended to look at my screen. 'You're smiling away at something.'

'It's nothing.'

My phone buzzed straight away, forcing me to check.

How's Friday early evening looking? xx

Perfect! I'll do food again xx

Cool xx

I slipped my phone away, fearing a bombardment of forthcoming enquiries based on the curious look on Tam's face. 'Sorry.'

James arrived with four pints of local cider. He plopped a tray on the table, and the drinks spilt a little on impact. Connie frowned at the order. It wasn't what she wanted as she sidled in alongside Tam.

James rolled his eyes and said his sister had taken too long to decide. He was in a spikier mood than usual and lowered himself onto the dark wooden chair opposite, a relief not to have his groin at eye level. 'Anyway, I've got some news.'

'Anything exciting?' Tam asked. It seemed unlikely.

James chuckled with a mildly disconcerting falsetto. 'I've split up with Elena. I mean, she split up with me, really.'

'Oh, James.' Connie cupped her brother's knee. 'Are you okay?'

'I think so.' James slapped his thighs. He took a long guzzle of his cider, sinking most of its contents. 'I always thought I would immediately go into a deep funk if it happened. And it's not been too bad. So far.'

'Aw,' Connie said and rubbed her brother's forearm. 'What about this girl at work you like?'

James shook his head. 'Jesus, Con.'

Our food arrived, breaking our quiet concern for James, who had disappeared inside a one-thousand-yard stare to nowhere. Perhaps the breadth of the break-up was hitting home in real-time. An enormous Sunday beef roast was placed before me, steaming away underneath a giant bowl-shaped Yorkshire pudding.

'Brian was texting someone earlier and smiling,' Tam revealed, perhaps trying to lighten the mood. 'I'm guessing it was a lady, the way he was smiling.'

Connie gasped, joining in. 'Not a lady friend, Brian?'

'Was it, Brian?' Tam said, full of mischief. 'We're all friends. You can say.'

'Probably Charlotte's sister,' James said as he spooned red cabbage onto his plate from a serving dish. 'I did warn him.'

It was a betrayal, having discussed the issue briefly with James at the pub a few nights before and then again at a showing of Jean Luc Godard's 'Breathless' at Totnes Cinema during their French New Wave season.

Tam held her mouth open as I attempted to subdue my creeping smile. 'Beatrice?'

I whispered, 'Maybe.'

'Maybe!' Connie tutted playfully. 'We leave Totnes for five minutes, and you're creeping around it like a Tom cat. It's undignified.'

'Nothing is going on,' I insisted. I attempted to describe the lesson I gave to Noah and how we had food together afterwards. But I tailed off, realising the detail was adding to their suspicion something spicier was happening. 'I'm just teaching guitar to her son. To cut a story short.'

'Not the way you were smiling,' Tam laughed. She sipped her cider tentatively and then nodded approvingly. 'No way.'

'Oh, it's romantic,' Connie said. 'Although I'm struggling to picture you two together.'

'Con!' Tam whispered sharply.

'I don't mean that in a bad way, Brian!' Connie insisted. She held the side of her head on my shoulder for a second. 'I mean, I know things. Her family know mine. It would be an adjustment, that's all.'

I shrugged as the others continued to jibe. 'I'm giving lessons to Noah. I'm a qualified tutor. I'm not even thinking about anything else.'

Of course, the *anything else* was all I had been thinking about.

After a day in post-cycling lactic hell, my legs had fully recovered when I rode across the bridge again on the bike I had acquired from the trip, with James insisting I should borrow it for a while. The sun was baking again, and they called the weather a heatwave when Beatty opened her yellow door after I rattled the knocker with a cheerful beat.

'Hey!' she beamed as if she was excitedly surprised to see me.

'Hey!'

We touched arms as I wandered inside. Beatty tied her hair up. She stared at the landing without calling for Noah. 'There's a chance of a storm at some point, I heard.'

'Right.' I wiped the sweat from my brow. There was so much. 'It needs to break.'

'Yes, it really does.' Beatty sniggered, sensing the comedy in our brief exchange. 'Sorry, are we a pair of pensioners catching up? Did you fancy a game of dominoes?'

I laughed. 'Sounds alright, actually.'

Beatty pulled in her lips, pensive suddenly. 'So, it's a bit of a weird situation. Mum came over to collect Noah an hour ago.'

'Oh, right.'

'Yeah. I'd forgotten my parents were taking him to Cornwall for the weekend.' She rolled her eyes. The trip had been planned months before and not mentioned in the last few days, which was the limit of where her short-term memory stretched.

'Okay.'

Beatty bit into her lip. Perhaps she had planned to take her cue from my reaction to the news, but it was digesting too slowly – as all sudden changes did now. Clearly, it had shifted the dynamic of my visit, and any pretence had been stripped away – if that's what it was.

'I had to tear around the house,' she explained. 'I was stuffing things into bags to take with him.'

'That sounds hectic.'

'Yeah. I was in two minds about whether to let you know or if it was too late.' Beatty laughed, and we continued to hover in the hall. 'We could hang out here if you wanted, I don't know. I've made food anyway. But it's totally up to you.'

'Well, it would be a shame to waste it.' I popped my guitar down by a coat stand with an umbrella protruding from its holder. 'Probably won't need that.'

'You never know.'

Beatty needed to check on the oven, and I followed her through the snug and pink dining room. We headed down into the enormous kitchen, where she knelt by a large cooker and peered through its glass door. She had found a recipe for a butternut squash bake using bits she had around and thought it sounded nice. I nodded, absorbing her lovely voice – how it cracked and cooed.

'You should record audiobooks for a living,' I found myself saying.

'Pardon?' Beatty frowned like I had said something mad. She fumbled in a drawer under the kitchen hob and handed me a corkscrew for the wine bottle on the worktop.

'You've got a nice voice.' I picked at the wrapping on the bottle, which didn't want to come away. 'You could narrate documentaries about train journeys. Or couples that love narrow boating. That sort of thing.'

'That's very specific.'

Beatty was still chuckling about my compliment when we were outside again, underneath the parasol at the white garden furniture. We talked about how we had filled the days in our time apart, the bike ride, and why I was walking so gingerly in case it alarmed her.

Beatty said her in-laws had been over without warning, having decided the boiler needed checking despite the hot weather. She blew a long puff of air – her previously good mood threatened. The three had argued about her plans to sell up and downsize. They said they wanted their grandson to grow up in a good home, and that's all it was, but she thought it was more sinister than that. The constant check-ins felt coercive. Perhaps they wanted control over her and Noah and that connection to their son, Mike.

'Mike is your ex?'

Beatty nodded. She sipped her wine and parked the glass on her folded arm. 'He's dead, by the way.'

'Oh.' I lowered my fork after a dispatching mouthful. 'Shit.'

Beatty laughed, short and uneasy. 'I never know whether to call him my ex-husband. It seems a bit literal.'

'Fuck.' My mouth dried as I chewed. 'Um. Recently?'

'Four years ago.'

'Do you mind me asking what happened?'

'Leukaemia happened.' Beatty glanced at the kitchen extension bulging from the building. There were perfect trails of flowers which hung like grapes above the glass doors. 'And now there's not much of me here. Do you know what I mean?'

I nodded. 'I think so.'

Beatty shook her head like she was freeing herself again. 'God. I'm sorry. I'm laying it all out.'

'Don't be sorry.'

An enormous boom of thunder banged above. Our eyes met, wide and alert. After peeking under the parasol, the sky had clouded without our noticing. We grabbed what we could, with plates on our wrists and wine glass stems between our fingers. A thick hammering downpour came as we ran into the kitchen, and the door clunked shut.

'It's like being in a church,' I said as the rain echoed in.

Beatty laughed. 'Okay.'

Our fingers glanced, and the sky flickered as we watched the storm unfold like a film. The downpour washed the glass wall as Beatty locked her hand in mine and pushed her face into my neck.

'Are you okay?' she inquired as if she had asked a very different question.

'Yes. Are you?'

'Yes,' she whispered. 'Do you want to come upstairs?'

We kissed – mere minutes after discussing Beatty's dead husband. And perhaps that was too much to process as we drifted through the house, up the stairs and inside a bedroom at the end of the landing.

The room was small and dark inside, and the day's boiled heat circulated as we kissed again. We fell on top of an iron-framed bed which spanned the width of the back wall. Its mattress was surprisingly buoyant as we removed our clothes like nervous teenagers.

A pulse of concentrated reality shocked me from nowhere. And suddenly, I was there, completely present, doing what I was doing: having sex with Beatty and not behind or in front of myself. It was overwhelming, the sense of obligation. I wasn't up to it, and she must have seen that – her wide brown eyes stared through me instead as we grasped at each other, evaporating all the time.

Beatty rolled over to face the wall when it was over, and the low, beamed ceiling stared down at me.

'Are you okay?' I asked when it seemed neither of us would speak again.

'Yeah, I'm fine.' Her voice wobbled as if she might cry. 'You had a worried look on your face.'

'Did I?' Beatty buried her face into the pillow. She started to sob quietly, and it was a nightmare. 'Beatty, you're crying.'

'Yes, sorry. I'm trying not to.'

'Was it that bad?'

'No, no,' she insisted, but perhaps it had been. 'I was just trying to work out why you were so worried.'

'Fuck. I'm sorry.'

'Oh, don't!' She rolled and pushed her nose into my shoulder, the moisture from her eyes on my skin. 'I feel so vulnerable, suddenly. It's not a nice feeling.'

'I understand. A lot is going on.'

'Yes,' she said and held a palm on my cheek. 'There's just a lot I need to shield myself from.'

I asked if I should leave, whether that would make Beatty feel more comfortable. But she moved her hand to my chest and asked me to stay. She said she couldn't face being on her own.

We didn't have sex again that night. A part of me had wanted to, perhaps to prove I wasn't a disaster at it. And after getting ready, we whispered to each other in the darkness where it was too warm to fall asleep. And then it was too noisy once Beatty fired up an antique metal fan to cool us.

'What was Mike like?' I asked, deciding to pick that scab.

Beatty half-smiled, her eyes narrowed like she couldn't believe the question. 'Why?'

'I was just wondering.'

'Okay. Um. He was a lovely, fun person and positive all the time. And he was beautiful with Noah, and that's the saddest thing.' A short nasal sigh escaped. 'There you go.'

'It's an awful thing to happen.'

'Yes. And it's why I want to get out of here. I can't even sleep in our old room.'

'Why?'

'Do you actually want to know?'

I shrugged. 'Up to you.'

She pinched her bottom lip. 'Well, I tried to find a hospice for him when he was terminal. But his parents insisted Mike was nursed there instead. Until the end.'

'Fuck.'

'Yes.'

Beatty fell asleep first, turning to face the wall. I switched to my back, and the ceiling was closer now. And I struggled to understand what had happened until I finally drifted away, too.

Perhaps those pre-sleep worries had provoked the insane nightmare which followed – where Mike had emerged from the room next door and watched from the landing where the door was open. A paralysis held me down – and I suffered his glare. And I couldn't move, not an inch.

ELEVEN

I was still in the previous day's clothes after slinking away from Beatty's in the early hours. Two strangers were sleeping in my bed when I got home, and there was little to do but clean the sizeable mess left in the kitchen and lean into every other distraction available.

'You sound far away,' Mum said via the speaker on my phone.

'I've got you on speaker.' The device was charging on the worktop next to a clutter of empty bottles. I squeezed a cloth into the kitchen sink, and a puddle of yellow washing-up liquid frothed underneath the hot tap. 'I'm just tidying up around.'

'Well, that's thoughtful of you.'

'Well, it's my house too.' I grabbed a stack of dirty plates and bowls from the draining board and dropped them into the foaming water. 'Hey. I was thinking about Terry earlier. Remember him?'

Mum groaned as if I had reminded her of a car crash she once had. 'Oh, why?'

'I don't know. I just remembered the bags of fizzy sweets he brought over.'

'Mhm.'

'And he was always taking us to Disneyland. He had a friend who worked there or something and could get a deal for us.'

'Oh yeah.' She tutted. 'It was always Disneyland. Full of promises, he was, Bab.'

'Yep. I wonder what he's up to now.'

'God knows. I don't like thinking about him or that time.'

'No, me either. I don't miss that cold flat.' I plopped my hands into the hot water and scrubbed at the plates, filing each onto the drainer. 'Or the smell from the chippy downstairs.'

Mum laughed. 'It was the lovely combination of boiled fat and Lynx for me.'

'I bet. It's funny how smells linger with you.'

'Yes. Layla and Paul were gorgeous, though, always inviting us downstairs to ask if we wanted their leftovers.'

'Yes. I practically lived on lukewarm chips.'

Mum sighed. 'They're both dead now, Bab. Car accident.'

'Shit! I didn't know that.'

'No.'

'That's a lovely way to round that anecdote off, Mum.'

'Sorry.' She tutted. 'It's such a shame.'

'Yeah.' Footsteps creaked across the landing above, the first signs of life in the house beyond me. 'I better crack on, really, Mum. Love you.'

'Love you too, Bab. Tarra-a-bit.'

Soon, Tam was shuffling into the living room, barefooted and arms folded – a dressing gown hood pulled over her head. 'I was just coming down to sort this,' she croaked as she joined me in the kitchen. 'Thank you.'

'That's okay. Guessing you had friends over.'

'Yes. I'm so hungover.' She slumped onto a dining chair at the table. 'You're wearing glasses.'

'Yeah.'

'I think there are people in your room.'

'Yes. I didn't notice them at first.'

Tam sighed. 'I did tell them not to.' She said Connie's friends had popped over late with food and alcohol, and the hours rolled away unnoticed until everyone was smashed. 'What happened to you? We were speculating.'

'Just got waylaid.' I dragged the heavy rubbish bag through the patio doors and despatched it inside the wheely bin on the concrete outside.

'Oh, okay!' she called. 'I'm hanging too much to be interested, anyway.'

I slipped back into the kitchen, where Tam stretched to a full span and then collapsed, spreading her arms over the table. I quietly pulled the patio doors together as she rested her head on the hard surface as if nuzzling into a soft pillow.

The frosted glass door squeaked open at the end of the room, and a suited Geoff wandered inside. His presence was so unexpected that I was ready to cast it off as a waking nightmare. He beamed as he clocked me in the kitchen and brushed the arms of a pinstripe suit jacket that clung to him in the wrong places.

'Alright, Bri!' he said, just as I assumed he might vanish and never speak. He twirled by the chocolate-coloured leather chairs. 'What do you think of the new get-up then?'

'Who's that?' croaked Tam, threatening to lift her head.

'Oh, it's just Geoff,' I replied in a daze, hoping that was enough information to calm her.

'Sorry, I didn't see you there, darling!' Geoff said as he reached us and spied Tam at the table. He laughed as she lifted her head, his barking laugh. Everything was so terrible. 'Has he worn you out?'

Tam peered at Geoff and then at me, the most bewilderment I'd seen on a human face. She levered herself upright, pushing down on the table. 'I'm going back to bed, Brian.'

'Okay,' I said. 'Best to sleep it off, I reckon.

Tam slunk past Geoff and drifted out of the room. Perhaps she was too tired and hungover to process the odd scene, although that seemed hopeful at best.

'You're wearing glasses, Bri,' Geoff said when the coast was clear.

'Yeah.'

'You look like Harry Potter.'

'Okay.' I shrugged. 'Why did you just walk in, mate?'

'We've got an all-dayer today, mate,' Geoff said like I had to know that already. 'Check your messages. I told me you to wear a suit.'

I unplugged my phone from the worktop. Perhaps I was going mad – but there were no missed calls or notes from Geoff – despite our casual agreement when he last visited. It was a relief, if anything. 'I genuinely don't have anything from you, mate.'

Geoff screwed his face. 'Who the fuck have I just been ringing then?' He slipped on a tiny pair of specs, pulled a mobile from his inside jacket pocket, and held it at eye line. 'Fuck!' He hung his head. 'Carl. Shit! He's been ringing me.'

'Okay.' I shrugged, and perhaps I was off the hook.

'I've just blocked him.' Geoff winced, the corners of his mouth stretched as if that decision would come back to bite him. He popped his phone away, along with his specs. 'Shall we do it, then? Your shirt's creased, but we'll keep you out of the way.'

I hesitated. 'Um…actually, I need a shower. I haven't had the chance to have one yet. I'm quite tired.'

'Oh, don't worry about that, Bri,' Geoff insisted, waving his hand. 'I can sort you out a shower when we get there.'

'Right.'

Perhaps Geoff had magical persuasive powers or an uncanny ability to knock me off balance whenever his mouth opened. And perhaps it was okay to do an all-dayer – whatever it was. It would occupy my mind, at least.

Geoff pointed up at the troublesome brown stain on the ceiling. 'Got a bathroom above here?'

'Probably. Possibly.'

'Yeah, you have,' he insisted. He checked his copper-coloured wristwatch. 'Shit! We need to go!'

'Okay.'

We hurried outside and jogged towards the van, where Jack leaned against the passenger door in a bow tie and waistcoat like he was off to play a snooker game. We climbed inside, and I was sandwiched between Geoff and his nephew again as the vehicle's rumbling engine awoke.

The colourful terraced homes vanished from view as we moved, and I was a confused hostage, unable to make sense of my circumstances. But it was good to have distractions. It was good not to think at all.

'Hey, Jack,' Geoff called as his nephew removed a handheld console from the glove box. The floor had been tidied since our last venture, with the cans and other wrappers removed. 'Wind the window down if you feel sick again. I'm not having a repeat of last week.'

'Okay,' Jack mumbled. He rested his feet on the dashboard and farted loudly.

Geoff nudged me with his elbow. 'That fucking Carl chap threatened to punch him last week.' He shook his head. 'Jack was sick on his trainers on the way home, and Carl blew his top. Not putting up with that, Bri. Come at my family, and that's only going one way.'

'Right, yeah,' I replied. 'No plans to punch Jack here.'

'Good.' Geoff chuckled and patted me on the back. 'Well, I can see you're not that type.' He removed his hand eventually, after an unsettling period where it lingered around my shoulders. 'Jack does get ill playing that when we're travelling. So keep an eye out.'

I nodded. 'Okay.'

The van hit a series of tiny winding roads as we headed further into Dartmoor. The lanes were so narrow it didn't seem possible for our vehicle to pass through, and Geoff's frustration grew each time we paused at a passing point for another driver to barely squeeze by.

'This is the problem with this time of year,' Geoff complained. 'It's full of grockles in their Chelsea tractors, getting into a panic with their SatNavs. They haven't got a fucking clue.'

'Right.'

The sun's warm glare peeped through the clouds as we turned onto a long, tree-lined driveway towards our destination. Pynnesbury Hall was a large grey-stoned Manor House half-wrapped in scaffolding and green netting as we approached.

'They've still got the scaffold up,' Geoff tutted as we parked. I hope these suckers are getting some of their money back. Imagine all of that shit in your wedding photos. Maybe they can photoshop some of it out. Who knows, these days.'

'Right.'

We were bang on schedule, Geoff announced. He turned his attention to the small notebook pulled from his top jacket pocket and reeled off the program ahead. Because of the dry weather, we were working on Plan A and would need the outdoor PA and mics for the ceremony inside a lakeside pavilion. Guests would then be led up onto the garden terrace for drinks, where we would provide them with some light touch background music. The remaining gear would be set up in the marquee for the after-dinner speeches and a disco to round off the day's entertainment.

'Perfect,' he said and slapped me on the back. 'What do you reckon, Bri?'

I nodded. 'Sounds good.'

A short blonde woman in a floral dress coat emerged from the building and made a beeline in our direction. Geoff tucked his notebook away and slipped on a pair of sunglasses. 'Here she is, Lady Lottery Winner of the Manor.'

He groaned as if the pair were old adversaries and pushed open the driver's door. 'Let's go, Bri.'

I hesitated, unsure why I had been summoned. 'Right.'

'Karen!' Geoff yelled as if the two were long-lost friends. We stepped out onto the gravel, and he stretched his arms before settling for a pat on Karen's shoulder.

'Hello, Geoffrey,' Karen replied, like a school teacher addressing a wayward pupil. She told us the main entrance to the building was out of action due to ongoing work, but we could access the venue via a gate to the gardens.

Geoff clicked his tongue, his gaze moving to the building. 'Is the scaffold staying up for the wedding?'

'Well, yes,' Karen replied. 'We don't want the home to collapse, do we?'

Geoff nodded. 'They'll have to keep the ugly netting out of the photos.'

Karen rolled her eyes. 'Yes, well, we are all professionals, aren't we?'

'Some are.' Geoff pointed his thumb in my direction. 'This is Brian.'

'You look like Harry Potter,' Karen said with a slight smile. 'I never know why you need all of these apprentices. It can't be that difficult. Kevin Dack does it all on his own.'

Geoff groaned. 'If you pay for Dacky, you'll get tacky. Everyone knows that.'

'All the discos are tacky, Geoffrey.' Karen smirked. 'We had a ceilidh last week, which was terrific fun. We might just encourage those from now on.'

Geoff shuddered theatrically. 'It's a crap fad. Embarrassing forced fun.'

'Well, we'll see,' Karen said. 'Anyway, I need to get going. There are important things I need to get sorted between now and later.'

'Okay, babe.' Geoff clicked his fingers and pointed at the van. 'Right, let's crack on then, Bri.'

'Okay,' I replied.

'Nice of her to threaten an entire industry like that,' Geoff grumbled as Karen wandered back towards the house. He unlocked the rear doors of the van, and they flapped outwards. 'She should know about tacky. Did you see that dodgy spray tan?'

'Not really.'

'And that face wasn't moving. Like the wind had changed.'

I shrugged. 'Not sure.'

'Where's this bitch?' Geoff shuffled through a series of hard-shelled silver boxes before locating a cube-shaped container. He tapped at it lovingly as if it soothed all of his worries. 'LED mirror ball simulator.'

'That's good.'

'You're telling me.'

After stacking the gear onto equipment trolleys, we pulled them into the manicured gardens after locating the gate at the side of the imposing building. I pinched my shirt collar. The chafing warmth of being in the previous day's clothes was unbearable. 'Do you think I'll still be able to have that shower?'

'What?' Geoff was incredulous. 'There's no time for poncing about in showers, Bri. Not with all the work we've got on.'

'Right.'

Jack stayed in the van to play on his handheld console as we headed to the lakeside gazebo, where staff were arranging white chairs on either side of a carpeted aisle. My role morphed into an equipment fetcher for Geoff, searching for specific items when he called for them and then waiting for him to wander over when I couldn't do that.

Geoff completed the set-up in the hexagonal wooden structure, installing the mics and mobile PA system there as I generally stood by, hands on hips. Once he was happy with a quick sound test, we moved the remaining equipment along the temporary fabric pathway towards the long white marquee.

'They've gone with the panoramic windows,' Geoff said, nudging my arm. 'Good choice on a sunny day like this. But you've got to open the sides up and let it breathe.'

'Right.'

'Maybe grab a beer in a bit,' Geoff said as we headed inside and wandered past a circular bar. The catering staff were dressing long tables at the back of the space. 'Nah. Not drinking today.'

'Right.'

'I'm assuming that's gonna be moved,' Geoff said as he inspected a top table assembled over a dance floor.

'Not sure,' I replied.

'Better be.'

After the marquee disco set-up, Geoff cycled through every light sequence from the new mirror ball. He was ecstatic with his purchase, grabbing my shoulders and shaking them with a barely controlled joy before finally securing it atop one of the speakers.

We headed out of the marquee, with Geoff announcing our departure to the staff there as if they were old friends. We wandered up the slope, pulling the remaining items to a wide stone terrace overlooking the expansive sloping lawns below. My crucial role was to kickstart a curated laptop playlist there once guests arrived for drinks and nibbles post-ceremony.

After a small sound test with the PA, Geoff returned to the gazebo, telling me to watch out for his signal. He hobnobbed with the wedding photographer, who was busy taking aerial shots via a drone.

I slipped into the main building to freshen up inside the communal loo. A muddleheaded fatigue set in as I wandered back into place, damp under my clothes and not remotely quenched from a panicked wash.

The venue had filled since my disappearance, and a top-hatted groom and his best man waited at the makeshift altar as wedding guests slipped into their seats. The sun warmed my eyelids as I gripped a low crumbly wall. My head bowed, and I was ready to slip away until a vibration in my pocket buzzed me awake.

I slipped my phone out, and there was a message from Beatty.

Did you get back okay? xx

Yes all good. How are you? xx

I'm okay. I slept for so long! xx

That's good xx

A 'Beatty is typing' note disappeared and reappeared as the Wedding March blasted below. There was little to do but remain fixed on my screen as that cycle repeated. An important message was coming, which was difficult for her to express.

It's okay for what happened not to mean anything xx

It was impossible to find an immediate reply when everything was so fogged. Was Beatty offering me a way out or a way in? Or perhaps she was offering nothing other than her honesty. We had sex, big deal. People have sex. They have bad sex, too. It's just sex.

Prospective responses to Beatty's message were still bouncing around after the ceremony, as the photographer led the married couple away for photos by the lake. Waistcoated catering staff moved onto the steps below with platters of drinks and hors d'oeuvres as the guests funnelled up the slope. Geoff's pre-agreed signal came from the gardens – a full-armed wave and I dutifully pushed play on the laptop so Damien Rice's 'Cannonball' could play.

'Well done, Bri,' Geoff beamed as he reached the terrace. He patted me on the arm like a proud dad and retrieved a stack of pale blue business cards from his inside blazer pocket. Each had the words *Disco Inferno - Text to Request* emblazoned in gold lettering with Geoff's number underneath. 'What do you reckon?'

'Good,' I replied and pretended to examine them closely. 'I like the gold.'

'Very swish. Absolute game changer, these.'

Geoff split the stack and asked me to distribute as many as possible to the guests milling on the terrace. He said it was a genius bit of marketing, something he had picked up from one of his major rivals. The guests received the cards with polite smiles and mild confusion as I handed them out in a daze.

I was still drifting along, sleep-deprived and confused, when we sat down for food in the marquee alongside the photographer and other periphery service providers. We had an undressed table to ourselves, away from the wedding party. Jack rejoined us there and launched into his meal like he hadn't eaten for days. His wet mouth chomping away was the only thing keeping me in the present.

'Three-course meal, Bri,' Geoff said, winking from across the table. 'Nice little perk.'

'Yeah.' I poked at my plate with a fork. 'Nice food.'

'Hell yeah.' Geoff peered at the small menu card on our table. 'Chicken breast, braised with wild mushrooms and a marsala wine.'

'Fancy.'

Geoff's eyes narrowed. 'Are you alright, Bri? Not been smoking something you shouldn't have?'

Jack farted before I could answer. The noise was loud and aggressive, like a surge of air released from an unknotted balloon. It was unpleasant enough for his tablemate to shift out of her seat with a hand cupped at her mouth.

'I'm fine.' I wasn't sure where to look, but Geoff remained poised for an answer. 'Just tired.'

'Well, it's a big one tonight, mate. I need you to be on top form.' He pointed at the bottle of water in his grip and winked. 'Taking no risks.'

The top tables were cleared away by staff once the pedestrian speeches had finished, leaving the dancefloor free of clutter. The wedding party assembled at the pagoda stand outside, where a bluegrass band played a series of bouncy, twee cover songs.

Geoff grumbled as we made final tweaks to the set-up, saying he couldn't focus with the music playing outside – it was impacting the levels. And he fretted the band had stolen our limelight and guests would head home before we could do our thing. He said it was Karen's fault for planting a seed in his head that discos were becoming old-hat.

A ukelele-led cover of Ed Sheeran's 'Perfect' finished up out of sight and to rapturous applause. It only occurred to me then that there was work to do as Geoff fired up the mirror ball light to remind the wedding-goers of our presence. A cascade of neon lights beamed around the primarily empty tent as he faded up Daft Punk's 'Get Lucky' with the clapping still ringing.

'Thank you to the guys,' Geoff roared into his mic. He smiled with relief as the marquee began to fill up, with some party-goers heading for the circular bar and others straight to the dancefloor. 'What a great support act to kick off the evening's entertainment. We are the Disco Inferno, rounding off the wedding celebrations of Peter and Louise Winterburn!' A huge cheer went up as the married couple held their hands aloft. 'I'm DJ Geoff the Deck Wrecker, here with Brian the Magic Man, and we'll be spinning the tunes from here on in. So grab your loved ones, get onto the floor and boogie your butts off.'

My new nickname *Brian the Magic Man* was firmly lodged into my brain, perhaps permanently, as Geoff peeled off his pinstriped blazer and threw it to one side. He pumped his fist and pulled on his curly red wig, a gimmick of his beyond my comprehension.

'Let's fuck some shit up!' he yelled, cupping his hand at my ear.

'Okay.'

'Do you want to take the glasses off? You look like a nerd.'

'Sure.'

Two young teenage girls tentatively approached the booth and lingered there. After some cajoling between the pair, one with multicoloured braces asked if we could play 'One Kiss' by Dua Lipa. Geoff stepped across before I could answer and explained they would have to text for requests or message us on the Facebook page. 'There's a lot of electrical equipment around,' he explained, handing a business card to one. 'It's for your safety. And ours.'

The girls shuffled away, bewildered.

My pocket buzzed with another message from Beatty, and I cursed myself for not responding earlier.

Sorry if you've been busy. I hope I didn't upset you xx

I tapped out a quick reply, deciding it was what she would have wanted to read.

Sorry! I have been busy. I agree it didn't mean anything xx

Geoff cupped his hand to my ear, the insanity of my message seeping. 'Are you okay, Bri?'

I nodded and returned the phone to my pocket. Perhaps my reply was clumsy, and I should have followed it up to clarify or soften what I had written. Perhaps there was a good reason I didn't do that. Perhaps a good instinct had kicked in my behalf.

'We need you, bro.' Geoff pumped his fist as Curtis Mayfield's 'Move On Up' captivated the unrhythmic bodies on the dancefloor, off-beat and out of step. 'Let's give these cunts a fucking part-ay!'

'Okay.'

There was an unhinged look in Geoff's eye as he lifted both hands, and the crowd raised theirs in return. They were his now, in his palm. And I shrivelled as a realisation hit home. I was Terry, and that's who I was or could be – a man with fizzy sweets and nothing else.

Geoff was manic and triumphant once we returned to the gravelled car park – grabbing my shoulders constantly as we packed equipment back into the van. 'Woah!' he yelled, tapping at my back as the rear doors closed. 'Look at that fucking moon up there! Look at that round bitch!'

Perhaps it was worth looking at as I finally turned – so gigantic and full. 'Wow.'

'I wish Karen was here, Bri!' Geoff said, his gaze lifted at the sky. 'I wanted to rub it in her face so bad.'

'Right.'

'With my dick.'

'That's nice.'

'Well. That's what happens when you pull a tiger's tail.'

There was no sign that Geoff's excitement would dissipate as we pulled away from the venue. Jack booted up his handheld console again, and 'Get Lucky' blared through the speakers as we hit the tiny black roads, with our driver keen to re-live the evening's proceedings.

Geoff switched off the music suddenly and pounded on the steering wheel like he'd had an idea. 'We need to organise a smash-up! Just us three. Are you old enough, Jack? We'll get shitfaced and see who can pull the first bird. My money's on Bri.'

'Don't know,' Jack replied. He parted his legs and farted, fast and angry, like a warning shot. 'I'm not eighteen yet.'

'Shit.' Geoff gasped in surprise. 'We'll have to get you a fake ID, won't we, Bri?'

'Maybe.' I slunk into my seat, wanting to fall asleep so the conversation couldn't continue.

Geoff tapped my shoulder. 'Are you tired, Bri?'

'Yes.' I folded my arms. 'Sorry, mate. Long day.'

'I'll let you get some rest, brother. You've earned it.'

'Thanks, mate.'

It fell quiet for a while – only the lulling rumble of the van and the tapping from Jack on his game.

'Are you okay, Jack?' Geoff asked, waking me from a half-sleep I had slipped into. 'Jack?...Jack?...Jack!? Wind the window down if you're ill, Jack! Jack!!'

My eyes opened as the panic in Geoff's voice rose. Jack was groaning, small and involuntary, as the console tumbled from his grip.

'I think we need to pull over, Geoff,' I said

The vehicle stopped, and Jack was heaving when I reached past him to push the passenger door partway into a spiny thicket. Geoff exited via the driver's side and ran around the front until the greenery blocked his progress.

'Sorry,' Jack muttered between his retching.

'Don't worry, Jack,' Geoff said, flashing his phone torch at the puddles between Jack's feet. 'It's just puke. Did he get any in the van, Bri?'

'I don't think so,' I replied, not straining to see.

'That's not too bad then.' Geoff switched off his light and made his way back inside the van. 'At least he hasn't ruined his new waistcoat.'

We pulled away once more.

'Geoff,' I said. 'I don't want to do this again.'

TWELVE

The sky above her was pink, Mum said as she lit a cigarette from her favourite spot at the balcony table. I was her defacto smoking buddy now Bill had given up, a thousand miles away on the lime sofa where I rearranged the sagging cushion.

'How is Bill?'

'He's alright. He's finding it a bit hot at the moment.'

'Right.' I shuffled into place, happier now. 'Sometimes I wish he had come into our lives earlier.'

Mum frowned. It was a heavy subject change. 'Why's that, love?'

'I don't know.' I rubbed at my face, unsure whether to continue. 'Maybe I'd be less up and down.'

'Don't say that.' She tutted. 'You'll make me feel guilty.'

I bit my thumbnail, breaking a shard away. 'I'm not trying to make you feel guilty. It's just the reality. How hard it was for a while.'

'Well, I had to work two jobs.'

I nodded. 'Exactly.'

Mum blew a trail of smoke from one side of her mouth. 'I feel terrible we didn't spend as much time together as I wanted.'

'It's fine, Mum. That wasn't the point of what I was saying.' I picked and peeled away the nail fragments from my thumb, unsure if I should continue. 'I used to have this dream where you married this moustached pilot. Is that weird? He would take me up in his little red plane and do loop-the-loops and spirals. So vivid.'

Mum laughed, her regular *pah!* 'That would have been nice.'

'Well, it *was* nice anyway –Bill was so normal with his gardening business. Just you know, a nice, unexciting guy.'

Mum laughed again until she coughed. 'I'll tell him that.'

'But, I liked that about him. He seemed dependable because of it.'

Mum smiled, red-cheeked. 'What's brought this on?'

'I was looking at those photos again last night.'

'Okay.'

'I found this picture of the three of us by the bar at one of our gigs in Camden. You know, when I lived around the corner in the shitty flatshare with Luke.'

'With all the water damage. God.'

'Yeah, just before everything. Bill's in his favourite salmon polo shirt, looking so awkward.'

Mum laughed with a *pah!* 'And his shorts with all the pockets, I bet.'

'That's right.' I smiled. 'Bill said he was proud of me after that gig. That's stuck with me for some reason.'

'Aww.' Mum's eyes dampened. 'He was proud of you.'

I nodded, thumbnail between my teeth again. 'Such a simple thing to say that he was proud. It knocked me out for hours.'

Mum stubbed out her cigarette in the yellow ashtray. 'You'll make me cry, Brian.'

'I'm sorry.' I exhaled an involuntary, wistful sigh. 'It's odd how some memories feel like yesterday and others as if they happened in a distant past life.'

'Hmm. Yes.'

There were voices in the hallway where Tam and Connie had gathered. 'We're heading out for drinks, I think.'

'Okay, Bab. Don't let me hold you up.'

'Love you, Mum.' Tam tapped at the frosted glass door, and I waved to let her know I was winding up. 'You should stop smoking.'

'Yes, I know, love. Tara-a-bit. Love you too, my boy.'

The first dose of summer arrived, with the weather turning cooler and wetter as the calendar ticked over. There were no further messages from Beatty in response to my reply or to book lessons for Noah, and I avoided her part of town after returning to my exercise routine.

I tried to write again when I wasn't working or running. But inspiration was in short supply, and my limbs had an odd tension humming through them – an odd heaviness. Planned sessions generally veered off quickly into an hour's worth of playing Beatles songs. Perhaps that helped to soothe a head bobbing just above the water.

There were fewer reasons to stay in Totnes, and yet such little mental energy to do anything other than bob along. It was as if I was waiting for my hand to be forced, and perhaps that was inevitable when Connie moved into the house. I convinced myself it wouldn't have been a big deal when the moment came – it would be the kick of reality I needed.

Events took a slight left-turn when Connie's parents decided to travel through Canada to celebrate her father's Sixtieth birthday, apparently something he had always wanted to do.

Connie and James promised to fulfil a booking for their parents' mobile pizza oven while they were away. There was a music and comedy festival not far, and we all chipped in to help – taking turns to man the converted horsebox in rotating pairs whilst the others went off to enjoy themselves. It was an odd bonding experience, especially for someone who had never made a pizza, but hanging out with the others was fun.

Tam invited James to move into the spare room temporarily on our return, and he accepted, insisting it was easier that way, but his sister knew he hated being on his own. Still, having him around re-balanced the house, and I was less of a third wheel. We started cooking for each other in the evenings, taking turns. We socialised together, too, with a sudden upswing in pub nights and parties. The strange droning in my body was leaving again.

Tam and Connie had all but stopped filming. But they decided to make a video where they talked openly about their relationship. Tam posted it to her social media accounts, her way of coming out to the people in her life who wouldn't have known, including her family and old London friends. She had preferred to keep her personal life to herself. That had been her instinct for a while. But she wanted the news to free her up. That's what she needed, she said.

Perhaps we were a gang when we returned from the pub after celebrating James's birthday. Tam and Connie balled up on the lime sofa, and I slumped inside one of the armchairs. James was almost passed out in the other. We drunk-argued because I wanted to pay a reasonable going rate for the room, and it was infantilizing that I wasn't. And when that simmered again, Connie suggested I play a song to cheer everyone up.

I retrieved my acoustic from upstairs, too intoxicated to be concerned about morphing into something terrible – a Guitar Guy.

I sat down again and fumbled for the zip on the nylon case. Tam noticed the creased Beatles songbook poking from the pocket and asked if I could play 'Let It Be'. It was a song Frank would play for her when she was small.

I began strumming, dropping out of the singing as Tam continued. She lifted the lengths of Connie's red hair as she sang with a lilting charm. The ground was firming, and the possibility of a tiny, unambitious life was beautiful – one where I would wrap myself in that house for the foreseeable.

Perhaps the ground was unstable again when Donna took me aside later that week to let me know my temporary contract wouldn't be renewed. Fryers were restructuring, and it was awful they had to let people go. She gave me a tight, familiar hug when I hoped she wouldn't, and I left the glass meeting room in a daze.

It was a surprise how much Donna's news knocked me off balance. Working at Fryers hadn't been the stuff of dreams, but I'd appreciated, at least, having a reason to get up in the mornings. And I had locked myself in the toilet cubicle and sobbed there – how much more upsetting it was to realise my paper-thin resilience.

That tension vibrating in my limbs was back, and I decided to disclose my news to Tam over dinner, the silliness of losing my temporary job. And she would laugh and give some good advice, and I would see the situation from her perspective, someone who had it together.

Tam shook off her umbrella underneath the Italian restaurant's awning, and I pulled the hood from my coat down. It was busy inside, but they found room for us in the far corner by the Specials chalkboard. It was just the two of us, with Connie away in Birmingham meeting with old uni friends and James confided to his room, struck down with a nasty cold.

Tam pushed her dark-cropped hair to one side. She wasn't sure how to grow it out, and when I came up short with suggestions, we talked about the house party we were throwing the following week. She said Connie had invited everyone they could think of, so the place could be rammed.

'Is there anyone from your work you wanted to ask along?'

'I don't think so.' Tam poured a glass of red wine each from the bottle when it arrived. She said it was a Pinot Noir when I enquired despite knowing nothing about wine. 'Actually, they've said they can't keep me around.'

'Oh, really?' Tam shrug-smiled like it wasn't a big deal, but her phone vibrated on the table and continued rumbling. We stared at the device until it stopped. 'That's weird. They're letting you go already?'

'Yeah.' I rubbed at my face, my arms heavy. 'I feel weird about it. Is that odd?'

The phone grumbled again. Tam answered this time, smiling and tutting as she spied the name on the screen. 'It's Con. She'll be wasted already.'

Our antipasti platter arrived when Tam ended the call with her excited girlfriend. The teenage waiter struggled with the Tetris required to accommodate our cheeses, olives and oily things, so we helped out by moving glasses and other adornments.

'How's Connie?' I asked when the minor ordeal was over.

'Yeah, sorry about that.' Tam gave a knowing chuckle. 'She let someone use our video for this Totnes Pride promo, and it's getting shared everywhere. Apparently, someone wants to interview us on a big podcast or something. It's ridiculous.'

'Wow.' I removed an olive stone after eagerly biting into it and almost losing a tooth. 'That's cool.'

'Yeah. I suppose so.' She pushed her hands together in prayer, her eyes smiling with excitement. 'I actually do have some other news I need to tell you.'

'Go on…'

Tam shuffled her head from side to side as she finished her mouthful. 'So, get this, I'm going to Berlin. After all. We both are.'

The news hit like a sharp stone flicking a windscreen. 'You and Connie?'

'Yes! Obviously.' She rubbed the chain over her shirt collar with a thumb. 'I wanted to let you know before next week. Because we're good mates now, aren't we?'

'Yeah.' Suddenly, it was a struggle to swallow a tiny mozzarella ball as my mouth rapidly dried. 'Like full-time?'

'Yeah.' Tam's eyes popped as if she were sensing the gravity of her plans. 'We're making an announcement at the party before we go.'

'Oh, right.' I forced a smile after lubricating my mouth with more wine. 'So, what's sparked this?'

Tam dabbed a napkin on her lips. 'Basically, I was offered a full-time gig with this graphics company I've been doing some work for. I was going to say no, instinctively. But then I discussed it with Con, and we got excited about it.'

'Cool.' I nodded. 'Is it soon? Probably not.'

'Actually, it's *really* soon. I've got to be over there in a few weeks and need to find somewhere to live.'

'Fuck....' I bit into my thumb knuckle and held my teeth there. 'Wow.'

'Probate should be done by the end of the week, and Paul said I can put the house on the market then.' Tam topped up her glass after I declined the offer with a raised palm. 'I want to make a clean break, you know? I don't want to be a fucking landlord or anything.'

'No.' The food was turning, congealing – my appetite collapsing. 'Shit.'

'Yes.' Tam smiled again but was watchful now – perhaps alerted by my poorly masked reaction to her news. 'I'm guessing you'll head back to London. Now you've had your break.'

'Yeah.' I rubbed my cheeks in circles, my hands numbing. 'I should do. I'll see what work is about, I guess.' My voice wobbled, an utter betrayal.

Tam tilted her head, perhaps sensing my worry though it was the last thing I wanted. 'You can stay until you get something lined up, or whatever your plans are. It takes ages to sell a house, doesn't it?'

'No idea. Never done it.' I chuckled nonchalantly and poked at a sundried tomato with a cocktail stick. 'God. It's so warm in here, isn't it?'

Our eyes met. The attentive concern on Tam's face was unbearable. 'Are you okay?'

'Yes.' I frowned like she was being ridiculous. Of course, I was okay as I pushed a finger into my ear to dull the sudden heat spanning from there. 'My ear keeps heating up for some reason.'

'Maybe you're getting this cold James has got.'

'Yeah. Is that a symptom?' My arms prickled as I gripped the sides of our table. Perhaps I was having a meltdown. 'Maybe, that's it.'

'Do you want to get some fresh air?' The rain was horizontal outside, tapping at the window across the room. 'Although it's raining again.'

'Would you mind?' I fumbled around in my pocket for my wallet. 'I probably need to get back, actually.'

'It's okay, don't worry,' Tam insisted, dabbing her pink lips with a napkin. 'I'll sort this. You've not touched much.'

'I just want to pay something,' I replied firmly. It was important to me now.

Tam waved her napkin. 'I'll sort it, mate. You get on.'

'I'm not a fucking charity case, Tam!'

I chuckled in a failed attempt to take the edge off my sudden eruption and placed a few low-value notes on the table, whatever I had in my wallet. I shuffled away from my chair off-balance. The exit seemed miles away as I narrowly avoided a collision with the serving teenager and a low-hanging copper light.

The rain slowed to a soft drizzle after escaping onto the high street. But I could breathe with a restorative moisture twinkling on my face. My head bowed towards the soggy reflections in the narrow pavements as I walked up the slope, inhaling and exhaling in rhythm. And we weren't a gang at all. We were all just passing by the entire time.

After pulling on a dry set of clothes at home, I propped myself on the bed with a half-baked strategy to reach out to old friends via dormant social media accounts. I would leave innocuous messages under their most recent posts, nothing too pathetic and grasping – just a reminder I was still in the world.

After a successful password guess, it was jarring for the app to confront me with an anniversary photo of a post-gig Dorothea group hug and from Frank's account of all places. He had taken the picture inside a tiny dressing room at the end of our first support tour. Luke has his arm around my shoulder, tired and triumphant. And there were no signs of the trouble beneath our weary joy – no indication we would drift so far apart.

God, it was so sad not to be doing the one thing I had only ever wanted to do – such a ridiculous compromise to settle for anything else.

My plan had been blown off-course as I scrolled and scrolled, and who were these ghosts? Anyone remotely sensible had long given up on oversharing intimate details of their lives. Those left appeared to have time on their hands, weary broad smiles with babies – trapped in an infinite loop. 'My World' in every caption. I love my family. I am happy. Please tell me I am happy. Please.

I was about to switch my phone off, perhaps throw it out of the window, when I stumbled across a picture of Esther where she had been tagged into a work night out at a fancy restaurant. Perhaps it was a forced-fun pic taken at the end of a long table, where she was nearest. But she was holding a glass on a folded arm and smiling so warmly and contended – it was like looking at home again.

There was a comment underneath from Esther's friend, Liz. 'You look lovely here, Es. Oh, and congrats to you and Nate. So amazing! xx'

Congrats to you and Nate…

I clicked on Esther's profile and stumbled upon a schmaltzy beachside photo posted a few weeks earlier. It was the sort of sentimental announcement she would have once made fun of, one where she was gazing up at Nate and his bushy eyebrows – out-of-focus white cliffs looming behind. There was a caption underneath; 'Nate proposed in Greece, and I thought it would be rude not to say yes!'

The hits kept coming, pummelling away the air left in me.

Memories rained in from nowhere. They were mundane, mostly, like when we stayed up late to watch one more episode of The Sopranos and how I poked Esther's chin dimple to make her laugh when she didn't want to. And the adorable way she said the word *chuffed*, the expectation once it had escaped from her lips again. And how much she loved being roasted for it and everything else and doing the same to me. And the fact I could always win her around. I could always win her around.

After locating his LinkedIn account, I trialled Nate's New Zealand accent out loud and in the darkness of my room – phrases like, 'How's it going, Esther?' and 'I like medical research', seeing as that was what he did for a living. I wanted to imagine what he sounded like to her – soothing, I decided.

There was a tap at the door, a rattle of finger taps.

'Come in,' I said.

Tam gave me a cautious smile once the thick carpet gave way. 'Were you just talking to yourself?'

'Possibly.'

She tossed my coat onto the foot of the bed and popped a packet of painkillers on the desk. 'I found those in the cupboard if you need them.'

'Thanks.' I rubbed at my face. 'I'm sorry for earlier.' I searched for an excuse, but nothing came.

'It's okay.' Tam was in a forgiving mood. She perched herself on the side of the mattress and crossed her legs like a concerned aunt. 'I don't remember this bed. Was it always here?'

'No. I bought it.'

'Oh, okay.' She glanced at the phone parked on my leg, where Esther's engagement picture was still expanded. 'Are you social media stalking?'

I switched the screen off. 'I don't know.'

'Because I'm into it,' Tam laughed. 'Who was that? You don't have to tell me.'

'Esther. My ex.'

'Oh. Fuck.'

I nodded. 'Yes.'

'Sorry. I'm being so nosy.'

'You're fine.'

'Aw, Brian and Esther. That's a cute pair of old people's names.'

I laughed. 'Yeah. We used to joke about that.'

'Budge up.' Tam shuffled further onto the bed, and we sat side by side. 'Is this why you were upset earlier?'

I hesitated, but it was an easy out to explain my behaviour. 'Probably.'

'She's pretty! I would be sad.' Tam wagged her finger. 'But this is why you shouldn't keep exes on social media, mate.'

Tam said she used to follow updates from an ex-boyfriend obsessively. She would get upset each time he found someone new like he always did, even though she didn't want them to get back together. It was absurd because she liked girls – but he was her first love, and it would still tie her in knots if she saw him with someone else. It was why I should delete Esther immediately.

'I just feel shitty about how it ended,' I said.

'How did it end?' Tam asked. 'Did you cheat on her?'

'No. I tried to kill myself.'

'Oh.' Tam let out a tiny gasping sigh. 'Fucking hell, Brian.'

'Well. I swallowed some tablets and called an ambulance. And then I just left without saying anything.'

'Fuck.' Tam's eyes widened as if she had connected a few dots. 'Well, I'm sorry, mate.'

'It's not your fault.' I drummed on my leg. 'Maybe I should congratulate her or something. Perhaps it would be a tiny way of apologising.'

Tam held a finger to her chin. 'Well, if you feel like you owe her an apology, give the woman a proper apology.' Perhaps it was obvious. 'Have you tried?'

'Not successfully, I don't think.'

'I mean, I wouldn't just message her out of the blue or write anything on social media,' she said. 'That's low effort.'

'Shall I write a letter?'

'Ugh.' Tam shuddered and chuckled to herself at the thought of it. 'God! I'd get so itchy if I received a handwritten letter from an ex.'

'What should I do, then?'

'Just be prepared to lay it out and be willing to cut your losses. Or you'll go mad.'

'Okay. By Morse code, then? Flags?'

'I don't know!' Tam chuckled and pushed at my shoulder. 'Maybe just message her and ask if she would consider a chat. And if she doesn't, then move on.' She clicked her fingers, remembering she had once read a blog that set out the guidelines for a good apology. Her phone was charging upstairs, but she would try to find it for me. 'One of the rules was to not ask for forgiveness because it's not yours to give. That's quite powerful, isn't it?'

I nodded. Perhaps it was. 'Yes.'

'But don't let it fester. You've done what you can at that point.'

'Right.'

'Otherwise, you'll be staring at these photos forever.'

I told Tam she was right because she was, most likely. She tapped me on the leg and scooted off the bed. There was a lot of sorting and planning to do.

I breathed as the door closed and typed a message to Esther, assuming it would be the last thing she wanted to see.

Hey. Would it be possible to call?

My phone buzzed minutes later, a link to the blog post from Tam. I had half-expected to read some glossy catch-all advice, but the piece was well-written and reasoned. I made notes on my phone in case Esther returned my call. I wanted to get it right. I needed to fix that hole. Perhaps I just had to keep fixing holes, and everything would be okay.

THIRTEEN

A churning wind whistled at the patio doors as I sat, phone in hand, at the kitchen table in front of a discarded bowl of cereal. Mum's eyes bulged in surprise when I finally accepted her video call. 'Oh, hi, love,' she said, placing her red coffee mug on the patio table. 'I didn't think you would answer.'

'Hi, Mum.'

'Happy birthday.' She wiped at the corners of her mouth. 'Did you get your gifts, Bab? Bill got you the DNA kit.'

'Yes. Thanks.'

'There's a man who makes straps at the market in the town, any name you like, and I just thought you'd like one.'

'Okay.'

Her brow furrowed. 'Well, do you like it?'

'As a grown man, that's probably an odd thing to have – a guitar strap with *Brian* written on it. My actual name.'

Mum tutted, and her cheerful smile disappeared. 'Oh, well.'

'Sorry, Mum. I'm not eight years old.'

Mum ushered Bill to join the call and waved at him frantically from wherever he was inside. 'He's hurt his back again.'

'Oh, dear.'

Bill shuffled into view, all red-faced like he had been in the sun too long. He winced as he lowered himself beside Mum like it was something they had rehearsed. 'Happy birthday, Brian.'

'He got his DNA kit,' Mum said, touching Bill's back.

'Yep,' I said. 'Thanks, Bill. It came on Tuesday.'

Bill said he was pleased. 'One of our friends said it shows where your DNA comes from on a map. And your relatives, too, if you wanted to tap into your Irish roots.'

I smiled. 'Cool. Thanks, Bill.'

'Bill's hurt his back,' said Mum.

'Oh, dear. Sorry to hear that, Bill.'

She cupped her mouth, having recalled something. 'It's twenty years, Brian. I meant to mention it before. Would you put some flowers down for me?'

'For Dad?'

Bill waved a sign-off with his head down – this was none of his concern. He shuffled out of his seat, breathing in pain as he slipped out of view.

'Is that okay?' Mum asked gently.

An unsensible rage boiled as I massaged my forehead with both hands. 'This is a lovely birthday chat, Mum.'

'Well, I was only asking because it was fresh in my mind.'

'Okay, but I don't want to think about Dad dying today. It's my birthday.'

'I see.' Mum nodded. 'It's just a shame the dates are so close together.'

'I know!' I slapped the table, and my spoon jumped inside the bowl. 'I know...'

Mum smiled, all wounded. 'Okay, I won't say anything else about it.' It was awful – such a wash of shame to upset her. 'You seem a bit down, love. Are you not celebrating later?'

'Not really.'

'Okay....' Mum's brow furrowed. 'Let me get you that plane ticket, love. Come and stay here for a bit.'

'No. I need to sort things out....' I checked the time on my phone. I was running late for work. 'Listen, I need to head off. I'm sorry for being miserable and ungrateful. It's turning thirty, I think. It's a big number.'

'It is a big milestone, Bab.'

'Yeah...But thank you for the presents. I am really sorry, Mum.'

'Don't be sorry. Tara-a-bit, then.'

'Bye, Mum. I'm sorry.'

Esther hadn't called in the days after my message. I had rehearsed what I wanted to say to her. But now it was my birthday, one week later, and I was far less sure we would speak again. And I didn't know what to do with that fact – now I had convinced myself it was the first hurdle to leap over.

A thinly bearded estate agent had been over one evening to measure up and take pictures, and the listing was up online barely a day later. The estate agents described the house as 'an exciting development opportunity with an open, modernised space downstairs' and my room as having 'an endearing view over surrounding trees and the street below'.

With the move to Berlin absorbing all of Tam and Connie's free time, I spent more of mine with James. The change seemed to unbalance him, too, and we never said that directly but quietly admitted feelings of being directionless instead. And then we wallowed like baby men when we drank together and smoked his dwindling stash of weed. We talked shit under those influences, so much of it, projecting and afraid to be alone. And Esther didn't get in touch during an uptick of ghost vibrations in my pocket. And I couldn't move on until she contacted me, as the water sloshed around my neck.

I left work late on the day of the leaving party, offering to help with a few last-minute invoicing enquiries first. I dragged my feet as I set off for home, not wanting to leave the small wire-fenced industrial estate on the edge of town. Instead, I took a windy detour onto the winding path beside the river and the walled paths leading to Totnes High Street. I shuffled past the antique shops and then onto the street, which bent towards our tall blue house.

A boom of raucous laughter bellowed as I opened the front door. A few of Connie's friends arrived early in the afternoon, and celebrations were underway.

'Brian's here!' Tam called from somewhere in the kitchen.

I paused over the first step of the staircase, my hand gripping the thin wooden bannister with no opportunity to slink away.

When I pushed the frosted-glass door open, there was already a sizeable group in the house – perhaps twelve fashion-forward unfamiliars strutting around the kitchen like they owned the place. Connie rose from a chair at the dining table peppered with empty bottles and glasses. 'Brian!' she yelled in excitement.

'Hi.'

I shuffled into the room as Connie hurried over, gripping a half-filled wine glass. She hugged me with her outstretched spare arm. 'You look so official in your office clothes. Like a high-powered business guy.'

'Right.'

Everyone stopped and looked our way as we stood under the beam between spaces with Connie's arm draped over my shoulders – presenting me to the group. I shrugged, having been pulled into her show with nothing to say for myself.

'Are you smashed already, Con?' laughed Tam.

Connie laughed. 'I think I am now I've stood up!' She drifted back to the dining table and perched on her girlfriend's knees. 'Oh Brian, do you need your room tonight?'

'Um. Yes,' I replied.

Tam tutted and soft-glared at her girlfriend. 'Of course, he does.'

'I was just checking!' Connie said. 'I didn't know if you were off on another escapade.'

'No, I need my room.' I chuckled in a failed attempt to soften my spiky tone. 'If that's okay.'

'Don't listen to Connie,' Tam insisted. 'Are you going to celebrate with us tonight?'

'Yep.' I looked only at her and squeezed a faint smile. 'I need to sort myself out first.'

'We're going to drag you back out of your shell later, Brian!' Connie boomed in her sing talking. 'We have powers of persuasion.'

'Cool.'

I smiled and slipped out of the room, fearing I had sucked all of the joy out of it. I trudged up the stairs and decided to reset with a shower. It sputtered and spat like it always did, and my head rested against the tiled wall as the residual water dripped into the tray long after I gave up on it.

There was a tap at the bedroom door, a wrap of fingertips a short while after I had returned to my room, dressed, and lay face down on the bed. I rolled over and shuffled up against the headboard.

'Come in.'

Tam pushed her way inside after struggling with the carpet. 'Hey, are you okay?'

'Yeah.' I nodded a lot. 'Are you alright?'

'I'm good.' She leaned against the door. 'Oh! Have you heard from your ex-girlfriend?'

'Not yet.'

'Ah.' Tam smiled thinly and played with the bangles on her wrist. 'You can camp out here if you're not feeling it. Might be loud, though.'

'No, it's cool.' I tapped at my legs. It was difficult to be a malcontent when I didn't want to be one, not for Tam. 'I might be down at some point.'

'Amazing.' She smiled again, warmer this time. 'I think it will be fun. James will be looking for you. You're best buddies these days. It's nice.'

'Yeah.' I scratched at my unshaven face. 'I'll see how I feel.'

I waited, perhaps for ten minutes, debating what to do before I slunk downstairs and found James at the leather armchairs in a thick-collard burnt orange shirt. It was a bold choice for a man with his complexion. We stayed together at the back of the room as the house filled with guests, and we drank dark rum and talked enough nonsense for a space to clear around us.

James was in a gloomy mood, having seen pictures of Elena on Instagram where she was out and enjoying herself. He wasn't sure he could handle it.

'You shouldn't follow your exes on social media,' I told him. 'It'll eat you up.'

'Yeah, maybe.' James poured rum into our glasses, more than a sensible amount. 'It's just that Lena knows I'd see her sitting on a dude's lap. You wonder if it's on purpose.'

'She's just having fun. Not everything is about you. You're not together.'

'Maybe. But, she should take more care…' James shook his head, perhaps realising how he sounded. He gulped down his drink and winced at its strength. 'I'm stuck in the Totnes bubble – everyone is everywhere else. I need to wake up.'

'Yeah.' I downed my drink, too, and held a fist at my mouth after. 'You should do that.'

Suddenly, Beatty drifted inside the frosted glass door like some dream. She was wearing metal-framed glasses, and we made eye contact, a sharp pang in my chest before she was hurried further into the room by her sister Charlotte. Tito and other familiar faces from the garden gang followed behind.

James clicked his fingers. 'Mate?'

'Yeah?'

'I was asking when you're heading back to London.'

'Right.' Beatty and her group funnelled through the patio doors towards the garden. I loaded up a pair of shots. 'Not sure.'

James waved open-palmed. 'What are you gonna do then, man?'

'Uh.…' We emptied our glasses, and I coughed as my throat charred. I was lit up and charged with a surge of assertiveness. Perhaps the answer involved Beatty. Of course, it did. 'Shall we go outside? It's a bit warm in here.'

I swayed on the third step from my seat, everything hitting, yet determined to capitalise on my mood change. And there were so many people in the house, too many, as I bobbed and weaved to reach the kitchen with James lingering behind.

The wind from earlier had mellowed to a light breeze as we walked through the open patio doors and into the concrete garden, where a spicy whiff of weed hung in the air.

Beatty was sitting in one of the rattan armchairs where slow-blinking fairy lights crisscrossed above. She paused from a cheerful conversation with the garden gang and stared at me with glassy-eyed amusement. 'Hey!' she called enthusiastically.

'Hey. How's it going?' I asked as if it was a surprise to see her there.

'Good. I was just about to get us some drinks.' Beatty held her hands out, and I took that cue to pull her upright. She wobbled slightly and flattened her skirt once she was more surefooted. 'You can give me a hand.'

'Sure.'

I followed Beatty back through the patio doors, and we slunk into the corner of the kitchen. We were out of sight once a group of unfamiliar bodies gathered by the dining table to pick at the food there.

Beatty cupped her hand at my ear as house music played from the speaker nearby. 'I think I'm a bit stoned.'

'Oh, yeah?'

'Yes.' She rested her cheek on my shoulder. 'I thought I was smoking a cigarette. We've been drinking since this afternoon, so I wasn't paying attention.'

I laughed. 'Right. Nice surprise.'

'No!' she said. 'I've got a sensitivity to weed. I'll probably pass out soon.'

'Oh, dear. Been anywhere nice?'

'Nowhere exciting. My in-laws have taken Noah to their place in Brittany, and I've been at Charlotte's.'

'Ah, nice.'

'Yes!' She snickered, frenetic and giggly, lifting her face inches from mine. 'What's wrong with me, then? Am I flat-chested?'

I frowned, having not expected the question. 'What do you mean?'

'Well, I am. Is that why you don't want me? That's a bit pathetic, Brian. Very shallow of you.' She pulled her glasses from her face and wiped them on the nap of her skirt. 'I've lost my contact lenses. I'm such a mess.'

'I do want you.'

'Oh!' Beatty laughed like there had been a hilarious misunderstanding between us. She returned her specs and looked at me with a wild intensity. 'You're handsome, have I told you? You're like a male deer.'

'A male deer?' I laughed. 'A stag?'

'No! Not a stag!' Beatty fell into a fit of silent chuckling. She vibrated onto my shoulder, forcing my head against the kitchen cupboard. 'I don't know what I'm saying. I think you're handsome, okay? Deer-like handsomeness.'

'Okay, thanks.' I cupped my hand to her ear, drunk and ready to overpay her compliment. 'I genuinely think you're one of the prettiest girls I've ever met.'

Beatty narrowed her eyes, suspicious and playful. 'I'm not pretty, Brian. And I'm not a girl, either. Don't be ridiculous.'

'Okay. But you are pretty. And I love listening to your voice.' I was ridiculous, sucked into the same chaotic mood. 'You're a lovely *woman*, and I wish I could fall asleep listening to it every night.'

We flinched in unison as a bang of static blasted through the speakers, an aux lead pulled from somewhere in the room. The surprise made us laugh as Connie rushed to the patio doors to call people inside in preparation for the much-promised announcement.

We leaned against the worktops as guests crowded into the living room and kitchen. Some were already filming on their phones as Tam and Connie stood arm-in-arm by the lime sofa at the back of the room. It was impossible to focus on anything other than my wanting to cocoon away with Beatty. Perhaps we were sozzled and lonely and recognised that in the other. Or perhaps we were in love, and the truth serum of alcohol allowed us to admit that now. Perhaps that made more sense. Love was the balm to smooth over the cracks in each of us.

'So, as you might know, we've got something to tell you all,' Connie announced, as party guests clapped and whooped. 'It's a happy announcement, but also a sad one, actually.' She looked at Tam, and they gripped hands. 'So, my wonderful girlfriend here has had an amazing job offer in Berlin.'

A hand rubbed my trouser pocket and moved over the top of my thigh and further across. 'Do you want to walk me home in a minute?' Beatty asked, whispering into my ear.

'Sure.'

Connie continued. 'So, this is a sort of goodbye party. We're heading off to live there for a while.' She smiled at Tam like nobody else was in the room. 'We're going to miss all of you so much. Like crazy.'

'Don't make me cry,' Tam said as Connie paused and held a hand over her eyes.

'I won't!' Connie laughed, bleary-eyed. 'Anyway, I wanted this to be short and sweet, or I will just blubber away. So, please have fun and make sure you come and say goodbye before you leave.'

There was a blast of applause with cheers and whistles thrown in. Guests rushed to surround and congratulate the couple. It was all too much, and I needed to leave.

A guttural howl rang out from the garden as we made our move. Charlotte was consoling James on the garden sofas there, his redhead bobbing as she stroked his hair, and Tito stood by with a vacant smirk. Everything was surreal.

'Let's go,' Beatty whispered, her chin resting on my shoulder.

Seizing our chance, we slipped past the crowd in the living room and sped-walked to Beatty's place, stumbling over the uneven pavements and past closed shops in a horny panic to get there. She asked what I would do to her as we crossed the bridge together and headed towards the pink buildings. I was terrible at sex talk in most circumstances, but the manic energy between us made it easy to play along.

We kissed in the hallway after slipping inside Beatty's house. Our hands locked as we sped past Noah's room and the double doors, which never opened. We moved into the dark characterless room at the end of the landing, my newfound erotic confidence evaporating again. Perhaps the moment was too big.

Beatty leaned onto the bouncy bed. Her arms splayed – all the weight onto her knees. 'Let's do it like this,' she said, reaching underneath her skirt.

'Sounds good.'

After fumbling around inside the side table drawer for condoms, it was suddenly all happening. Perhaps it was a bad idea as we struggled to find a natural rhythm.

'Hold up a second,' I said when Beatty's skirt slipped between us. 'I'll re-arrange this.'

'Shush.'

'Okay.' I re-positioned the troublesome garment over Beatty's lower back for the third time. Pushing it as far as it would go. 'Should we whip this thing off?'

'Don't worry about it!'

'Sure thing.' Beatty grabbed my spare hand, with the other prodding the fabric. 'I'll just keep at this pace, I think. Unless you fancy a change-up on the position.'

'*Shush.*'

'Yeah, of course.'

'*Shush.*'

'Sorry.'

'Just stop talking. Please.'

My eyes clamped shut as our bodies parted and collided back together again in perfect harmony. I drifted to a joyful place – a glow of happy endings trickling into my nervous system. Perhaps Beatty would ask me to move in when it was over. We would take things slowly, allowing the space we needed for our mutual love to flourish. Perhaps we would sell up and get a place together, something imperfectly perfect and away from the prying eyes of Mike's parents. I'd become a father to Noah there, the musical dad he needed – and we would sing together after every meal, the three of us plus Rupert, the cat.

Beatty squeezed my hand. 'I want to feel you go now.'

Her voice took me home as my back crashed against the mattress after – the crackled loveliness of it.

'God.' Beatty sighed. Her face buried into the white duvet as she spread her arms. 'I needed that.'

'No worries. Happy to deliver.'

'Shush,' she croaked. 'Why do you keep talking like that?'

'I don't know.' I pinched my thigh, annoyed with myself. 'I don't know what I'm saying.'

There was an ornate metal box atop the bedside table. I plucked a tissue protruding from it and scrunched my rubber inside before tossing the ball into a tiny metal waste bin across the room. Perhaps we would get down to brass tacks now, nothing too detailed, just a rough declaration of our love.

'God.' Beatty moaned, unhappy, as she shuffled over the side of the bed and planted her feet on the floor. 'Shit. Oh, Shit.'

'What's up?'

'Fuck.' Her head bowed, and she pushed her elbows into her knees, forcing her legs apart. 'Everything is spinning.'

I cupped her shoulder. 'Are you okay?'

Beatty flicked my hand away and whimpered, slow and wretched. She stood up, rubbed at her face and then ambled towards the door, where the landing light was peeping inside. Perhaps everything was going wrong again, and we weren't about to have our post-sex debrief after all – the one to lift the fog.

A bathroom door clunked shut out of sight, and enough time passed to dress quietly, rehearse what I wanted to say, and then panic when Beatty didn't return. And perhaps the fact she had been unwell would add to the charm of it. It was a sloppy love story now, something to laugh about when we told it.

'Are you okay?' I asked, tapping the closed bathroom door with a knuckle.

'Yes.' Beatty's voice echoed as the toilet flushed. 'Don't come in.'

'Okay.' I paused, unsure what to say or do. 'As long as you're okay.'

'I'm not okay.'

I slunk onto my knees so we could be at the same level. 'Right. That's not good.'

'I can't function.' Beatty spat into the toilet. I'm not a functioning person at the moment.'

My forehead pushed into the door. 'You're just wasted. We both are.'

'Well, I shouldn't be wasted.' She was defeated now. 'I need to get it together.'

'We will,' I insisted and decided to take my chance. 'I want to take care of you. And Noah.'

'Oh, for fuck's sake! Stop it.'

I hesitated. 'What's up? I want to look after you.'

'I don't want to be looked after! Jesus fucking Christ, Brian.'

'Okay…what do you want, then?'

'Well, I don't want this conversation for a start.' Beatty retched again, another small puke. 'Look, I feel really fucking embarrassed. Do you think you could leave?'

FOURTEEN

I returned from the shower with a towel around my waist. My phone illuminated the room as it vibrated on the bed. Mum was calling again, and I flicked at the screen with a damp thumb to answer. I set the conversation to speaker and pulled a shirt on.

'Hi, Mum.'

'Hello,' she muttered, fretful. 'You've not been replying to my messages.'

'Sorry. I've just been busy.'

'Did you want to video chat?'

'No, I can't, really.' I dried my feet on the edge of the bed and tugged a pair of socks on. 'The Wi-Fi signal is no good up here.'

'Okay….'

'And we're dropping Tam and Connie at the airport soon. I'm already running late.'

She sniffed. 'Have you decided what you want to do, love?'

'Not yet.' I stood up and pulled on a T-shirt and the rest of my clothes. 'But I'll have time to plan something out after today.'

Mum sighed loud enough to make the speaker crackle. 'I don't like the thought of you on your own. I'm worried you'll do something silly.'

'Why's that?'

'Because you don't sound right, Bab.'

'I'm fine.'

'Now, don't take this the wrong way, but I'm worried you'll get all druggy again.'

'Christ!' I pulled the handset to my ear. 'Mum, I'm thirty years old now. Please, can you just let me sort something out? You don't need to be on my case.'

'Well, I have to be on your case. It goes wrong when I'm not.'

'This is my point! I just need space to sort things.' A tap of fingertips rattled at the door, and an inquiring call came from behind it. The others were ready. 'I've got to go. I'll call you soon. I promise.'

We travelled back from Bristol in the old brown Volvo estate James had borrowed from his dad, just the pair of us now. There had been a joyous send-off inside the terminal a couple of hours previous, propelled by Connie's endless enthusiasm. But none of that excitement returned with us, only the road ahead. And I would miss Tam, especially. Our time was relatively short, but we understood each other.

With no stereo to fill the nouse, the lumbering rattle of the old car became the soundtrack home as slow traffic hindered our return to Totnes. Workers and machines were laying a new surface behind the coned barrier in the closed outside lane of the motorway. It was easier to reflect than contemplate an immediate or any future. It was so easy. I didn't need to think about anything else.

'Have you always worn glasses?' James asked. They were the first words spoken since we had left the airport car park.

'No.'

'You look a bit like Harry Potter.'

'Okay.'

James's head turned to study more closely. 'You don't, really.'

'Right.'

'I'm heading back to mum and dad's tonight,' he said, nervously sucking his lips. He had accepted terms with Fryers and was heading to Bath with his redundancy money to flatshare with an old friend. 'I've got a lot to sort out.'

'Fair enough.'

Perhaps I was too worn down to be angry with James for him to leave, too. And obviously, I was aware of how childish that impulse was. But the development had scuppered a hastily drawn-up plan to hire a van and drive to Berlin with Tam and Connie's things. It would have been a fun road trip. Perhaps we would have stayed a few nights and fallen in love with the city. Perhaps we would have remained there for a while or forever.

James grumbled as we slowed to another stop. 'Cannot fucking wait to get this leaving thing out of the way.'

I nodded. 'The whole office will be there, I heard.'

'Yeah. It'll get messy, the way some are talking.' He sighed and rested his forehead on the steering wheel.

'You alright, mate?' I asked. 'Can't be that bad, surely.'

He shook his head. 'I'm sad about Connie, man.'

'Right.'

He laughed, short and sharp. 'I bet it seems weird for a guy to be close to his sister.'

'I thought that was pretty common in Devon.'

James snorted. 'Fuck's sake! You know what I mean. We've just always been great mates. I think some people find it weird. I've always been very protective of her.'

'Right.' I hummed in agreement, although I had seen their relationship the other way around – that Connie had a maternal instinct towards her older brother. 'I think it's nice, man.'

We moved again, and James re-arranged the continually slumping rear-view mirror. 'We've always got on well. She's just fun, isn't she? Tam, too, once you get to know her.'

'Yeah. It's a shame.'

'Not for them, I bet.' James rubbed his face with one hand, either tired or trying to comfort himself – perhaps both.

'Imagine hanging out with us in Totnes to living in one of the most exciting cities in the world.'

'Yeah.' I scratched at my week-old facial hair. 'Yeah.'

'Probably millions of lesbians there, man. It's what it's known for.'

'Okay.'

James nudged my arm. 'All-night sex parties.'

I slunk into my seat, in no mood for the subject pivot. 'Fucking hell!'

James looked over. 'What?'

'That's your sister, for a start.'

'I'm not getting off on it!' James shook his head like he couldn't believe what I had insinuated and returned his gaze to the road. 'That's the vibe in Berlin. Google it.'

'Jesus, shut up.' I held my hands over my eyes. 'You are fifteen years old sometimes.'

'Cheers, mate.'

Perhaps it was rough to have been grumpy and then allowed the rest of the journey to play out in silence. But perhaps it made sense to create some distance between us, too – to prepare.

It was my last week at Fryers, and I spent each evening after work on the green sofa, alone – sometimes choosing to sleep there. And the Estate Agents performed house tours whilst I was there. Sometimes I would smile at the prospective buyers as they shuffled around, but generally, it was easier to pretend I was invisible.

I agonised over whether to send a follow-up message to Esther, perhaps to prompt her in case my note slipped past by mistake. And somehow, I was stuck there again, learning I couldn't. It didn't matter how delicate my new enquiry might be as I tried to tiptoe that spider silk. At best, I was a nuisance now. At so much worse, I held some awful power over her – a menace, a blight capable of ruining her day with the gentlest reminder of my existence.

After sinking half a bottle of wine, the last remaining alcoholic item in the house, I headed to the leaving-do at the Waterfront restaurant that Friday evening, reversing a plan to no-show. It was too dangerous to be inebriated and alone, and a message from James arrived to slap me out of that slump.

Hey man it would be great to see you tonight if you could make it.

I was late when I arrived, but the group from Fryers weren't difficult to spot at a table alongside a windowed wall. A shaven-headed ball of muscle named Liam challenged me to an arm wrestle as I was slow-clapped for arriving late. I politely declined the offer as he flexed the triceps bulging from underneath a tight white shirt.

James waved me over to a vacant spot at the far end of the table. It was quieter there, free from the rowdiness.

'Here he is,' James said, slightly sheepish in his yellow shirt. We hadn't spoken in days. 'I saved you a spot.'

'Thanks.'

James pushed a beer across the table as I sat on the furthest available chair opposite the turquoise tufted banquette. There was wine on the table too, he said and introduced me to Natalie from the sales team, next to me. She gave a cautious nod, as did her turtle-necked husband, Phil, one along. I met Claire next, from the Client Management team. Her face was impeccably round, like a dish, reminding me of someone I couldn't place. She smiled with oversized canines from her spot next to James.

Claire was someone James had mentioned often, although I had never spoken to her until now. He had often crowbarred her into discussions during our lunch breaks and any other chance he got.

'Claire is keeping a low profile,' James said as Natalie and Phil left to smoke outside.

'I am,' Claire agreed, in her tiny west country voice. She had tried to give herself a 'beachy wave', but her curling iron had broken. Now her pale blonde hair was neither straight nor curled. She leaned in. 'Is Liam staring?'

The arm wrestling had continued at the raucous end of the table, where a drinking element appeared to have been incorporated. But there was no sign that Liam was gazing intently in our direction, James assured. 'I'm more worried he'll get me with a dirty pint later,' he said.

Claire screwed her face. 'What's a dirty pint?'

'Just some dumb send-off tradition,' James explained with an eye roll. 'What they made Pete drink when he retired. All the dregs from other drinks.'

'God, I remember that. He was so ill.' Claire reapplied her lipstick in a pocket mirror. Some of the group were heading out to Torquay later, she said.

James chuckled like that was a terrible idea. 'Fuck that!'

Our pre-ordered pizzas arrived, and we dug into the food and complimentary wine. Perhaps I had loosened up when Donna stood at the far end of the table with her trademark specs on with blue lenses for a light-sensitivity condition. She tapped a fork on a wine glass and then muddled through a speech written on her phone where she referred to me as her 'little tech man' several times. She then presented me with a gift from the team, a GoPro, for the bike I had inherited from James.

'I need to give you some money for your bike before you head off, James,' I said, shuffling into my seat again.

James shook his head. 'Nah, man, I don't need it.'

'Well, I'm going to.'

Claire leaned across the table after returning from the bar with vodka shots. She fastened the button on my shirt, which had popped open. And when Natalie and Phil declined theirs, we crossed arms as we sunk the spare drinks, with James watching closely.

There was an urge to be chaotic and reckless, to flirt with Claire and say things I didn't believe. 'Did you hear Holly had a whole week off when her cat died?' I looked around at the group. 'I don't think any man would get that time off.'

'Who's Holly?' asked James.

'Just someone on my old team.' I flashed a boyish smirk at Claire and then at Natalie, who had tuned in. 'It's weird that only women are allowed time off work for stuff like that.'

Claire laughed and wagged a finger. 'Oh, my God.'

'He's got a point!' Phil said. He leaned in like he had been waiting all evening to hear some casual sexism. 'Some of the women at my work get away with murder.'

Natalie tutted at her husband. 'For God's sake, Phil.'

I casually poured more wine into Claire's glass, our eyes locking. 'You would be the first to laugh at any guy who did what Holly did. Pure double standards.'

She opened her mouth in playful outrage. 'No, I wouldn't! You're an idiot.'

'I'm just being silly,' I assured her, already smiling at what I was about to say next. 'You are the best-looking girl in the office, Claire. I've just realised.'

'Oh, my God! Not I'm not.' Claire rolled her eyes, a slow smile spreading. 'I look so awful with my hair like this.'

A beery cheer rose as a group gathered around us, and Liam plonked a pint glass with a swirling burgundy liquid on the table. 'You can't get out of it now, James,' he crowed. 'Don't worry. I didn't spit in it.'

A small chant broke out around the table. Some were already videoing the event with phones as they gathered around. Others stood up to watch. But I was ready to shut them up. I was wild and ready to implode as I guzzled the drink, tipping the glass and rising to my feet simultaneously. The unmarried concoction sloshed unhappily down my throat, some escaping my lips and spilling onto my shirt and floor.

I slammed the glass back down, cold sweat drenching my back. My throat burned. I was on fire, out of control now and thirsty for anarchy.

'What the *fuck* are you doing?' Liam yelled, somewhere between anger and respect. 'Claire, you'll have to suck him off in a minute to make him feel better.'

'Shut the fuck up, Liam,' Claire snapped.

Liam laughed, a horrible baying chuckle. 'Brian, you should wear the GoPro when you shag her later.'

I wiped my mouth. 'Shut the fuck up, Liam.' My blood was up, and my fist clenched. I wanted to punch something, Liam's smirking face preferably. And then I wanted to be punched in return, repeatedly, endlessly and into oblivion.

'Jesus, calm down, mate,' James pleaded. He moved around the table and stepped between us, fearing an overmatched confrontation.

Liam swiped James to one side and patted me on the chest as we squared up. 'Do you honestly think I'm going to waste my time with you?'

Donna started screaming as bodies jostled, and Liam walked away, laughing. We funnelled outside to the venue's tiny concrete car park when the excitement was over, and the owner asked us to leave. Embarrassed farewells were exchanged before a minibus cab arrived for those headed to Torquay. Others departed by foot, leaving just three of us perched against the iron fence railings outside the restaurant.

'Are you alright, man?' James asked. 'I genuinely thought you were going to hit Liam. I was excited to see it, in a way, because he's such a cunt.'

'Right.'

'But it would have been a hassle to visit you in the hospital tomorrow.'

I stood up, a rush of blood to my head as I did. James offered to call me a cab, but I told him it was ridiculous, given the distance involved. 'I don't know what I was thinking drinking that shit.'

'Not much is my guess,' James chuckled. He pointed at the road opposite, which bent behind the stately cream-coloured Royal Seven Stars Hotel just ahead. 'Claire, I'm heading up Coronation Road if you are.'

'I'm not sure yet,' she replied.

'Right, this is me, then,' James said. He patted my shoulder. 'We should catch up soon, mate.'

I nodded, still clinching onto the fence railings with both hands. 'Yeah, definitely.'

James gave Claire a light hug. 'Catch you around, guys.' He gave a sheepish thumbs-up after reaching the opposite pavement and then drifted past the bowed outside walls of the old hotel.

I scooped up my leaving gift from the ground and set off for the cobbles at the foot of the high street, with Claire's heels clopping alongside.

'Thanks for standing up for me earlier,' she said.

'No worries.'

She hooked her arm through mine as we walked past the drinkers on the terrace outside the hotel. 'I need to hold onto you for balance,' she snickered.

'No problem.'

Claire's arm remained attached to mine as we wandered up the slope of the high street. Her heels clipped against the ground as we moved, a percussive rhythm to keep me going. We walked under the street lights, past the closed shops and art galleries, until we reached our curved street.

We stood beneath the orange light of a lamppost, the blue home opposite with its For Sale sign propped outside. Claire smiled sweet and hopeful, and it was almost unbearable.

'It feels like we've been on a date,' she laughed and fingered the coils at the tips of her hair.

'Does it?'

'Yes.'

'You look like someone,' I told her. It had been bothering me all evening, and suddenly a name had clicked into place. 'Have you ever seen The Newsroom?'

Claire frowned. 'No. I don't watch the news. I find it depressing.'

'No, it was a drama set in a newsroom. I didn't like it, but my girlfriend did.'

'Okay.'

'And there was a woman called Maggie, or Margaret. I think.' I drew a circle in the air with my finger. 'Same face. Almost.'

'I don't know what that is.' Claire squeezed her bottom lip, her brow furrowed. 'Did you say you've got a girlfriend?'

'I used to.' I rubbed my face. 'I really miss her.'

'Aw.' She hugged me. 'It's sad when you break up with people.'

'Yes.' We were squeezing and swaying. 'I feel so fragmented without her, you know?'

Claire laughed. 'I don't know what that word means.' We looked across the street together. The house was unhappy with its lights off. 'Is this where you live? It's fancy here.'

A tile was missing in the pitched roof above Tam's window. I half-expected to see her there. 'Yeah. The blue one.'

'Do you want me to come inside, then?' Claire bit her lip. 'Just to check you're okay.'

I nodded. That sounded nice. 'Yeah, that would be lovely.'

I flicked the lights on as we stumbled through the front door and into the hall, dazzled by the change in brightness. We drifted into the living room, and I slumped onto the colossal sofa, wanting to melt into it as Claire placed her folded leather jacket onto its arm.

Claire gasped. 'Oh wow, this place is so nice.' She walked along the wall of framed photographs, examining them as if she were in a gallery. 'I like these pictures.'

'My friend took them.'

Claire ventured into the kitchen and opened and closed the cabinets there. 'Do you mind if I make myself a glass of water?'

'Sure.'

'I'll make you one as well.' After identifying the correct cupboard, Claire retrieved a pair of drinking glasses and filled them under the kitchen tap. 'I always drink lots of water if I've been out.'

'Good idea.'

She returned with our drinks and placed them on the coffee table at my feet. 'You've gone all quiet.' She slid in next to me and sipped from her glass. 'Are you feeling okay?'

'Yeah.' I smiled at Claire's smile. I wanted her to hold me and tell me everything would be okay. 'You're lovely, Claire.'

'Thank you.' She climbed onto my thigh and placed a curious thumb-tip between my teeth. 'We could go up to your room. If you want to.'

'Could do.' It wasn't easy to speak around her inserted digit. 'Or maybe we should snuggle up here and fall asleep together. I'm quite tired.'

Claire giggled as if she were in on a joke. 'I'm not tired.' She stood and pulled at my hand. I staggered to my feet and gripped the sofa arm to stabilise my footing. 'Sure you're okay?'

'I'm fine.'

I wasn't fine as my glass of water spilt onto the carpet as we bounced upstairs. The orange street lights were peeping through the undrawn window as we headed to the bedroom. I tumbled onto the bed, spreading my arms out.

'You've got lots of guitars,' Claire said as she ran her fingers over the strings of one. 'Can you play them all?'

'Yeah.'

'Wow. Like Ben Howard?'

'I don't know. Maybe.'

'He's from Totnes.'

'Right. Yeah.'

Claire knelt on the bed and stroked my hair. 'Are you from Totnes?'

'No.'

'I didn't think you were.' Her eyes narrowed like she was struggling to read me. 'Did you want to do something?'

'Yep.' I gave her a reassuring smile, but I didn't really. 'Definitely.'

She kissed my forehead and lips, then rolled onto her front. It was such a hassle to get on and off, she said. I did what she asked, and she shuffled onto her back again to pull the outfit over her feet.

Claire whispered, 'I know what'll perk you up.' A knee landed next to my cheek as she straddled my face and placed my hands on her breasts. It would have been an exciting moment in any other circumstance as my dry tongue rolled dutifully. 'You're good at that. Keep going.'

'Cool. Okay.' I didn't want to keep going, having grown nauseous. I couldn't breathe. Perhaps I was about to pass out or be violently unwell, and nothing in between. 'Claire?'

'Shush.' Claire leaned forward and gripped the headboard, her weight on my face. 'Just…keep going.'

'I don't think I can.' My voice strangled as nausea took hold. I pushed at Claire's inner thigh. She moved to un-straddle herself as my head lifted, gasping for oxygen as her knee swung and collided with my eye socket – a perfect full whack. The pain was instant, screaming through the haze. I jumped up. 'Fuck!'

'Oh, God! Sorry!' Claire shrieked. 'Are you okay?'

'Fuck!' I stumbled onto the landing, bouncing off the door frame and stumbled sea-legged into the bathroom. My left eye was already hot in the speckled mirror – visible in the other. I held my face, the shock of it. 'Shit. Shit.'

There were hurried footsteps on the landing, and I rushed to the bathroom door.

'Are you going?' I asked.

Claire froze at the top of the staircase, fumbling with the zip at her back. 'My dad waits for me when I'm out, so it's best. I was twenty-three last week. It's sad, really.'

'Do you not want to stay for a cuddle?'

'I can't.' Claire winced, unable to disguise her unease. 'Oh, my God. You should get your eye checked out.'

'Maybe.' I shielded the left side of my face with a hand. 'It's worse than it looks.'

'Hmm.' Claire stomped down the squeaking stairs in a hurry. 'I feel awful! Sorry!'

The front door slammed shut, out of sight. I stumbled back into the bedroom and sat on the bed, clamping my eye. And what should I do? I couldn't be alone. I reached into my pocket, deciding then to call Esther. And she wouldn't have wanted to hear from me at first. It was late, and I was out of it, and I was me. She would have protested, but I would have talked her around – assured her I needed to close it all out. We could move on unless she wanted something more from me.

But my phone had disappeared. It must have tumbled out at some point in the evening and could be anywhere. It was useless, and my head was yelling, splitting into two. I pulled myself from the mattress and swallowed a handful of painkillers from the packet left on the desk – knowing it wouldn't be enough. I needed to knock myself out.

I slid the wardrobe door open, leaning my knee into it and retrieved the packets of sleeping tablets from the front pocket of the suitcase parked inside. I shuffled back onto the bed, cracked the pills from their foil shells, and washed them away with the sips left in my glass. And I kept going after dry swallowing more of each. I wanted to black out and not panic. I wanted there to be nothing.

My head slid between the pillows after swimming on my back to get there. It was essential to seek comfort and relax enough to switch off. My breathing lost its depth as the cracks in the ceiling widened all the time, and the mattress sank by my feet. Dad was back, silhouetted in his ribbed vest and staring at the wall. I wanted to see his face with my one good eye, but my head wouldn't lift – the muscles in my neck were slack.

'Dad…Dad.'

But it was Frank's face staring back at me when Dad turned, bearded and serene. 'Don't worry,' he said, smiling. 'I'm sorting it all out.'

'Frank…' My chest was no longer rising. 'Why did you fill me with that false hope, man?'

There was a pulsing by my leg, my missing phone vibrating against my shin. It beamed like a lantern and bought news of an incoming call. My thumb flicked at the screen through the rapid blurring of my vision. Perhaps it was Esther calling after all. Perhaps I would tell her I was sorry before drifting away. Perhaps there was something poetic about that.

'Hello?'

'Hey fucker!' A familiar voice yelled from the speaker, but it wasn't Esther.

'Geoff?'

'Yeah! We've just driven by your place, and the lights were on. I wondered if you were still awake.'

'Geoff…'

He sighed. 'It's not the same without you, Bri.'

'Geoff….'

'Yes, Bri? You sound like complete shit. No offence.'

'Geoff. I've taken too many tablets. Can you please come over? I think I'm in trouble.'

'What?'

'The door's unlocked.'

The phone dropped from my grasp and slapped onto my ribs before tumbling on the bed. And I sank into the mattress, between its coils, plummeting through the floor until it was black. And there was nothing until Geoff's West Country tones penetrated the pocket of shadow I had fallen into – screaming underwater.

'Oh, God! Look at his face, Jack! It's fucked up!'

'Geoff.'

'Bri! It's okay, man,' he insisted. 'Stay calm. I'm trained in first aid.'

Violent nausea pummelled away as Geoff pulled me into a sitting position, his arms around my stomach. He was in stereo now as I puked and choked there, a thick vomit squeezing from my throat and slipping over my stomach and legs.

'Watch his head!' Geoff warned.

'Okay,' Jack replied.

Jack's eyes were grey and frightened as his hands clamped around my armpits. My body swayed and clanged into unseen obstacles before being greeted by the cold outside and then the familial rumbling of Geoff's van.

'Just keep tapping his face!' Geoff demanded as Jack sobbed over the noise of the van.

'Okay,' Jack replied, sobbing.

'Don't cry, Jack,' Geoff said. 'It'll be alright.'

'I'm sorry, Jack,' I whispered, and I wanted to cry with him.

FIFTEEN

Eleven missed calls.

An oxygen mask hissed in rhythm from the patient in the next bed as my finger traced the thin tube winding from a vein in the back of my hand. Our ward bay was small – six beds until the friendly porter arrived to wheel one away with its occupant screaming and his forlorn family trudging behind.

Phil from the crisis support team popped by, and his wiry grey head nodded earnestly throughout our conversation. There was no fight, and I assured him when he asked about my eye, only an accident I couldn't quite describe. And when he inquired about the overdose, I told him I had been upset about a relationship ending. We agreed it would be a good idea for me to see a GP as soon as I could and that I would seek medication for depression.

Mr Leonard in the bed opposite yelled again, as he had all morning intermittently. He was sprawled out, bare-chested and twisted up. 'Dirty fuckers!' he shouted.

A nurse moved from her station. 'Are you okay, Mr Leonard? Do you need something for the pain?'

'I don't want to be here!' he yelled, balling an angry fist.

'Okay,' the nurse replied, unflustered. 'Just let me know if you need some painkillers.'

After pulling the fabric curtain around us, the exhausted doctor returned with good news. She said I was fortunate there were no apparent signs of organ damage. The black liquid had worked well. The constant puking probably helped, too. But my eye was in bad shape. Something had broken inside the socket, and I needed an X-ray to check the extent of the damage before I could leave.

A familiar voice rose out of sight after the doctor departed. Geoff was bounding onto the ward bay with a little girl, no older than five, holding his hand. She had a red balloon on a plastic stick with the other.

'Here he is,' Geoff said as they paused by my bed. 'This is Bryony, look. Brian's got a bad eye, baby. Don't stare.'

Bryony was a little doll, chubby and perfect. Geoff asked her to say hello as they had practised. He said I had a name like hers, and she placed her nose barely an inch from mine.

'Hello, you,' she laughed in a silly low voice.

'Give Brian his balloon, look,' Geoff said.

Bryony held the balloon aloft like the Olympic torch and let it drop onto my bed. 'Here you go, sick man.' She chuckled as it bounced and then settled by my legs. 'It looks like your eye.'

I thanked Bryony for the present as she stared at my neighbour in the oxygen mask. He waved to her with extended fingers, and she did the same in return. It was sweet, but there was a growing uneasiness at her being there, considering what had happened.

'Go with Nanny and get some food then,' Geoff instructed. An older nurse was waiting by the ward entrance. Bryony ran towards her and hugged her around the waist. 'Mum's on a shift here. They're off to the canteen.'

'Oh, okay.' I bit my thumbnail. 'They don't know why I'm here, do they?'

'God, of course not, Bri.' Geoff plopped himself onto a green visitor's chair beside my bed. He pulled a sandwich with crumpled cardboard packaging from his coat pocket. 'I just told Mum you had, you know, a urinary infection.'

'Right. Okay.'

'Oh, yeah.' Geoff's eyes widened, remembering something. He balanced his food purchase between his knees, pulled my house keys from a trouser pocket, and placed them on the side table. 'I went back to tidy up last night. Seeing as it was such a mess.'

'Oh, wow. Thanks, mate.' I smiled, sincerely touched and yet mildly unsettled at the thought of Geoff alone in the house. 'You didn't need to do that.'

'No worries.' Geoff ripped open the packaging from his snack, and a pungent whiff of egg wafted from it. 'It's up for sale, I noticed.'

'Yeah.'

'I was worried I would scare your housemate again.'

'She's gone to Germany. Just me there now. Until it sells, I guess.'

'Oh.' He took a bite from his sandwich. 'Hey, it confused the doctor. With your eye all messed up. I parked up outside the A and E here, fucking handbraked it. Then we ran in with you, and I was shouting *medic* and all that shit.'

'Right…'

'You said you had taken a lot of tablets.' Geoff shuffled forward, his eyes filled with curiosity. 'But then you were talking about your dad in the van. Weird stuff.'

'Was I?'

'Yeah.' Geoff picked flecks of egg and crumbs from his stringy beard. 'So, I told them you must have argued with your dad or something. That's what I was trying to work out. Whether he forced some tablets down you and you had a punch-up. That's what I told them. Was I a million miles off?'

I nodded. 'Yes. You are a million miles off.'

'Oh, well.' Geoff puffed his lips and took a bite from the other sandwich, preferring to speak with a full mouth. 'Did you just take too many tablets by accident, then?'

'I'm not sure.'

He nodded solemnly. 'Ah, okay, well, that doesn't matter. Do you think you'll be here for a while?'

'I might be able to leave today, they said. It depends on how things look.'

'Oh, wow. That's good, then.' Geoff wiped more crumbs from his chest and lap and placed the empty packaging into a waste bin by his feet. 'I could give you a lift home if you want. Or fetch some more stuff for you. Whatever you need, bud.'

'Maybe…' I hesitated. Perhaps Geoff had done more than enough already. But it was also an incredibly convenient offer for someone with few other options. 'Well, if it doesn't put you out.'

'Not at all, Bri,' he insisted. He stared at me, a tongue lolling inside his cheek. 'Hey, I've got a spare room at mine. Come and stay for a day or so. I don't have anything on. Except for work.'

I hesitated, unsure. 'Oh right.'

'I was just wondering if you've been down in the dumps. You might not want to return to that house on your own.'

'Hmm.' I scratched at my face, ignoring an instinct to reject the offer outright. Perhaps he was right, even if the alternative meant living with Geoff for a few days. And he seemed different now, perhaps just a chaotic man with a kind heart. 'Are you sure?'

'Hell yeah, Bri.'

'Okay, then,' I said, with absolutely no conviction. 'Thanks, mate.'

Geoff beamed and pushed at the arms of the chair. 'It'll be two buddies hanging out. Until you're bored of me.' He laughed. 'Probably tomorrow.'

'Right. Yeah.'

We smiled at each other, and it fell quiet, and perhaps I hadn't thought our agreement through at all. Geoff tapped the bed again before he stood. He said he needed to relieve his mum, who had to return to work. I thanked him for his help, and we shook hands awkwardly before he backpedalled with his thumbs raised.

'I'll be back later then, maybe,' he said. 'Drop me a text.'

'I will.'

'Dirty fuckers,' yelled Mr Leonard as Geoff disappeared from the ward. 'I want to go home.'

'You're not well, Mr Leonard,' replied the doctor as she attempted to pull a troublesome curtain around her patient's bed. 'You've got an infection.'

Mr Leonard banged on his mattress. 'You're keeping me here without my permission. I've got a chicken in the oven!'

'Well, we'll take care of the chicken.' The doctor yanked harder at the long dividing cloth that was catching above. 'Don't worry.'

The X-ray revealed a fracture in my cheek, and a jarringly cheerful surgeon decided it was stable enough that I wouldn't need surgery – not now, at least. Instead, he gave a series of instructions I was bound to forget the second he was gone. I was to hold ice to it every few hours until the swelling was down, chew slowly, keep my head above my chest level when lying down, sneeze with an open mouth if I had to, and finally, I should not blow my nose.

I called Geoff once I was ready to be discharged and met him in the car park when his van dutifully rumbled in. We stopped by the house to clean and tidy and then pick up some clothes and essentials. Bryony and Geoff played hide-and-seek there as I packed and cleaned, a creeping dread as I did that – being back at the crime scene.

It was a grey, drizzly late afternoon when we finally pulled up in a communal parking area in a part of town I didn't know existed. I followed Geoff and Bryony as we strolled towards a cube-shaped house and its flat-roofed porch. The home was grey and had a smoke-burnt patch spreading on the plaster above the downstairs window. Attached houses on either side were immaculate in comparison, painted peach with neatly potted flowers out front.

There was a strict shoes-off policy, Geoff explained after we dodged the brambles and spiny weeds at the porch door. We slipped into the living room, where a vast library of vinyl lovingly had been stacked floor to ceiling along the back wall. It was at odds with the chaos elsewhere, the eccentric furniture choices and empty boxes strewn over the floor.

Geoff dived into a tiny cupboard under the staircase and rummaged inside. 'We're running low on leccy, Bryony,' he announced before re-emerging. 'I'll pop to the shop in a bit. Do you want to come with Daddy? I'll get some pizzas and ice lollies.'

'Yes!' Bryony shouted, jumping up and down. 'Yes, yes, yes!'

'Okay, let me show Brian his room. Do you want CBeebies? Let me put CBeebies on for you.'

I lumbered behind Geoff as Bryony jumped into a small beanbag armchair to watch children's television. Rough chipboard rubbed against my feet as we climbed the stairs, with only the loose webbings of carpet in patches.

'Probably needs a hoover,' Geoff said as we stopped outside a narrow yellow bedroom. 'And I'll get those bags out, as well.'

'This is fine.' I wandered inside and perched on the single black-framed bed with a red sleeping bag folded on top. 'Thanks, Geoff.'

'I'm sorry it's not bigger,' he said, leaning against its door frame. 'Jack's got next door, and Bryony has her little bed in my room when she stays. She won't sleep here on her own.'

'I hope I'm not kicking her out, mate.'

'No, no,' he insisted. 'Trust me. It's a bit of a dumping ground, this room.'

'Right.' I didn't care about the condition of the room, and I certainly wasn't going to be sneery about it. 'Thanks for having me over.'

'Pleasure.' Geoff winced as we looked at each other. 'God, Bri – your eye looks awful. No offence.'

'Oh well.' I laid down, and the bed rattled under my weight. The painkillers were doing their thing. I needed to close my eyes and nothing else. 'Would you mind if I caught up on some sleep, mate?'

'Sure, Bri.' Geoff backed his way out. He winked and pulled the door closed behind him like a dad finishing off a bedtime routine. 'Get some rest. I'll let you know when it's dinner.'

'Thanks.'

I climbed inside the sleeping bag and wriggled to get comfortable. Sharp coils in the mattress stabbed into my back, but I was determined to doze through it anyway. I disappeared into the deepest sleep before a curious tapping at the door woke me again.

'Bri. I've got us some pizzas downstairs,' Geoff cooed. 'I know you're probably whacked out, but I didn't want it to go cold, bud.'

'Okay,' I croaked. Everything throbbed as I unzipped my sleeping bag. 'I'll be there in a second.' After fishing around in my rucksack, I dry-swallowed the painkillers I had been prescribed and clomped down the stairs.

'Here he is,' said Geoff.

'Hey.' I raised a palm as the sticky orange vinyl floor clung to my socks. I joined the other three on a green plastic chair at a square dining table. The room was in disarray, with doors missing from wall units and piles of crockery left unwashed in the sink.

Geoff folded a pizza slice and almost took it whole. 'Jack's here, look.'

'Hi, Jack,' I said with a weary smile.

Jack nodded with his mouth full and then unleashed a huge, muddy burp, which threw Bryony into hysterics. He was off to play computer games in his room, he announced

'I got the garden furniture in,' Geoff said as Jack left us. He stared intently at my face, unable to hide his discomfort. 'Looks okay, actually.'

'Cool.' I nodded, shielding my eye. 'Have you got any frozen peas, Geoff?'

He sprung to his feet and fished out an opened bag of mixed vegetables from a small fridge freezer, spilling piles of frost onto the floor. 'Is this okay?'

'Great.' I balled it up and held it to my cheek. 'Perfect.'

Geoff put Bryony to bed shortly after our food and a lengthy round of bedtime stories. I wandered into the living room, holding the frozen vegetables to my swollen face and wedged myself into the low beanbag armchair. The carpet was within touching distance, with thick dust and scattered crumbs in its pile. And what would I do now? Perhaps it was best not to think about that at all.

Geoff joined me in the living room after I had dispatched the mixed vegetables into the freezer to cool again. He fell onto the vacant tan leather sofa and popped open the can of beer I had fetched for him after declining one for myself. He switched on the TV with the remote, and we settled on a film after flicking through the channels – 'Feeling Minnesota' with Keanu Reeves and Cameron Diaz.

'I must have had a thousand wanks to Cameron Diaz,' he said, sipping from his can.

'That's a lot.'

'Yeah.' He peered down at me over the sofa arm. 'Sure you don't want the sofa, Bri?'

'No, I'm fine down here.'

'That's a kid's chair, really.' He took another swig of his drink and placed his can on the floor. 'I can't believe Bryony went off with no stress. We must have tired her out.'

‘That’s good,’ I said. ‘She’s a funny kid. Is she excited like that all the time?’

‘All the time when she’s here.’ Geoff laughed, barking. ‘A ball of energy, that girl.’

Geoff turned forty when Bryony was born, he explained. He had always wanted children, but it looked like it wouldn’t happen for him. Then, after meeting his daughter’s mother through his job at the supermarket, the pair enjoyed a summer of mutual lust, culminating in a pregnancy and a hasty offer of marriage. They tried to make it work at first, but it all fell apart as quickly as it came together before Bryony was born.

‘I’m sorry, mate.’

‘Don’t be. Bryony’s never known any different. She’s just this little sunny girl all the time. I have no idea why.’

‘That’s nice.’

‘Yeah, it is.’ He re-arranged himself on the sofa, laying on his side. ‘So, what do you think of the place, really?’

I hesitated, unsure whether it was too early to tell Geoff a truth he needed to hear: that he was living in neglect. ‘Yeah, it’s nice.’

‘Well, it needs a spruce up.’

‘A bit.’

‘Definitely.’ Geoff said he needed to get rid of the cardboard lying around. He had gotten into a bad habit of ordering new gadgets for the disco when left to his own devices of an evening. ‘It’s an arms race, the disco business,’ he explained. ‘I’ll see Colin has a new truss system, and I want that. Or Simon Rogers has bought one of those confetti cannons, and I’ll want that, then. I don’t have any money for anything else. Other than those two upstairs.’

‘You’ve already got lots of good stuff, mate.’

‘Yeah. But you can’t rest on it.’ He swirled his beer can and pointed at the TV on its wonky corner stand. ‘Freddie’s tipped off the police, look.’

‘Which one’s Freddie?’

‘Cameron Diaz. Keep up.’

‘Right.’

‘Fuck.’ Geoff shook his head, fully invested now. ‘She just wanted to be a dancer in Vegas. See, you’ve got to live out your dream, Bri. Whatever it takes.’

‘Yeah.’

I pulled out my phone and typed out a message.

Hey Mum. I’m okay xx

SIXTEEN

My phone vibrated on the pillow, waking me. I had fallen asleep in the afternoon again – a sapping fatigue perhaps caused by a re-adjustment to antidepressants. And the tiny bedroom was dark and breathless as I swung my clammy legs around, with a new blackout blind trapping the humidity inside.

'Hi, Mum.'

'Hello.' She puffed on a cigarette. 'You sound so whacked out.'

I rubbed at my face. 'Well, I've been asleep.'

'Shall I put the video on?'

'Not right now.'

Mum groaned like she suspected something. 'You're not using drugs again, are you?'

I sniggered. 'Not fun drugs, no.'

'Oh.' It was quiet momentarily, with Mum presumably absorbing what that meant. 'And you're still staying with this friend?'

'Geoff. Yes. Just until I can get things sorted.'

'What does he do for a living?'

'Mobile disco stuff.' I rubbed a thin sheet of sweat from my face. 'He works at the supermarket as well.'

'Right. What's he like?'

'Um, nice. A bit eccentric.' I laughed because boiling Geoff down to a condensed description was so challenging. 'Listen, I'm going to wander outside to get some fresh air. But I'm okay, Mum. You just caught me during a nap. I'm fine.'

'Okay. It's a good idea to get out a bit, love.'

'Yes, it is. I'm trying to.'

'Good.'

'Bye then, Mum. I love you.'

'Tara-a-bit, then. I love you, Bab.'

After registering at the local surgery, I booked an appointment to see a local GP. The cheek was okay, he surmised, healing well. But then we spoke about my overdose, and I knew what was coming having been through the process before. It wasn't a friendly chat, more of a clinical cross-examination where I answered questions about what happened leading up to the latest sad attempt to end my life, or whatever it was, and how I was feeling now. Not great was the gist – not suicidal, just subdued and flattened.

Geoff was out at work when I got home that day, saying I could stay as long as I liked only that morning. The offer was genuine – enthusiastic, even. He liked having me around. And the vinyl clung to my socks as I made coffee in the kitchen, the sink dry and filled with hard-speckled dirty crockery. I spun the tap and began scrubbing and cleaning what hadn't been for some time. Suddenly, I was mopping the kitchen floor, hoovering the carpets, and tidying the lounge – flattening and removing the cardboard.

Perhaps the motivation behind the big tidy-up was selfish, to bring order to my immediate surroundings should I be there for a while. But Geoff was bowled over by the change in the place, seeing what he couldn't bring himself to do, and there were genuine tears in his eyes when he was back from work that evening.

Between us, we tidied and cleaned the house by routine and scoured local adverts for furniture bargains, anything we could bring back to life with some care. We absorbed DIY videos posted online by beautifully dull repair guys and used them to strip and paint the walls and fix door handles and hinges. We became an odd couple pulling each other up, taking incremental steps and achieving our short-term goals.

During a morning of strimming in Geoff's overgrown wedge-shaped garden, the estate agents called to advise that an offer had been accepted on the house and that the sale should go through quickly. A removal company had hoovered up the remainder of Tam's items some time ago, but many of my belongings were still there.

The slats on Geoff's bed had broken, so I lent him mine after we headed over in the van. The yellow room was too small to house it anyway. And we picked up my bike, guitars, amps, and pedals – the last of my belongings to come over. Then, after a quick drive to the estate agents, I returned Frank's key. And it was strange to do that, jarring for it all to have ended that way.

I continued to stay at Geoff's place, helping with his weekend gigs when the swelling around my eye had retreated, and the days were bookended by cooler autumnal mornings and evenings. The change of scenery provided an escape and, if nothing else, a reason to leave the house. It was nice to pay him back in such a small way, as he had been kind enough to open up his odd nest. And there was something remedying in watching others being carefree and having fun.

Perhaps the gentle excitement of the discos provoked me to play again. At first, I just wanted to remember the licks and parts from the Dorothea days to know it was all still there. But then I started playing like I used to, retreating to my room when Geoff was working – picking, detuning, and strumming in search of something to catch my interest. One evening, I became immersed in a rolling chord sequence I liked that I hadn't noticed him watching in his green supermarket gilet by my bedroom door.

'This is quality,' he said, stopping me in my tracks. 'Like watching Ben Howard, mate.'

I winked as our eyes met. 'Thanks, mate.'

'He's from Totnes.'

I nodded. 'I heard.'

'What's that chord there?'

I checked my fingers on the fret. 'Um, C diminished 7th.'

'Diminished what?' Geoff frowned like I had blown his mind. 'That's some next-level shit, isn't it?'

'Nah.' I chuckled and tried to pick up from where I had been, picking thumb to finger, but it was no good. 'I like to throw in a diminished now and then – to inject a bit of darkness.'

Geoff puffed his unshaven cheeks. 'I don't know what you're on about.'

'It doesn't matter.'

Geoff pulled his phone out and showed me the website of an acquaintance he knew from the wedding circuit – a drummer who performed in a covers band and gave lessons on the side. 'That's Lenno.'

Lenno was a large man with bleached, spiky hair and a matching soul patch. 'Right.'

'You ever thought about teaching?'

I nodded cautiously. 'Sometimes.'

Perhaps Geoff's question was a polite prompt for me to start contributing, and that would have been entirely fair of him. And with peaks of twitchiness sprouting, big questions were beginning to peck away along the same theme – what the fuck was I doing? What should I be doing? I would find myself outside when that became too much. And it was restorative to do that, to walk or cycle and spend that energy out in the elements. Those clustered thoughts would sometimes organise then.

One late afternoon wander took me onto a high street closing down for the day. There were new arts flyers in the window of The Watercress café as I strolled towards it and stopped to read them as I would. And on this occasion, there was also a neatly hand-written sign on the glass panel of its teal door – *Help Needed, Please Enquire Within.*

A slender man with unruly hair emerged from behind the counter inside. He held a spray bottle under his arm and tied an apron over a stripy t-shirt. A sudden burst of assertiveness had me pushing the door open, and it was heavier on the hinges than I had expected.

'Sorry, we're closed,' the man said as he wiped a circular table by the window.

'Oh.' My fingers clung around the door handle to prevent it from banging shut like it wanted. 'I was just going to ask if you were still looking for help.'

The man looked up. 'Fucking hell!' He was dumbfounded – eyes wide like I was playing a prank. 'Anna!'

A short woman with blue hair and stretcher earrings appeared via a door behind the counter. She stopped suddenly and yelped. 'Oh, my God. That is freaky! Is this a wind-up, Tim?'

'He's asking about the job,' Tim said. 'Can you Adam and Eve it?'

Anna rested her elbows on the counter. 'Well, sold. Let's get him in here.' The pair must have been together. They had their routine. 'What's your name?'

'Brian,' I replied, almost intimidated into never speaking again.

The man waved me inside. 'Come in, Brian. I'm Tim, and this is my partner, Anna.'

I released my grip on the door, which swung shut with a clatter.

'Get this,' Tim said, with one eye on the bang at the entrance, 'you are a doppelganger of the guy who left us last week. You don't have an identical twin called Ronan, do you? He's just about to travel around South America.'

'No.' I held my hands at my hips, unsure where to place myself. 'Does he look like Brian Cox? The scientist on TV.'

'Not really.' Tim wiped a pair of thick-framed glasses on his apron and returned them to his face. 'Or, maybe he does, thinking about it. I'm not entirely sure who that is.'

Anna's mouth was still open, perhaps for comic effect. 'So, what's your experience? We need someone who can hit the ground running, really.'

'Well, I used to work in a café,' I said, recalling the fortnight I once spent working in a local Costa Coffee as a teenager.

'That's good,' Tim said, nodding. 'Any other hidden talents? Can you juggle?'

I shrugged, not knowing if it was a genuine question. 'Um, I can play the guitar.'

'Oh, I love that, Anna,' he said. 'I bet we could use that.'

'How flexible are you?' Anna asked. Her eyes narrowed. She needed more convincing than her easily-pleased partner. They needed someone Monday to Thursday, she said. They had Saffy, who helped on Fridays and Saturdays.

'That sounds great,' I said, not overthinking whether it was. 'Ideal, actually.'

'The fact he does look exactly like Ronan would be great comedy value,' Tim noted. 'I mean, I have to squint to see it now. But only a tiny bit.'

'You haven't done any major crimes, Ronan?' Anna asked. She held a hand at her mouth, realising her error. 'Oh God, it's Brian. See! I'm already doing it.' She collapsed into laughter and pushed her face into a rested arm. Tim laughed, too, but without a hint of joy on his face. It was slightly unnerving.

'Well, I did write *Mr Tucker Sucks Ass* on the playground in Primary school, and my mum got called in.' There was more laughter now. Perhaps I was one of the gang already.

'Okay, how about you come in tomorrow for about seven?' Tim asked.

Anna winced. She wasn't sure. 'Um, maybe. If we agree, it's on a trial basis.'

'I mean, we need someone, Anna, desperately.' Tim bowed his head like he was exhausted. 'Everyone else asking about it has been an oddball, and I just want to keel over.'

Anna rolled her eyes and smiled. 'Fine,'

Tim gave a thumb-up. We were on. 'Just don't be late. I hate tardiness, Brian.'

'Yes, Ronan was tardy,' Anna noted. 'Always in Tim's bad books.'

'Yes. And sorry if we don't sound like we know what we're doing, we don't really,' Tim added. 'Well, Anna does. She's the brains. I'm very much winging it.'

Anna laughed. They couldn't afford to pay me a huge wage, she said. They just needed a utility person like Ronan was – a bit of serving, cleaning, washing up, prepping food, and taking orders. 'What else? Making hot drinks and dealing with unfounded complaints. Does that sound okay?'

I nodded casually – perhaps it did. 'Fine by me.'

'Cool,' Tim said, with a clap of his hands. 'Let's shake on it now, and we can sort the details tomorrow.' He walked over with his hand outstretched before pulling me in for a hug. 'I'm a hugger, mate. I tricked you. Come on, Anna.'

Anna bounded through the hatch door at the counter, and we had a three-way hug for longer than was comfortable.

SEVENTEEN

Pink wispy clouds scattered the early morning sky as I free-wheeled into the courtyard behind The Watercress with my phone clamped to my ear.

'You do sound happier,' said Mum.

'Well, that's good then.'

'How's the job? Something to keep you busy, I bet.'

'Yeah.' I parked my bike in its regular spot at the red brick wall beside the old industrial bin. 'It does.'

'And the owners are nice?'

'They're a lovely pair of hippies.'

A windchime clanged above the rear kitchen entrance, but the door was locked – too early again. With no sign of life inside, I headed back onto the narrow passageway to begin the loop to the café front.

'I can tell you must like it,' Mum said. 'There's some enthusiasm in your voice again.'

'Well. I do feel happier.'

'Good.' Mum gasped a happy sigh. 'It's cheered me up, you saying that.'

'Good.' I exited the narrow path and rounded to the pillared walkway on the high street, where an elderly dog-walker was chiding a yapping terrier. 'I've been thinking about doing some guitar lessons, you know, on the side. To bump up my earnings.'

'Well, that's a good idea!' Mum clapped her hands. 'I'll tell Bill. He'll be pleased. He was just saying how nice it would be for you to do something with your talent again.'

'Yeah. Well, it's just a thought.'

'Do you remember that little workshop we had in our garden?'

'Yeah, where he kept stapling old bits of carpet to the walls.'

'Aw.' Mum chuckled fondly. 'The neighbours used to get annoyed with the noise when your friend came over.'

'Yeah. And Bill would always argue with them and staple more old carpet.' I waved to Anna, who was tidying at the counter when she spotted me between flyers at the café window. I turned to show her the guitar on my back, and she beamed and pumped her fist. 'He was good like that.'

'He missed hearing you play when you left, you know. He said it when we looked at our little garden for the last time before we left.'

I paused, with the door handle in my hand – suddenly no strength in my arm. 'That's really nice, Mum.'

'Yes.'

I gave the door the push it needed, leaning my shoulder in. 'I need to do some work now.'

'Okay, Bab. Tara-a-bit. Love you. Just keep going.'

'I will. I love you too, Mum.'

Despite its fun-loving and relatively self-aware owners, The Watercress was still very Totnes. According to the twee hand-painted sign in the window, it described itself as vegan-friendly and community-focused. It knew its audience well, who were generally environmentally conscious and affluent but not necessarily. It championed local produce and the importance of sustainability. It was lots of things which might have nauseated in less sincere hands.

I squeaked through the trial period, where the learning curve had been steep, and my ability to turn up on time had impressed if little else. I discovered our customers often asked, in great detail, about the ingredients in their orders. Eventually, I stopped heading into the kitchen to ask Tim – who grew weary of my constant questions. Learning it all by heart was easier and a valuable time saver.

The passing tourist trade was winding down as we headed into late Autumn. But the café would still get busy, although it was no longer overwhelmed during the peak periods of the day. I found myself at ease with the general comings and goings of the place and the quirks of our dedicated regulars, who continued to call me Ronan long after I had given up correcting them.

Tim had recently recalled my mentioning of being able to play the guitar when we first met and badgered me to learn a couple of songs for 'Bounce and Rhyme' – a parent and toddler sing-along session held twice per week. I couldn't tell if it was an elaborate wind-up. That was always possible with him as he enjoyed throwing people off balance. But I had arrived prepared that morning, just in case.

After the early morning rush dissipated, parents funnelled inside with their youngsters as they would. Some with tiny ones would park themselves at tables further away from the performance space, in front of the children's bookshelf. Those with older toddlers usually wanted to be inside the heat of the action and placed themselves near that far corner, where we would clear tables away to make temporary floor space.

'We have a special guest today,' Anna announced as if she were mid-way through a headline festival set. 'Brian will accompany us on the guitar for this next song, which is everybody's favourite.'

There was a tiny smattering of applause, mainly from Anna and one overexcited toddler, as I wandered to the corner with my freshly tuned acoustic guitar. We performed a storming rendition of 'Wind the Bobbin Up', as pre-schoolers completed the actions either note-perfectly or in a chaotic freestyle, depending on their personality. A small girl with a cartoon octopus t-shirt kept reaching up to touch my guitar throughout the song, and she would smile sweetly when I looked at her.

Once we had finished, a woman in a bright orange headscarf headed over. 'I'm so sorry, she was banging on your guitar,' she said apologetically. 'I didn't notice until the end.'

I smiled, charmed by it. 'She's absolutely fine. As long as she's having a good time, that's the main thing.'

'She loves musical instruments and gets very excited.' To illustrate, Mae reached up to stroke the strings again and stopped to watch them vibrate. 'Mae, baby, it's fun, but we must stop now.'

'Sorry, Mae.' I lifted the guitar out of reach and shaped to head back to the counter. 'Hey, I like your scarf, by the way. It's a cool colour.' A sharp panic tingled when I stopped speaking. It was so out of character to be throwing out compliments to strangers. Perhaps it was the antidepressants speaking on my behalf or the buoyant afterglow of the performance.

'Thanks,' the woman said with a sweet anxious smile. 'I've got alopecia, so I've always got a few I like to try.'

'Cool.' I smiled and quietly fretted my compliment had backfired. 'Well, it's a good choice.'

'Thanks.'

I retreated to the counter to relieve Tim, who had stepped in to serve the small queue of customers and was mildly annoyed I had taken my time.

'I didn't know you could play the guitar, Ronan,' said an elderly man at the front.

As I continued the array of duties that morning, my gaze drifted to the headscarfed woman whose face was alive like she was in more than one place at a time. She was sitting at a window table in the corner with an older lady, possibly her mother, given their likeness, and little Mae. Our eyes locked for the tiniest moments, and I shifted my sight line by inches in a panic and pretended to drift off – pathetic, really.

After closing, I retreated into the tiny chrome galley kitchen to join Tim, where we cleaned and made the compotes, granolas and parfaits for breakfast in the morning. After cashing up, Anna squeezed inside to join us and began rifling through the freezer under the counter, where she grumbled about having to feed the cat of one of the café regulars away on some yoga retreat.

'Did you see it in there earlier, Anna?' Tim asked. 'It was electric. That's a huge song, and Brian gave it a real edge.'

Anna hummed in agreement. 'It was a big hit.'

'I think we could phase him in more,' Tim suggested. 'You're pregnant, and I think Brian has what it takes. It'd be like Ben Howard at Glastonbury every Thursday.'

My phone buzzed, and I pulled it from my pocket. Having expected another hilarious video from Geoff as he liked to send, there was a message from Beatty instead.

Hey! Are you still in Totnes? I promised Noah I would ask xx

I froze, bunting the phone against my chin.

'He's got his mobile out again, Tim,' Anna tutted.

'Oh, dear,' Tim groaned. 'Always when my back is turned.'

'Sorry,' I said. I continued from where I had been, rough chopping dried pecans and walnuts with a head now swimming.

'As I was about to say,' Tim continued, 'those toddlers were really winding those, what are they called? Dobbins?'

'Bobbins…' I replied.

Tim gasped in mock horror. 'Jesus, Brian. There's no need for language like that. There are pregnant women present.'

Anna chuckled. 'He keeps walking into your dad jokes, Tim. I bet you were sat on that all day.'

'Yes!' Tim admitted. 'I was.'

Anna rested her hands at the end of the workstation. 'Are you listening, Brian?' Anna asked, chuckling. 'You've gone quiet.'

'Sorry,' I said, filing my phone away. 'I am listening. It sounds good.'

I was still unsure whether to reply to Beatty's message as I hung my cycle helmet on the new coat rack in the porch after riding home.

'Alright, Bri!' called Geoff, as he would. He was bounding down the stairs with a pair of shiny black loafers in his grip as I entered the living room.

'Hi, mate.'

His thinning hair was dripping wet as he perched on the bottom step. 'Jack's here, look.'

'Hey Jack,' I chirped. But Jack was snoring on the tan-coloured sofa, hands held across his stomach.

'He's asleep,' Geoff noted. 'He's been at college. It's whacked him out, I expect.'

'Right. Are you off out?'

'Yeah.' Geoff fished out the tissue paper scrunched inside his shoes. 'I've got a date tonight. Remember Helen?'

I racked my brain. 'From that first wedding we did?'

'Bingo!' Geoff tied his new shoes and slipped on the pin-stripe blazer hanging from the staircase post. 'She messaged the other day, asking how I was, and I just asked her out. Bam, no messing.'

'Smooth move.'

'That's how it is with me, Bri.' He patted his chest with both hands and winced after realising how damp he was underneath his thin white shirt. 'I'll stick the fans on in the car.'

'Okay.'

He pulled open the porch door. 'I had a last-minute shower, but I'll dry off there, won't I?'

I nodded. 'Um, yeah. Probably. You're looking good, though, mate.'

'Thanks, buddy.' Geoff smiled and backed his way out. 'There's pizzas in the fridge. I got the four-cheese one you like.'

'Lovely.' I gave a thumbs-up, although I couldn't recall ever discussing my topping preference. 'Good luck, mate.'

'Cheers.' He winked and pulled the door shut. 'Don't wait up!'

'Wow. Okay.'

I eased onto the office chair at the new workstation under the stairs. We had recently picked up the items from a neighbour who was having a garage clear-out. I stared at Beatty's message there, pondering what to do.

Jack coughed and spluttered. He sat up like a corpse being shocked into life. 'Woah.'

'Alright, Jack?' I reached over to the wall and flicked on the living room light. 'Fancy some pizza?'

'Yeah.' He stretched and scanned the room like he wasn't sure where he was.

The kitchen floor no longer wanted to glue itself to my feet as I headed to the kitchen and bent to turn on the oven. It took an age to heat up like it always did, and I pulled my phone out again to type a quick message.

I'm still around. How are you? Would Noah like a lesson? xx

EIGHTEEN

After accepting Mum's offer to set our call to a video chat, I waved at the phone screen. She was in her usual sunny spot on the balcony with a fag in one hand and the other holding onto a sun hat buffeted in the breeze.

'Why am I small on the screen and you're big?' she asked, returning to a favourite topic.

'It's the other way around for me, Mum,' I said. 'I've explained this.'

'Can I switch it around?'

'You would prefer to stare at your own face during our conversations?'

'Hmm.' She blew smoke from her cigarette, which wafted sideways in the wind. 'Not now you've said it like that.'

'Right.' I repositioned myself on the bed, my back against the wall with my legs over the side. 'You okay?'

'Yeah.' Mum frowned. 'That room is so small, Brian. You'll need your own space soon, surely.'

'Maybe.' I tapped at my teeth. The subject had been on my mind of late. 'I'd need to work out what I could afford. Or whether I should just leave and go back to London.'

'Well. You must be doing better now with these lessons.'

'Probably.' I scratched my face. 'It's taken off more than I thought it would.'

'Well, that's a good thing. We are proud of you.'

'Thanks.' There was a tap at the door and a gentle enquiry from Geoff. He pushed inside until he saw me with the phone and then lingered on the landing apologetically. 'Anyway, I better head off, Mum. We're off out in a bit. I'll speak to you soon.'

'Yes, okay. Love you, Brian. Tara-a-bit, Bab.'

'Love you.'

We were one song away from the evening's climax when Geoff announced he would 'fire up the Cameo' again. Our pared-down set-up was on a raised stage at the back of a local cricket clubhouse, where framed team photos of yesteryear lined the walls, and a polystyrene-tiled ceiling almost grazed our heads.

Darude's dance classic 'Sandstorm' was hitting its stride as Geoff's new toy pumped red and green beams from a tiny box. But only four revellers were left on the shiny wooden dance floor, which stood between us and the Seventies stone-clad bar beyond. Most of the party had ventured outside to watch a fireworks display on the cricket pitch, and of those who remained with us, three were doing separate ironic robot dances. The fourth was on her knees, trying to slice the rays with her bare hands.

'Look at the precision on the aerials, Bri,' Geoff gasped. 'You could cut your steaks with those.'

'Yeah. You could.' I shook my head in performative disbelief to meet Geoff's relentless enthusiasm. But perhaps I had reached my limit on trying. 'Almost seems a bit wasted on a venue like this.'

Geoff glared at me like a disappointed teacher. 'Are you saying these people aren't good enough for us?' The woman flipped onto her back to do imaginary snow angels when one of the robot dancers tripped over her arm, and they laughed on the floor together.

'No, I'm not saying that,' I replied. 'It's just a bit dead in here.'

There was a thumbs-up from a scarfed man returning from outside as Geoff pulled on his comedy red wig, a gimmick of his I never understood.

'I love you, Bri, but you've got to stop turning your nose up. Everyone deserves the best we can give them.'

'Right. Yeah.'

Geoff picked up the microphone, and I faded the arpeggios from Darude's finest moment. 'Right, we are sadly close to midnight here,' he announced in his DJ voice as a stream of missing guests fanned back inside. 'But it's been a great night. We've been DJ Geoff, The Deck Wreck Machine, and The Boy Wonder, Bri Broski. Please take the time to log onto our Facebook and Instagram, the Disco Inferno. Make sure it's our page in Totnes, and please leave us a review. A big thanks to everybody who stayed late celebrating Wayne's fiftieth birthday. Fifty years young, give him a final cheer, everybody.'

A boozy cheer erupted around the room.

'We've got one more song dedicated to you, Wayne, from your lovely wife, Julia. It's a number which is your favourite song.'

I faded up the piano-lit opening bars of 'Don't Stop Me Now' by Queen as Wayne led a conga of his friends and family, which snaked around the dancefloor and then between the tables and chairs.

Geoff put a hand on my shoulder as the revellers continued their fun. 'Sorry, Bri,' he said. 'I didn't mean to get funny.'

'That's okay, mate.'

'I feel like you're too busy with all your lessons and the café.'

I nodded. 'A little bit.'

'And you don't enjoy this as much as I do.' Geoff pulled his wig off, perhaps sensing the gravitas of the moment. 'Am I hitting the nail on the head, or what?'

'Well, I'm a bit tired.' I rubbed my face nervously. 'But I don't want to upset you, mate.'

'No, no. I understand.' Geoff bowed his head solemnly, like a dad finally accepting his son was destined for another path. 'It doesn't upset me, Bri. I'm proud of you.'

I nodded. 'That's good, then.'

'Yeah.' The conga morphed into a circle around the edges of the tiny dancefloor. Wayne was a joyful pot-bellied man and danced away inside its middle. He pointed at his family and friends with a full pint in his other hand. 'Hey, everybody loves this guy, look.'

'Yeah. Must be nice.'

Wayne pinched at his eyes when it became too much for him. His wife rushed to hug him, and he picked her up, spilling his drink down her back and onto the floor.

'What a lovely feeling that must be for them,' Geoff said.

Packing up the van didn't take long when the evening's festivities were over. Jack had ventured inside on schedule, and we had the whole routine down to a fine art between us. Geoff was brimming with contentment as we pulled away from the venue and cheerfully hummed the tunes we had played that evening.

'I'm in love,' he announced, verbalising a swell of happy thoughts. 'There's no other word for it, fellas. I love Helen. I love that woman.'

'That's good, mate,' I said.

'And I've got to be honest, Bri. I love banging her as well.'

'Right. Good.'

Geoff laughed and tapped on the steering wheel. 'Seriously though. I cannot believe my luck sometimes. It's like we've known each other forever.'

I smiled quietly, resisting an urge to preach caution. Geoff was an all-or-nothing guy, and I couldn't do much to change that about him.

Perhaps it would have worked out differently with Beatty had I been more unfearing, like Geoff. And perhaps it was too jarring to have been reminded of the mistimed thrill of whatever we had as I tripped into the For Sale sign angled by her yellow door on my first trip back.

A familiar rush of excitement surged when Beatty opened her door, her dark hair now towards her shoulders. We hugged briefly in the doorway, and the buzz of electricity dispersed into a shared chuckle as we parted. After she beckoned me inside and called for Noah in the same breath, I thanked her for putting the word around regarding my lessons.

'Brian!' Noah burst from his room and charged down the stairs.

'Hey mate,' I said as he reached the bottom of the stairs and stood there with a big toothy grin.

'Come on, let's go!' he yelled, sprinting across the floor.

We retreated into the blush-pink dining room, and Noah studiously tuned his guitar without prompting. Beatty left to make coffee after I accepted the offer. She retreated to the snug after, with classes to plan for the following day and only returned at the lesson's end to announce Noah needed a bath before bed. Our eyes met as I packed away, and Noah sprinted off. She smiled, and it was gentle – a cue for me to leave and nothing more.

The rain was light and horizontal as I set off on the ride back to Geoff's house, and it was always a surprise to head back there. But then it thundered overhead, and suddenly, I was pedalling through a downpour that slapped the river as I rode back across the bridge. And it was so heavy it was difficult to see or even stay upright under the sheer force of it.

After unlocking the porch door when I was home, I slammed it shut again as the rain reverberated on the plastic roof above. I gasped for breath as water dripped from my clothes and guitar case and pooled on the floor.

There was no response from inside after calling, so I headed into the kitchen with sopping clothes balled into my arms, confident I was alone. After feeding the damp items into the washing machine, I flicked through the cupboards for something quick and easy to eat when my phone rumbled on the worktop. I retrieved a packet of dried pasta, planting it on the worktop as the message from Esther beamed.

Do you still want to talk? x

I snatched my phone.

Sure x

Are you free now? x

I hesitated, my body shivering and wet.

Give me one minute. I'll call you! x

I rushed to my room and slunk under the bed covers, hugging them for warmth before I braced myself. Esther was upbeat when she answered, immediately asking for my address to redirect any mail still trickling through. 'I just thought I'd ask right away, so I wouldn't forget.'

It made sense, I told her, and with formalities out of the way, I decided to take the initiative. 'Congratulations on your engagement.'

'Oh, thanks.' Esther's voice muffled like she was chewing a nail. 'I didn't know if you'd heard.'

'Yeah.' I gave a quick, knowing snicker – like it was mad for us to be talking about it.

'Is that why you called?'

'Sort of,' she said. 'Actually, it was my counsellor's idea for me to speak to you. Well, we both decided.'

'Oh. Wow.' I placed a pillow between my back and the metal bed head. 'What spurred this, then? The counselling.'

'Nate has a friend who mentioned going to see her, and I just thought I'd do it quietly and discuss a few things. They say everyone should go, don't they.'

'Right. Yeah.'

'What have you been up to, then?'

'Um.' Various flickers of how I had been doing shuffled around – so few suitable anecdotes to share. 'I've been teaching guitar to a couple of kids recently. Nothing too taxing.'

'Oh, that's lovely.' Esther sounded so pleased. It was nice. 'Finally come in use, then.'

'Yeah. Maybe a third soon. A friend's daughter wants to try. It's just finding the time to fit everything in.'

'That's so good,' she said. 'So are you staying down that way forever? I can't imagine that.'

'Um. No idea.' A series of uncertain hums filled the silence. There was so much and so little to say at the same time. 'So, when is the wedding? Are you planning something?'

'Yes...' Dates regarding Nate's working visa had pushed timelines forward, she said. It made her stressed about the optics of it all and organising everything on short notice. And now they were writing invitations, he wanted to invite an ex-girlfriend who had become a mutual friend of theirs. 'It made me wonder if something similar might be possible for you.'

I laughed like it was ridiculous. 'Are you trying to set us up?'

'No. No.' Esther sniggered, sharp and nasal. 'I don't think you'd get on.'

'Fair enough.'

'Would it be weird to ask if you wanted to come, then?'

I pondered the question for mere seconds. 'Probably. It would, wouldn't it?'

She hummed in agreement. 'Especially now that I've said it out loud.'

The conversation threatened to fall quiet when the blog Tam had shared bounced into my head. 'Actually, can I apologise to you, Es? Because I am sorry. About what happened. I'm just really sorry.'

'Oh…' She was surprised. 'It's okay. I feel like I can see things more from your perspective now. Just a horrible situation, wasn't it?'

'Maybe. But I shouldn't have left you to deal with everything. It wasn't fair.'

'Okay.' She hummed for a moment. 'I think we both just want to move on, don't we?'

'Yes.'

A door slammed downstairs. Geoff was home and bellowing about the awful weather outside to no one in particular. I slunk out of bed carefully to avoid it rattling and crept over to shut my door. Perhaps he would see that as a barrier, a request for privacy – although it hadn't stopped him before.

'Are you in a better place now?' Esther asked as I slipped back into the bed.

'Yep.'

There was a stomping up the stairs, and my heart sank, sensing Geoff was about to knock at the door before he did. Suddenly I was caught between telling him I was busy and alerting Esther to an odd domestic situation.

'Bri? Are you alright?' Geoff asked, and he tapped again. 'I'm fucking soaked, mate!'

I cupped the speaker. 'Okay, mate.'

'Who's that?' Esther asked.

'Um.' I trailed off. 'Just a housemate….'

Geoff barrelled inside just as I hoped he wouldn't. His thinning pate was dripping wet from his travels, and he stopped in his tracks, perhaps jolted by my shirtless self enjoying a phone call in bed.

'Is that your mum again?' he asked.

'No.' I pointed at the phone, expecting him to get the hint and leave.

'Ooh.' He nodded and winked like we were on the same page. 'Enjoying a bit of phone sex, are we?'

NINETEEN

I drew the long curtains at the living room window as the lightbulb fizzed and blinked intermittently inside the floral ceiling shade. Geoff was DJ-ing at a school disco with Jack, and I returned to the grey fabric armchair we found on eBay a week earlier.

'I can't stop winking,' I said, my laptop propped on my legs.

A mischievous grin grew on Mum's face. 'You did say *winking*, Bab?'

'Jesus. Yes, Mum.'

Mum's lips burst, a full cackle as she tapped her cigarette at an ashtray. 'Well, who are you winking at?'

'I don't know, customers at the café mostly.'

Mum's giggling rose to a peak. 'Oh, well, be careful – you'll get fired for that!'

I laughed, too. Hers was infectious. 'I genuinely think this is the worst conversation I've had. Already.'

Mum pinched her eyes with a thumb and finger. 'Sorry, love. I must be in a funny mood.' She took a deep breath, and her chuckling sputtered to a stop. 'Now, then. What's happening with getting your own space?'

'I don't know. I need to look.'

'Well, it'll be good if you can.' Mum stubbed out her fag and sat back. It was serene where she was, with a gentle sea hushing out of sight. 'Because I don't think you've stood on your two feet, have you?'

'Alright.'

'I'm serious.' She wagged a finger. 'Now, don't take this the wrong way.'

'Go on....'

'Esther was the more forceful one in your relationship. You were very laid back.'

'Maybe…I see where this is going.'

'Well, that's normal for most relationships, Bab. There's one organiser. If there's two, you don't get along so well.' Bill's hand placed a red mug on the bistro table in front of Mum, and she squeezed it before it disappeared. 'So, you need to be less passive now, Brian. Now it's just you.'

'Right.'

'Because it'll be good for you to manage your lifestyle. You know, budget, take care of the bills. Do all the boring stuff. That's just growing up.'

I pinched my lip. 'Yes.'

'Right, well, it's late. I should go to bed.'

'Okay, love. Love you, Brian. Love you, my boy.'

'Love you, Mum.'

Only a smattering of die-hards had made it to The Watercress in the morning as I leaned onto the counter with no customers to serve. The late autumnal rain drummed on the windows, interrupting my thoughts – reminding me where I was.

Anna popped in from the kitchen and stared glum-faced into the room. 'There's nobody here, Brian.'

'No.'

She gripped her sides and stretched her back. 'Oh,' she said, wide-eyed and recalling. 'Are you still unhappy about your living circumstances?'

'Possibly…'

Anna said the owner of the cat she was feeding had decided to extend her travels into India and was looking to rent the place out. She had emailed Anna to ask if she knew someone.

'We could go after work,' she suggested. 'I'm going there anyway. The cat is massive.'

The offer was far too convenient to decline outright and likely too good to be affordable.

Anna stretched from side to side as I slipped away to tidy vacant tables. And I hoped for better distractions as the rain came again, preferably the woman with the array of head scarves I now knew as Pip. I had managed to ask her name during our routine after Bounce and Rhyme, where she would wander over as Mae hit the strings on my guitar. It was common for her to come in at least twice per week and always on Tuesdays, which is what day it was.

There was a flash of bright green from behind the heavy door, and suddenly, Pip was pushing Mae's bright buggy inside. I wandered from behind the counter to help and greeted the three of them there as they dried their feet on the mat and hung wet raincoats on the rack.

Pip's mother, Winnie, journeyed over to the counter after they settled into their usual spot by the window in the corner. She ordered their regular breakfast of chia seed puddings, tea, and some oatmeal pancakes for Mae. I had learned it all by memory, and she never deviated.

'Phillipa doesn't know anyone in Totnes,' Winnie said suddenly. We were off-script now as I poured boiling water into two small metal teapots.

'Oh, right,' I said. 'Has she been here long?'

'Not long. She's staying with me and her father. She's lonely, I think.'

'Has she tried speaking to the other parents?'

Winnie chuckled and shuffled across to meet me at the low counter. 'Mae is her brother's daughter. Her niece.'

'Oh, okay.'

She turned to look at her daughter. Pip shielded her face as if she knew what was happening and was mortified. 'I said I would ask you because you often talk to her.'

'Okay.' I scratched at my face, unsure what the question was precisely. 'Do you want me to ask Pip if she wants to be friends?'

Winnie nodded. 'Phillipa, yes. Not Pip.'

It was an odd conversation to have had with the mother of a grown woman, but Winnie gave me a crumbly smile before she headed to the corner with the tray in hand. She was satisfied with its conclusion, so perhaps I had to fulfil my end of the bargain now I had agreed to it.

Tim had earlier mentioned a band playing at the Lighthouse Ballroom that coming Friday, a group of local musicians everyone seemed to know and love. He had tickets but couldn't go, and after discovering they were still available, I decided I would ask Pip if she wanted to go. She could have politely declined the offer if she wished to, or impolitely, it didn't matter. I had held up my end of the bargain.

The café busied a little as we headed towards lunchtime, and the rain sputtered to a sprinkle. I was cleaning a nearby table when Mae skipped towards the door in her red wellies, holding her grandmother's hand. Pip gripped the folded buggy behind them as Anna took an order at the counter.

I seized my chance, sliding over to hold the heavy door which genuinely wanted to kill people.

Pip turned after following the others outside. 'What was Mum saying to you earlier?

'Um. We were just chatting.' I smiled as Winnie ushered Mae away from the scene so her grandaughter could jump into the puddles on the high street. 'I think she wants you to make friends.'

'Oh, my God.' Pip laughed, a shushing noise, like a jolly librarian. 'She's such a maverick.'

'Yeah.' She shaped to leave as I blurted out my cobbled plan. 'There's a band playing just up the road on Saturday. I don't know if they're any good.'

'Okay.' She folded her hands into the pockets of a long raincoat. 'That sounds fun.'

'Cool.' I was so surprised she hadn't dismissed the idea, I didn't know what to say next. 'That's good, then.'

'Yeah. We should go then if you want.'

'Definitely.'

We exchanged numbers in the doorway before Pip rushed to catch up with the other two, who hadn't quite made it out of earshot. She locked her arm inside her mother's as Mae jumped into a massive puddle with both feet.

'Oi, Mr Flirty, get back to work,' yelled Anna from behind the counter.

'Sorry.' I closed the door softly and continued my tidying from before.

Anna had an amused grin on her face. 'Did you just score a date?'

'No.' A smile of my own creeped out. 'Not a date.'

'It bloody seemed like it,' she laughed. 'I was spying on you.'

'We're just going to see that band Tim was talking about.'

Anna laughed. 'Oh! Well, that's a date!'

'No. Her mum asked me to. It's a friend thing.'

Anna held a hand at her mouth. 'Oh my God, that's so sweet! Really?'

'Yeah.' I shrugged as I stacked plates and cups into a neat pile.

'That would be an incredible story to tell your kids one day.'

Suddenly Tim poked his wavy head through the kitchen door. 'What's going on?'

'Brian just scored a date, Tim,' Anna said.

I was in trouble now. Tim had only stopped calling me 'Marmalade Man' because I spread some on my toast my first morning there. 'Not with one of our customers, surely,' he groaned. 'I told him not to mix business with pleasure.'

'Good point,' Anna said, performatively rolling her eyes. 'And our customers won't return here once he's broken their hearts. He's going to bankrupt us.'

'It's not a date, Tim,' I insisted. 'As I told your lovely wife.'

Anna gasped. 'Oh, he's calling me lovely now! Did you hear that, Tim? He's trying it on with everyone.'

'She's a pregnant woman, Brian! Leave her alone,' Tim deadpanned. 'That sort of stress could bring on an early labour.'

After prepping for the following morning, I walked with Anna along the dark, bumpy walled lane behind the high street to see the flat she had been talking about. And when we reached the converted old grey schoolhouse at its end, I popped my bike into its tiny courtyard and followed her inside.

The property was on the ground floor, and we entered via a door to the kitchen. Two tall arched windows stretched over two floors across the room, looming above a jumble of mismatched wooden furniture, with Inca patterned throws and erotic pencilled artworks on the wall.

'It smells of joss sticks,' Anna said, heading for a wonky corner staircase, giving off amateur carpentry vibes. 'Come up here.'

'Wow, there's an upstairs?'

'Yeah. Sort of.'

Perhaps I had already moved in as I followed Anna up the disconcertingly frail steps. A nest of a bed was up on the next floor, taking up much of the mezzanine. And there was a sleepy fat black and white cat lying on top, showing her ample belly.

'Don't be fooled,' Anna said as I perched on the mattress. 'That cat hates people.'

'I'm good with cats,' I assured her. But sure enough, the creature named Pumpkin hissed and swiped at me after I brushed her head with my fingers.

'Told you!' Anna laughed. She rested her arms on the wonky wooden railing facing the tips of the tall windows. 'It's quite cute, isn't it?'

I joined her there and wobbled the chunky balusters in the wooden barrier. The entire length of the barrier was unsafe. 'How much does she want?' I asked.

'Well, not much, I don't think.' Anna smiled and pinched her ear-stretchers. 'It's crass to talk about money, Brian.'

'Only if you don't need to.'

'I suppose.'

'There's a big picture of a vagina on the wall downstairs.'

'Yeah. I'm looking at it.'

A pang of guilt buzzed when I cycled back to Geoff's after, deciding to be up-front and let him know I needed my space. He was at the computer as I walked inside after hanging my helmet in the porch – his half-rimmed reading glasses perched on the end of his nose, like Homer Simpson.

'Hey, Bri,' he chirped as if my return was a pleasant surprise. 'Working on the old bookings spreadsheet.'

'Hey, mate.' I pretended to look at the screen and nodded approvingly. 'Could I have a word about something? When you've got a sec.'

'Sure.' With Bryony watching children's television in the new armchair, he gestured towards the kitchen with his thumb. 'Let's go somewhere a bit quieter.'

Geoff closed the knotty pine door behind us and folded his arms where the black marble worktops met. Helen was supposed to be coming over but had a headache. It was a shame, we agreed. 'Anyway, what's up?' he asked.

I hesitated, not wanting to compound any disappointment. 'Well, I'm thinking of getting some space of my own.'

'Oh.' A tongue lolled around Geoff's mouth. 'I thought it might be that.'

'It's just a bit tight in that room with all my stuff.'

'Yep.'

'And there's a place I could have, just in town. The owner has gone to India on some yoga retreat thing for a while. So I'd look after her cat there.'

Geoff folded his arms. 'Okay. Okay.'

'And there's a lot of her artwork on the walls, self-portraits where you can see everything.' I forced a chuckle to try and get him onside. 'Everything.'

'Hmm.' Geoff sighed through his nose. 'Sounds a bit fruity.'

'It's a bit eccentric.'

'Disgusting, actually.' He sighed like the world was against him, his eyes on the floor. 'If that's all it is, Bri, I need to get back to it. As you could see when you strolled in, I'm trying to make ends meet.'

'Right. Yeah.'

He brushed past and swung the kitchen door open. 'Some of us have normal lives with responsibilities.'

A tense atmosphere lingered at Geoff's house over the coming days, and I spent the downtime inside my room between shifts at The Watercress and cycling to and from guitar lessons. But then Friday arrived, and suddenly I was pushing my hair around in front of the bathroom cabinet mirror and fretting about my outfit choice and the grey buttoned cardigan and plaid shirt I'd thrown together. I had only two looks left, 'office intern' and 'mature art student', and landed on some concoction of the two.

Geoff was lingering by the kitchen as I reached the bottom of the stairs. 'Hey, mate.'

'Hey, mate.'

'You off out, then?'

'Yeah.' Bryony suddenly clung to my leg from nowhere, as she liked to. She laughed, almost out of control, as I plodded around the living room, and she held on for dear life.

'I bought home some Ice Cream Mars Bars from work,' Geoff said as I tickled Bryony from my limb. It was a very Geoff-style peace offering.

'Oh, nice.'

'I'll hide you one with the fish fingers,' he said. 'Otherwise, Jack and Bryony will nick them all.'

I nodded. 'Good idea.'

An enormous fart rang out from the tan sofa where Jack was engrossed in his handheld console. Bryony laughed, her head tilting back. 'Jack!' she yelled. 'Fart boy.'

'Where are you off, then?' Geoff asked as I drifted towards the porch door. 'You look smart in your cardigan. Off to a book club?'

I laughed politely. 'I'm off for a date, thing.' It was strange to say that out loud, like it was happening. 'Not an actual date. Just going to see a band with someone.'

'Wow, well, that's a turn-up for the books.'

'Maybe.'

Bryony clung to Geoff's leg now, and he dutifully stamped around the room to see if he could shake her loose. 'You should have said about that band,' he said, reaching down to tickle his daughter. 'I'd have come along.'

'Well, it looks like you've got your hands full.'

'That's true.'

I seized my chance and pulled the porch door open. 'See you later, then.'

'Good luck, Bri.'

'Cheers. Bye Bryony, bye Jack.'

Pip had suggested meeting for food before the gig and had booked us a table at a wine bar called The Panda. It had always looked cosy and slightly too upmarket whenever I had travelled past on my commutes, with its navy blue façade and fancy awning.

I was early after a long, chilly walk conducted at a nervous pace. After peeking through a lattice window, I ordered a bottled beer at the bar and placed myself on a stool there. With distractions needed, I delved into my phone to attend to the lesson-related admin in my emails. Chasing up payments had quickly become its most tedious drawback.

Suddenly, there was a tap on my shoulder. Pip had arrived, and we enjoyed that I hadn't noticed immediately. She unzipped a hiking jacket, and we discussed how cold it was.

'You look great,' I said, standing to greet her. We hugged briefly, and it was odd to do that – strange to acknowledge whatever this was.

'I wasn't sure what to wear,' she replied and tugged at a pale blue overshirt matching the colour in her headscarf. 'I haven't been out in ages.'

'Me either.'

Pip ordered a glass of wine, and we were shown downstairs to a basement restaurant with a low arched bricked ceiling and lit candles on tables. Ours was next to a fireplace filled with wedged timber. We laughed together after taking our seats, preferring the breezier atmosphere upstairs.

'How old are you?' Pip asked. She looked up from the menu and then shush-laughed at her directness. 'Sorry. I've been trying to work it out.'

'Thirty…' I frowned. It was a huge number to say out loud.

'Oh. I'm thirty next year.' Pip pouted. 'How do you feel?'

'Old.'

Pip was a secret talker; I liked that about her – it took the pressure off. We talked about my recent habit of winking at people, and she said she'd noticed that I had flashed an eyelid at the young waiter before he left. We joked around and exchanged ideas on how I might ween myself from my new quirk.

We ordered food when the waiter returned, and Pip watched intently to see if I winked as I handed my menu back.

'Have you always lived in Totnes?' she asked, still laughing.

'No. I moved from London earlier in the year.'

'Okay, I don't have to be too careful then.' Pip said her parents had recently retired to Totnes to be nearer her older brother, Michael and their granddaughter, Mae. It was a big move from their Kent village with her dad Lin unwell. 'It doesn't feel like a real place sometimes. It's a bit mad, but I think I love it.'

'Yes. You get used to it.'

'And I see the flyers in your café, all the stuff happening. It's so vibrant for a small town. It's nice.'

'Yeah, I probably haven't made the most of that.' I polished off my beer. 'Do you mind me asking why you're staying with your parents?'

'Not really.' Pip said she was taking a break from her university job in Cardiff. Pressures at work and a relationship breaking down had added to the stress. 'And my hair started to fall out too, which was another thing to worry about.'

'Shit. I'm sorry.'

'It's fine.' She micro-adjusted the bow at the front of her head scarf. 'I can tie these properly, thanks to videos online. I've spent so many evenings watching them. Make-up, too, I was never into it much before, and now I love it. I'm getting good at realistic eyebrows.'

'They look great.'

'Thanks.' She laughed. 'Yours need a bit of a trim.'

I shielded my forehead. 'Shit.'

Our food arrived, and we complimented each other's choices. I prodded the long leafy vegetable that accompanied my ravioli, a panicked last-second order. I had no idea what it was, I admitted, but Pip seemed to think it was a type of kale.

'You look like you should be wearing a headscarf,' I told her, returning to the subject from before. I prodded at my food in a quiet panic, unsure if I had complimented or assessed unnecessarily. 'They suit you. Is it weird to say that?'

'I guess not.' She smiled and collected salad on a fork. 'I'm still getting used to them. The only downside, bar the obvious, is people who think I'm having cancer treatment. Or that it's religious garb. I get so many frowny *poor you* faces and sceptical sideways glances.'

'Oh, dear.'

'Brian!' a familiar nearby voice called. Suddenly, Beatty's sister Charlotte was beside our table, her arms outstretched. I reached up to accept an unexpectedly friendly embrace. 'Beatty said you were still in Totnes. How lovely!'

'Yes, I am.' I wasn't sure what to say other than give a clumsy introduction to Pip.

'We're over in the corner,' Charlotte said. She pointed at a long table at the far end of the room, where Tito was leaning out of his chair, sporting a sizeable salt-and-pepper beard. Other familiar faces were there too, from the various comings and goings at Tam's house over the summer. 'Come and sit with us! There's space.'

I was about to politely dismiss the offer when Pip enthusiastically accepted on our behalf. Before I knew where I was, Charlotte had flagged down the passing waiter, and the wheels were in motion.

Despite my misgivings, the impromptu reunion with the garden gang was surprisingly lovely in how the others took to Pip after we squeezed in at the table's end on opposite sides. It was freeing to be around outwardly friendly people again, perhaps a relief for it to have reduced the intensity of socialising one-on-one.

Charlotte crept around the table when Tito departed for a toilet break long after we had locked ourselves in for dessert and more alcohol. She slunk down at our end, eyes glazed, gripping the table for balance.

'It's Titi's birthday soon,' she whispered and fished strands of hair from her mouth. 'He's going to be forty, the old beggar. We're having a party in a friend's barn. They rent it out for weddings and all sorts. We're so lucky to have it.'

Pip smiled. 'That sounds lovely,'

'Will you guys come?' she asked, eyes wide and sincere. 'I just want to fill the place out and do it justice.'

'Sounds amazing,' Pip said. 'We'll go, won't we?'

I shrugged ever so slightly as our eyes met. 'Yes. Sounds good.'

Charlotte squeezed Pip's hand. 'Amazing! It's going to be so good.' She held her mobile to eye level and frowned at the device like it no longer made sense. 'What's your number? I'll send you the details and add you to the WhatsApp group.'

Tito rubbed his wife's shoulders when he returned from his break. He clicked his fingers and pointed in my direction. 'I know you!' he bellowed as if we hadn't spent the previous hour in each other's company.

'Yes, Titi,' Charlotte laughed. She stood up, her message vibrating in my pocket. 'It's Brian. You're so observant!'

Tito looked at Pip and then back at me. 'Is this your girlfriend?'

'No,' I replied, smiling politely. 'This is my friend, Pip.'

'Not yet.' He belly laughed, his bulbous cheeks exploding. 'We'll see.'

Charlotte tapped Tito's arm. 'Stop it! He's so embarrassing.'

Tito shook Pip's hand. 'You need to watch him. I know about him!'

A frost twinkled on the pavement outside where our group said fond goodbyes underneath the awning before filing off in separate directions in twos and threes, up and down the slope of the high street. I stretched and yawned as we pondered whether to catch the remainder of the gig up the road. The long days were catching up, and I admitted that to Pip. She suggested I walk her home instead, and it seemed like an excellent compromise.

A penetrating wind bit between my ribs as we walked by the white terraced cottages at the tip of Castle Street. 'You must be freezing,' Pip said, balled up inside her sensible puffer coat.

I gripped the arms of my cardigan. 'I'll warm up in a bit.'

'You know you winked at your friends when they left.'

'Yeah.' I groaned. 'I was hoping you hadn't noticed, to be honest.'

We wandered underneath the arched North Gate overpass and towards the tall Victorian chimney looming by the train station where Pip's parents lived nearby. We talked about small things underneath the street lights along the way – Mae, primarily, the funny things she did and how much being around her was cheering Pip up.

We paused on a grass verge as we reached a piggledy cul-de-sac with every type of house. 'This is me,' Pip said. She pointed at a square bungalow where two stone cats sat on either side of its driveway on concrete plinths.

'Cool.'

'I had a nice time, thank you.' Pip yawned and stretched. 'I've caught your tiredness.'

'Sorry.'

'That's okay.' She gave me a sleepy smile. 'Your friends seem so lovely.'

'They're not really my friends,' I admitted. 'Just people I've bumped into a few times. It's that sort of town, I think.'

'Oh! Well, they were nice anyway.'

'Yes.'

We bungled goodbyes, touching shoulders and glancing hands before Pip turned to walk between the stone cats. She paused underneath a cheerful canopy porch above the front door, her hand poised with a key. 'Why do I need to watch you, then?' she asked, smiling.

I shrugged. 'No idea. I think that guy enjoys a bit of mischief.'

'Yeah…' Pip closed one eye, playfully suspicious. 'See you, then.'

I waved. 'Bye.' And I didn't wink.

TWENTY

Mum's happy round face appeared on my phone screen after I prodded it to accept her video call request. I was standing on the creaky staircase in my new rented flat, half-expecting it to buckle, when she waved from her usual balcony spot.

'Well, are you going to give me this tour?' she asked.

'Sure,' I replied.

'You look exhausted, Bab.'

I rubbed at my face. 'Yeah, I cycled miles to and from a lesson last night. It's getting a bit much.'

'Oh, dear. And it's stressful moving.'

'Yeah. It is.' I flipped the camera around to pan the space downstairs, the narrow living area and the tiny kitchen underneath the mezzanine. 'Here it is.'

'Ooh.' Mum hushed approvingly. 'It's very bohemian.'

'Yes.'

'What are those pictures on the wall?' She laughed. 'I saw some boobs.'

'Oh, yeah. The owner is an artist. I think.'

'Ooh, lovely....where's your bed?'

I backed up the stairs and pointed my phone at the bed there. 'There it is.'

'Oh, you've got a little upstairs. That's very cosy. And a lovely fat cat.'

'She's not that lovely when you get close. I keep making that error.'

Mum laughed. 'And you couldn't buy anywhere, love?'

I sniggered. 'No. Surprisingly, my budget didn't stretch that far.'

'Well, you've got everything you need. Well done, Brian.'

'It'll do me for a while. Until you know…' I tailed off and prodded at the wobbly balcony, pondering how to fix it.

'Anna said it might get chilly at night with the big windows. They're original, single-glazed. And there's an old heating system which charges at night or something.'

'Oh, okay.' Mum was drawing on a cigarette as I flipped the screen back. 'Just put on an extra jumper or a pair of socks. Like we used to.'

'Right, yeah. Great days.'

Mum tutted. 'But I bet it's lovely to have your own space.'

'Yeah, it will be when I've tidied.' The front door clicked open from downstairs. 'Right, I better go, Mum. Still lots to do.'

'Okay. Tara-a-bit then. Well done, love. Love you.'

'I love you too.'

Geoff plonked a wrapped package onto the chunky dining table, which separated the kitchen and living area. 'Come on, Jack,' he said as his nephew shuffled inside with his favourite grey PlayStation cap on and a tuft of hair poking through the loop.

'Hi, guys,' I said, walking down the steps.

'Hi, Bri.' Geoff nodded at the table as I slalomed the piles of my things on the floor. 'We've got you something. They wrapped it in the shop, didn't they, Jack?'

'Yep,' Jack confirmed. 'They did.'

'Oh wow.' I pulled the tape along the folds. There was a plain, unwrapped box underneath.

'It's a vase inside,' Geoff confirmed. 'You could probably use it as a milk jug. I don't know.'

'Oh, well, thanks, mate.' I removed the bubble wrap from the cream ceramic and placed the jug on the table. 'Thanks, Jack. And both of you for your help.'

Geoff's brief smile evaporated. He had been frantic all morning, simultaneously gloomy and yet overtly helpful. 'It's a bit of a hippy crib this, Bri,' he said. He pointed at the nude portrait on the back wall above the small sofa with its Inca-patterned throw. 'You get a lot of that shit in this part of town. I would have warned you if you said you were looking this way.'

I shrugged. 'I'm sure it'll be okay.'

'It's just a bit much that, the legs open and seeing it all.' He tutted. 'Tits are out over there, too. I couldn't bring Bryony here.'

'No,' I agreed. 'Maybe I'd turn that one around beforehand.'

'Hmm. And the others.'

A chafing silence fell as we peered around the room, our feet planted on each side of the table. Jack then broke the tension with an angry fart – a loud *BRRRAAAPP* which echoed with the high ceiling.

'Right.' Geoff's cheeks puffed, his focus seemingly re-centred by the noise. 'Let's get you to your mum's, Jack. I need to get ready for work.'

We drifted towards the pale blue front door in the kitchen, which Jack opened and then disappeared into the communal walkway.

'Is he okay?' I asked as Geoff stepped outside. 'He's been farting a lot this morning.'

Geoff tutted. 'Well, he's a big lad, and he gets nervous. What do you expect?'

'Right. Fair enough.'

'And he's mopey.' He knelt to pet the barrel-shaped cat rolling at my feet before she hissed at swiped at him – a classic move of hers. 'My brother's appeal was turned down. Jack was hoping he would be out for Christmas.'

'That's not good. Poor Jack.'

Geoff sighed and rose to his feet again. 'He's gone in on himself, won't even get his hair cut.'

'Maybe he's growing a mullet.'

'Maybe.' Geoff's eyes brightened, remembering something. 'Oh. I've dug out my fishing rods from the shed. We could go soon if you're still up for it.'

‘Definitely.’ I nodded several times so he was sure. ‘Yeah, that sounds good.’

‘Okay.’ He half-turned to walk off. ‘It’ll be quiet in the house, now.’

‘I’m sure it won’t be that quiet with Jack there. And Bryony when she’s over.’

‘Hmm. Guess not.’ He smiled weakly. ‘I’m off, then. Have fun.’

It was strange to be alone when the door clicked shut, with no surge of relief at the freedom my new home promised – an odd deflation instead. Perhaps it was the guilt gnawing from Geoff’s departure, the unbroken worry on his face. Perhaps I hadn’t done enough to reassure him this wasn’t an abandonment. Perhaps a selfish part of me hadn’t wanted to.

I perched on the sofa, the first time I had sat down all morning, pondering what to put where. My phone buzzed in my pocket. It was Pip.

So are you all moved in? xx

Yes! Lots to sort xx

I’m excited to see it! xx

You should come over!

Pumpkin bumped at my legs again. I headed into the kitchen, pulled a square tin of her food from the enormous stack in the low kitchen cupboard, and minced it into her bowl as Anna had shown me.

After a long sorting and tidying session, I yanked my bike from its spot against the wall between the tall windows and wheeled it towards the front door. It was freezing as I rode out along the shadowed, uneven lanes with the guitar on my back and an icy wind stinging my bare hands. Perhaps the exertion of it all was taking its toll as I free-wheeled across the bridge towards the pink buildings, and the warmth of Beatty’s house beckoned.

I rattled the knocker at the yellow door, my wrists numbed and locked. Beatty's hair was tied up when she pulled it open, the ghost of laughter on her lips.

'Brian!' She slapped a hand on her cheek, surprised to see me there. 'Oh my God, is it time again?'

'Afraid so.'

'Um.' Beatty looked over her shoulder and back at me again. 'I keep losing track of all these things. Come in, come in.' I stepped inside, and she called for Noah as I blew into my closed hands to warm them.

'I'm in the toilet!' he called in return.

Beatty laughed. 'He'll be here when he's finished, then.'

'Yeah.'

'I'll quickly set up the room.' Beatty shuffled down the narrow hallway and disappeared through the door at its end.

A toilet flushed upstairs after a short wait, and Noah came bounding down the stairs. He slapped my outstretched hand as we greeted. 'Don't worry, I've washed my hands,' he said before speeding down the hall.

I followed on into the toasty snug where Beatty was sat cross-legged on the mustard-coloured sofa facing into the room, and a sizeable unknown man poked at a wood burner with a thin log. His presence was so unanticipated it halted me in the walkway between spaces.

'This is Noah's guitar tutor, Brian,' Beatty said with a flustered chuckle. 'I'm an idiot and forgot he was coming over.'

'Hey, dude. I'm Andy,' the man said, raising a giant paw. It was the deepest sound, like a talking double bass. 'How's it going?'

'Good,' I replied, hands in my pockets. 'Yeah, really good.'

It was difficult to look at Andy and his rugged handsomeness – how emasculating, it was to do that. And how broad his shoulders were – like sails. And how a receding hairline somehow worked in his favour. And how all of that and a Celtic accent had women running to their doors looking their best.

'Andy's just got back from Scotland,' Beatty said.

I nodded. 'Oh, cool.'

'Yeah.' She sipped from a coffee mug with both hands. 'And he's already telling me how environmentally unfriendly my wood burner is.'

'Yeah, these are awful,' Andy said, shaking his head. 'I'll help you rip it out.'

'As long as you're paying!' Beatty scoffed.

He laughed. 'Maybe I will. Do you want to help me, Brian?'

I smiled, unable to think of anything worse. 'Not sure I'd be much help.' It was enough chafing small talk to join Noah in the dining room next door, where he was dutifully tuning his guitar. I pushed the handle down when Beatty clicked her fingers.

'Oh, Brian! One of the music tutors who does private guitar lessons at the school is retiring soon. He's getting old, and he's been unwell.'

'Right, okay,' I replied, not absorbing her news. 'That's useful to know.'

'I thought it might be.'

'Right.' My hand pushed at the handle. 'Better get on, then.'

'Hold on!' Noah called. He asked me to wait outside to prove he could tune his instrument without help. 'Almost there.'

'He's so bossy!' Beatty laughed.

'Yeah.' I chuckled along, unsure where to look – directly at Andy, apparently. 'So, did you have a good time in Scotland?'

'Not that great, really.' He frowned. 'I was home looking after my mum until she passed. She's had cancer.'

'Oh. Shit.' I unhooked my guitar case and held it in my grip. 'That's not good. Sorry, man.'

'Nah. You're alright.' Andy prodded at the fire again. 'It's nice to be back, at least. And to see my boat again.'

I nodded. A fucking boat. 'That's good. To see your boat.'

'Yeah.' Andy smiled, an amusing thought popping into his brain. 'I thought you had come to serenade us just now.'

'No, no.' I chuckled politely as my eyes caught Beatty's. There was a flickered shared acknowledgement of something – perhaps how weird this was. 'Just giving a lesson to Noah.'

'Brian used to be in a big indie band,' Beatty said.

'Oh, wow.' Andy sat up on his knees. 'That's impressive.'

'Well, we weren't big,' I insisted.

'What were they called?' Andy asked. 'I'm a bit of a muso myself.'

'Dorothea.' I smiled, expecting nothing. 'We were going to support The Arctic Monkeys on their US Tour before we split up. Apparently. A long time ago, now.'

'Oh.' He stroked his dark bristly stubble as he thought. 'No. Sorry, mate.'

'That's okay.' Twangs from Noah's guitar were still pinging next door, taunting me now. 'Sounds a bit crap, as claims to fame go.'

'Sounds like you made it up.' Andy laughed a bit too much. 'Actually, a friend of mine knows a guy who used to be in Ben Howard's touring band.'

I nodded. 'Oh, cool.'

'He's from Totnes.'

'Right.'

Andy looked at Beatty and shook his head disbelievingly. 'Noah's grown so much.'

'Oh, I know.' Beatty's eyes popped. 'I swear he's an inch taller each time I look at him.'

'Brian, come in!' Noah yelled, finally. 'I've finished.'

Beatty chuckled at her son's youthful straightforwardness. 'Non!'

'You better do as he said,' laughed Andy, turning to me again.

'Yeah.' I smiled thinly, and Big Andy could fuck off for ordering me around.

Noah was strumming the F chord he had been practising when I shut the door and fenced us off. 'Look.'

'That's good, mate.' I slipped onto the vacant dining chair opposite and pulled lesson worksheets from the pocket of my guitar case. 'Excellent.'

'I keep trying to play it without looking.' He smiled with missing front teeth. 'But my fingers are in the wrong place when I check.'

'Well, it's good to keep trying,' I told him, shuffling the sheets into the correct order. 'You'll be able to do it without thinking soon.'

My concentration cracked as the lesson began, and howls of laughter rained from the snug – an echoing glee pounding from behind the door. Perhaps I was jealous, and it was enough to throw me into an hour of messy, contradictory instructions, with Noah's toothy smile fading.

The joy from next door quietened when I was packed and ready to leave quickly. 'All done, then,' I called before reopening the door. It was a warning shot, really.

Beatty smiled, hugging her knees from the same spot. 'Oh, good. Thank you, Brian,'

'See ya later, mate!' Andy said, still prodding the fire.

Noah sped past as I winked at Andy because, of course I did. I headed into the hallway cursing myself, and Beatty followed, closing the snug door behind her.

'How was it?' she asked, perhaps inquiring about something other than the lesson.

'Yeah, fine.' I slipped the guitar case straps over my shoulders. 'A Minor and E today. He's linking them with a new fingerpicking technique. He needs to work on that this week if he can.'

'That's good, then.' She tapped at her chin, ready to say something else without doing that.

'Everything okay?'

She shook her head like she had been in a trance. 'My mum isn't well.'

'Oh.'

'It's nothing bad,' Beatty said, clarifying that it was just a migraine. But her mother was supposed to babysit while Beatty and Andy headed to Charlotte's for dinner. 'It wouldn't be appropriate to ask you, would it?' She pinched her bottom lip, pulling it as far it would go. 'It's only because he likes you. You know, and you're here.'

I smirked because it was ridiculous, and Beatty laughed, presumably for the same reason. 'Um. I probably could do.' Perhaps I said that because I liked her. Or perhaps because I didn't know how I felt about anyone or anything.

'Really?' Beatty's expression oscillated between joy and hesitancy. 'Are you sure?'

'Yes.' I nodded, completely unsure. 'I don't mind.'

With the reality of our impromptu childcare agreement sinking in, Beatty launched into a long list of instructions. Noah needed a bath but could have one in the morning if he protested too much. He still needed to wash properly and understood what that meant. Then he could get into his pyjamas and play for a while. She speculated that he would probably entertain himself upstairs and wouldn't bother me much. But she would appreciate it if I could check that he had brushed his teeth before bed. It was an ongoing battle.

Perhaps I was dazed as Beatty and Andy headed into the frigid night air in their heavy winter coats. Suddenly I was alone with a child I was responsible for and had no real frame of reference to lean on. And teeth, he had to brush his teeth.

After heading into the massive kitchen, I made coffee in Beatty's fancy machine before returning to the snug, sitting where she had been. And with Noah presumably happy upstairs, there was only the tick-tocking of a grandfather clock in the corner for company.

I pulled my phone out and messaged Pip.

Hey. What are you up to? xx

Just cooking with Mum. How about you? xx

Babysitting apparently xx

What!? Who are you babysitting? xx

One of my students xx

What? Is that an extra service you provide? xx

Haha. Not normally xx

Oh! Have you messaged the parents about your plans yet? Xx

Not yet! I will do xx

Inquisitive footsteps cascaded down the stairs out of sight, and tiptoed along the hallway. Suddenly Noah was bounding inside the room in his grey rocket-themed pyjamas. 'I've washed already,' he announced.

I gave a thumbs-up. 'Well done, mate.'

He perched on the wide sofa arm adjacent to mine. 'I've got forty-seven dinosaurs now in my collection.'

'That's cool. I didn't know that.'

'Yep.' He stooped up and front-flipped onto the furniture cushions. 'What dinosaurs do you know?'

I flexed the memory banks, closing one eye. 'What about a pterodactyl, the flying dinosaur? Have you heard of that?'

'Er, yes, Brian.' He rolled into a headstand, his legs against the sofa's back. 'I think I learned about pterodactyls when I was three.'

'Wow, three. That's impressive.'

I sipped my coffee and replaced the mug on a side table. Simply saying the names of basic bitch dinosaurs out loud wouldn't cut it with Noah. But as soon I had plucked the word 'Allosaurus' from somewhere, he had pivoted to shouting song titles to see if I knew how to play them on the guitar. Suddenly, I was unzipping the case to counter an accusation I was being untruthful, and that then morphed into an extended two-hour guitar lesson to make up for one earlier.

After asking for the time, Noah announced he should have been in bed an hour earlier when I checked my phone. We downed tools, and he agreed to brush his teeth, but only on the condition I read from his favourite book. It seemed like a fair deal, and I found myself tidying his room as I waited, shifting piles of LEGO from the floor into a large red plastic tub.

After a series of loud spits and spatters from the bathroom, Noah slipped into his bed with a small library built into its base. I perched on its edge and read three chapters from 'The Invention of Hugo Cabret' – two more than initially agreed.

'How's that, then?' I asked. Noah's eyes were heavy this time.

'Good.'

'Great.' As instructed, I replaced the plastic bookmark and popped the paperback next to a Pokemon-themed nightlight, which needed to be left on.

'It's a really good book,' he whispered, rolling away to face the wall.

'Yeah. It is,' I whispered, too. 'Sure, it's not too bright in here for you?'

'Yes.'

'Cool.' I crept towards the door.

'Brian?'

I paused. 'Yes?'

'My dad bought that book for me.'

'Oh.' A lump bulged in my throat. 'You'll have to look after it, then.'

'Yes,' he whispered. 'But you did the voices wrong.'

‘Oh. Sorry, mate.’

‘It’s not your fault. You did your best.’

I retreated down the stairs and slipped back into the snug where the wood burner was still chugging away. After slumping back onto the mustard sofa, I sent emails and texts to the parents of my students to inform them our lessons would take place at my new address from now on. I would turn the risque artworks around before they arrived or carefully hide them upstairs.

I fell into a doze after browsing through my phone. My hands clasped the device at my stomach before it vibrated. Pip, again.

I’m going to Dartmoor tomorrow xx

I sat up and checked the time. It was late, but there was no sign of Beatty.

I thought you always went to bed before midnight xx

Sometimes I can’t sleep in this tiny room. A giant stuffed polar bear stares at me xx

That sounds terrifying xx

It is. So do you want to come with me? xx

Yeah! xx

TWENTY-ONE

I was sitting at the dining table with my lesson spreadsheet on my laptop, having put it together using the skills learned from my time at Fryers'. My phone buzzed again, pulsing against my coffee mug – a video call request from Mum.

'Hi.'

'You're back home, then?' she asked, her hair flapping gently on the balcony.

'Yep. Just trying to organise my bookings.'

'That's good. Were you out with this girl?'

'Pip?' I sipped from my coffee mug. 'Yeah, just for a quick drink.'

Mum smiled as she drew on her cigarette, all mischievous. 'Just a quick drink, was it?'

'Yeah.' I smiled at Mum's smile. 'She's convinced me to send that DNA kit off.'

'Are you, you know, together, Bab?'

'I knew that question was coming.'

She laughed, a trail of smoke blowing from the side of her mouth. 'Well?'

I sighed. 'We are a just man and woman hanging out.'

'Well, I haven't seen any pictures of you together on Facebook. Or do you use something else now? It's just for us oldies, I heard.'

'I don't use social media, Mum.' I quietly flicked the screen back to continue the tweaks I had been making to see if I could multitask. 'It's actually quite freeing not to document everything like that.'

'It's not good for me.' She chuckled. 'I'm nosey.'

'That's true.'

It was quiet for a moment, and when I switched the screen again, Mum's eyes were lost in thought. 'I miss us spending time together. It was nice to be able to just pop on the train to see you and Esther.'

'Yeah. It was.'

She hummed wistfully. 'You were always such a daddy's boy when you were little. I used to worry we wouldn't have that sort of bond.'

'Right.'

'I suppose it was the only good that came from what happened. That we were so close after.'

I nodded. 'Are you alright, Mum?'

'I'm fine.' She laughed nervously. 'I suppose I'm wondering what I'm doing out here.'

'You're enjoying life.' I smiled, trying to reassure her. 'Shall I send you a picture of Pip and me together? Would that cheer you up?'

'Yep.' She nodded and stubbed out her cigarette. 'I think it would.'

'Okay, I'll try. But don't stick it on Facebook or whatever. Pip's on long-term sick.'

Mum sniggered. 'Okay, Bab. I don't think we would have any mutual contacts.'

'Well, you never know.' I closed down the spreadsheet. It was late. 'I better get on before I go to bed. Early start and all that.'

'Okay. Tara-a-bit, love. Send that photo, then. Or a few.'

I laughed. 'Yep, okay. Love you, Mum.'

'Love you too.'

A tiny low-powered sun beamed as a cold breeze bit again. I met Pip in her pink woollen hat on the cobbles at the bottom of Totnes High Street, outside the Royal Seven Stars hotel.

'Did you know this hotel used to be an inn in the seventeenth century?' Pip asked.

'I didn't.' I shrugged. 'Sorry, I wasn't expecting trivia questions.'

'Well, it was.' She flashed a wry, playful smile. 'I'm full of incredible facts.'

'Exciting. Will there be more?'

She laughed. 'Maybe.'

We set off, with Pip wanting to explore the town from the bottom of the high street to the top before we headed to Tito's party later.

'What does Tito like?' Pip asked as she paused to peer inside the crisscross windows of a miniature art gallery.

'Um. Drinking, I think.'

Pip sighed. 'Well, we can't buy him alcohol. That's very low effort, Brian.'

'An original artwork might be slightly high effort, though.'

'Yes. But I'm going to nose anyway.'

Pip knew all about Totnes, how it was a shame the neighbouring Dartington College of Arts had closed. A thriving student population had been part of the town's tapestry since its peak counterculture days, and now its edges had been smoothed over – with boutique shops and fine dining establishments moving in.

We walked underneath the East Gate Arch and its cheerful cream clock and turreted roof window. Pip said it had been rebuilt after burning down in 1990 as we emerged on the narrow pavement beyond.

'It's like being on a guided tour,' I told her.

'Well, I am a historian,' she beamed. 'I love it.'

'Is that what you do in Cardiff? Just realised I've never really asked.'

'Yeah.' Pip peeked inside an interiors shop with neat fish scale tiling above its entrance. 'A bit of lecturing, teaching and other bits. I'm one of those students who never left, I guess.'

I followed Pip as she entered the shop, which was crowded with abstract artworks, nicknacks, and pot plants hanging on ropes. She was sure we would find something inside and immediately pointed at a pair of porcelain lamps. They had been made by a local artist, using local clay according to the notes on a display card, which included a short poem.

'These are so beautiful,' Pip said and pretended to stroke them with a finger.

I checked the price tag and winced. 'Yeah, and three hundred and fifty pounds.'

'Aw, but it's nice to give gifts which show some thought and effort.'

'Um. Maybe.'

We browsed the soft furnishings in a darker back room, where Pip picked up a wide velvet cushion featuring a stork surrounded by pink and green flowers. 'What about this?' She squeezed it to her chest. 'I don't know why. I like it.'

I shrugged. 'Okay. So, that's what we are bringing tonight? A cushion. For Tito.'

'Yes!' Pip shush-laughed. 'I've decided.'

Tito's eccentric gift was too large to fit inside Pip's rucksack, so I carried it under my arm as we continued and stopped to look inside every outlet on both sides of the street. She had an affinity for quirky gift shops, the type of place where logjams formed in tight spaces and strangers panicked at the prospect of touching each other.

After our shopping spree, we retreated to a tiny café on the tip of the high street. We ate quiche and drank green tea at a bar table facing the street. A protest was taking place outside, a long procession of young teens drifting past demanding action on climate change – some were holding banners with signs asking, 'Where's my future gone?'

'My mum loves you,' Pip said suddenly. She rearranged the bags at our feet, filled with nicknacks and Tito's cushion, a child-sized ukulele bought for Mae and a card book about a missing duck. 'Did you know that?'

'Not really.' I smiled at the conversation pivot. 'How come?'

'I don't know, maybe because you're polite to us when we come in.

'That's a low bar for your mum's love. Me just doing my job.'

'I know, but when we head to the café now, she's like, *let's go and see Brian.*' Pip chuckled onto her teacup. She was lovely in profile with her long, thin neck and perfectly square chin. 'She asked if I wanted to go to Michael's today. But I said I was meeting you, and she was so insistent on that instead. She thinks if I make friends here, I won't rush back to work.'

'She's probably enjoying having you around.'

'Yeah….' Pip said her parents had been lonely in the small town where she and her brother grew up. A growing sense of isolation peaked when her father, Lin, was diagnosed with a severe form of dementia, Pick's disease. 'Mum keeps saying he's improving, but he can't. It's impossible.'

'I'm sorry, Pip. That's rubbish.'

'Yeah. It is.' Pip played with a gold bee-shaped earring – her eyes lost to the window. 'I was shocked at how far downhill he had gone before I came here. I hadn't seen him in six months, not face to face, and he literally can't speak now.'

'That must be awful.'

'Yes, and he was such a good talker, always great with advice if needed. And he was good at languages too, being part of an older generation of Singaporeans who could speak four or five. He could just switch in and out whenever he wanted.'

'Wow, that's impressive.'

'Yeah.' She sighed with her shoulders. 'Now he lolls around in his pyjamas, not speaking – just grunting.'

I finished my tea and plonked the cup down. 'What's going to happen?'

'Well, we need to find him a home. If Mum can face up to that reality.'

'Right.'

Pip turned to face the street again as the last banner disappeared from view. 'It's so active here. I love it.'

The wind had picked up when we stepped outside again and decided it was time to head to the flat with our hands full.

'I do like your flat,' Pip said as I closed the front door. She parked her rucksack on the kitchen table and stared at the enormous portrait above the sofa. 'It's so bold, isn't it?'

'It looks quite hairy to me.' I snickered after Pip groaned at my dad joke, the reaction I had hoped for. 'I was thinking of sticking it away because turning it around is a hassle. But it's so big, and I worry about damaging it.'

There was a thud from upstairs, the familiar sound of Pumpkin dropping from the bed on the quest for food. She bumbled down the steps next and nuzzled into Pip's legs.

'Hello gorgeous, Pumpkin,' Pip said as she reached down to pet the cat with her fingers. 'So aptly named.' The pet quickly abandoned her small display of affection and wandered into the kitchenette. 'It's all pretend.'

'Yep!' I wandered over to the cat cupboard as the staircase creaked out of sight. 'Are you walking up my stairs?'

'Yes. Is there anything you don't want me to see?'

'Um. Just how untidy my bed might be….'

'Okay, I won't look too closely.'

After Pip had finished her brief exploration, we retreated to the dining table, where she wrapped Tito's present in tissue paper and ribbon. Superfluous to requirements after a generous offer of help, I reached for the guitar propped against the sofa arm and started noodling there.

'I want to do Dartmoor properly as we're so nearby,' Pip said, smushing the cushion at its sides. 'Did you like our trip there?'

'Yeah. You're an outdoorsy person, right?'

'Sort of.' Pip snipped a length of tape and held it in her mouth momentarily. 'I used to go hiking and climbing with my ex. Wales is amazing for that, so I guess I miss it. It's the fresh air, I think. It's good for thinking.'

'What happened there? Was he a dick?'

'No. Not really. It was a mutual thing.' Pip frowned, a full face-shrug as if she hadn't worked it out. 'We still worked in the same faculty after, so it went from living together to working alongside each other. And then my hair started falling out. It just became an awful, humiliating time.'

'God, I'm sorry, Pip.' I winced. 'I keep saying that. Embarrassing, really.'

'No, no.' She rolled her eyes. 'I've been droning on all day. Just tell me to shut up.'

'Don't be silly.' I smiled gently. 'Why would I do that?'

'I don't know. I message friends and my flatmate a lot, but that's limiting. And I love Mum, but in her mind, there's a quick solution to every problem – a change in diet or rest.'

'Right.'

'Sometimes I just want a long chat, you know.' Pip flattened the tissue paper around the gift to ensure it was tight. 'I told her about your music lessons, and she's started referring to them as Brian's Music School. That's sweet, isn't it?'

'Yep.' I grinned and plucked at the guitar. 'Brian's music school. That sounds incredible.'

'It does!' Pip fastened the ribbon over the wrapped cushion. She held up the wrapped gift, neat as a pin. 'It's lovely to have a skill you can turn to like that. You could take it anywhere.'

'A bit like your present wrapping. That's genuinely amazing.'

She squeezed our gift. 'That's my student years spent working in John Lewis over several Christmases.'

‘I’m genuinely impressed.’

My phone buzzed with a group text from Charlotte advising us to ignore SatNav instructions close to the venue and that plans to release sky lanterns had been cancelled. The note was a helpful prompt to get ready, and we took turns in the small bathroom next to the kitchen. It was surreal we were going at all, having initially expected to let the date slide. But Pip had been excited about socialising again, so that couldn’t happen now – especially when she needed cheering up.

The location wasn’t far, an affordable cab ride to a tiny hamlet in the South Devon hills. Pip read out details from the event’s dedicated website as we made our way along the dark winding lanes, and our driver muttered about the poor state of the road surfaces there. The event was grander in scale than I had imagined as we pulled up inside the grounds of a large gothic Victorian house. Pip gave me a look before we exited the vehicle, eyebrows raised – a shared *what are we doing?*

A posh woman with arm-length gloves called Jennfier introduced herself as the party coordinator. She took our gift and ushered us towards a gate at the side of the building where others were also funnelling. We walked with our group along the path by a paddock until an enormous black structure loomed – nothing like the rustic outbuilding I had pictured from the description.

We were dropped off outside the enormous barn, surrounded by better-dressed guests milling and half-watching a scantily clad performer juggling flaming batons. The building was tropically warm as we drifted inside, past the stage with an assembled drumkit in front of a checkerboard dance floor. Long tables stretched from there to a swanky neon-lit cocktail bar at the other end.

Pip pointed to the brightly coloured lanterns hanging from the wooden rafters above us. 'Wow, someone has made a lot of effort,' she said.

'Yeah, it's wild.'

I chewed my thumbnail, an unease gnawing as we ordered drinks and sat at the back of the room where a magician performed close-up magic. Providing he left us well alone, it was a good spot to re-group and perhaps hide away long enough before slipping away.

Pip slipped an evening bag across her black dress with tiny printed flowers.

'I like your dress,' I said as she planted it on the seat beside her. 'I forgot to tell you earlier.'

'Oh, thanks. I bought this a couple of years ago.' She arranged her skirt over her knees, and the venue swelled with party-goers in ball gowns and tuxedos. 'I'm so underdressed compared to some people.'

'I know what you mean.'

Pip laughed and squeezed my arm. 'You look so tense.'

'Yeah, I'm not sure what we're doing here.' I sipped my green cocktail. 'It's like some high society thing.'

'Just relax.' She leaned her head to mine and took a picture of us, showing it after. 'That's a nice one, isn't it?'

A momentary calm washed over me. 'Can you send me that?'

'Of course.'

I peeked at the photo again when it arrived, as the comparably attired George and Hetty sat opposite. They had recognised Pip from our night together at the Panda Bar, and the three talked about the dress code and whether we had missed something. I popped my phone away and smiled, and nodded along.

Suddenly, Charlotte hurtled over in a flowing pink gown, her arms outstretched. 'Oh my God, you've come, and I'm so happy.'

'We're just re-introducing ourselves,' George said. 'And hanging out.'

'Hanging out. I love it!' Charlotte beamed and thanked us again for coming by squeezing each of us in turn. And when Hetty asked if there was a more formal dress code, she insisted there wasn't – people were free to wear what they liked.

'You've done an amazing job,' Pip said, and we hummed and nodded in agreement.

'Oh, bless you.' Charlotte held a hand to her chest. It was down to her friend Jennifer, really, who had thought of everything. She said a band was playing later and wanted to see us on the dance floor. 'We'll all have a mingle there.'

Charlotte moved off to have a near-identical exchange with a group seated further down. And as Hetty and Pip discovered they had a miracle mutual acquaintance on social media, George re-tied his ponytail – his eyes fixed in my direction.

'You were in a band, yeah?' he asked, leaning across the table.

'That's right.' I polished off my drink. 'A while ago.'

Perhaps sensing my unease, the conversation quickly pivoted to his smallholding, where he made artisan cheese. He said there were plans afoot to distil gin there and convert outbuildings into eco homes. With little to add as the one-sided conversation continued, it was a relief when Beatty and Andy appeared, fresh from the bar.

After hugging her friend Hetty, Beatty smiled in my direction, cheerily bemused by my presence. Andy's giant hand then enveloped mine with a warm shake and said he was glad he wasn't the only one not wearing a suit.

Beatty was amused and annoyed with her sister about the dress code situation and whether there was one. Pip joked that she could sit with us fellow scruffs, and suddenly, I was introducing her as my friend and Beatty to Pip as the mother of one of my students.

It should have been a jarring experience as we settled in together, six of us alongside and across, where we chatted without silences and took turns to the bar for refills. And it was odd later, as Beatty rubbed Andy's back just as he had professed his love of Talking Heads, and we shared a bonding moment. And it was strange how quickly a sharp pang of jealousy gave way to an uncorking relief.

We were interrupted by a sudden pop and hiss of a microphone switching on. Charlotte was standing on the stage and thanking everyone who helped her to organise the event. She beckoned her husband to join her there, and guests whooped and clapped as Tito took the microphone in his white tuxedo, a spotlight shining on him.

'Thanks, guys, thank you,' Tito said, his voice cracking. 'Thank you to my beautiful wife for organising this. Even this morning, it was a surprise to me. I'm forty and still young, so let's party and have a good time.'

We sang 'Happy Birthday' as Jennifer wheeled out an extravagant three-tiered cake, and the mere sight of it was a step too far for Tito. He held a hand over his mouth as Charlotte kissed his head. Pip caught my eye, and we smiled together, disconnected and slightly endeared. What were we doing there?

A besuited party band came onto the stage and launched into a jaunty cover of David Bowie's 'Let's Dance.' Pip lobbied our group to hit the dancefloor, and we were among the first to head there – setting the tone for the unexpected fun which followed. And we stayed until it was late, and it was somehow great and ridiculous, against all odds.

Pip groaned after we climbed into the back of our cab after stumbling our way back to where we had been left. 'I feel drunk.'

'Oh, dear,' I muttered, similarly intoxicated. 'Shall we wind the window down?'

'No…I can handle a good time.'

I smirked. 'Sorry. I just thought you were a massive nerd.'

'No!' Pip playfully swiped at my arm, and the vehicle pulled away onto the tiny black lanes. 'That was an entertaining night. Funny too. God bless wealth.'

'Yeah, it turned out okay.'

'Hetty asked if we were married.' She leaned across and rested her head on my shoulder. 'Shall I be your pretend wife?'

'Sure.'

Pip left her head there as we travelled home on what was now a heady, unfathomable journey. And it was fun to be ambiguous with each other until she suddenly shuffled up in her seat as we headed closer to Totnes.

'Oh,' she said.

'What's up?'

Pip stared at her phone. 'Mum messaged earlier to say she's locked up and gone to bed.'

'Ah, okay. What does that mean?'

'I don't have any house keys with me. I didn't think I'd need them.' Pip tipped her head back and shush-laughed. She said she thought it was hilarious, but her brow furrowed, and I wasn't sure if it was.

'Is it a problem?'

'Yes…' Pip groaned, pushing her thumb and finger against her eyelids. 'I can't get in the house, Brian.'

'Well, stay at mine if you want,' I suggested. 'I'll just sleep on the sofa.'

'Hmm.' Pip gasped a troubled sigh like that wasn't a good option. 'I'm not sure what Mum was thinking. Maybe she thought I had a key.'

'What do you need?'

'I don't have my nightcap,' she said, and her voice wobbled. 'And I can't remove my make-up.'

'Don't take it off then. Is that an option?'

'No, Brian. Stop it!' she tutted. 'My skin can't handle it.'

'Okay. Sorry.'

'Plus, you know, everything else. My toothbrush, clothes. Oh my God. I have such a long bedtime routine.'

I told Pip I had a spare unused toothbrush, having bought a pack the previous weekend. It made her fret less than she had been, but she still debated whether to wake her parents, who would have been asleep for hours based on Winnie's last message. And it would be unseemly to stay at mine, she said, uncomfortable then to explain to her mum where she had been.

We arrived back at the flat when that was the best of two poor options for Pip. But it was freezing when we got inside – the night's chill breathing through the thin glass of the large windows. I prodded at the input and output dials on the old storage heater on the wall beneath as she took a shower in the small bathroom, where she planned to remove her make-up with water and cheap shower gel.

With the old heater lifeless, I ran upstairs and flicked on the portable radiator up there.

'You don't have any hot water,' Pip whispered as she exited the bathroom with one of my old t-shirts on.

'Fuck.'

She shielded her face as we passed each other on the stairs, her white head scarf tied at one side. I ignored an instinct to tell her she didn't need to worry. And it was tough to get that balance right – who was I to say how she should feel? And so, I said nothing and headed to the bathroom to ready myself for bed instead.

Washed and ready for bed, I slipped underneath the patterned sofa throw, which was immediately too thin. And the furniture wasn't wide enough to accommodate my body fully stretched. 'Are you okay up there, Pip?' I asked.

'Yes,' she replied, hushed and sleepy. 'I feel embarrassed now. Sorry.'

'It's okay,' I told her. 'I had a nice night.'

'Me too. The band were so good.'

'Yeah.' I drew my knees in to get warm. 'They were okay.'

'Oh, my God.' Pip tutted, sensing my caution. 'Why only okay?'

'Um.' I snickered at how ridiculous I was about to sound. 'The singer's guitar was out of tune a lot.'

Pip shush-laughed. 'Well, nobody noticed.'

'And the bassist kept dropping notes.' I paused. It was a losing battle – but I went again anyway. 'It's a musician thing, I suppose. You have a sensitivity to these things.'

Pip groaned like I was an idiot. 'Oh, well, poor you! Must be terrible to carry that burden around.'

The sarcasm was stinging. 'Sorry. A fucking dumb thing to say.'

'I'm just messing with you,' she said. 'Are you cold?'

'Little bit.'

'Come up if you want. You don't have to be chivalrous to the point of getting pneumonia.'

I paused for a moment. 'Wouldn't it be weird?'

'I'm sure we can sort some basic house rules. You sleep on one side of the bed, and I'll sleep on the other.'

'Only if you're sure.' I crept up the stairs where it was darker, pulling my arms out through my t-shirt where they had clung to my body.

'Hey.' Pip shuffled over to make space as I stopped to warm my hands on the heater. 'Jump in, then.'

'Okay.' I slipped underneath the heavy duvet, brushing the mattress lip with my shoulder and staying near its edge. 'It is a bit weird, isn't it?'

'A bit.' She glanced at my forearm with the back of her fingers. 'You're freezing.'

'I know.'

Pip's hand slipped towards mine, and our fingers clasped automatically. She pulled me closer until my arm lay over hers. And I was glad she was there, happy she existed as her warm body radiated to mine. Odd, then, for more to happen beyond a selfless heat transfer – for us to have enjoyed that closeness and sought more.

TWENTY-TWO

My phone was clamped between shoulder and cheek as I arranged my week's washing on the clothes horse inside. Mum said there had been storms all night above Tossa, and she had watched them from the balcony until the crashes and claps were too close to home – like a bomb exploding.

'Pip does have a pretty face,' she said, pivoting suddenly.

'Yeah, she does.'

'Does she not want to wear a wig, then?'

'She doesn't like them.'

'Well, I think she looks lovely.'

'Yep.'

'You do remind me of your dad.' Mum dry chuckled before taking a quick draw on a cigarette. 'You can be very coy.'

'Can I?' I retreated to the sofa and popped my feet on the hexagonal coffee table. 'I guess I don't have strong opinions about wigs.'

Mum laughed. 'Hmm. Not what I meant.'

'I have been thinking about Dad again, actually.'

She hummed cautiously. 'It's not making you feel gloomy, I hope.'

'No. Um. I just feel like I want to know Dad now.' Pumpkin jumped onto the sofa and half-parked herself over my stomach and the spare cushion. 'I know things about him. But they are just things. You know.'

'Right.'

'I mean, he was married in Ireland before he came over. But who was he before that? Where did he grow up and go to school? I should know these things. I mean, who was that guy?'

'Right. I see.'

'I'd ask you, but you were weirdly incurious about a man you had a child with.'

'Well, I wasn't incurious.' Mum tutted. 'You had to tease information out of your father. He carried a lot of guilt with him – maybe that's the Catholic upbringing. I don't know.'

'Hmm.' Pumpkin nuzzled into my palm as I petted her head. Perhaps we were good friends now. 'Maybe.'

'And actually, it was nicer to talk about what we were doing than what we had done. He was always much happier that way.'

'Yeah.'

'And you came along so quickly. It wasn't a planned thing. One minute, your dad was fixing my little car, and suddenly, we were having a baby. So there was adapting to that new situation and giving up my nannying.'

'Yeah. It was fast.'

'It was a whirlwind! But we were happy, Bab. And you were brought into the world with love. That's all that mattered.'

'Yes….'

Mum sighed as our conversation faltered into silence. 'See? You're not saying much now. This is what I worry about. That information gets too much for you.'

I chewed my thumbnail. Perhaps she was right. 'Yeah.'

'I wish you didn't close up.' Mum sighed, and her voice softened. 'I worry it's because I wasn't more generous with you when you were little.'

'You took good care of me, Mum. If that's what you mean.'

'But it was that extra time I wanted. To be with you more. To talk to you all the time. So much of that was taken up by working horrible hours and keeping us afloat. I suppose I was fortunate you were mature for your age, and I could leave you.'

'Right. Yeah.'

'But I do feel bad about it. I'll always feel bad. That I neglected you.'

'You didn't!' I insisted, keen to get off the subject. 'Anyway, I thought it would be nice to go to Ireland, that it was something I should do. Perhaps I would fall in love with it.'

'You might do, Bab. It's a part of you.'

'Well, my name's Brian O'Malley.' I laughed. 'I used to tell people I was Irish because it was easier when they laughed at it. But, I might find something I've been missing, people I've been missing – somewhere I've not been lost.'

'Maybe, Bab.'

'Yes, maybe.' I sighed. It was hopeless talking about these things in the end. 'I'm probably just talking shit.'

'Language, Brian.'

'Sorry. I have enjoyed this conversation, though. It's therapeutic to talk about this stuff, Mum. I'm supposed to talk about it more.'

'Yes.'

The Watercress was quieter when winter arrived, but there was enough in the way of local clientele to keep it ticking over. Anna had been feeling unwell late into her pregnancy, which meant my workload there didn't decrease in the way I had expected. And Pip's relentless organising of my downtime, which was hers too, meant the plan to take on more lesson bookings was on hold.

We had a weird set-up, venturing onto Dartmoor at almost every opportunity, often bringing the family's rescue dog, Macho. And we watched the sunset and moon rise on Haytor Rocks, freezing ourselves with tea-filled flasks. And we braved the icy fog at the summit of Brent Tor and peered inside the unlikely tiny church at its peak. And we strolled along the West Dart River and wandered into Wistmans' Wood and its crooked fairy tale trees.

Beyond our outdoor escapades together, we spent evenings with the garden gang after stumbling onto the periphery of their social circle. We attended local theatre productions, art exhibitions, and spoken word evenings. Nothing was off limits. And not all of the entertainment on offer was enjoyable – a lot of it was weird. But I was with Pip, and that didn't matter.

It must have seemed like we were together to others, doing such intensely couple-like things. And our friendship was more than platonic, propelled by a tacit acknowledgement that we might have explored its romantic possibility in another time and space. Perhaps that was okay when we spent every spare minute together, and I dreaded the thought of it stopping.

One evening, after back-to-back lessons at the flat, Pip came over with takeaway food and Christmas decorations her Mum was about to throw away. There was a manic energy about her that night. She was fidgety and talkative – like she wanted to be distracted. My DNA kit had been processed that morning, with the results posted online, and she was excited for us to view the findings together.

'I found an article written about your band from last year,' Pip said as we plated our Chinese food at the table. 'A sort of *Where Are They Now?* thing.'

'Oh, yeah.' I nodded like it was nothing and moved the empty foil containers to the kitchen worktop. 'Have you been Googling me?'

'Maybe.' Pip laughed as she unscrewed the wine bottle. 'It was a good piece, an ongoing blog series about all the music this journalist loved when she was a teenager.'

'Yeah.'

'I thought it was interesting. I didn't realise how close you came to getting quite big.'

We sat at the table to eat at right angles from each other. 'I'm not sure about that.'

A knowing smile grew on Pip's face as we tucked in. 'I feel like I know lots of things about you now. Things I'm not sure I could prise out of you otherwise.'

I laughed. It was a running joke that I hadn't been as forthcoming about myself. 'Not very flattering things, I suppose.'

Pip shrugged. 'You were all very young. That's what I got from it, mainly. And that it was sad that you don't talk to each other anymore.'

'Yeah….'

'And that your old bandmate seemed nice.' Pip covered her mouth as she finished a mouthful. 'She was very reflective about how it all ended, I thought.'

'Amber. Yeah.' My mouth was dry, and I sipped my wine to lubricate it. 'It was interesting to see it from her perspective.'

'What is your perspective?'

I wasn't sure I had a perspective any longer, I told Pip, relenting. It changed as time passed, and I switched angles to try to make sense of it. But I lost the plot then, and that was true. We all did in small ways. The touring was relentless, with Frank wanting Dorothea to forge its reputation as a live band – always ready to add dates and festival spots at short notice. It was where the money would come from, eventually.

Perhaps it was the exhaustion that drove a wedge between myself and Luke. I kept prodding him, and I don't know why – perhaps to check he still cared. I would catch him letting things slide, playing sloppily momentarily, or forgetting words to songs, and he would do the same to me. It was ridiculous because we were improving, and the workload was sharpening the musicianship. But rarely would we leave a gig without an argument and a round of finger-pointing after. Even with the sound of joy ringing in our ears, the tiniest mishaps would throw us into war.

'Doesn't sound healthy,' Pip said.

'No. But we all thought the atmosphere would improve in the studio when it was time to record the album we had always wanted to make.'

'But it didn't?'

'Well, we went from not speaking to me punching Luke and him breaking my forearm with his guitar.' I prodded at my food. 'He said he was leaving the band after, and we thought it was a joke or an empty threat. And then we waited until it was neither.'

'Must have been difficult.'

'Yeah.'

'Did you not want to do it anymore after that?'

'Not really,' I said. 'I lost my best friend. And I realised I couldn't do it without him. Sadly, he didn't feel the same.'

After food, we finished the wine and moved to the sofa, pulling the laptop across our legs. 'Have you heard of the Totnes Orange Races?' Pip asked as the DNA website loaded.

'I don't know what that could be.'

'The Totnes Elizabethan Society organises it. Can you believe it exists?'

I sniggered. 'Rock'n'roll.'

Pip tutted. 'You can be so cynical.

'I'm being silly.' I gave her a stupid grin.

Her eyes narrowed, part angry and amused – perhaps we were flirting. 'It's not attractive.'

'I'm sure they'd let you join.'

Pip sighed. 'But I can't, can I?'

I'd have been happy if we had abandoned plans to go on my 'DNA Journey', as the website put it – but Pip joked that she was too nosy to let it slide. We stared at the pie chart breakdown of me by geographical area – more Irish than English and a smattering of other unexotic traces over northern Europe.

There was a pinpointed geographical area heavily linked to my DNA. It was on the west coast of Ireland and centred over Galway. I had matches to relatives there with Irish surnames, including my own. Pip suggested I send polite messages to the second cousins I apparently had now. Some lived in the city where Dad was from. And we browsed through images, imagining wandering along the wild beaches and colourful winding streets.

'We should go,' Pip said, excitedly shaking my shoulder.

'Yeah. Maybe.'

The repaired storage heater popped and hissed as the cold from outside penetrated the tall, thin windows.

'I could stay here tonight.' Pip said, like she needed some company, and slid her head onto my shoulder. 'I bought my bag.'

'Sure. Of course.'

We slipped into a bleary-eyed bedtime routine like a long-established couple, taking turns to use the bathroom. I offered to sleep downstairs, but Pip said she didn't want to deprive me of my bed again. I joined her there when I was ready, and we whispered in the softening darkness until Pumpkin left the duvet crevice between our legs, and the cat flap squeaked open.

I played with Pip's ear as she rested her head on my inside shoulder. It was nice to have somebody there, especially her. And she pushed at my chest until we faced each other, heads on pillows and her eyes widening in the low light. 'Can I tell you something?' she asked.

'Yeah. Of course.'

She rubbed her face. 'I'm feeling a bit panicked, actually.'

'What's the matter?'

She took a big sigh. 'I'm only telling you because I need to speak to someone.'

'Okay.'

'I've got a weird feeling. It's similar to something before.'

I smiled. 'Are you about to tell me something really fucking weird?'

She didn't laugh. 'No. Listen.'

'Okay. Sorry. Just say.'

'Fine.' She rubbed her face again, saying she didn't know how much detail to go into. I didn't mind, I told her, whatever it was. 'I had a tiny bleed just before my period was due, and then I didn't get my period. A proper one.'

'Okay,' I whispered. 'And that's happened before?'

'Yes. I had a termination when I was nineteen. That's what happened then.'

'Oh.' Pip stared at me intently, watching for whatever reaction I was determined not to give. 'Must have been hard.'

She shook her head. 'No. Not really.'

'Okay…okay.'

There was a buzzing from the floor, my phone vibrating like someone was calling. We waited for it to stop, still looking at each other.

'What's up?' Pip asked when I didn't speak after.

'Um.' I bit my thumb knuckle. 'Are you saying you might be pregnant or something else?'

'I'm saying I'm scared and don't want to check.' She rolled onto her back and sighed. 'And I'm annoyed because I stopped taking the pill to give myself a break. And we were stupid.'

'So it's possible?'

She tutted. 'I'm telling you this to get it off my chest, Brian.'

'Okay.' I held her hand, and she squeezed it like a stress ball. 'I understand.'

'It might just be my cycle adapting to the change. I don't know.'

The rumbling started again, and Pip nodded like I should see what it was. Amber was calling, her name illuminating my phone screen. It was jarring to see it there, as if the heavy conversation from earlier had willed her into my orbit again. I answered quietly, escaping the bed and perched on the staircase.

'Brian!' Amber said, her voice worried.

'Yes.' I yawned over the back of my hand. 'Are you okay?'

'I'm sorry, I know it's late.'

'That's alright. What's up?'

Luke was in the hospital, she said, after hearing the news from her mum. The details were sketchy, but he had been hit by a car after getting into a fight. She was going to see him in the morning with Mo. Perhaps I should go too, she suggested, if I could. Pip was watching from the bed, and the avalanche of news filled my head, leaving me incapable of understanding it.

'Yes, I will. Of course.'

'Okay. Cool. Love you, mate.'

'Love you too, mate.'

Pip stared as I zombie-walked back to the bed and slid beside her again.

'What's happened?' she asked.

I tapped the phone on my chin. 'Not sure.'

There was a look of genuine concern on Pip's face, and it almost tipped me over. Perhaps I could tell her anything, how I had lost control over my life and that I was falling like a pinball, sometimes ascending again but clattered there by no force of my own.

'Do you want to come to London with me in the morning?' I asked.

TWENTY-THREE - HOSPITAL

It was a raw, wintry morning when we ventured outside under the orange streetlights, waiting for the caffeine hit to shake me awake. Dead leaves circled at our feet as we trudged towards the train station on glazed empty pavements – unable to hear each other over the whistling wind.

The sky was waking up when we reached the tall chimney of the old pumping station, which loomed over our destination. Pip fretted about whether to come as I prodded at the ticket machine on the platform. She pondered whether she could escape somewhere to take the call she had scheduled with the University's senior management team. But I was alone when the train pulled away, in an all-but-empty carriage that wobbled in the gusts as we hit the open green landscapes.

I took my phone out and messaged Pip.

Let me know how it goes xx

And when there wasn't an instant response, I followed it up.

I like you Pip xx

It was probably a stupid thing to have written, so nothing when her news the previous night had been left unresolved. And what to make of that other than to understand that she wanted me to share in her worry without inviting me in. And what if she was pregnant? What would that mean? I barely knew her, really. The timing would be so wild, but so what? And if I were to lean into my thoughts, I might like the idea – the purpose it would give me, the loops it might close.

My phone buzzed. It was Pip.

I like you too xx

It was odd to bumble between thoughts as the carriage buffeted and new passengers stumbled to their seats. And as the train pulled away again, and then again, my focus swayed to what was coming and seeing Luke.

Unlike many foggy days since the band ended, Dorothea's short existence was committed to memory in the fullest colour. It was easy to fold my arms, fall asleep, and return to the Cambridge Junction, where our final never-ending tour began. It was where I had been happiest, where the crowd had sung along to our older songs, the first occasion that had happened. And by the time we launched into our new set-closer, 'I Giggled' and its extended outro, Moses had thrown off his shirt. He was locked in and serene, sweat raining from his tattooed torso as he pounded his kit. And Amber couldn't stop smiling as her bass drove us on, her eyes closed to drink it all in. And when mine met Luke's, our blood was connected – odd to feel that close to anyone. We were alive and powerful, and I've never felt like that since.

After the train reached its destination, I hopped onto the tube at Paddington and stepped off again at Whitechapel, where Luke was a patient at Royal London nearby. I wandered past the busy street market on Whitechapel Road with its striped gazebo stalls. It was exciting to be in the capital again, with a chill in the air and the sun overhead. And it was madness to do that after being couped away in a small Westcountry town – to be in the city again, to sense its power and possibilities. And what was I doing anywhere else?

I slipped down a narrow side street after crossing the double traffic lights to get there. The hospital appeared, almost menacing the skyline with varied blue windows in its LEGO towers. Luke's ward was on the twelfth floor, said the cheerful woman at the help point desk inside.

After stepping into a lift, nerves surged about surprising Luke with my visit – unsure if I would even recognise him by sight. I had witnessed his appearance alter from afar during his post-Dorothea musical forays, glimpsing it in various media, sometimes seeking it out when curiosity got the better. His face had changed over the years, the additional flesh hiding his high cheekbones and sharp jawline. His hairline had slowly receded, too, along with his musical accomplishments.

'Brian, Jesus!' came a call after I rounded onto the ward bay. It was a fractured noise but familiar as I turned towards it. And there was Luke, in a yellow beanie hat – his legs splayed out on a bed, one in plaster and the other inside a circular cage.

I waved as I approached. 'Hey, man.'

A tiny, olive-skinned woman with librarian glasses stood from an adjacent patient chair. She shook my hand as Luke covered his face long enough for a passing nurse to ask if he was okay.

'This is Sel,' he said after giving a thumbs-up.

Sel smiled. 'It's not Brian, is it?'

'Yes,' I replied, and we shook hands. 'Nice to meet you.'

'No!' Sel held her mouth. She couldn't believe it. 'He's just been talking about you. And now you're here.'

Luke buried his face in the nook of his folded arm. 'I manifested you, man. It's insane.'

I laughed along at how mad it was. 'How's it going, mate?'

'Really shit, actually.' A raw graze streaked down his cheek when he moved his arm. His mouth was cut up and swollen. 'Sel's from Spain. If you were wondering about the accent.'

Sel lifted her elbow, 'Catalonia.' A red and yellow striped tattoo of the region's flag extended up and over her forearm. 'I've got the flag, look.'

'Yep. She always makes that distinction.' Luke chuckled and held his face after as if it hurt him to do that. 'I saw Mo and Amber earlier. You just missed them.'

I shook my head. 'Oh, damn. That would have been wild.'

'Yeah.' He snickered at how unbelievable it was. 'Man, you should see those guys now. It's like they've been through some societal integration program. So different.'

Sel announced that she was heading off to get some lunch. She said it was too stale to hang around a hospital ward all day and would bring something nice back for Luke. After declining her kind offer for the same, I perched on her vacated chair.

'She seems nice,' I said.

'Yeah. We're engaged.'

'Ah, congrats.'

Luke sniffed. 'Cheers. She's amazing.'

I asked where he was living now. It was an uncomfortable question, based on how much he shuffled and fidgeted in response. They were between places, he said, with friends in Bermondsey until they figured things out.

'I suppose you want to know what happened,' he said.

'Yeah. If you want.'

Luke said he had been arguing in a bar with a random stranger over money placed on a pool table. He had forgotten about the encounter when he stepped outside at closing and was cold-cocked, presumably by the same person. He staggered into the road after the blow, and the driver of an oncoming car didn't see him there.

'I'll live. Look at this.' He forced his damaged lips apart, and his bottom front teeth were missing. 'I swallowed them, mate.'

I winced. 'Shit. Do you get them back again soon?'

'No idea.' Luke laughed, and his arm vibrated as he reached over and gripped my hand. 'Frank said you were working with computers in Devon. I didn't know if I could believe that.'

I shrugged. 'I sort of was, for a tiny bit…' It was a difficult thing to explain away neatly. 'I've been teaching guitar there more recently, to kids mostly.'

'Man, that's lovely.' He shook his head like it was a wonder. 'Do you like it?'

I shrugged again. 'I actually don't know.'

'Well, it sounds idyllic to me right now.'

I tapped Luke's arm, and he finally withdrew his hand. 'I guess you heard the news about Frank.'

Luke sniffed. 'Yeah. We were speaking before it happened.'

'Yeah, he told me.'

'He said he'd heard my band split up and asked if I fancied a Dorothea reunion. He told me you were up for it, and I was surprised, to be honest.'

I nodded casually but was eager to learn more. 'What did you say?'

'I told him I was interested after thinking about it. But he didn't reply, and I assumed it was Frank being Frank or that he was too busy. Then I found out he fucking died, and it took me out, honestly.'

'Yeah. It did me as well.'

Luke sighed, a long gusty withdrawal. 'I can't stop thinking about our little band now, man.'

'Yeah.'

'Did you see that article about us? Frank sent it to me.'

'Yeah.'

'She was one of our little Camden crew, man. Remember them? How funny.' Luke scanned through his phone, excited and scrolling. 'Listen to this: *It feels cruel they achieved so little. Of all the bands I watched live as a lost, infatuated spotty teen, I think I loved them the most. I was Amber on that tiny stage with my gang of boys, although I had no musical talent of my own. And they spoke to dweeby kids like me. They made us feel like we had a place in the world.'* Luke rubbed his eyes. 'That bit made me cry.'

I nodded. 'That's nice.'

'Seems like alchemy to me now.' He tilted his head backwards. 'I feel like I'm always chasing that again. Is that how it feels for you?'

I pinched my lip. 'Sometimes. We were young, weren't we?'

'So young.' He perked up suddenly, his eyes brightening. 'Amber and Mo got a train up from Brighton. Man, I was so touched. Did you know she grooms dogs now?'

I smiled. 'No. I didn't know that.'

'She loves it. So weird what time does.' He sniffed and then again. 'And they bought their little boy in. Did you know they had a kid?'

'Yeah. I knew that.'

'They're so happy, man.' Luke grabbed the fancy wireless headphones under his arm. 'Guess what I've been doing?'

I shrugged. 'No idea.'

'Beatles, mate. I'm obsessed.'

Luke said he had been listening to the band's entire catalogue, through and back again. He couldn't stop himself. Of all the music takes we agreed on as teenagers, they were this one bone of contention. And perhaps my love for them only existed because of Dad, I told myself then. At the very least, it heightened my affinity.

'You used to call them the most overrated band in history,' I said. 'They made shitty circus music for kids. Something like that.'

Luke laughed. 'Well, you can change your mind. Especially when you do the leg work.'

'Yeah.'

Revolver was the one he insisted, their tightest album. 'Imagine listening to 'Tomorrow Never Knows' in 1966.

That's when England won the World Cup, wasn't it? Think how long ago that was, how old that event feels in comparison.'

'Different era.'

'And for the biggest anything in the world to have dreamt it up – this timeless beam of light flowing overhead and into the future.'

I laughed. 'Steady on, mate.'

Luke chuckled and banged his bed with a palm. 'I don't have these conversations anymore. Why can't I talk like this all the time?'

'I don't know.'

The nurse was back and, this time, wheeling a machine to take Luke's blood pressure. She pulled the green curtain around us and strapped the sleeve around his arm.

'Am I dying?' Luke joked as the sheath inflated.

'No.' She smiled, jotting down the result. 'I think you'll make it another day at least.'

The nurse pulled the curtain back again and moved the machine to the next patient as Luke shuffled and stretched. It was impossible to relax with his legs like that. And he was restless and rubbed the bristles of a shaggy blond moustache. 'It's got me thinking lately,' he said, unprompted, 'with climate change looming.'

'Right.' I nodded slightly. The unexpected topic change was jolting.

Luke winced as he reached for a ring-bound notepad by his side. There were biro sketches of underground structures inside, with connecting tunnels and walkways. 'What do you think?'

'Hmm.' I rubbed my chin, leaning across. There were so many drawings scribbled on that same theme. And perhaps I didn't understand the question. 'What am I looking at here?'

Luke hesitated, a tongue lolling inside his cheek. 'Well, it's going to be too warm to be outside during the day, right?'

'Right.' I wasn't sure what to say. Perhaps it was a joke with a lengthy set-up – only Luke's blue eyes were so wide and frantic it was unlikely. 'I guess so.'

'So, like, where are we going to go?'

'Underground?'

'Bingo!' He sniffed. He was sniffing all the time. 'We've got to build cities and infrastructure down there. They've been doing it for hundreds of years in Turkey, man.'

'Right.'

'You look confused.' Luke's concentration broke. Sel was back on the ward, heading in our direction with a pair of fancy brown patisserie bags in her grip. He started whispering. 'She doesn't want to know. But, I think I might show them to my local MP.'

I nodded. 'Okay…'

Sel sidled up to the bed to show off her baked purchases. 'How are you two?' she asked. 'Getting along? Isn't it amazing?'

'Yeah!' Luke replied, sliding his notepad to where it had been. 'We're so good.'

I gripped the chair's arms as I half-stood, unsure whether Sel would want to reclaim it. The nurse then reappeared before we could come to a decision. The doctor needed to see Luke, and she looked at me expectedly, like I would have to leave.

Suddenly we were all exchanging incomplete goodbyes. Luke reached up and squeezed my hand again, grabbing it with his other. 'Thanks for coming, man.' His black eyes were wet. 'All that way from Devon. I'm so, so touched.'

'No problem, man. It was good to see you again.'

'Yeah.'

I moved to leave as the tall, spectacled doctor arrived, and the nurse pulled at the curtains. Luke called out. 'We should do it all again, I reckon!'

I gave an instinctive thumbs-up before the fabric wrapped him from sight.

A hand grabbed my arm after reaching the long curved desk at the nurse's station by the ward exit. It was Sel, and she wanted to give me Luke's new number.

'Was he showing you his pictures?' she coyly asked as I tapped it into my phone.

'Um. A little bit…'

Her eyes lowered. 'That's just the cocaine talking.'

'Oh. Okay.'

'It's a problem for him.' We made eye contact again. 'He's crazy here. I told him, no more.'

I nodded. 'Right.'

She gave a sad smile before hugging me, patting my back with both hands. 'Luke needs his friends. We need to look after him.'

'Yeah. Of course.'

We shared half-smiles, and I moved out into the maze of that hospital, overloaded and lost in its bright corridors. And I kept making wrong turns, the blue signs hanging down no longer making sense.

I barrelled through the revolving door at the main entrance after reaching it, finally. A swell of tangled emotions threatened to overspill when my pocket vibrated. Pip was calling when I pulled out my phone. I just wanted to be with her and nothing else.

'Hey, are you okay?' I said, answering.

'No!' she replied, fraught like she had been terrorised. 'I've been trying to get hold of you.'

'Why, what's up?'

'Dad's missing…'

'What do you mean?'

'He left the house when we were shopping, and now we can't find him.' Pip started crying. 'I don't know what to do. What the fuck do I do? We shouldn't have left him.'

'Oh, fuck. Have you called the police?'

'Yes, of course! They're out looking for him, we all are. Mum's losing her mind. She's convinced he's drowned in the river.'

'I'm sure it's fine.'

'I'm scared, Brian. What if she's right?'

'Shit. I'm sorry, Pip.' I was panicked too. 'It'll be okay. I'm coming back. We'll get it sorted.'

TWENTY-FOUR

There was no urge to move as a chill penetrated the tall uncovered windows. The cat was by my feet, occasionally stretching across the bed and clawing at my toes. And Mum called again, the pillow vibrating. This time I answered, pushing myself up against the fabric bedhead as Pip's fairy lights blinked along the wonky wooden railing.

'Have you not heard from her, love?' Mum asked.

'Just that she's heading back to work in the new year.'

'Oh.'

'And she's got to support her Mum in finding somewhere for her dad.'

'Is he okay now?'

'I think so.' Pumpkin arched her back before plopping onto my legs. 'But, you know, it's been traumatic for them.'

'Yes, well, it would have been.' There was a short *pfft* as she drew on her cigarette. 'You sound awful, Bab. Shall I put the video on?'

'Um, not now.' I scratched at my unshaven face. 'I feel a bit shit.'

'Oh.' Mum tutted. 'It'll be alright, love. You'll get past it.'

A doubtful snigger escaped. 'I can't even get past things that happened twenty years ago.'

'Brian...'

'I've just got no resilience, Mum. Nothing.'

'Don't say that, Bab. We should put the video on.'

'I really can't, Mum. It's dark up here, and you wouldn't see much.'

'Okay.' She sighed, sad and weary. 'I just worry about you when you're not communicative.'

I pinched my lip. 'It's okay. I'm being responsible.'

'What do you mean, Bab?'

'I'm taking antidepressants.'

'Oh.' Mum sighed, gasping and nasal. 'I didn't know that.'

'It's a good thing, really.'

'Okay.' Mum sniffed. Her voice was wet. 'I just feel so far away from you.'

'It's fine.' I played with my hands, regretting being so candid. 'Anna and Tim have invited me over for Christmas, and they've had a baby. A little girl.'

'Oh, lovely.'

'I'm doing things. I'm okay. It's not like I'm sitting around wallowing all the time.'

'I just want to give you a cuddle, Bab.'

'I know you do. I'm sorry. I feel like I'm always upsetting you.'

I woke up in the previous day's clothes – an unsanitary warmth hovering. I rubbed the gack off my teeth with a finger and checked the time on my phone. My new student was due soon, and I ran downstairs to the tiny bathroom to scrub my teeth and body there.

There was a tap at the front door after getting dressed. I quickly moved a plate and cup from the dining table to the sink when a second tap came, almost angry in its insistence.

'Right, here we are,' said a short, broad woman after I pulled the handle open. She gripped the tense shoulders of a young boy holding a long soft leather briefcase in his hand. 'We're here for Wilfred's lesson.'

'Right.' I clapped my hands together. 'Yes.'

I ushered the pair inside after a handshake with each. Mrs Collins-Lake had emailed and called several times to tweak the agreed time for our first lesson booking. Now she was here, every bit the eccentric character from her written communication style – with her rosy cheeks and an explosion of wiry grey hair.

'Are there many children here?' she asked.

I shrugged. 'Not that I've noticed.'

'We school him at home, you see.' She removed an enormous fabric bag from her shoulder and thudded it onto the dining table. 'So we're trying to socialise him where we can.'

'Well, it's just me here. Lessons are one-to-one.'

Wilfred sighed theatrically and retreated to the sofa, slumping and kicking his feet. 'Nanny, call me Fred, please,' he requested.

'Oh, yes.' Mrs Collins-Lake was already busy rifling through her bag, pulling wool and wooden needles. 'You like that better.'

'Would you like tea or coffee, Nanny?' I asked.

'Well, I'm not *Nanny* to you,' she chuckled. 'But no, thank you.'

'Oh, right,' I said. 'So you're Fred's grandmother?'

'No!' She started knitting, tapping needles attached to a giant ball of dark green wool. 'I'm Fred's mother. Now, why do you think I named him Wilfred?'

I scratched at my ear, caught off balance. 'Not sure.'

'Wilfred Owen.' She smiled like it was obvious. 'We raised him on the poets, darling.'

'Right...' I moved the dining chair from the table into the room and slid the antique case from underneath Fred's feet. 'Is your guitar in here?'

He nodded. 'Yes. If you can call it that.'

I unclipped the latches on the odd case. 'Have you played before?'

Mrs Collins-Lake snickered. 'I haven't heard a note from it. We bought it as an early birthday present from a fair last year. And I wouldn't have thought Wilf would be an exceptional player. He's tone-deaf. But do people praise Bob Dylan for his playing? I would think not.'

I removed a violin-shaped acoustic guitar. Its strings were bowed and rusted, and the tuning posts corroded. 'I think we might struggle with this one.'

'Jesus Christ, Nanny! I told you.' The boy slapped a hand over half his face. 'What is my fucking life?'

It was an uncomfortable start to the day, and I scuffed through an hour of instruction with regular interruptions from Mrs Collins-Lake. Perhaps on another day, I'd have asserted myself and asked for quiet – but my head was fogged and heavy. And so much, a midday journey to a shingle beach on the south coast, the best for winter fishing according to Geoff, was barely a flicker as he drove us there.

Suddenly I was squeezed into a ragged portable chair, never steady with its feet dug into the tiny stones. A pair of fishing rods rested on a tripod, wavering in the breeze and under the lumpy grey clouds – their lines long tossed into the English Channel.

'Right. What's up, Bri?' Geoff asked. He crouched over a small sports holdall, zipping it up after retrieving foil-wrapped sandwiches. 'You're not speaking, bud.'

'Sorry,' I replied after my food package landed on my lap. 'I'll wake up in a minute.'

'Cheese and pickle.'

I nodded. 'Thanks.'

'Your favourite.'

Thin rain and sea spray doused us as Geoff's annoyance grew at my lack of enthusiasm – the lingering stares and occasional arm grabs to gee me up. And I felt terrible for him that I had allowed my upset over Pip to filter in. She had withdrawn after her father was found in the supermarket with a pint of milk in his hand. He had been crying in his pyjamas, and I knew this because Geoff, of all people, had found him.

Perhaps Pip was complicated and didn't want the space she had asked me for. Perhaps she was overwhelmed and had also received the bad news she feared on top of everything else she was dealing with. Perhaps she wanted me to share her anguish, and I should have ignored her wishes and cold-called at her parent's cube-shaped bungalow. Perhaps we would have gone to Totnes Christmas market together like she had wanted to. And she would have rushed to answer the door, tears already streaming. Perhaps we would have sunk to our knees and held each other, and everything would be okay. Perhaps Winnie would have wandered in from another room. 'Brian, you came,' she would have said. 'I hoped you would.'

Perhaps I could feel my depression again, pushing down at my shoulders as the slow green sea bubbled and rolled. And the water was hypnotic. It was easy to lose myself there, to have waded in and drifted underneath those waves – to dissolve, the salt remove my flesh.

'Jack would have loved this,' Geoff said suddenly.

'Yeah.' I nodded and finally took a bite of my sandwich. 'It's a shame he couldn't make it.'

'His IBS is flaring up.'

'Yeah.' I stared at my food, the grated cheese flecks falling into the foil. 'You said.'

'Irritable bowel syndrome.'

I nodded. 'Yeah.'

Geoff said it was unlikely Jack would be able to help at the Christmas party he was DJing at the following day. It was a 'max set-up' event and perhaps too much for one person alone.

'I would ask you,' he said glumly. 'But I suppose you're busy.'

'No. I can help, mate.'

Perhaps I needed distractions, and I had been a lousy friend to Geoff. And we stayed late until the waves grew and a biting wind swirled. One of the upsides of antidepressants, it seemed, was that I wouldn't descend into detachment.

There was a baseline somewhere above that I could thud into, where I could still function and hope for better days.

I told Geoff there was a tug on one of the lines, as we were about to call it a day. It had quivered for a second time – although I couldn't be sure, having studied them for so long. He flicked his head torch back on and agreed that something was happening after an inspection. He lifted the rod from its pod and waved to the other fisherman down the shore. Perhaps that was the convention. But no sooner had he started to reel in the catch. But then he stopped again – the tension gone.

'Shit,' he said, despondent. He kicked at the shingle. 'There's fuck all in here, Bri.'

'Yeah.'

He ripped his head torch from his head. 'When I was a kid, I'd come here with my dad and brother, and we'd whip a hundred whiting out of there.'

'Right.'

'They've all fucked off. The earth is dying.'

The Disco Inferno had been booked at the Torquay Plaza the following evening, and the Christmas party was a shared event for local businesses. The journey there was quiet, and we stopped for drive-through fast food on the way. Geoff was unusually pensive as if there was nowhere useful for his manic energy to go. He tapped his teeth as we continued, tutting impatiently at temporary traffic lights and grumbling that the event would be a 'shagfest' and its guests wouldn't care about the music.

The venue was surprisingly grand when we arrived at the large white Victorian hotel on the hillside facing out to sea. But, with no practical side entrance to slip in and out from, we were forced into lengthy trips from the car park out front to our set-up on a raised theatre stage at the back of the main function room.

Despite the dated decor, it was a grandiose space with high ceilings and chunky square pillars, surely once designed with more ostentatious events in mind. And it was strange to be so high up relative to the dancefloor below and the banquet-style long tables beyond where oversized silver balloon arrangements were dotted.

Geoff had purchased several new gadgets since our last disco together, including a pair of flaming torch-themed lights, which he placed in front of the speakers. The LED infernos fluttered away as he shared his quiet joy with an impressed pony-tailed security guard who had stopped by to chat.

We played a low-energy Christmas-themed playlist for the guests as they tucked into their festive sit-down meal. Their ears were adorned with the likes of Frank Sinatra's 'Have Yourself a Merry Little Christmas' and 'Santa Baby' by Eartha Kitt. Many revellers had arrived in high spirits, filling the air with boozy excitement.

After the staff had cleared the tables, the house lights were switched off, and it was disco time again. Geoff fired up the lasers and kicked off the event with a series of mid-tempo classics. 'There'll be a lot of high-ups in here, Bri,' he said gravely as the dancefloor began to fill. 'A lot of money in the room tonight.'

'Right.'

'And they'll notice any mistakes. Trust me.'

I waited for Geoff's odd mood to shift, for any trace that it might, as the mirror ball light twirled and 'We Found Love' by Rihanna, featuring Calvin Harris, packed out an enthusiastic dancefloor. But he was dull in his presentation, not buoyed by the festive joy below us or the Santa hat he donned for the occasion.

Unexpectedly, one of the more inebriated guests decided to jump on the stage with us. He was a rail-thin, ratty-faced man, everything pointy. 'Oi. Play some fucking Pitbull!' he demanded in a piss-yellow shirt.

Geoff waved him off. 'It's texts for requests only. I said that at the start.'

'Alright, calm down, fat bitch,' the man snapped. He pushed at one of the torch lights, and it wobbled momentarily. 'Look at your tacky shit, mate.'

'Tacky?' Geoff banged the desk, red and furious as our friend jumped down again. That particular insult had cut through. 'Tacky.'

'He's just had too much to drink, mate,' I insisted. But Geoff's phone was out, and he was texting furiously.

'Where the fuck is Barry?'

The security guard re-appeared with a burly colleague clutching a comically large walkie-talkie. Geoff pointed out the troublemaker on the dancefloor, and a crowd of bystanders filmed on their phones as he ran for it. After a solid ten minutes of diving under tables and hiding behind pillars, our friend tripped over a giant set of balloons and was dragged out of the room in a headlock.

Geoff's mood evaporated into a quiet gloom as the event hit its summit. He was poised, arms-folded with the mic in his grip as Mariah Carey's 'All I Want for Christmas' entertained the remaining partygoers. They sang to each other in private dance circles and posed for group photos.

'Have a lovely Christmas, folks. That's all from us,' Geoff announced after fast-fading the remaining few bars. His sign-off was transactional and joyless, with no excitement or weird nicknames. I missed those now.

We were headed for a fraught journey home as we packed away silently with no Jack to help. Guests were milling in the thin rain outside as taxis arrived in convoys, and we pulled our carts out to the sloping asphalt. Geoff trilled his lips as we headed to the far corner, where we left the van by a row of palm trees.

I pulled out my phone to check for any messages from Pip in case I had missed a pocket vibration within the previous half an hour. Geoff's pace quickened as my eyes dipped, almost breaking into a sprint with the stacked boxes on his cart wobbling behind him.

'Nooo!' he yelled suddenly. 'No!'

I looked up. 'What's up?'

'Nooo!' Geoff butted the side of his van. The vehicle was slumped and tilted. Large gashes had been knifed into the tyres when I arrived. 'No. Fuck. No.'

'Shit.'

'Fuck.' The headbutting slowed to a stop. Geoff rested a cheek on a side panel and spread his arms wide as if he were comforting an injured loved one or beloved pet. 'Why would anyone do that, Bri?'

I shook my head. 'I'm not sure.'

The rain thickened, and Geoff climbed into the cabin to call a local recovery service. 'They're gonna take me for every penny I have at this time of night,' he moaned before slamming the driver's door.

I pulled my cart back to the venue to fetch the remaining equipment. My clothes were heavy and drenched when I pushed the items inside and pulled the rear doors together. The van's engine was rumbling when I slipped onto the passenger seat and held my hands to the fans blowing tepid warm air.

'They're on the way,' Geoff murmured. He placed his elbows on the steering wheel and pushed his hands into his cheeks. 'Apparently.'

'That's good, then.'

'Hmm.' He drew a long nasal breath, his whole body exhaling after. 'Are you going to tell me about this lady-friend then, Bri?'

I wiped the moisture dripping onto my face. 'What do you mean?'

'That religious woman you've been hanging around with. I waved at you from my van by the train station, and you didn't wave back.'

I frowned, not recalling. 'Oh. I don't remember that.'

Geoff sighed. 'That's because you've forgotten about me, Bri.'

'What do you mean?'

'It's okay. I knew it would happen as soon we finished Breaking Bad. Then you moved out. I knew it would.'

'Geoff, don't be silly.' I squeezed the water from my shirt sleeves. 'I've just been so busy. It's got nothing to do with Breaking Bad.'

'Too busy to reply to a text, is it?' Geoff screwed his face as he turned to look at me, a swell of acidic bitterness overtaking him. 'You're like all the artsy knobs in Totnes, posh attention-seekers, swanning around and thinking they can dictate how it is to the rest of us.'

'Pardon?'

'Well, it's my town, too!' He pounded the steering wheel with an open palm. 'Some of us don't have the time to ponce around in top hats and scream about, lecturing others. Some of us are struggling, Bri.'

I was confused and blindsided by the rant – how specific the details were. 'Geoff, I'm sorry I've not been in touch.'

'Am I no use to you anymore, Bri?'

'Of course you are. Come on, man. You fucking saved my life. That means something.' Perhaps it was cheap to have bought that up, but a ball lodged in my throat. Perhaps I had only appreciated the scale of that, then. 'It's what happened.'

'Yeah.' Geoff leaned back in his seat, arms folded as his chin fell onto his chest. He was deflated and unimportant. It wasn't how he was supposed to feel. 'It's just crap, Bri.'

'I know…'

Geoff started to cry, a sputtering, embarrassed weeping. And the palm trees fluttered in the wind outside my window, my wet hair dripping onto my face.

'I am sorry, mate,' I whispered. 'I've been a bad friend.'

'It's not just you, Bri.' Geoff wiped his nose on his leather jacket sleeve and rubbed at the trail it left. 'I asked Helen to move in, and she needed thinking time. It's been ages now. It must be over.'

I gripped Geoff's shoulder, and the leather from his jacket squeaked. 'I'm sorry, mate.'

'It's okay.' He shook his head and trilled his lips. 'I just can't make anyone like me, Bri. Not for long. I'm too intense. I overdo it, don't I?'

The recovery vehicle arrived before I could answer, its amber roof lights blinking in the wing mirror. The rain calmed to a horizontal drizzle after we stepped outside. And we watched the van being fixed to the long shelf of the truck and climbed inside its cabin once it was secure.

I became sandwiched between a despondent Geoff and a shaggy-haired recovery driver who waved us into his cabin. He was an avid talker and quickly revealed himself as the worst possible person for that moment. And I nodded as we travelled, and he had launched into a story about the ghost in his village who was moving pot plants and deflating bike tyres. He said he had seen the apparition waving to him from an abandoned phone box at the end of his road, but the council wouldn't do anything about it when he called. Now he worried he knew too much.

'That's how they get you,' the driver said.

I nodded, wishing I was anywhere else. 'Right.'

'And I fucking hate my neighbours,' he continued, pivoting unexpectedly.

Geoff was tuned out, his head bobbing against the passenger window.

'Oh,' I replied, eventually. 'Do you?'

'Yeah,' he said. 'They're Romanian, but that's got nothing to do with it.'

'Okay…'

A muffled, pulsating dance tune pounded away out of sight. Geoff wriggled around to free a phone from his jacket pocket, and the device lit up the cabin as he examined the screen.

'Hey, baby,' he said, answering excitedly. He waved his free hand in small arcs, signalling us to be quiet as he took the call. 'What's up?…No, it's fine. I've been gigging, always up late…Yeah, I'm good. How are you?…Oh, that's good…They're both fine, good as gold. Bryony and Jack miss you…Well, you know I'd wait for you for a million years if I had to…I've missed you too, so much.'

The driver nudged his arm into my side. 'He's gonna start wanking soon the way he's speaking. He better not.'

'I've missed you so much, baby,' Geoff continued. He sobbed again but with none of the despair of before. 'I've been praying for a miracle…No, you're my miracle…Yes, you are. You are my Christmas miracle…I'm crying now… I love you, too. I love you, baby...I'm just on my way home with Bri.' Geoff wiped the tears from his eyes and gave me a thumbs-up. 'Helen says hello, Bri.'

'Hi Helen,' I replied.

'Did you hear that? Bri said hi…Yeah, he's got a soft voice…I can't wait to see you…It means the world to me…I love you too, so much…Okay, bye then…You go first…Okay, I'll go then…I love you…love you…love you...'

Geoff held his phone to his forehead when the call was over.

'Everything alright?' I asked.

'Yeah.' He tapped the phone on the bridge of his nose. 'That was Helen.'

I nodded. 'I guessed that.'

'It's back on, Bri.' He clenched his fist. 'Would you believe it? It's back on.'

'Who's Helen?' the driver asked. 'Has she got big tits?'

TWENTY-FIVE

'Happy Christmas, Brian,' Mum said through the phone screen. She had wrapped herself inside a fleece blanket from her usual spot. 'Can you see me?'

'Yeah, I can.' I propped myself up against the bed head and picked the hard sleep dust from the corners of each eye. 'Happy Christmas, Mum.'

'Bill says *Happy Christmas*. He's making me a fry-up.' She pinched her cigarette and held it at the camera. 'This is my last, hopefully. I'm having hypnotherapy.'

'Good,' I said. 'Happy Christmas, Bill.'

Mum craned to pass on my message. 'Brian says *Happy Christmas.*'

'Did you get the gift I sent, Mum? I hope it got there in time.'

She cupped her mouth. 'Oh, Brian. It got me emotional. It's the three of us at Earlswood Common, right?

'Yeah. I got it printed and framed in town.'

'Aw. It's a lovely, chunky frame. Bill hasn't aged, has he?'

'No, he's stuck in his late forties.'

'I know.' She blew smoke from her lips, whimsical glazing in her eye. 'Are you going to book your flight with that voucher?'

I nodded. 'Yes, Mum. I will. Thank you.'

'I can't wait to see you!' she said. 'Are you still seeing your friends today?'

'Yeah. It should be good.'

Mum smiled. 'Aw, it's lovely they've thought of you.'

'Yeah. It's nice.'

'Are you going to speak to them about cutting down your hours?'

'I might. See how it goes.' The cat flap pinged from downstairs. Pumpkin was back from an early morning trot and was heading my way to demand breakfast as per our routine. 'Are you up to much?'

'Well, we're seeing our neighbours across the way – John and Irene. They're Irish, from Cork. Which is in the south, they said.'

'You asked them if they knew Dad, didn't you?'

'Well, yes.' Mum gave a knowing chuckle. 'You never know. The Irish are much more friendly and outgoing by nature.'

'Right.' The cat jumped up and butted at my legs. 'Do you like living in Spain?'

Mum paused for a moment. 'Yes. Why?'

'I don't know. I just wouldn't change it.'

'Okay.' She stubbed out her fag in the yellow ashtray. 'What's all this about?'

'I was thinking. Maybe we don't need to speak as much as we have been.'

'Oh,' she said. 'Why is that, Bab? I like our chats.'

'I don't know. Maybe it would be better if we staggered it out more. Maybe that would be healthier, and we would have more to discuss.'

'Okay, love.' Mum hummed to herself before she smiled as if she agreed. 'Yes, okay. I better go, love. My breakfast is ready.'

'Okay. Love you.'

'Love you, too. Tara a bit, then. Have a lovely day.'

The cat meowed, an odd *ekk-ekk* noise with her whole face scrunched, the one she made when she wasn't willing to wait any longer. I slipped out of bed, sliding from a cosy warmth to greet the cold with a phone buzzing in my grip.

A festive message had arrived from Luke.

Happy Christmas mate – love from Sel and me

I typed a quick response after forking the cat's food from the tin and dry-swallowing my fluoxetine.

Hey! Happy Christmas! How are you?

Better. We've moved in with the folks for a bit.

Oh cool. Nice to spend Christmas with them.

Definitely. Sel's pregnant! It's all happening.

Shit! Congratulations!

Cheers. I'll tell you more about it when we come and see you next year!

I'd love that!

I checked the time and was behind schedule on plans to wrap up my last-minute purchases before heading to Tim and Anna's.

There was a scrunch of ice beneath my trainers when I finally entered the frosty courtyard behind The Watercress with my plastic bag of gifts. Tim was waiting at the back door in an elf's hat. 'Merry Christmas, Brian,' he yelled. 'I was wondering where you had got to.'

We shared a brief hug as I reached him. 'Sorry, mate.'

'Let's get merry.'

Christmas music was blaring as Tim ushered me to the flat upstairs and the living room, where ivy and mistletoe hung over the obscure action paintings on the walls. Much of it was Anna's, who had been an artist in a former life.

'Have you met Ross?' Tim asked.

A squatty, shirtless man rose from a chord beanbag and shook my hand. He had a fleecy chest and two large nipple rings. It was an unexpected sight, enough for my mouth to stop working.

'You've taken your shirt off, Ross,' Tim said, examining his friend.

'Yeah. You know me, mate.' Ross rubbed his furry torso. 'I get so overheated.'

'Fair enough.' Tim scratched nervously at his upper lip. 'But are you okay with popping something on in a minute?

Verity will be up soon, and we've got our elderly neighbour popping down.'

'Yeah, no worries at all!' Ross retrieved a leopard print silk shirt draped over a reclined armchair and slipped it on. 'I've cooled down.'

Tim had made mulled cider, he said, and I accepted his offer for some as he retrieved Ross's tankard from a coffee table. I quietly slipped the presents from a plastic bag and placed them with the others beside a small potted tree decorated with string-threaded fruit slices. Ross laughed as I lowered myself onto a wicker rocking chair, with its seat creaking as if it might collapse under my weight.

'Might snap,' he said.

I smiled. 'Feels like it.'

He reached behind his beanbag and stroked a greyhound's long nose protruding from behind it. 'Got my dog, Wilf. He'll be everyone's best friend by the end of the day.'

'Oh, that's good then.'

Ross nodded towards the other end of the room, where a vast library wall bent around a festively decorated dining table. 'Got a lot of books here.'

'Wow, yeah.'

'Must read a lot.'

'Yeah.' I nodded. Must do.'

The stilted small talk continued as we waited for Tim's return. Ross was in the Salvation Army, he said and played the trombone in their brass band. I suggested it must be a busy time of year for them, and he confirmed it was.

'Brian's here!' yelled Anna, entering the room. She wore a pair of comedy antlers and jigged baby Agnes along to Paul McCartney's 'Wonderful Christmastime'. 'Do you want to hold her?'

'Sure,' I replied, a baby already landing in my arms.

I rocked Agnes lightly in my chair. Her big blue eyes had turned green since I first saw her, and a tuft of black hair stood at the back of her round head. Ross wandered over and tickled her under the chin like a pet.

'She's cute,' he said.

Tim danced back inside. He handed out the tankards of mulled cider and told me to watch out for the brandy. 'Rosalind will be here in a minute,' he said as I handed over Agnes in exchange. 'She'll want the recliner chair.'

The doorbell rang as if, on cue, a high-pitched rattle. Tim escorted his elderly neighbour into the room in her clashing shades of pink. She paused as she caught sight of us. 'Oh, there's men here, Tim,' she said wearily.

'That's okay,' Tim replied, jigging Agnes. 'Two lovely men, Rosalind.'

'Well, you didn't say anything.' She pulled a pair of fluffy slipper boots from a bag for life and popped them on. 'I'd have made more effort.'

'I think you look lovely,' Ross said.

Rosalind wagged a finger. 'Oh, don't you be ridiculous.'

Tim left again to check on the food. Rosalind was having trouble with her sciatica, she said, and also the recycling bins, which the council kept forgetting to collect. And why did she need to recycle at her age, she asked. It was ridiculous.

Tim's teenage daughter, Verity, then stumbled to join us bleary-eyed with her short pink hair wet from a recent shower. 'This is a random gathering,' she noted after looking around the room. It was a fair observation. She stretched herself out over the vacant beaten-up brown sofa. 'I think that's a good thing, though.'

Tim returned with brandy in his grip for Rosalind. 'Look, Verity. Your hair matches Rosalind's outfit.'

'Is she allowed to have her hair that colour at school, Tim?' Rosalind asked, sniffing at her drink as if she was suspicious of it.

Tim shrugged as his daughter death-stared. 'I don't know. She'll find out.'

'I think it looks cool,' Ross said.

'Thanks,' said Verity. 'Dad said it looks crap.'

'I just don't like that shade of pink,' Tim said, smirking. 'Naff, isn't it, Brian?'

'I like it,' I said diplomatically.

Tim winked. 'Verity said she's getting into K-pop now. She's a K-pop Stan, she told me. She might have to give up your lessons.'

Verity rolled her eyes. 'Dad, please. I'm begging you to stop.'

Tim laughed. 'Well, I will stop because dinner is almost ready,'

I offered to help plate up the food to escape the jolting small talk, if nothing else. Soon we were laying out a mishmash of serving dishes on the table with roast potatoes, parsnips, carrots, red cabbage and creamed leaks for people to help themselves.

Rosalind frowned as we shuffled into our seats, all in the same room at last. She stared at the domed cranberry and lentil pudding on her plate like it might grow arms and throttle her. 'No turkey at Christmas, Tim?'

'We're meat-free in the flat,' Anna replied, jogging Agnes in her Moses basket with one hand. 'Sorry, Ros.'

Rosalind huffed like it was a disaster. 'I didn't know you were all vegetarians. I could be having a pub lunch.'

'Worse than that, we're vegans,' Anna added, amused by it.

'I'm not anymore,' Verity announced. 'I have dairy, now and then.'

'Honestly, this town.' Rosalind laughed. 'It's full of nutters. Absolute nutters.'

Tim winked at Anna. 'We're all mad here.'

'Well, I just feel sorry for the farmers,' Rosalind huffed. She prodded at her plate, still unimpressed. 'You're putting them out of business, and they're shooting themselves in droves.'

'This is lovely, Tim. Thanks,' I said, perhaps to soften the mood. And it was true. The food was delicious. He had a gift. 'Thanks for having me, both.'

Ross held up his wine glass. 'A toast, I think, with thanks to Tim and Anna and a lovely Christmas for everybody.'

We clinked glasses and pulled the crackers laid out, crossing our arms to do it properly after Tim insisted.

'It does taste nice, Tim,' Rosalind said after a tentative forkful. 'Very nice. Thank you.'

After washing up with Anna in the narrow kitchen, we gathered in the living room, where more mulled cider was consumed, and Verity played postman to distribute the presents under the tree. It was warming to be buried inside that rocking chair, understanding it wasn't about to collapse. And I slowly untuned from Ross's one-sided conversation with Tim, where he discussed the bird feeding station he was making in his metal workshop.

Suddenly, my pocket buzzed, and I quietly slipped my phone out. There was a note from Pip, and I had been so lulled I didn't know what to do.

Hey! Are you having a nice Christmas? xx

Yes! How are you? xx

I'm okay. Are you free to catch up tomorrow? xx

Yeah! I'd love to xx

Maybe we could go for a walk. It's supposed to be dry and I need some fresh air! xx

Sounds good! xx

'Are you being antisocial?' Anna asked, lightly rocking my chair. She had crept up from behind after putting Agnes down for an afternoon nap.

'No,' I replied. 'Just tending to my Christmas messages.'

'Okay.' I mirrored Anna's smirk as she curled beside Tim and Verity on the old brown sofa. 'I'll allow it.'

Buoyed by the prospect of seeing Pip again, I tapped out a quick festive note and sent it to every contact stored on my phone – just like I used to on Christmas Day.

Merry Christmas. I hope you're having a lovely time xx

'I forgot to tell you, Tim,' I said, sliding my device away. 'I think Ben Howard came into the café the other day. A customer pointed him out to me.'

'Everyone's met Ben Howard,' Verity laughed. 'This is Totnes.'

My pocket rumbled with vibrations on my phone, and I grew curious about the notes dropping in. And when Ross stood to take Wilf for a quick walk around the block, I slipped into the kitchen to finish off the pans left to soak.

I prodded at a roasting tin bobbing in the sink and scrolled my phone with a free hand. Perhaps it was the time of the year that had driven a glut of responses to my note. There were enthusiastic replies from Esther, Geoff, Beatty and Amber and older friends I hadn't seen in a while who were shocked to have heard from me. *We must catch up* and that phrase, over and over. Perhaps I wanted to do that now.

A message from Tam flashed as I was about to turn to the sink full-time.

Brian! Are you still in Totnes? We're there for New Year's xx

I'm still here. How are you? xx

We're great. How are you? xx

We continued messaging back and forth as we caught up. Tam was spending Christmas with her mum and Connie, and they were headed to Totnes next. Suddenly we were arranging to meet at The Ballroom's '80s-themed New Year's Eve party in town. She said James would be there too, and they could get me a ticket if I wanted. And she loved her life in Berlin, and I should come over and visit them. They were excited for us to meet again, and I was too.

When I returned to the room, Rosalind was asleep, with her chair fully reclined. Ross wandered inside with Wilf in tow. He quietly sat on the beanbag again with the dog tucked in behind. It was warm, he said, pulling at his shirt.

'Well, you've been outside,' Tim suggested, perhaps fearing another shirtless moment. 'You'll cool down soon.'

We stayed among the hotchpotch furniture until it was late, playing an outdated version of Trivial Pursuit and then some word games Tim appeared to invent on the fly. And the moon was red and pleased when I wandered home with a hazy head.

A tiny burgundy hatchback was chugging in the winding street behind the bumpy lanes behind my building. It was early morning as I opened its passenger door, bleary-eyed, and Pip immediately roasted me for my outfit choice – the shorts and thin bomber jacket I had on.

'What are you wearing?' she laughed, uncocking the handbrake.

'I don't know. Something outdoorsy.' I pinched the sleeve of her hiking puffer coat. 'I didn't realise we were going for a four-day trek in the Alps.'

Pip laughed and pointed at the thermometer on the dashboard. 'It's three degrees, Brian.'

'Ah, well.' I rubbed at my bare legs. 'It might warm up.'

Pip was still chuckling when we left Totnes and hit the open roads with bare bark trees and defrosting fields on either side. She asked what I had been up to recently, getting there before I did. And Christmas Day aside, the answer was not much, with the café closed until the new year and no tutoring until then. But Beatty had reminded me of the retiring music tutor during my previous lesson with Noah. It was official now, and the parents of his students were already emailing me to enquire about availability.

'So you're expanding Brian's Music School?' Pip asked.

I shrugged. 'I suppose I have to think about it.'

'Do you enjoy it?'

I nodded, not entirely convinced, but perhaps more than I had been – perhaps now I knew half the kids would give up mentally, if not actually, after a few lessons. I had stopped taking that personally, mainly because of the few who had fallen in love with its potential and were happy to be crap for a while. I was that kid once, draining whatever little money Mum could scrape together on her insistence. And it was beautiful for me to discover something I loved doing like that, she would say, and for it to be completely mine.

'Does that mean you're hanging around Totnes for a while?' Pip asked.

'I think so. My landlady called early last week to check on the cat and said she wasn't planning to be back for at least six months. Maybe I'll reassess then.'

'That's a good idea.'

I nodded. Perhaps it was. 'How are you?'

Pip wrinkled her nose. She said her extended family had been over to stay, making her parents' home feel unbearably small. 'There's been such a weird atmosphere there, with it being Dad's last Christmas at home. And we've tried to make it fun for Mae because it's the first year she gets it, but Mum kept leaving the room to cry.'

'Oh, dear,' I said. 'How is your dad?'

'Well.' She puffed her cheeks. 'We've found him somewhere for the new year. It's close and easy for Mum to get to.'

'I'm sorry, Pip.'

'That's okay.' She sighed like it wasn't really. 'It needs to happen, at least.'

'Right.' I scratched at my face, unsure whether to ask what had been playing on my mind. 'What about the other thing?'

She tapped at the wheel. 'I plucked up the courage to do a test yesterday. I'm not, you know, pregnant. It was negative.'

'Okay.'

'Sorry. That was a weird way to say that.'

The arms of the morning sun were reaching through a freezing mist when we arrived on the grounds of Castle Drogo, a country house owned by the National Trust. According to Pip, there was a circular walk we could do nearby, which stretched down into a gorge and through woodland alongside the River Teign and back again.

After exiting the car park on foot, I immediately slid on the dewy grass by a wooden kissing gate at the trail's start point. Pip laughed as I examined the worn tread on my trainers. 'You need some proper hiking boots,'

'I did have a browse when you suggested it.'

'And?'

'I don't know.' I smiled, knowing how Pip was about to react. 'They all look like something a scout leader might wear.'

She rolled her eyes, chuckling. 'Oh, my God. You are thirty years old, Brian. You need to start thinking about practicality.'

I laughed along. 'I know.'

The grassy path morphed into a stony trail tracking the edge of a deep valley where a puffy white cloud was slowly rising out. 'It's beautiful,' said Pip, taking photos on her phone.

'It is.'

'Come here,' she insisted, pulling me close to take a selfie. I closed one eye, with the sun's glare beaming down. Pip examined the picture after, showing it to me on her screen. 'Aw.'

It was colder when we descended into a steep wood which screened out the sun's warmth. We passed dog walkers and families returning uphill, all suitably dressed for the occasion with their heavy jackets and wellingtons.

'I'm just going to buy you a pair of boots,' laughed Pip as I stepped gingerly down the slope. The ground was loose and peppered with knotty tree roots bulging out from it. 'I'm going to turn you into a hiker. So that you don't embarrass me.'

We hit the bottom of the path, where parked cars lined the edges of a road, and yellow helmeted canoers carried their boats towards a waterway bubbling nearby. A stone block bridge met us at the end, arching over a river. There was a large country inn on the bankside across with benches on its terrace that were dry enough to enjoy the flasks of coffee in Pip's rucksack.

Pip placed her gloves on our table and scrolled through her phone. 'I put that picture of us on Instagram. Do you mind?'

'No.'

'People are asking me who you are.' She winced and angled her phone across the table. 'It's been, like, twenty minutes. So nosy.'

'What did you say?'

'A friend.'

An older man in a beige duffel coat paused after squeezing past us with his collie dog. 'My sister passed away from cancer a few years ago,' he said, nodding at Pip's head scarf. 'So best wishes to you.'

Pip gave a sympathetic smile. 'Sorry to hear that. I don't have cancer, thankfully. My hair just fell out.'

'Oh.' The man grimaced. 'Well, I hope it comes back,'

'I live in hope.'

I shielded the glare with a hand as the sun moved between tall trees, and the man wandered to the bridge with his dog to stare out onto the river.

'I'm going back to Cardiff tomorrow,' Pip said, sipping casually from her flask.

'Tomorrow?'

'Yeah.' Her eyes bulged like she couldn't believe it. 'I just want to escape before the new year and get myself sorted.'

'Right.' I nodded, the news not yet penetrating – merely hanging. 'Makes sense.'

Pip said she just wanted to return to her job. She missed it and the people in her life back in Wales. And she had spoken to her brother Michael, their first long heart-to-heart in years. The situation with their parents weighed heavily, but he was around with his wife, Jane, and Mae. And Winnie had been integrating herself into the Buddhist community in Totnes. People were looking out for her. She would be okay.

'I'm sure I'll speak to her all the time,' Pip said. She laughed knowingly. 'We bought her a new iPad for Christmas, and she said she wants to see my face on it every day.'

I laughed. 'That's nice.'

'And I'll be back to see her and Dad when I can.' She bit into her nail. 'We'll still see each other if you want.'

'Yeah.' I nodded. 'Of course I do.'

Pip smiled like it was a relief to her. 'Maybe it'll be interesting to see how we feel, with some distance and space for everything to shake itself out.'

'Definitely.' I nodded. 'Good idea.'

'I'm sorry I've not been in touch.'

I shrugged. 'That's okay. You needed to work stuff out.'

'Yes.' Pip said her ex had called on the night her dad went missing. He had offered to come down to see her, and she thought it was what she wanted until it wasn't. 'It feels like I've been on a strange holiday, you know?'

I nodded. 'I know what you mean.'

'I just need to get back into a routine and get my head straight.'

We stood up with the empty flasks packed away again. Pip joked that we were hurtling towards middle age and held my hand as we headed for the bridge to begin the loop around the river. It was nice to be there, especially with her.

Perhaps my prospects had turned around and had done so in small, unexpected ways. There were happenings to look forward to, and it was amazing what that could do for someone accepting certain aspects about themselves – having scraped along my limits and been saved by good fortune and the kindness of others. Perhaps the water would always be there somewhere, and that was fine. But the tide was receding, for now, and leaving the tips of my toes.

Acknowledgements

Thanks to Isabelle, Damian, Gabby, Si, Aimee, Amanda, Mum, and James for your help, ideas and encouragement.

Printed in Great Britain
by Amazon

53131883R00182